salamander

j.robert janes

SOHO

First published in Great Britain by Constable & Company Ltd.

Copyright © 1994 by J. Robert Janes; first published
in the United States of America in 1998

Published by

Soho Press, Inc.
853 Broadway
New York NY 10003

Library of Congress Cataloging-in-Publication Data

Janes, J. Robert (Joseph Robert), 1935–
Salamander / J. Robert Janes.
p.   cm.
ISBN 1-56947-157-6 (alk. paper)
I. Title.
PR9199.3.J3777S25   1998
813'.54—dc21   97–49702

10   9   8   7   6   5   4   3   2   1

Salamander: from the realm of the mythical, a creature that lives in fire and enjoys it. A lizardlike, scaleless animal whose skin is moist, soft and slippery, and whose tail is long.

A creature that can change the colour of its belly and back to a shimmering, iridescent blue when trapped.

A creature that can vanish.

To my memories of Stevie Leacock Jr. and old Fred Pellatt, Sir Henry's brother. To the gold pocket watch Stevie left with his teeth-marks imprinted, and to the million German marks old Fred gave me that were absolutely worthless at the bank. Both men were of what this world is about and both, in their individual ways, would have been greatly bemused to find me writing. Indeed, they would, in retrospect I'm sure, have thought it quite in keeping with my playing tunes from the '20s and '30s on my trombone at all hours of the night.

Author's Note

Salamander is a work of fiction. Though I have used actual places and times, I have treated these as I have seen fit, changing some as appropriate. Occasionally the name of a real person is also used for historical authenticity, but all are deceased and I have made of them what the story demands. I do not condone what happened during these times. Indeed, I abhor it. But during the Occupation of France the everyday crimes of murder and arson continued to be committed, and I merely ask, by whom and how were they solved?

1 THE STENCH WAS TERRIBLE, OF PISS-SOAKED wool, wet ashes and death, that sweet, foul, clinging odour of burnt flesh, excrement and human hair.

Jean-Louis St-Cyr let his gaze drift over the corpses that lay in two great mounds at what had once been the curtained doorways to the foyer. Some, too, were scattered about the charred, soaked seats that now lay in ruins under ice.

Some had tried repeatedly to force the exit doors—there were corpses there, too, lots of them—trampled again and one could see how that seething mass of terrified humanity had run to those doors and then had tried to escape through the foyer.

'Louis, how the hell are we supposed to go about sorting this thing out?' demanded Kohler angrily. Hermann was looking desperate and ill behind a blue polka-dot bandanna that had been soaked in cheap toilet water and disinfectant. Contrary to popular belief, many Bavarians were known to have weak stomachs, this one especially.

[handwritten annotations:] ora- who travel around Detectorie / Police Inspect- Maigret occasionally France in "job" worked with Fly Squad

2 **robert janes**

Concerned about him, St-Cyr nudged his partner's arm. 'Try not to think too much about the loss of so many, *mon vieux*. Try to go carefully, eh? Remember, we don't have to pull them apart. Not us. Others.'

Louis was always saying things like that! A chief inspector of the Sûreté Nationale and a detective of long standing, he was the other half of their flying squad such as it was and always seeming to be on the run. '*Verdammt!* It's nearly Christmas, Louis! Giselle and Oona . . . they were expecting me to be at home in Paris for the holiday.'

Ah *merde*, no concern for his partner, and how, really, were they to begin? wondered St-Cyr, wishing he was elsewhere and looking desperately around at the carnage, telling himself that Hermann was better off if a little angry. It helped the stomach.

One couple clung in a last, desperate act of love. Ice encased everything, and the fire that had come before had removed all but scraps of clothing. Even the woman's garter belt was gone, the elastic adding its tiny contribution to the conflagration, the wires now embedded in her thighs.

Others had cringed under the seats, covering their heads and trying to protect their faces. Still others had been trampled by their fellow human beings. Now those who had done the trampling lay atop the piles of tangled bodies, their stark, empty-eyed expressions caught and kept by death and the encasing ice.

A cinema . . . The Palace of Pleasure of the Beautiful Celluloid. Whoever had set the fire—and it had been set—had made certain of the carnage. Both fire doors had been padlocked, though not, he thought, by the arsonist. The cinema had been packed—two days before Christmas 1942, a Wednesday evening performance, the fire set at about 9.15 Berlin time. The City of Lyon, the German Occupation of France but not a cinema reserved for the Wehrmacht, not one of the *soldatenkinos*. Railway workers and their families. Humble people, little people. Loyal fans, the film a favourite of all railway workers, *La Bête humaine*, The Human Beast.

In the scramble to escape, 183 patrons had died, an unofficial estimate. 'Ah, *mon Dieu*, Hermann, to come straight from the railway station to a thing like this!'

Icicles were everywhere—hanging from the balcony and a brass railing that had come loose under the crush. Even from the cornice of the projectionist's booth, even from the backs and bottoms of the seats. Charred timbers showed where portions of the roof had gone. The sky above was empty and grey. Icicles hung up there—great long things that, with the fifteen degrees of frost, appeared dirty grey and savage.

There was glass underfoot from the skylights above, and plaster in chunks with laddered bits of once-painted wood whose charred alligator pattern might have been used to trace the progress of the fire had one not been told exactly where it had started.

'Right at the head of each aisle, Louis. Simultaneously or very close to it. Gasoline, though God knows where they got it.'

'Molotov cocktails?' asked the Frenchman.

Kohler shook his head and nudged the bandanna farther up on a nose that had been broken several times in the course of duty and elsewhere. 'More subtle than that. Two women were seen entering together. One carried a woven rush bag large enough for the shopping.'

'And those two women?'

The Bavarian's gaze didn't waver. 'Seen leaving in a hurry, Louis, just as the fire struck. They were the first to get out.'

'Two women.'

'Yes. They came in late, and the usherette found them seats at the very back, the right aisle, left side, nearest the aisle.'

'It's not possible. No woman would do this, Hermann, and certainly not two of them.'

'Then talk to the usherette. See if you can get any sense out of her. The poor kid's still so deep in shock, she couldn't even tell me her name. I told her to go home and think about it. All the others had buggered off. She alone had stayed.'

Hermann was really upset. The faded blue eyes that could so often hold nothing but saw everything, were moist and wary. Frost tinged the strongly boned brow round the edges of its bandage—a bullet graze there from a last investigation and blood ... blood everywhere, some still seeping through. Too worried to even change the dressing. Yes, yes, that last case and what it had revealed to him about the growing resistance to the Occupation. Provence and a hill village. Murder then and murder now, and no time to even take a piss. Just blitzkrieg, blitzkrieg, because that was the way the Germans wanted everything solved. No time even for Christmas and a little holiday.

'We'll leave the usherette for now, Hermann. The relatives will want the dead released for burial. It's the least we can do.'

'Then you take this aisle, I'll take the right one. Meet me in front of what's left of the stage.'

'Look for little things. House keys, cigarette lighters, bits of jewellery, brass buttons, anything that might let us get a feel for what really happened here. Then we will know better how to proceed.'

'Guns?'

'Yes, guns. They were railway workers. Communists. Resistants. Perhaps the fire was an act of vengeance after all.'

'Gestapo Lyon wanting to get even, eh?'

'Perhaps, but then ...'

Kohler snorted sarcastically. Always Louis couched things by saying Perhaps but then ... *mais alors* ... *alors* ... And of course Gestapo Lyon could well have lit the bloody thing just for spite to nail a couple of Resistants yet would try their damnedest to blame it all on someone else!

Worried about him, St-Cyr watched his partner and friend pick his way between the seats. No row gave easy access to the far aisle, but once committed, Hermann moved deliberately, stepping over a corpse, pausing to examine something. A big man with tired, frizzy hair that was not black or brown but something in between and greying fast. A man with the heart and mind of a small-time hustler. A petty thief when need be. These days, food and everything else was in very short supply and ration tickets often unavailable to one who was not a 'good' Gestapo but a damned good detective. Hermann lived with two women in Paris, so was always on the look-out for things. Unfortunately there was a third back home on her father's farm near Wasserburg, the wife. But 'his' Gerda was suing him for divorce, having taken up with a conscripted French labourer, and the Gestapo's Bavarian detective was feeling betrayed by his own kind. Ah yes. Gerda's uncle was a big shot in Munich. Gerda's uncle had pull enough to see that the divorce went through in spite of all the laws against such a thing. Problems . . . there were always problems and they had only just got word of the divorce.

When a bit of roof came away, Hermann jerked his head up and froze in panic with a hand inside his overcoat, clutching the pistol in its shoulder holster.

Yes, Hermann was just not himself. The German Sixth Army was surrounded at Stalingrad. In North Africa, the Americans had landed. It was only a matter of time until the Germans packed up and left, and they both knew it.

Uneasy at the thought of their parting and what it might entail—a shoot-out perhaps, though they had become more than friends—St-Cyr went back to work. A child, a girl of six he thought, had tried to escape by worming her way under the seats. Her hair had caught fire, she had tried to get to her knees but one of the seats had held her down.

The mother's hand was still firmly about the child's slender wrist. She'd been racing to reach the daughter, had gone down on all fours and had scrambled between the next two rows of seats only to flatten herself as the fire had swept over them, and to reach out to the child.

The ice that encased her body had cracked. A gossamer of dirty, whitish-grey lines now made an angular web over the charred back and blackened head.

The child had been trying to reach the stage but had only got about one-quarter of the way. Had the mother seen her dive beneath the seats? Had she simply been searching madly for her daughter by the light of the flames and suddenly come upon her at the last moment?

And why, please, had the child been here at all? *La Bête humaine,* madame? Marital infidelity and murder? Was there no one to look after your daughter, or did you think it necessary for her to see that railwaymen were really human? That among them there could be both good and evil, just as there is in any other class or occupation? That they, too, could lust and hate with passion?

There was little left of the woman's purse, no chance of readily determining her identity, though he knew her flesh and skin would be better preserved next to the floor and that if he turned her over, parts of her clothing might still remain.

From across the bodies and the ice-encased wreckage, Kohler secretly watched as Louis tried to rationalize the child being with the mother. He'd be 'talking' to them, he'd be asking questions of the mother. Louis was stocky and tough, rarely belligerent and normally the diplomat even in very tight situations. Plump and chubby in the face, with the brown ox-eyes of the French and a broad, bland brow that brooked no nonsense. The hair was thick and brown and needing a trim, the scruffy moustache wide and thick. A fisherman, a gardener, a reader of books in winter when he could get the time, but now year round since fishing was no longer allowed under the decree of June 1940. *Verboten* to drop a line in the Seine of a Sunday. *Verboten! Gott im Himmel,* what had they been thinking of in Berlin when they'd written that decree? It had baffled the Bavarian half of their partnership as much as the French, and they both had had the idea then that this lousy war could not possibly last for ever. Take away the potatoes and you create, hunger; take away a man's right to fish and eventually he'll begin to question why.

Against all odds, Louis and he had got on—common crime:

murder, arson—oh yes, arson!—rape, extortion, kidnapping, et cetera, et cetera. None of the rough stuff—not that kind anyway. Not Gestapo brutality. Ah no. Only its witness in passing.

Decidedly uncomfortable and uneasy at the memory of a naked seventeen-year-old girl horribly tortured by the Gestapo but a few days ago in Cannes, Kohler tried to put all thought of the French Resistance out of his mind. But as he searched among the wreckage, he had the thought his two sons would die at Stalingrad and he'd never see them again. Gerda would leave him, she'd get her divorce, and there'd be no one at home to run to when this whole sad business was over. He'd be tarred Gestapo along with all the rest. God forbid that Louis should still think, as he had at first, that their partnership would have to end in one of them killing the other.

Ironically, there was a revolver lying under the ice, an old Lebel, Model 1873, a swing-out six-shooter exactly like the gun Louis still carried.

'Ah, shit!' swore Kohler, exhaling the words exasperatedly. 'I forgot about his shooter and Louis didn't remind me of it!'

As the Gestapo member of the flying squad, Kohler was to keep their weapons under German control at all times. Well, at least until the shooting started and the time for questions was over.

Swiftly Kohler sought him out again. Louis had gone back through one of the gaps in the rear wall and was now standing in what had once been the foyer. The grey light of day was louvered with shadow. Just his head and shoulders were visible beyond that tangled, horrible pile of humanity he was calmly studying. The brown felt trilby was yanked down over the brow for warmth and as a warning of determination. He'd get who-ever had done this. One could read it in him in spite of his calmness.

The head and shoulders vanished and Kohler realized that Louis hadn't wanted to be seen just then.

Merde again! 'If we can't trust each other, we're done for,' he said, muttering it to himself. With difficulty he freed the revolver and, looking about to see that he was unobserved, quickly pocketed the thing, determined to drop it in the nearest sewer.

'There's no sense our getting Gestapo Lyon all worked up. Hell, they'd only rip the town apart and shoot thirty or forty hostages we might need to question.'

Kohler knew that if Louis had found the revolver he, too, would have hidden it away and said nothing of it, but Louis was French and had every reason to do so, whereas his partner was . . .

When the revolver had disappeared, and Hermann had busied himself elsewhere, St-Cyr heaved a contented sigh. For a moment, he'd thought Hermann undecided. He was glad that they were beginning to think alike on this issue, but of course, Hermann might yet weaken and quite obviously there had been Resistants in the cinema. Railway workers were notoriously Communist, pro-Russian and therefore anti-German.

Distracting himself from such an uncomfortable thought, for things would be far from easy if the presence of the Resistance was as obvious to others, St-Cyr went back to searching the ruins. There were rings of gold and those of silver. If anything, the fire had deepened the colour of the gold wedding bands, while that of the silver had either been dulled by oxidation or swept clean by the flames. One gold wedding band had fallen and rolled ahead of its owner and he wondered about a last act of contrition. An illicit love affair? The wedding ring removed and then . . . then the fire and the realization that the ring would have to be put back on the finger or else . . .

He thought of Marianne, of how she must have removed the ring he'd given her on their wedding day. How she must have slipped it into a pocket only to guiltily put it back on when coming home late, satiated from the arms of her German lover. Yes, *lover*!

But Marianne was dead and so was their little son Philippe, killed by *mistake*! A Resistance bomb that had been meant for him. Ah yes, they had had his number—still did for that matter.

They thought him a collaborator because he worked under a German, a Bavarian, and for the enemy. What else was he to have done, eh? God had frowned, and God had not thought to tell the Resistance otherwise.

With difficulty, he freed the ring and managed to force it back on the proper finger. He said to himself, Hermann was watching me just then. He has realized I've kept my gun and said nothing of it.

There was one corpse whose hand still clutched the clasp knife the man had used to kill those around him in his struggle to get out. The blade was a good fifteen centimetres long and not exactly what he should have been carrying around. Ah no, most certainly not.

Railwaymen! he said to himself. Ah *nom de Jésus-Christ,* how on earth were they to settle this business? How could they possibly hope to catch this ... this maniac, this Salamander who had supposedly set the fire? *Salamander,* the telex from Mueller, Head of the Gestapo in Berlin, had read with all the brevity of a command from on high and all the warning too. 'Find him before he kills too many more,' Boemelburg had said in Paris. The Sturmbannführer Walter Boemelburg, Head of Section IV, the Gestapo in France. Hermann's boss.

Two women, not one man, a Salamander, had been seen. It made no sense to tell them so little yet expect them not only to find out everything in the space of one or two days—would they have that much time?—but also to put a stop to the arsonist or arsonists immediately.

And how, please, had Berlin found out about it in the first place?

Back inside the cinema, Kohler came upon what must have been a priest. Only the top of a richly jewelled cross protruded from tightly clasped hands that had been roasted. The corpse was jammed between two rows of seats and on its knees facing the foyer. A chain, of many links and stones, was wrapped around the right hand, and why must that God of Louis's make him do things like this? Gingerly he broke the encasing ice away and teased the cross free. It came quite easily, the flesh clinging a little, but unravelling the chain was more sickening. His fingers trembled. His breath was held. He knew he was on to something.

Rubies and sky-blue sapphires and diamonds . . . tiny fleurs-de-lis in gold . . . 150,000 marks? 175,000? Renaissance? Was it that old?

No ordinary priest. The Bishop of Lyon's secretary? he wondered. A cardinal perhaps or some ambassador from the Vatican? But why wear a thing like this to a film? Surely he must have known robbery was a distinct possibility?

Had he come fearing the worst, the fire, and then knelt to pray it would not happen even as it did?

All around him were the remains of dinner pails, boots, goggles and heavy leather-and-asbestos gauntlets, indicating that some of the men had only just come off shift from the marshalling yards in Perrache, right in the centre of the city not far from here and on the end of the tongue of land that lay between the Saône and the Rhône.

Gestapo HQ Lyon was in the Hotel Terminus facing the Gare de Perrache, an uncomfortable thought. Questions . . . there were bound to be questions. The Resistance thing if nothing else. *Verdammt!*

Two women and a priest, but no ordinary cleric. A large handbag woven out of rushes. A bag for the market, though nowadays market pickings were slim unless one dealt on the black market and had things to sell or trade.

A telex from Mueller, an order from Boemelburg. Shit!

Kohler sought the seats where the two women must have sat but, of course, they were now under a pile of humanity. Surely the priest could not have been looking their way. Not at the last. But had he known of them? Could it be possible?

Pocketing the cross, he moved away, found a broken wine bottle and another dinner pail, wondered again at the avidness of the railwaymen. Clearly they'd all agreed to gather to see a favourite film, but since the film had first come out in 1938, presumably most had seen it already.

Then why the gathering? he asked himself. Such meetings could only mean trouble.

He began to search further. Nearly everywhere there was the rubbish of railwaymen or members of their families. The gun he had found weighed on his conscience and he experienced a spasm of cold panic. He saw again that girl in the cellars of the Hotel Montfleury in Cannes, saw the blood trickling from her battered lips and nose to join the swill of vomit and excrement on the floor. Dead . . . dead at such a tender age. She'd known nothing, hadn't even been involved. Well, not really.

'Hermann . . .'

He leapt. 'Louis, good *Gott im Himmel*, what the hell do you mean by startling me like that?'

Ah *mon Dieu*, Hermann was really not himself! 'Nothing, *mon vieux*. Nothing, eh? Forgive me. The fire marshal wants a word.'

'Then talk to him. I'm busy.'

'Don't be so gruff. His German counterpart is present and speaks no French. Kommandeur Weidling requests your presence as interpreter.'

Kohler pulled down a lower eyelid and made a face behind the bandanna. 'Doesn't he trust you to do it accurately?'

'Please don't give me horseshit, Hermann. Both men are nervous and not without good reason. They are afraid this will happen again and soon.'

'Then there really is a pattern and there have been other fires?'

'Ah yes, a pattern.'

'The Salamander?'

'Perhaps.'

'Did you find anything?'

A shrug would be best. 'Just little things. Nothing much. We'll look again, eh? After the conference.'

'Piss off! The Feuerschutzpolizei back home can't know anything about this, Louis. What the hell's he doing here?'

Again there was that massive shrug. 'Ask Gestapo Mueller; ask Herr Weidling but proceed gently. We can use all the help we can get.'

'A visitor from home who just happens to be a fire chief and on the scene of a major fire? The son of a bitch shouldn't even be here, Louis, not with all those incendiaries the fucking RAF are dropping at home!'

Hermann always had to have the last word. It was best to let him so as to avoid argument, but . . . Ah, what the hell. 'Then let us have a look at our surroundings first, so as to have everything in perspective. Please, I think it is important.'

Kohler's grunt was answer enough. Picking their way past the ticket booth, they stood a moment at the entrance, gazing out across place Terreaux. Bartholdi's four magnificent horses were caught frozen in their imaginary flight to the sea. Shrouded in ice, the Goddess of Springs and Rivers looked unfeelingly down from her chariot at the corpse of a man who had run to her in flames for help.

French police and German soldiers kept the crowd at bay behind a rope barrier. The debris of firefighting was every where. Pumper trucks, whose snaking hoses were now collapsed and clinging to the icy pavement, were being attended to by exhausted firemen whose disillusionment at having failed to save so many was all too evident.

The square, one of the finest in Lyon and right in the centre of the city, would normally be busy in the afternoon, even under the Occupation. Now the curious and the grieving huddled around its periphery and, in places, beneath shop awnings that had been folded out of the way.

Collectively the mood of the crowd was one of outrage and fear. They'd be blaming the authorities. They'd be whispering

How could you let a thing like this happen? Why were the fire doors padlocked? It was that bastard who owned the place. He did it for the insurance. No, no, it was a sadist, a maniac. It's going to happen again. Oh yes it is!

A murmur intruded, a disturbing puzzle for it was not coming from the crowd. Now and then the sporadic chipping of firemen's axes broke through the hush and the murmur as the hoses were freed for coiling.

Unsettled that he could not readily find the source of the murmur, St-Cyr scanned the length of the square. The Hôtel de Ville, the city's seventeenth-century town hall, faced on to it at the far end, with a domed clocktower rising above and behind the entrance. The Palais des Arts—the Palais Saint-Pierre— took up the whole of the opposite side of the square. Eighteenth century. All solid, well-built buildings. Staid but baroque too, and emitting that singularity of purpose so evident in the Lyonnais character. Good business and sound banking: silk and explosives, leather tanning and many other industries. A city of about 700,000, with blocks and blocks of nearly identical, shoulder-to-shoulder buildings from three to five windows wide and from four to six storeys high, as were some of these. The stone grey or buff-grey, the stucco buff-grey to pale pink. The roofs of dark grey slate or weathered orange tile, the chimneys far more solid than those of Paris and of brownish-yellow brick with chimneypots that were rarely if ever canted because the people here would have seen to them.

Mansard roofs with small attic windows and tiny one- or two-room garrets for servants, shopgirls, clerks and students were to the left and right. Below them were ornamental iron railings before tall french windows behind which most of the lace or damask curtains were now parted. Drop-shutters were pulled up and out of the way or, in a few places, lowered to half-mast like weary eyelids, and in one case, closed completely as if to shut out what had happened

'The location is perfect, Hermann. Maximum exposure if fear of repeat fires is what was wanted.'

'Publicity. Someone who knows the city well,' grunted Kohler. 'A pattern, Louis.'

'An uncomfortable thought and an arsonist totally without conscience. But for every fire there is a reason, no matter how warped.'

'Or sick.'

Again the murmuring intruded but now there was that unmistakable feeling of never knowing if they were being watched by the arsonist.

'Louis, our visitor is feeding the pigeons. There, over there. Behind the fountain.'

The stiff woollen greatcoat was Prussian blue, the rubber boots, whose tops were folded down, were well used and black, of pre-war vintage. Little more could be seen of him beyond the stallions with their flailing hooves and wild-eyed muzzles, but the murmur increased and became more excited. The black leather gloves had been removed and stuffed into a pocket. The left hand held a torn loaf of white bread—white, no less and seldom seen on the streets these days!—while the fingers of the right hand ripped off bits and tossed them to the pigeons, his little friends.

'Does he keep doves at home?' hazarded Kohler, baffled that, in the face of such a catastrophe and hunger among the civilian population, anyone could be crass enough to unthinkingly undertake such a sentimental task.

'Maybe he's homesick,' offered the Sûreté

'Maybe he wants to show you French exactly how unimportant you are!'

Such inflammatory statements from Hermann were best ignored but why should they be? 'Is it that he has seen it all so many times before, Inspector, or is it that he needs to find release from the horror in such a simple task?'

Kohler grinned at Louis's use of 'Inspector' The Frog was

one up on him in rank and always pulling it. 'Hey, Chief, cut the crap. He's budgeting the crumbs. He's making sure that the weak and not-so-weak get their fair share but like all good Nazis he admires the brave and the strong. See how he flicks the extra bits down at his boots as a reward.'

It was St-Cyr's turn to grin. 'You're learning, *mon ami*. Being stuck with me is good for you. Let's hear what he has to say.'

'Let's ask him exactly why the fuck he's here and what he intends to do about it!'

The grunt of acknowledgement from the fire chief was terse, the bread summarily ripped into four large chunks and thrown among the pigeons so as to equalize the fight. 'Leiter Weidling at your service, Herr Kohler. Lübeck, Heidelberg and Köln. This one's done it all before. Same technique, same pattern. Gasoline poured on the floor to run under the seats and around the shoes and boots of the unsuspecting. Then across the entrances to the foyer or across the staircase. Then the match or cigarette lighter.'

'But . . . but the usherette has said there were two women . . . ?' began St-Cyr in German that was far from rusty.

Unimpressed that a Frenchman could speak his native tongue, Weidling fastidiously brushed crumbs from thick, strong fingers before pulling on his gloves. Again he spoke only to Hermann. 'Lübeck first, in late May of 1938. A cinema in the student quarter near the university.'

The blue eyes were lifeless in that rosy, apple-cheeked countenance. A man of sixty or sixty-five, a father probably and a grandfather. The lips were thin.

'Heidelberg in early July of the same year, a crowded lecture hall, a Party meeting. The first fire killed sixty-seven, the second only twenty-eight. Then Köln and a night-club in mid-August— again the same technique, again a good number—sixteen to be precise—but most escaped through the stage doors and I count the thing a failure.'

Was he really telling them everything? 'Two women?' asked Kohler, watching him intently.

Weidling returned the look. 'Perhaps, but I happen to think not.'

'And since those fires?' hazarded the Sûreté.

Again he was ignored. 'Nothing of a similar nature, Herr Kohler. Other arsonists, of course, but now this, yes? A student perhaps who visited the Reich in 1938 and then went home to Lyon. My people are checking into things and will send me the case files. You can read them yourself.'

A student, a citizen of Lyon . . .

'Leiter Weidling is to become a professor at the Fire Protection Officers' School in Eberswald. We are fortunate to have him with us. He's the only fire marshal in the Reich to have been decorated three times for bravery beyond the call of duty.'

This had come in French from Lyon's fire marshal, Julien Robichaud.

'On holiday, is he?' snapped Kohler in French, for that was the way one got things done quickly.

Weidling grinned, for though he hadn't understood a word, he had understood only too well the drift of Herr Kohler's thoughts. Hero firemen sometimes lit their own fires. 'Here for the International Fire Marshals' Convention and staying on a few days.'

It was Kohler's turn to be unimpressed, but he tried hard to hide his feelings by offering precious cigarettes all round and insisting Louis take one. 'A coffee, I think, and a glass of *marc*?'

Robichaud strode over to the nearest pumper truck and returned with a thermos jug, four tin cups and a bottle. 'Emergency rations, messieurs,' he said, gritting his teeth self-consciously. 'It's not a day for alcohol but . . .' He gave the shrug of a man uncertain of his position and definitely worried about it. 'But one has to have a little something, eh? to settle the stomach.'

Kohler took the bottle from him and uptilted it into his

mouth, shutting his eyes in blessed relief. '*Merci*,' he said, wiping his lips. 'Louis?'

St-Cyr shook his head. 'In the coffee, I think. Yes, yes, that will be sufficient.'

They were a pair, these two detectives, thought Weidling. Gestapo Leader Mueller's telex from Berlin had said to watch them closely. Gestapo Boemelburg in Paris had been emphatic: St-Cyr was a patriot and therefore untrustworthy; Kohler a doubter of Germanic invincibility. They'd been in trouble with the SS far too many times. They had made disparaging remarks about some of its members and had held them up to ridicule.

Weidling helped himself to the bottle. The coffee was good—the real stuff—the brandy barely passable, the French fire chief nothing but a nuisance to be got rid of quickly. 'You will need a list of all those who were in the cinema, Herr Kohler, both the victims and those who escaped.'

'It'll be impossible to get a complete list.'

'Nothing is impossible. Get one. Also the employees, the night-watchman and the cleaners, the concierge if that's what they call him, the manager and the owner and their closest relatives. Also all previous employees over the past four years. Grudge fires are not uncommon.'

Kohler grinned. 'I thought you said it might be a student? Lübeck, wasn't it?'

'Or Heidelberg or Köln. *Ja, ja*, you will still require the lists. It's best that way. Find out if the staff have been turning any-one away. Sex in the back rows. Some filthy Frenchman or Algerian exposing himself to women and little girls or boys. Some black or brown bastard making suggestive remarks. A woman betrayed by a husband with a lover. A Jewess. Those are always possibilities but you are correct, Herr Kohler, hero firemen could very well become 'hero' arsonists to advance themselves, but not this one. You will find me at the Bristol. Inquire at the desk. Get a list of the tenants too. There were apartments above the foyer and behind the balcony and projectionist's booth.'

Brusquely he shook hands with Robichaud and made excuses about having to tidy up for dinner. 'The wife,' he grunted. 'She'll have purchased the last of her silks by now and I must examine them. Have the lists compiled, Herr Kohler. You can bring them over at dawn. Gestapo Mueller wants this solved before it happens again and wishes me to give the matter my fullest attention. Even here in France people have a right to know they are safe under our administration. Heil Hitler.'

Shit!

They watched as he strode the short distance to his car. Robichaud sucked grimly on his cheeks and held his breath in exasperation.

It was Hermann who said, 'You have our sympathies.'

Lyon's fire chief nodded. 'But you have not had to introduce him at far too many banquets, monsieur, and you do not have to answer for your sins or blame yourself for letting this one happen. You see, messieurs, I was in the cinema. It was myself who turned in the alarm and unfortunately he knows of this.'

There was dead silence but only for a moment. St-Cyr took the bottle from him and cautiously filled the fire chief's cup. 'Two women?' he asked, pleasantly enough.

There was a hiss. 'Of this I am certain! I saw them vanish into a tram-car right over there.'

Right across the square beyond the fountain and obscured by it at the moment of escape, right in front of the Palais des Arts.

It was on the tip of St-Cyr's tongue to ask, Why did you not blow your whistle and summon a gendarme to chase after them? but he let the matter rest Obviously Robichaud had had his hands full.

Finishing his cigarette, he carefully put it out, then handed the butt to Hermann for his little tin. These days tobacco was in such short supply it was the least he could do. The crowd seemed intent on their every move. Again he cautiously looked around the square—always there was the possibility that the arsonist would hang about to watch the fun and come back again and again. Sometimes they would offer help or pitch right in unasked. Sometimes they would even turn in the alarm and make suggestions as to how the fire might have started. But not Robichaud, never him. Other things perhaps but not arson.

No one seemed out of the ordinary until St-Cyr spotted a lone girl with a bicycle. She had only just arrived and now stood uncertainly where Herr Weidling's car had been. She had come up the rue Paul Chenavard. Her carrier basket held a cloth bag that was square and no doubt full of books. About twenty-five or-six but looking a little younger. Still a student? he wondered apprehensively, but thought not. Of medium height, with short, light brown hair and a fringe. The deep, wide-set eyes earnestly searched. The pale oval of her face was not wide or narrow but something in between. There was no lipstick or rouge that he could discern from this distance. A bookseller? he asked. A librarian? A girl in a cocoa-brown beret and long white scarf that was tied under her chin and thrown over the shoulders of a fawn-coloured double-breasted overcoat. A grey plaid skirt and dark grey woollen argyle socks that would come to her knees. Flat-heeled, brown leather walking shoes, not winter boots. Knitted beige gloves gripped the handlebars. Gloves were not so easy to knit, and he wondered if she had made them and thought that perhaps she had. Trained in those arts, then, he said. Yes, she has that capable look about her. Not beautiful, not plain. Does she keep house for someone in addition to her job? Two women . . .

'Hermann, wait here. I'll be back in a moment.'

'She's already turning to leave, Louis. She's seen you looking her way, *dummkopf.*'

'Damn!'

Lyon's fire marshal said nothing but he, too, had noticed the girl. Robichaud seemed a decent enough fellow. Tough and experienced and carrying a cross no fire chief would wish to bear. A man of middle age and grey, a veteran with the ribbon of the Legion of Honour to prove it. A father? wondered St-Cyr. A man who, like most these days, worried about his pension and had gone to work under the Nazis grudgingly, no doubt, but out of necessity and to ensure that pension. We French are realists, he said sadly to himself, especially the Lyonnais.

It was Kohler who, having gathered up the cups and the thermos, returned them to the pumper truck, then led the way back into the ruins. Only the neck of the cognac bottle protruded from his already bulging overcoat pocket.

The girl with the bicycle might have a relative among the victims. Perhaps a husband she didn't want or a former lover? he asked himself.

Crime . . . it brought out the worst in one. It made one see motive behind everything, even the most insignificant of things.

Yet the girl continued to haunt him as her presence would Louis. Why had she come for such a brief look? Why had she fled before their eyes?

No shred of film had escaped the fire. Funnelling flames through to its skylight, the projectionist's booth, never roomy at the best of times, had been turned into an inferno. Bent and twisted film canisters and other rubbish were now heaped in the far corners and against that wall by the pressure from the last hoses. Only the twin projectors, once magnificent pieces of complex engineering, stood sentinel but in ruins on their jackleg pedestals whose tripod feet were securely bolted to the floor.

A lover of the cinema and a cinematographer at heart, St-Cyr ran his eyes ruefully over the control panel. Eighteen Bakelite-handled switches had operated the lights, the screen, the curtains and the sound system. Subdued lighting at the sides, please, behind torch-bearing Venuses that were no more. Spotlights on the manager if some sort of an announcement were to be made—an air-raid warning perhaps. Starlight on the ceiling. Now the full or half-moon and the shooting star. The magic of the cinema.

At once, the whole thing was there before him, that sense of power and control the projectionist must feel, that sense of boredom too, for how many films—even a masterpiece like *La Bête humaine*—can be seen thirty or forty times?

Picking through the canisters, he uncovered the charred remains of the projectionist's stool and beneath it, a woman's shoe that had survived only in its spiked heel and shank. Had someone been in the booth alleviating the boredom? There were no bodies. Presumably the projectionist and his visitor had survived. Perhaps the shoe was from an earlier time and had no bearing on the case.

Searching, he found a warped cigarette case, not expensive. With difficulty, he pried it open but there was no name. A woman's, he said, pocketing it and the remains of the shoe.

A fountain pen was next. Had the woman come for payment? Had the projectionist been writing her a cheque? Had she forced him to do so?

All manner of possibilities came to mind, the cinematographer discarding most of them as soon as they flashed on the screen of his mind. Once the feature film had started, the projectionist would have rewound the newsreel on the other projector before placing it back in its canister. Since all newsreels these days were German and from the Propaganda Staffel, this had to be done carefully, but had the woman arrived by then? Was she sitting on the stool? No cigarette smoking would have been allowed up here but plenty broke the rule and some had suffered as a consequence. Photographic and motion picture film had a nitrate base that made it highly inflammable. Perhaps she had taken out her cigarettes and he had told her to put them away?

Those two women had come in late. The feature film had

already been in progress ... Had this woman been one of them? Was it too much to hope for?

A lipstick was uncovered, the thin tube still bearing traces of its fake gold plating. A cheap compact followed, its mirror gone, the thing open—dropped—had it been dropped in panic at the cry of Fire?

He thought it had, and saw her sitting on the stool, bundled in her overcoat, hat and scarf. No heat in this place—no heat anywhere these days but in the rooms of the Nazis and their collaborators. She was touching up her face, turning a cheek sideways. She was doing her lips, a corner ... yes, yes. The projectionist had paused in coiling the newsreel's leader on to the spool. He was looking at her, grinning. He knew all about her little hopes and desires. He had seen her naked many times, had heard her saying ... saying ...

Only the sound-track of the film came to St-Cyr along with the whirring of the fans that sucked air past the lamp to cool it. But that could not be, not now.

The door would have been closed. Yes, it had a simple hook and eye. Would Lantier and his partner have discovered the hotbox that was to keep their beloved locomotive from returning to Le Havre, thus triggering the story? Had the film progressed much further? Had Séverine kissed the husband she would later beg Lantier to kill, having first had sex with the engineer in a railway shed among the boxes of bolts and piles of oily rags?

Had the engineer betrayed his true love, La Lison, the locomotive, for that of the innocent though shrewd and calculating Séverine?

In Zola's novel, Lantier had been born with an obsession to kill women—his cousin first. In the film, a passing train had stopped Lantier then, and later, when Séverine had asked him to kill for her to cover up the murder she and her husband had committed, the engineer had found he couldn't. She had told him their affair was over—*fini*—and he had snatched up a knife and had plunged it into her throat.

La Bête humaine ... the Human Beast. An obsession ... three fires in 1938 in Germany, two women and now this A Salamander ... The cry of Fire.

The film had been set totally in the world of railwaymen, its scenes so vivid one could still thrill to the power of the locomotive beneath one's feet and lean out to see the track ahead racing inevitably towards the story's horrible conclusion.

Even the smell of hot engine oil was still with him, even that of coal dust and the stench of sulphur dioxide.

One hundred and eighty-three deaths—450 in the audience, all with separate stories of hope and desire, deceit and avarice or pain and struggle. Always there were these stories, only the more so in cases like this because the victims' last moments had to have meaning, the substance of individual lives. That woman and her daughter; the one who sat up here but could well have escaped unscathed; the one who had frantically remembered to replace her wedding ring only to lose it as she fell under the feet of others.

The man who had murdered in his fury to escape; the one who had climbed a dry fountain, hoping its stone goddess would offer succour.

One thing was certain. The cinema was not the usual for railwaymen, its location too expensive, its seats too posh, yet they had come *en masse*.

Clearing away the ice from one of the portals, St-Cyr peered down into the cinema. There was no sign of Hermann, no sign of anyone but the dead, yet as sure as he was standing here, he felt there had been Resistance people in the audience. A meeting. Ah *merde*, was it a complication or in itself reason enough for the fire so as to kill the lot of them?

And if so, how did this business of the Salamander fit in? Mere coincidence, or was it that the arsonist or arsonists had known someone in the audience and had wanted to get rid of them no matter the cost?

A Salamander. A person or persons so elusive only a code-name could be attached to them.

A directive from Berlin, and now a visiting fire chief who claimed to know all about it. *Merde!*

Kohler nudged the door to the toilets open and shone the light over the ice-covered walls. Four men and two women had been trapped in here—locked in. Yes, *verdammt!* The key was still in the lock, the bolt sticking out. Out! The firemen had had to use an axe to get in.

The bodies were fully clothed. Overcoats, heavy sweaters, corduroy and twill trousers, beige paint on bare female legs instead of silk stockings, a wrist-watch that had stopped.

Two of the men had their faces crammed over the squat-holes in the floor, hoping against all odds that the sewer gas would contain enough oxygen to sustain life.

One of the women was bent double over the deep wash-basin at the far end, her head still under the faucet she clutched. Purse spilled open on the floor, pillbox hat and veil in ruins.

Another of the men had tried to cling to the tiny air vent high on the far wall but had finally had to let go and was now slumped against the corner.

The last woman and man had lain directly behind the door, trying to cover their faces with handkerchiefs.

Not liking what he'd found, Kohler fingered the lock and key in doubt. One toilet for both sexes, that was the norm, so nothing out of the ordinary there. A three-holer Turkish with trough urinal for the boys and a cracked mirror so they could comb their hair and try to watch the ladies at their peeing. But why lock the door on them? Why? Was the arsonist or arsonists so sick in the head, he or she or they could think to do a thing like that in addition to everything else?

The bodies had been untouched by the flames and lay

exactly as they'd been found, except for the two behind the door. He stepped over them and nudged the door closed. He set the torch down on the floor and turned the man over, sucking in a breath as he did so.

There was a rolled-up sheaf of paper in the right hand, the grip so tight it was only with difficulty—a foot pressed down hard on the knuckles—that it was released.

Railway schedules, ah *merde*. Lyon to the internment camp at Besançon and on to the German border near Mulhouse. Lyon to Paris. Lyon to Tours, to Bordeaux, to Marseille and Toulon . . .

The locations of bridges, viaducts, tunnels and switching yards . . . the lines black and clear under the torch beam. A siding at Dijon had been circled with red ink; another at Mâcon. A water tower at Moulıns, a coal depot at Nevers . . .

Switches . . and more of them. The locations of flatbed cranes to lift track or wrecked locomotives and railway trucks out of the way. *Verdammt!* What had the bastards been planning? To blow up everything?

Were the papers to have been sent over to England?

Dragging the woman back against the door to hold it closed, he went to work. First the identity papers of every one of them, then the contents of the men's pockets and the women's purses.

None of the men were over the age of forty-five. The women were in their late thirties. Not young, not old, not beautiful but ordinary . . Why did he have to look at them that way?

Madame Madeleine Roget of the passage Mermet in Croix Rousse, the hill between the rivers and home of the silkweavers . . .

Kohler yanked her head up from under the tap. 'What the hell did you think you were doing, madame? Plotting terrorism? You were a courier. Come on, answer me! You were going to take those plans to someone else. Two women would split the risk, the one going north, the other south.'

He let her head fall. He tried to get a grip on himself. Louis . . . ? he asked. Louis, what am I supposed to do? Tell Gestapo Lyon or keep silent about it?

Behind the projectionist's booth, and facing on to the place Terreaux, there were three flats. A corridor led across the width of the building to the now-open doorways and the narrow staircase to the street. St-Cyr hesitated. Ah *nom de Dieu*, there was no sense in risking life and limb, yet he had the feeling there was something he should see and asked angrily, 'God, why must you do this to me, eh? A simple detective? Roasted children on the Eve of Christmas! Mothers straining to reach their daughters! How much more do You think a man can take?'

As was His custom, God did not answer. One of the occupants had leapt to his death. The others had either made it down the stairs or had been taken down the ladders.

Gingerly stepping on to a joist, St-Cyr began to pick his way along the corridor, turning first to the right and then to the left when things got shaky.

The middle flat had not been occupied by the man who had jumped. There was nothing, no furniture, a puzzle until he noticed the charred buckets that had once held paint or glue for wallpaper, the remains of the ladders and bags of patching plaster. Redecoration in these times of shortages? The black market for·materials. He heaved an immense sigh of relief at the prospect of finding no more bodies.

When he came to the doorway on the other side of the building, he hesitated, then ran his eyes swiftly over everything, for here the fire had left a few things: toppled, high-backed armchairs that would have had lace antimacassars, the jade-green fabric scorched and then drenched by the hoses; a marble-topped table, now cracked in half, an alabaster vase and bust, both broken and on the floor. In spite of the stench, he imagined he could smell the place as it must once have been, the dust of ages, the closeness of faded linen mother or grandɹother had left to an only daughter, the sharpness of camphor, wine, cheese in days past, and once-forbidden cigarette smoke. Dust filtering slowly through the sunlight that would, on those rare days, have streamed in through the windows.

Ornate, three-globed lamps on tall, thick standards of Napoleonic brass had been toppled over and smashed. Family portraits had been flung onto the floor and were now jammed into the corners behind all the rest of the debris.

The brass of a ruby-coloured chandelier had been blown right off its moorings by the pressure of the hoses.

Again that feeling of dread came to him, tightening the stomach muscles and telling him his instinct had been right. Smoke damage was everywhere. Hot ... it must have been so hot.

The bed frame was of iron, the coverlet and blankets soaked through and yellowed. Only a sodden curl of dark brown hair showed. Cursing his luck, he eased the covers back and saw at once that the woman was naked. Flat on her stomach, with her arms stretched out above her head and all but hidden beneath the pillows, ah *merde*.

Her wrists were tied to the ironwork, her ankles too Her hips, thighs and seat were chunky. A woman of forty-five or fifty, he thought and when he found her purse, found her name and asked, Why did he not free you?

There was a rag in her mouth, the jaws clamped so tightly they would have to be broken to free it. Breath held in outrage, St-Cyr began slowly to examine her back and buttocks for signs of a whipping.

Finding none, he asked, Did the fire interrupt things? And then, gently and aloud, 'Who was he, Mademoiselle Aurelle? The one who jumped, or someone else? You were lonely, isn't that right—please, I'm only guessing, of course. But ... but you invited him in for a yuletide glass of *marc* perhaps, and a cup of that lousy acorn water everyone hates but is forced to call coffee. You were thinking of a little romance, even sex perhaps, but had planned to tell him you would have to go to the late-evening Mass.'

Terrified, she would have lain there stiff with fear, begging him not to hurt her until, having heard enough, he had stuffed the rag into her mouth to shut her up. Then had come the cry of Fire, and he had left her.

Ah *nom de Dieu*, such were the ways of some, but was the murder—he would have to call it that—more directly related to the fire?

There was nothing of importance in the other flat. Downstairs, there were only two flats, one much larger than the other and therefore better furnished. The owner's? he asked himself, flicking a doubtful glance at the ceiling, still thinking of that woman. Asking again, Who was he, madame? Someone you had only just met by chance or someone you met on the stairs nearly every day?

A copper bathtub rested on a black-and-white tiled floor, the bidet and toilet in another room as usual. A Meissen clock, Louis XV armchairs with tapestry coverings . . . A settee in plush maroon velvet, a large canvas of a street scene now in shreds. Smoke and water damage everywhere. It was as if the *pompiers* had taken out their anger on the place, hammering everything in sight with the force of their hoses.

Again he thought of the woman upstairs, of how she must have tried to scream for help and strained at the ropes. She would have been only too aware of what was happening to the building.

The place Terreaux was now deep in darkness, with only the blue-washed glass of occasional streetlamps and pinpoint torches to guide the way. The black-out, of course. On November eleventh, the Wehrmacht had crossed the Demarcation Line thus ending the existence of the Unoccupied Zone and bringing with them the SS, the Gestapo and all the rest of it.

He wondered if the girl with the bicycle had come back. Suddenly the need to find her was overwhelming and he went down the stairs to the street, and quickly out across the square. Stood where she must have stood, asked, Why did you run away?

Though the crowd had thinned, there were still onlookers, their silhouettes dark and muffled in the darkness. He shone his light around. He gasped, 'Mademoiselle .. ?' She threw up a forearm to shield her eyes. For perhaps two seconds panic gripped her, then she ran with the bicycle, hopped on, even as he yelled for her to stop and ran after her.

It was no use. The ice ... the ice. Ah *merde*! He slipped and fell heavily. Even so, the memory of her face lingered, the fear in her eyes, the tightness of her lips, the dismay at being discovered.

She had dropped something and when he saw it clearly, he said, 'Not you, mademoiselle. Ah no, not you.'

It was the yellow work card all prostitutes must carry.

They shared a cigarette, just the two of them, in the darkness of the square beyond the fountain. 'Louis, this student of Wei-dling's, this Salamander of Gestapo Mueller—hey, where did Berlin get a code-name like that?'

It was a problem, Berlin's knowing things they ought rightly to have shared. 'Salamanders are slippery, Hermann. Some can change the colour of their skins so as to blend in with their surroundings.'

Kohler handed him the cigarette. 'Stop being so evasive. You found something.'

And so did you, said St-Cyr to himself. 'A visitor, yes. I am almost certain a woman went up to the projectionist's booth.'

'One of our two women?'

The cigarette was returned. 'Perhaps, but then ... Ah,' he shrugged, 'nothing is definite, my old one. Nothing. There was another woman, but that is a separate matter and I think the two are unrelated.'

'What about the girl with the bicycle? Did you find anything?'

'Me? Ah no, nothing. A student perhaps, but a teacher, I think.' He would keep the yellow work card private for the moment. 'And you, my friend? What did you find?'

Kohler knew he would have to say something but he need not reveal everything. 'A Lebel. The old Model 1873. I dropped it into a sewer over there.'

'*Merci.* I am most grateful, Hermann. The less fuss the better.'

'Leiter Weidling wasn't telling us everything, Louis, and neither was Robichaud.'

The cigarette had now burned down to the fingernails and could be passed only with great difficulty. 'Lübeck, Heidelberg and Köln,' said St-Cyr as if lost in thought and asking questions of himself. 'The same technique, Hermann, yet I must ask why gasoline was not splashed so thoroughly on the staircases to the balcony? Was it that the arsonist, this Salamander perhaps, or one of those two women who came in late, wanted to save the other?'

'Who was upstairs visiting the projectionist?'

'Yes.'

'A prostitute, Louis?'

'Perhaps, but then perhaps not. At the moment nothing is clear except that the Resistance were here in force, Hermann. Me, I am certain of it, and that revolver you found says so.'

Merde! The bastard had the nose of a ferret. 'There was a priest, Louis, and a cross.'

'Yes, yes, a priest,' said the Sûreté, impatient with him for not revealing all. 'And a girl on a bicycle, eh, Hermann?' he taunted.

'What about the fire doors that were locked? What about the owner?'

'What about him indeed? Let's find the owner and ask him.'

'No sleep?'

'Not tonight. Not yet anyway. Not while the Salamander, if

he or she even exists, is out there, Hermann, waiting to see what we will do.'

Louis seldom had the last word but the prospect of being watched was uncomfortable and Kohler let him have it. There was also Gestapo Mueller's interest to consider. Shit!

In silence they returned to the cinema to find Robichaud and ask him where the owner might be found. It was not far.

THE BISTRO ALBERT BRÛLÉ WAS ON THE QUAI DE la Pêcherie, overlooking the Saône and Fourvière Hill, if one could see them through the darkness. There was only a tiny blue light above the entrance to signal anything out of the ordinary behind the black-out curtains, yet three *vélo-taxis* and two horse-drawn cabs were waiting in the freezing cold. The foyer held a bar and coatcheck. The restaurant was jammed, the talk earnest and everywhere. A businessman's place but several women were about, all well-dressed, gay and vivacious. Excited.

Mistresses? grinned Kohler, inwardly nodding as Louis hushed the head waiter and negotiated Sûreté business. The men would be showing the girls off to their competitors and associates. Not a whiff of tobacco smoke in the place—a real chef then. A fanatic in these hard times. If you want to smoke, go elsewhere. Don't *ruin* the taste of my cooking! And wasn't it marvellous what a person could do on the black market?

The clientele obeyed the no-smoking rule. Perhaps fifty customers were seated. There were two long rows of marble-topped tables placed end to end. Knees touched. A hand was on a woman's silk-stockinged knee. Ah yes, she was good for a little feel. Island tables elsewhere had electric lights turned down to give atmosphere, not to save on power as per the regulations. Panelled mahogany walls held oil paintings of nearly naked girls running through moonlight, and of others bathing in the buff while eating grapes and thinking of more tasty things, perhaps.

There wasn't a word of the recent catastrophe, not a mention of little girls in flames. Why spoil dinner?

'Remember to let me make the overtures, eh?' cautioned the Sûreté, gruffly putting his badge away and removing his fedora. 'There is absolutely no sense in throwing your weight around in here, Hermann. These people will all have well-placed friends in the SS, the Gestapo or the Wehrmacht. Indeed, several of those types are here tonight, so, *please*, do *not* make a disturbance! We've been in enough trouble and must get this over with.'

'Just remember I'm older than you and still the boss.'

'Then perhaps you would be good enough to tell me what it was you found so disturbing in the toilets of that cinema?'

'Nothing. Absolutely nothing, Louis. You know how my stomach is. So many bodies, the smell of roasted fle—'

'*Hermann!*' St-Cyr grabbed him by the arm. 'A cognac,' he hissed at the barman. 'Hurry, idiot! Before he vomits all over the place!'

Visions of braised human ribs came to Kohler, of a woman's shapely buttocks, the skin now crisp and brown, the juices running through the cracks. He smelled the sweetness of death, the putrefaction. He saw a set of white, white teeth, red lips parting in laughter and wanted to choke that laughter off!

The Prunier was downed in a gulp—aged thirty years! The ragged cheeks, with that terrible scar from the left eye to chin and memory of a rawhide whip, slowly began to lose their pallor. St-Cyr gripped his partner a moment more before releasing him. 'Is the news that bad?' he asked. 'Ah, *nom de Jésus-Christ! Résistants*, Hermann? Come, come, *mon ami*, out with it, eh? We've been condemned to work together. It's best I know everything.'

The Bavarian's eyes were smarting. He swallowed another brandy with difficulty. 'Then you tell me what you didn't, and I'll tell you what I didn't.'

That was fair enough. Always there was this hedging on both sides of the partnership. 'Later, then. Let's see what our Monsieur Artel has to say about his cinema.'

The woman who had laughed followed Kohler with her bright eyes, doubt growing in them. He knew she would swiftly lose spirit but had to tell her something.

Leaning closely, he whispered into the sweet shell of her scented ear, 'I'm sorry if I frightened you, mademoiselle, or is it madame and your husband off somewhere else? A POW camp in the Reich, eh? Hey, more than a million and a half Frenchmen still languish behind barbed wire in spite of all the promises to let them go home. The poor buggers dream of girls like you but have to masturbate.'

Devastated, she dropped her fork and seized her napkin, so, good! '*Bon appétit*, madame,' he said and tossed the rest of the party a nonchalant wave.

The meal at Artel's far-corner table was being consumed by four Lyonnais businessmen in almost identical, nondescript blue serge suits and subdued ties. They talked of business, were solicitous towards their host while privately holding their own thoughts. They spooned with stolid indifference the *potage velouté aux truffes*, the boneless fish soup painstakingly made by pressing the steamed fish through a fine wire sieve and blending the result with long-simmered fish stock, a creamed sauce of beaten eggs and flour, and the truffles of course. Ah *mon Dieu*, it made the digestive juices run to watch them.

Now and then a double chin was hastily wiped with a large,

white linen napkin, a glass of red Beaujolais nouveau was reached for or a crusty loaf from which a generous chunk would be ripped by pudgy fingers and perhaps dipped in the soup before being eaten. On one little finger there was a jade signet ring. All the left hands had gold wedding bands . . .

'Louis, they haven't even noticed us.'

'Don't feel so put out. You're not dressed properly. Observe, eh? Tell me which is the notary, which the banker, which the insurance agent?'

'And which is our man, Monsieur Fabien Artel?'

The owner of the cinema.

'Monsieur Artel? Monsieur Fabien Artel?' asked Louis quite pleasantly.

The man hesitated. 'Yes. Yes, that is me.' He threw the head waiter a scathing glance. 'What is it you want of me?'

St-Cyr took the table in, nodding to the others. 'Messieurs. No, please, continue with the soup. It is very good, is it not?'

Artel tossed a dismissive hand. 'You're from the police. This is neither the time nor the place. Please leave.'

Ah well, a stubborn one. 'We'd rather not, monsieur. It's Christmas Eve and we'd like to get home.'

'The préfet—'

'Fabien, go easy. As your legal adviser—'

'Don't interrupt me, Martin. Guillemette is right over there, dining with the Obersturmführer Klaus Barbie. I need only give a nod, and he will see to it.'

Ah *nom de Dieu*, Klaus Barbie! 'Monsieur, do not try my patience,' breathed St-Cyr. 'One hundred and eighty-three have died in your cinema. A few simple answers are in order if we are to stop the arsonist from committing another, and perhaps even more horrendous crime.' He let his gaze move to the insurance agent—one could tell them apart at a glance—but continued. 'Surely it is to your advantage to co-operate?'

'He's right, Fabien. Co-operate,' said the agent.

The banker nodded curtly at the wisdom of this and

motioned to the head waiter. 'Monsieur Jules, some chairs, please, for our guests. An apéritif, messieurs? A little of the Moulin-à-Vent? Yes, yes, that would be most suitable.' He turned to the sommelier. 'Étienne, you may bring the Moulin now for Monsieur Artel.'

Kohler was impressed. Louis was doing all right for himself. The banker got up to formally introduce himself. 'Jacques-Yves Durant, messieurs. Crédit Lyonnais. This is Armand Clouteau of Montagnier-Suisse, one of our principal insurance companies, and this is Martin Lavigné, one of Lyon's foremost notaries. Gentlemen,' he indicated the chairs. He sampled the Moulin-à-Vent and, declaring it near-perfect with the upraised forefinger of slight doubt, said, 'The 1933, eh, Fabien? You do us proud.'

It was by just such little slights that the establishment maintained their positions among themselves. St-Cyr indicated that they should finish their soup but already, at a glance from Artel, the waiter was clearing the plates. A pity.

'So? Proceed,' said Artel. 'My cinema is in ruins and you do not wish such a thing to happen again?'

Implying how could this be possible, eh? 'It's a directive from Gestapo Mueller in Berlin,' said Kohler, leaning forward a little. 'He doesn't like Christmas to be spoiled.'

'Hermann, please. Monsieur Artel knows only too well that if he should invite the préfet and his distinguished guest to join us, others would be certain to hear of it.'

Touché, eh? thought Artel. So, *mes amis*, a pair of gumshoes from Paris. One from the Gestapo, the other from Belleville perhaps, and what's it to be? The squeeze in public or the softening up for later? 'Arson? It's not possible. What are you people saying?' He gestured, looked at them both, then hunkered down for the fight. 'It was a surge in the lines, messieurs. Excess electrical power causes the wiring to heat up and puff! my cinema is in flames and Robichaud cannot get his *pompiers* there fast enough. Oh *bien sûr*, it's the factories these days, their demands for electricity. Those old buildings around the place Terreaux . . . Lovely, but of course . . . Ah, what can one say?'

'That's interesting,' breathed Kohler. 'An accident? Is that what you're saying?'

'Yes. Yes, of course it was an accident. Arson . . .'

'Can take years to settle. Louis, I think he's going to be sick.'

'Monsieur, your fire doors were padlocked.'

'Padlocked? But . . . but this is impossible! *Impossible!* Why should my fire doors have been padlocked when the theatre was full to capacity?'

St-Cyr tried the Moulin and found it perfect. Would the next course bring the *quenelles de brochet*, the dumplings made with a forcemeat of river pike served *au gratin* in kidney fat and eggs perhaps and a sauce of mushrooms and cream? 'The doors were padlocked, monsieur. Perhaps you could explain why this was so.'

Ah *merde*, the Sûreté! They were always after dirt, always interfering and most of them crooks anyway. 'I gave explicit instructions to Monsieur Thibault, my manager, that the fire doors were to be unlocked during every—*every*—performance at my cinema.'

St-Cyr nodded solicitously and sought succour by examining the lifeline of his right hand. Gabrielle had been upset that he had broken his promise to keep Christmas with her and her son at the château on the Loire. A chanteuse, a patriot, much taller and much younger than himself, she had the body of a goddess but would share it only with one man. It was yet to be shared, alas. 'Your manager has told the fire marshal that you expressly forebade him to do so, monsieur. Were some of the patrons likely to cheat and let their friends in? Messieurs,' he looked gravely around the table, 'those doors, they are a problem.'

Artel was swift. 'Then ask the Préfet and Obersturmführer Barbie to join us, Inspector. Communists, yes? Potential terrorists and saboteurs? I think you will find little sympathy at that table.'

The Sûreté heaved a sigh. The lifeline was not good. Gabi might hold it against him, his being away at such a time. 'It is not that table which concerns me,' he said sadly. 'It is all those lives, monsieur, and perhaps those of others yet to come.'

'Then find him!' hissed Artel. 'Find the man who did it, eh? Come, come, my fine messieurs from Paris. Get on with your work!'

The *quenelles* were waiting. The *côte de boeuf garnie à la lyonnaise* would be overdone. Braised beef ribs and stuffed onions in a white sauce with quail-egg-sized potatoes that had been sautéed in butter. *Butter!*

'Present yourself at the Hotel Bristol at eight o'clock tomorrow morning, Monsieur Artel. My advice is that you come prepared to answer fully all questions pertaining to the fire, including . . .' St-Cyr fingered his wine glass delicately. Ah, he would have liked another taste. Perhaps Hermann could acquire for him a couple of bottles, a little present for Gabi, not that she would let the offer sway her. 'Including, monsieur, that of murder.'

'Louis . . . ?'

'Hermann, it is time for us to leave.'

Outside in the freezing cold and darkness along the quai, the memory of those four men came clearly. 'Four Burgundian trenchermen, Hermann, with merchant hearts of stone. They would as soon cut each others' throats if advantageous yet are solicitous of our friend. Now each of the others will begin to think it best to leave our fly alone on the wall and he, in turn, will tell us everything or try to run.'

'A murder?' asked Kohler, his breath billowing.

'Yes. One of the tenants. We shall want to know exactly where Monsieur Artel was at the time of the fire and perhaps for the hour or two prior to it. Also, of course, the whereabouts of his insurance policy.'

'There was a priest, Louis.'

'Yes, yes, I saw you take a cross. Valuable, was it?'

'Quite.'

'Then find us a taxi, Hermann, and we will pay the Bishop of Lyon a little visit. Use your Gestapo shield if necessary but do not tempt fate.'

'Not Barbie's then?'

'Ah no, that would be most unwise. One of the *vélos* perhaps, if its driver has legs strong enough for Fourvière Hill. We must attend the late-evening Mass.'

'You really do want to have the last word. Hey, me I'm going to let you have it!'

'Good!'

'Then tell me how you knew beforehand who each of those bastards was at that table?'

The Sûreté's sigh betrayed impatience. One had to do that now and then with Hermann. 'It was more in their posture than in anything else. The banker carries himself well and has his corset and breeding to thank for this. When he sits, his back is stiff and his food taken with precise movements. He is more vain than the others. A man who knows women and manipulates them. Shrewd, calculating, determined and believing success is his right due to birth. His nursemaid introduced him to sex and ever since then he has favoured the employer-employee relationship. Were I a woman, I should not wish to work for him. Were I his wife, I would employ a straight razor!'

'And the notary?' snorted Kohler. It was good for Louis to get it out of his system. The Frog needed that every once in a while.

'Secretive—oh they all are—but this one the more so. He's used to property deeds, to wills, to marriage contracts in which each packet of linen or towels or cutlery, no matter how old or worn, is recorded in the most meticulous detail. His is a safe of secrets, Hermann, and he could well know things about the others they themselves do not know or have forgotten. He strained his soup through his teeth in case of a misplaced fish-bone. His wife is miserable. They rarely if ever refresh their marriage vows because he is too tired. She dreams of taking a lover but knows he will discover the expense, no matter how trifling.'

Kohler longed for a cigarette. 'You're cruel. You're enjoying this.'

'But of course! And why not, since you have asked? The insurance agent was nervous but tried well to hide this, though the others were all aware of it. Several million francs are riding on this policy he was fool enough to have written for his friend. How could he have listened to such a one? The director will be certain to rake him over the coals. A demotion at the least, Hermann, an outright dismissal if he is not fortunate. He alone does not have a mistress—that would be far too risky. Instead, he contents himself with infrequent visits to one or two of the city's most discreet houses. He insists only on the cleanest girls and slips the doctor who visits them a little something for the inside information. He also has a slight catch between his upper eyetooth and his first premolar. This traps food and he has become so accustomed to sucking at it, he does so even when there is no need.'

Kohler shattered the air with expletives. 'Come on! You couldn't have seen all that! How'd you really know which was which?'

'Experience. When you have had to examine people as much as I have, Hermann, you learn. Have patience. That banker sat and ate like a banker; the insurance agent like one of his kind; so, too, the notary.'

'And the owner?'

'Ah yes, Monsieur Fabien Artel. The fleshy lips and closely shaven cheeks blue with shadow. The dimpled chin, eh? and the puffy eyelids whose eyes were hooded beneath arched, dark brows that were not thick. The rapidly receding hairline, the touches of grey that have been patiently hidden. The arrogance of that nose, the corpulence—the wedding ring that should most certainly have been cut off and expanded to prevent loss of circulation were he not so parsimonious and busy. Whereas the banker's eyes might hold a momentary trace of sympathy for a needy client, untrue of course, this one's could never hold any. He views the world as a notecase and asks only how much is in it for him?'

'Suffers from a crisis of the liver, does he?'

'And the misused prostate!'

Good *Gott im Himmel!* 'Don't hate him, Louis. Don't let all those bodies get to you. It's best not to.'

'Then ask the mother who tried to reach her child, Hermann. Ask the woman who was tied to a bed she had probably slept in every night of her life. Ask your priest who it was that lit the fire. Ask him why he was in the cinema and not about his duties at such a busy time.'

'Ask the Bishop, Louis. Ask the one who employed him.'

'That is exactly what I intend to do when he gives me the wafer, Hermann. You're learning, eh? A few more months with me and I will consider you polished enough to go home.'

Normally Hermann would have risen to such bait and loudly proclaimed the Thousand Year Reich was in France for ever. Instead, he walked away into the night and when he commandeered a carriage, he asked first if it was waiting for the Préfet of Police and the Obersturmführer Klaus Barbie. 'Then we have need of it, my friend,' he said. 'Gestapo Central, Paris. Don't argue or you will face the wrong end of my pistol.'

The carriage was only of limited use and that was probably just as well. Dropped at the foot of the montée des Chazeaux, St-Cyr made excuses—the terrain, the height and steepness of Fourvière Hill, the narrow, medieval streets of Vieux Lyon, the impassibility to carriages beyond certain points, the Roman origins of Lugdunum and prior need to defend the city from them by fortifying the heights. 'Ah, so many reasons, Hermann. Please, it is but a little climb up to the Basilica.'

'*Little?* I see nothing but a steady stream of penitents bundled in black on a pitch-black night and mumbling over their beads with regret.'

'The funicular is closed. A power failure of Germanic origins— *i.e.*, punishment for some slight. Probably graffiti splashed on some wall in stolen white paint that ran *Vive le Général de Gaulle, Vive la France libre*, or some such thing.'

'If you French had guts you would have levelled this hill! I can't understand why the Romans didn't. Christ, it's cold!'

They started up the 242 steps of the montée, no sand on the pavement as a special treat in these frozen times. Shuffling old ladies, old men grinding their false teeth and carefully budgeting their cigarettes, coughing, spitting, hawking up their guts, boys, girls, babes in arms, single mothers, grass widows, war widows and older men with younger wives, one of whom was painfully pregnant and could no longer button her overcoat. Triplets? wondered Kohler anxiously. The rope around her belly was frayed. She'd worn three aprons beneath it to help keep the cold at bay. Piety shone in her eyes and the *flic* on duty hadn't the heart to warn her to extinguish her candle.

'*Gott im Himmel*, you French are stupid!' seethed Kohler. 'If it isn't ten thousand steps up to some rathole of a fucking flat in Montmartre or Saint-Denis, it's an elevator with a two-strand cable that ought to have been replaced ten thousand years ago!'

'We are going up to the Basilica, Hermann. Correct me if I am wrong, but I do not think they had elevators then, though I am *positive* they came into use about 1850.'

'Another lecture, eh? Then let me tell you, you French have been using the same goddamned elevators ever since!'

Hermann hated using the elevators in Paris or anywhere else. He had been caught once, left hanging by a hair, and the memory of that near-catastrophe was always fresh. Always! Now he would use the stairs but, as he *hated* them too, there was no solution short of parachuting him in. And he hated heights more than anything.

As if ashamed of his behaviour, Kohler mumbled, 'Madame, permit me, please, to offer you and your husband a little assistance. The steps are steep and I gather there are far too many of them.'

In alarm she dropped her candle, let out a shriek, gasped, '*Georges!*' and fainted. Christ!

It took fifteen minutes to bring her round and get her back on her feet. In all this time the shuffling stream never stopped, but only pinched down as it passed them, then opened up again. Shoulders rubbing shoulders. Coughs chasing coughs. Step after step. Christmas Eve, 1942.

'Your face, Hermann. She saw your face. The mark of that whip, eh? The scar, it is still too fresh. The frost must have made it glisten.'

'She knew I was Gestapo, Louis. She was so damned scared, she practically dropped her babies right there. Could we have delivered them?'

'Of course. Under the Third Reich all things are possible.'

'I did once. Did you know that? She'd been knifed and was dying, Louis, and I held her little boy up for her even as she closed her eyes and smiled. Berlin, 13 June 1939, right after one of the rallies. Always there were the rallies. Thinking he'd be safe in the crowd, some son of a bitch had to let her have it for no other reason than that she looked a trifle Jewish, I guess. We never knew the reason and we never caught him.'

'Remind me to buy you a drink and a bit of supper, eh?'

'Those ration tickets Marianne left for you are now at least a good four weeks out of date, idiot! I'll find us a place. I'm not hungry anyway.'

'That priest just knelt and let it happen, Hermann. He didn't try to save himself like all the others.'

'Did he tie the woman to her bed? Is that what you're wondering?'

'Or did he know the Salamander would strike and is that why he was in the cinema?'

There were so many questions, so little time in which to get things done. At the top of the montée they began yet another steep climb, the switchbacks of the Sacré Coeur snaking through scant woods where the nubby branches of the trees reminded Kohler of battlefields long passed and of sanctuary woods after weeks of constant shelling.

The French always pruned their trees too much. They liked them wounded into stumps and fingerless fists.

'That priest was going to sodomize the woman, Louis. Guilt stopped him and he went downstairs into the cinema only to find the flames of hell had descended upon him.'

'We'll ask the bishop. We'll tell him the Church's secret is safe with us.'

For some time now the litany of the Mass had had a lulling effect. There was far less coughing and clearing of the throat or blowing of the nose. More rhythm to the responses, more unity of intonation and automatic signing of the Cross.

Prayers were offered for the victims of the fire, pleas for the arsonist or arsonists to give up and come forth to receive God's forgiveness. Prayers for those who had been badly burned and disfigured—somehow they must find it in their hearts to forgive. So, too, all those who had lost their loved ones.

Yet had it been wise to hold the Mass? If ever an opportunity for disaster presented itself, it was in this packed congregation. Each person's shoulders touched at least one other's. It was now so hot and stuffy in the unheated church, overcoats had been unbuttoned, mittens, gloves and scarves removed to cushion bended knees. A simple cry of Fire would cause untold panic and the Salamander, if he or she or they were bent on another disaster, would know this.

St-Cyr sat nearest the right aisle, about a quarter of the way from the altar and beside one of the blue-grey marble columns that rose to the vaulted ceiling high above where gorgeous frescos were sumptuously gilded. Consecrated in 1896, the Basilica exemplified the very soul of the merchants and bankers who had built it. Gold was everywhere, so, too, polished semi-precious stones. Its altar was immense and resplendent with silk and silver and gold. There were paintings and mosaics, beautiful stained-glass windows. Everywhere there was candlelight or the warm glow of scented oil lamps.

Clearly the Bishop of Lyon had spared nothing on this eve of eves. In defiance of the black-out, the Basilica must glow like a beacon. Not content, he had insisted on holding the Mass at midnight as had been the Church's custom for centuries.

With the curfew at midnight, and all tram-cars and *autobuses* stopped at 11 p.m., he had forced each and every person before him to break the law, which would drive the German authorities half crazy trying to arrest them all should they so choose.

Resplendent in his finery, Bishop Frédéric Dufour was a man to be reckoned with. His wrists were strong and bony, the hands big, shoulders wide and square, the feet always braced as if God were up there some place on the mountain and he but a humble shepherd. The short, wavy hair was iron-grey, his brow and face wide as if cut from granite, but he was still a man who could enjoy a good time among simple people, a man much accustomed to circulating in the world of salons but one who always remembered his roots. No fool, he must have gauged the metal of the Nazi High Command and gambled they'd say nothing beyond a mild rebuke to himself.

But, again, one had to wonder if it had been wise to hold the Mass? All eyes would be closed in prayer or on the hymnal or the Bishop and his assistants, the altar boys, the swinging censers, the choir that sat among stupendous columns of rose-red marble, the Cross above the altar, the Virgin to one side.

All but Hermann's. Hermann would be busy in the wings looking for possible arson or scanning the crowd for a chance sight of that girl they had seen on the bicycle.

Two women . . . Had she been one of them and why, please, had she dropped the yellow work card of a prostitute?

A priest, but no ordinary cleric. Were the two connected? Could that be possible?

And were they to have another fire so soon? Ah *merde*, Hermann. Be careful.

The smell of gasoline was strongest here, high above the altar in one of the four octagonal towers that formed the corners of the Basilica and rose to belfries more Gothic than Byzantine. Stealthily Kohler crouched in the pitch darkness and ran anxious fingertips over the cold marble floor. Gingerly he brought them to his nose, each microsecond frozen in time, his mind and body functioning too slowly—he knew this now. The floor was awash.

Stairs . . . there would be stairs to the belfry but surely they would not have started pouring the gasoline from up there? Surely those two women would be below him among the congregation, waiting . . . waiting for the right moment?

When he came across a jerry can lying flat at the top of the stone steps, he ran a hesitant finger around inside its open neck, felt the threaded metal, each groove sharp and precise. Saw at once the four towers in flames; saw the panic inside the church, the trampled; heard the terrified screams.

Verdammt! He shut his eyes and tried to calm himself. He thought to ring the bells—knew that this would only warn the arsonist or arsonists.

A door would be opened into the tower, a lighted candle would be dropped on the way out.

When he came to a narrow gallery, he stood in shadow looking down the length of the crowded nave. He searched, he asked, Where are you? He wanted to shout, *Raus! Raus!* Get out! before it was too late.

Prayers came up to him and he hesitated. Satisfied that all heads would be bowed and he wouldn't be seen, he stepped quickly through to the railing to look down at the seats nearest the door to the tower. Two women . . . What would they be wearing? Would they sit side by side? Had they even had anything to do with the cinema fire? Had they really?

It all looked so ordinary. Where . . . ? Where the hell are you? he wanted to shout.

Four belfries . . . four of them.

Slowly he retraced his steps. Again he looked uncertainly up through the darkness to the belfry, again he felt the gasoline on the floor. Had it only just been dumped? Had they heard him in the tower? Were they still waiting in the darkness at the top of those stairs?

He began to climb, and when he reached the top, eight tall and narrow arches gave out on to the night, the darkness there a little less. Freezing, a breeze came softly. It did not stir the heavy bronze bells. He must go around the bells. He must make no sound, give no sign of himself. They mustn't know he'd come back. *She* mustn't know. She? he asked.

Two women . . . a strong smell of perfume close, so close and layered over that of the gasoline because of the breeze. He waited. Silently he asked, Well, what's it to be, eh?

She'd have the matches ready. She wouldn't care if she or they died in the fire. Perhaps that's what she wanted. He crouched and ran his fingers lightly over the floor.

When he touched a woman's high-heeled shoe, he leapt inwardly but found himself asking, How could she wear such things on a night like this?

She didn't move. She did not even know he was here.

The fucking shoes were empty! She'd left them side by side and had splashed perfume on the stone sill to fool him!

Ah *Gott im Himmel*, Louis . . . Louis, where the hell are you when needed most? Down on your knees praying to that God of yours? Asking why He has to mock his little detective, eh?

Waiting . . . waiting just like everyone else.

* * *

The Mass was taking forever. Why had they simply not sent a messenger to the bishop with a note, wondered St-Cyr? Urgent consultations. A cross . . . an exquisite masterpiece of mid-to-late Renaissance art. Four square, blood-red rubies at its ends, four magnificent square-tabled sapphires at the crossroads and well-faceted, round Jager diamonds, each of at least three carats, the stones all set in raised collets on chased quatrefoils whose four-leafed petals were filigreed in dark blue and gold enamel.

The rope of gold was with rubies and enamelled cushions between the links. The bishop could well have refused to see Hermann and himself. Made excuses, sought to divert the inquiry . . . ah, so many things might well have happened. There was also Dufour's reaction to the shock of being confronted so unexpectedly. Ah yes.

At a nudge, St-Cyr awoke from the turmoil of his thoughts to join the shuffling line in the aisle. The bread, the wine, the blessings and genuflections came as each parishioner received the Blessed Sacrament, none now asking why that fire had had to happen, none worrying that it could just as suddenly happen here. Hermann . . . where was Hermann?

'My son, that cross . . . ?'

Doubt and fear, then realization and sadness swiftly entered the dark grey eyes of the shepherd whose cheeks were rugged. 'Jean-Louis St-Cyr of the Sûreté Nationale, Bishop. Please forgive the inconvenience, but it is imperative that we talk.'

'Here? Now? But . . . but . . .' Ah damn! 'Yes, yes of course. One of the confessionals.' Dufour indicated the ornately carved boxes on the far side of the church and said, 'Follow, please.'

There was no time. Clearly that was evident; so, too, that the bishop wanted the least possible notice taken of them.

No sooner were they inside and seated, when he hissed, '*Why have you come here like this with that in your hands? Have you no sense of decency? Father Adrian had nothing to do with that fire. Nothing! How could he have?*'

'Then why was he in that cinema, Bishop? Why was he on his knees facing the worst of the flames?'

'Facing the flames?'

'Yes. The others had blocked the only exits. Some had tried to run into the foyer but had collapsed in their panic or from the smoke and flames. The others then fell on top of them.'

'He must have known he could not escape.'

'But to exhibit such calmness and strength of will is quite remarkable, is it not? Why was he a martyr?'

Dufour considered this. When he asked to see the cross, St-Cyr handed it to him, and for a moment their fingers touched. He felt the trembling in the bishop and knew Dufour was either frightened of the outcome or deeply grieving over the loss of his priest.

They could not see each other's expressions. Had he suggested the confessional for this very reason? Had he?

Indeed, the confessional had always seemed to single out the confessor, using that same remoteness to pigeon-hole the sinner's soul. Uncomfortable . . . it had always made St-Cyr feel uncomfortable, the mind flitting back to boyhood days and things like cakes and pies best left unstolen.

When the bishop spoke again it was as if to God, humbly begging His forgiveness. 'This cross was far too ostentatious, Inspector. For quite obvious reasons I forbade Father Beaumont to wear it except on very special occasions. Adrian . . . Adrian was my personal secretary. We'd been together for years. When that happens, the right hand usually knows what the left hand is about, isn't that so? He understood he was not to wear this outside the Basilica. I could not have him causing envy among my other priests or with the cardinals and other bishops, could I? Father Beaumont agreed—he was that kind of man. Honest, diligent, absolutely trustworthy, and my humble servant at all times, be it night or day. I kept the cross in the safe in my office, and I know for a fact that he has left it to me in his will.'

Ah *nom de Dieu*, a will . . . 'Why was he there, Bishop? By rights he ought to have been busy. The sick, the wounded, the old, the poor . . .'

Something would have to be said. Dufour sighed heavily. 'Our housekeeper will tell you Father Beaumont received an urgent telephone call, Inspector. Mademoiselle Madeleine Aurelle. Yes, yes, I had already anticipated a visit from such as yourself. The Préfet . . . Ah, of course he has telephoned to warn me of you. News gets around quickly, does it not? So many people, so many deaths . . . My housekeeper, Mademoiselle Béatrice told me the details of the telephone call. Mademoiselle Aurelle is in her middle years, you understand. Father Beaumont was her confessor—that is to say, Inspector, that one was fond of him. As the men of my village used to say, she had hoarded her little capital for far too long and had not bought any gold with it.'

Her virginity . . . Her 'little capital . . .' and this from a bishop!

'The silly woman was always after Adrian, Inspector. She badgered him constantly. The crisis of the heart, the chest, the earache, the back, the rent. He suffered her constant need for attention and quite often . . . Oh, *bien sûr* I myself have heard him calming her fears many times over the telephone. Always a kind word, a promise to talk to the owner of that building, to call in at the pharmacy for some little thing, the greengrocer's, the tea-shop or send someone round to the flat, himself most often. He had the heart and patience of a saint. He understood her and forgave her always.'

'Then why was he not with her? Why was he in the cinema on his knees, holding that cross before him?'

'I don't know, Inspector. *La Bête humaine* . . . it's an excellent film. Perhaps, after he had attended to Mademoiselle Aurelle, he . . .'

'She was naked, Bishop. She was tied face down to her bed. A rag had been stuffed in her mouth.'

'Then why did you not say so at once?' Angrily Dufour thrust the cross back only to find his hand gripped tightly. Ah damn the Sûreté and their filthy minds! Always against the Church! Always looking for dirt! 'Had she been violated?' he asked, hating himself for having said it.

St-Cyr savoured the moment, having obtained the answer he most wanted without having to ask for it. Violation had been entirely possible. 'Could the call have been made or prompted by someone else, someone known to them both?'

'The arsonist or arsonists?'

It was a plea to God for help. One could not have that woman violated by a priest, particularly not by a bishop's secretary, a saint! Ah no, of course not.

'The cross, Bishop? He should not have worn it to the cinema or to visit this . . . this nuisance who had not had the wisdom to spend her little capital much earlier in life.'

'God ought to guard my tongue, Inspector, particularly as in regards to my humble past. The cross was given to Father Beaumont some years ago. It can have no bearing on the fire.'

'Then why did he wear it? Come, come, Bishop Dufour. There *has* to be a reason for everything.'

'Ah, do not be so difficult! You people from Paris . . . For most things there is often no reason other than impulse.'

'Then how did he come by it, eh? A wealthy parishioner—a gift like this? Did he save some family from scandal? Did he get the unmarried daughter into a convent so that she could have her child in secret, eh? In each house there is always a closet, Bishop, even in God's house.'

'Especially so, is that what you're implying, eh?' It was. Ah damn. 'Monsieur Henri Masson gave that cross to Father Beaumont, Inspector, but he's been dead for several years. Ten, I believe, or is it twelve? Now, please, I must return to my duties. Father Beaumont would not have harmed Mademoiselle

Aurelle. It was just not in his nature to harm anyone, least of all myself and the Mother Church.'

Kohler touched his lips in doubt and fear. *Gott im Himmel*, with what were they dealing? The bitches were still playing with him. The wash of gasoline was all around him now in the store-room below the belfry. And God *damn* the Führer and his invincible Reich. The fucking torch in his hand was useless!

He knew the arsonists were close to him—closer than they'd ever been. The place reeked of gasoline. His shoes, leaking at the best of times, had let in the gasoline. The turn-ups of his trousers, would they be wet too?

They were. Ah *nom de Dieu*, Louis, why can't you come and find me? Two women . . . *Two*, Louis!

Not liking things, he got down on his hands and knees and crept forward. The room, off to one side of the tower, seemed full of paintings in richly carved and probably gilded frames that only brought memories of that last case, of Provence and an antique shop, of a dealer who had complained about the French using such priceless pieces for firewood. *Firewood, verdammt!*

There were canvases—far too many of them. And he knew then that some of the wealthy, thinking their paintings safer with the bishop, had brought them here rather than let the Occupying Forces steal them.

Cautiously sweeping the floor with wide motions of his hand, Kohler touched excelsior—fine wood shavings, a wren's nest of them. He found the candle stub in its middle, fixed to the floor—no more than one-and-a-half centimentres of that—found seven wooden matches, their heads arranged in a ring, all close to the candle so as to speed the instant of ignition, not that they would have been needed.

Trembling, he dropped the matches and had to pick them up. He put them and the candle stub *and* the excelsior into a pocket and stood up slowly. The message was all too clear: See what we can do to you or to anyone at any time.

Two women . . . had there been two of them? Had he frightened them off?

Clearly they were dealing with a case of madness.

Shadows flew about or were pinned to the walls. Robichaud, the fire chief, looked up into the belfry timbers and sharply drew in a breath. The beam of his torch faltered, then came back to settle on the jerry cans. Dull brown and pale green with their camouflage, each was still slowly dripping a trickle of gasoline. Stolen . . . they must have been stolen.

'Regulation issue,' he grunted. 'The fuel depot at Delfosse or one of the others over in Croix Rousse, the Fort Saint-Jean or the Saint Vincent along the quai.'

All fuel was under German control. The two jerry cans had been lashed to timbers that ran above the bells. Each would have weighed a good twenty kilograms. Who could have done such a thing? 'Ah *mon Dieu*, Bishop, this . . . this . . .' He swung his light down to indicate the trail of gasoline that crossed the belfry floor and ran to the empty can Herr Kohler had found at the top of the steps. 'This is the trailer from the storeroom downstairs. Light the lower one, Bishop, and the flames, they race along this trail and right up to those.'

Stains from the dripping cans high above them had spread down other timbers to the floor. 'It's a miracle the Salamander didn't set it off,' said Guillemette, the Préfet of Lyon.

'My pumpers . . .' began Robichaud. 'The lines up here on Fourvière Hill—oh for sure, Bishop, my men can fight a normal fire but this . . . this? Ah no, no. It's impossible. *Impossible!* The mains would collapse, isn't that correct, Guillemette? Well, isn't it? For years I've been trying to tell you all that new and far larger water mains are needed. More pressure. A new station up here, two new crews. *Men!* Where am I to get them, eh? *Where?* They're all off in Germany either in the prison camps or the forced labour brigades.'

'Easy, Julien, go easy, eh?' snorted the préfet. 'We all know how much you care but you are not the only one to consider when the budgets come round.'

The light swung, pinning shadows to the walls as Robichaud turned on him swiftly. 'Then what about you stopping this one, eh? You have yet to visit the temporary morgue we have set up in the Lycée Ampère. Ah, you've not thought it necessary to inform the children who have lost their parents, is that it? How are we to find them, eh? Lists ... that bastard Weidling demands *lists*? Let him pull the limbs apart himself. Let him examine the teeth and hope for dental records.'

Bishop Dufour stepped forward. 'Julien, go down to my study. Have some of the port, then take a glass of the Calvados my sister sent me. Please, I must insist. You're exhausted. There is no need to be ashamed. Your tears are quite understandable.'

'Are they, Bishop? Are they?' The beam of his light fell to the floor at their feet.

'Now, now, Julien, control yourself. Please, I beg it of you. Say no more. We have enough trouble as it is.'

Patting him on a shoulder, the bishop led him to the top of the belfry stairs. 'Auguste and Philomena will wash this down and be most careful.'

'That old caretaker and his wife? Don't be silly. My men will handle it.'

'Then do as I say. You need to sleep. Look at you, you're still dressed for a fire. Have you forgotten time? Please, I promise I'll awaken you in a couple of hours. At least do that for me.'

Robichaud started down the stairs then swung his light back over them before settling it on the préfet.

Blinded by it, Guillemette said nothing, only waited.

'Hermann, go with him,' said St-Cyr quietly. 'See that he does as he's told. You'll find me on the terrace in front of the church.

I'll be looking out over the city trying to figure out what has happened here and where our Salamander could be hiding.'

'If it was those two women from the cinema, Louis, they know all about how to start a fire.'

'It's the mark of a *professional*!' hissed Robichaud. 'Surely our préfet must have the names of all such people. Ask *him* to provide them. Give *that* list to Herr Weidling when you join him for breakfast!'

St-Cyr drew the bishop aside. 'A small problem,' he said, glad that the edge of light from his torch just touched the bishop's eyes. 'Three fires in 1938, Bishop, in the Reich, and now this. Was it to have been number two, I wonder, or was Father Adrian the target and our Salamander did not realize he had been killed?'

'I . . . I don't know what you mean, Inspector? N . . . no one would have wanted to kill Adrian. No one.'

'Good. I just wanted to hear you say it, but it is odd, is it not, that the Salamander should know the workings of the Basilica so well? None of the other towers were touched. Only the one with the paintings.'

'An insider . . . ? But . . . but . . .' Desperation haunted the bishop's eyes until, at last, he said, 'It's not possible. No. No. Absolutely not.'

Again the detective said, 'Good,' but this time he grunted it as he abruptly turned away in dismissal and went down the stairs before another word could be said. Ah *merde*, the paintings . . .

The city was in silence but now the skies had cleared. Up from the rivers came an icy ground fog to hug the streets and blocks of flats in silver-grey and hide the infrequent pale blue lamps.

St-Cyr stood alone. Christmas . . . it was Christmas Day! Ah *maudit*, what were Hermann and he to do? Lyon—old Lyon— was a rat's nest of narrow streets and passageways, the *traboules* that darted from a side entrance down a long and arched tunnel, up a spiralling flight of stairs, through buildings three and four hundred years old to yet other streets and lanes and other passageways. Dark and filthy, most of those passages, with doors here and there and iron-grilled windows and cries in the night. No lights. Not now, and not much evident in the past either.

Though old and venerable, its citizens more Swiss-like in their attitudes than French perhaps, Lyon was also very much an industrial city. Its railways linked it to every corner of the country. One could come and go so easily if one knew how—oh for sure there were the controls, the sudden spot checks, the Gestapo or the French Gestapo, the German and the French police too, and the harsh demands to see one's papers. *Papers, please.* Your *carte d'identité*, your *laissez-passer*—the *ausweis*, the *pass*! all travellers had to have to go anywhere—anywhere—outside their place of domicile. The work permit too, and ration tickets—books of these each week, the colours constantly being changed so as to confuse Allied agents and foil counterfeiters. The letters of explanation, too, that one had to carry at all times. Those that freed one from 'voluntary' labour service in the Reich; those that gave the medical history if needed. A valid military discharge for being wounded at the front in 1940. Papers and more papers.

If one hesitated, the suitcase or handbag or both would be ripped from one's hands and dumped out on to the street no matter what the weather, the crowd, the traffic, time or place, or even if one was in a hurry and would miss their bus or tram-car or the Métro.

But forged sets of papers were now becoming much, much better and far more commonplace. Those two women ... the Salamander ... could have provided themselves with false papers. They could come and go, and could already have left the city, having left their warning here, if such is what it was.

Close ... far too close for comfort.

'Well, Jean-Louis, we have the pleasure of your company again,' said Préfet Guillemette 'yet in spite of the urgency you do not call at my office? You do not exchange greetings or ask for assistance? A car, the ration tickets, some little thing? Ah no, not you. Well then listen, my friend. *Listen*, eh? Things have changed here. Be careful.'

The tramp of hobnailed boots came up to them from a Wehrmacht patrol somewhere on the side of the hill. 'Préfet, let us bury the hatchet and not be so territorial. This case demands our every co-operation no matter on which side of the fence we sit.'

St-Cyr would never change. *Never!* 'Fences? You talk of fences? Is it so wrong of me to invite the Obersturmführer Barbie to dine with me, eh? *Especially*, my friend, as he is in charge of countersubversion and I must work with him and show good faith in public.'

'Don't try to make excuses, Gérard. I know all about your kind. Fence sitters, ah no. You and the others have always been in bed with them.'

'*Bâtard!* And Kohler, eh? What of him? Isn't he Gestapo? Won't the Resistance still be aware of your association with him? Pah! I'll do as I please and tip them off if necessary.'

'Don't threaten me, Préfet. Please don't.'

'Then don't be a fool. Try to understand how it is. No mouse can fart for fear the lion will step on him.'

'But you're no mouse; you're one of the lions? What did Herr Barbie want, Préfet? Your thoughts on the cinema fire, on this Salamander and Gestapo Mueller's interest, or more Jews for you to herd on to railway trucks to Nowhere? Was the round-up of last August twenty-sixth insufficient? One thousand, I heard. Was it one thousand you contributed to the forty-odd that have so far been taken? You sent them to Vénisseaux, to buildings that had long been abandoned, and then they were deported.'

Ah *nom de Jésus-Christ!* St-Cyr would never listen. 'Shot or deported, it's all the same with them. Like Robichaud, Louis, your tears are admirable but out of place.'

'Then please do not light that cigarette, there is gasoline on my sleeve.'

Suddenly furious with him, Guillemette angrily stuffed the

lighter and cigarette away. Much taller and bigger, a *flic* all his adult life and proud of it, he leaned on the railing, blocking St-Cyr's faint view of the Croix Rousse. 'Herr Barbie could not help but notice that little exchange you chose to have at the restaurant with Monsieur Artel and his associates, Louis, but that one, he did not ask me about it, you understand. The Obersturmführer acted as though completely unaware of the furore.'

'He didn't want to spoil his dinner.'

'*Cochon!* Did you not think when Herr Kohler borrowed his *fiacre*?'

His carriage. 'Don't call me a pig, Gérard. Please, let us try to work together, eh? The city demands it.'

'*My* city, Louis. *Mine!*'

Ah *nom de Dieu*, was there no common ground? At sixty-two years of age, Guillemette had been Préfet of Lyon for the past twelve years. A hard-fought post. One had had to oil the way there but he was shrewd and clever, a force to be reckoned. An enemy that was definitely not needed. 'Robichaud has had a hard time of it.'

Guillemette faced him bluntly. 'Then start by asking the right questions. How is it he escaped to send in the alarm? Surely he should have stayed to direct people out of that building?'

When no answer came, the préfet clenched a ham-hard fist and raised it defiantly. 'He panicked, Louis. He *ran* to save himself. That is why the tears, my friend. That is why he is so upset.'

Guillemette blew out his cheeks in exasperation. 'Robichaud's every action is being called into question, Louis. There are several who are saying he should be dismissed.'

'Herr Weidling?'

'Yes. Most certainly.'

It would be best to get it over with. 'Where was Robichaud sitting, who was he with in that cinema . . . ?'

The préfet snorted lustily. It was always refreshing to get the better of Paris! 'One of my crows tells me he was in the back row, off the left aisle with his mistress, Madame Élaine Gauthier.'

The crows . . . the informers. Without them the police could not survive for long or advance up the ladder of command. Clearly Guillemette had been having the fire marshal followed. 'I should like to meet this crow. Did he stay for the flames?'

'You listen, Louis. Listen hard! Now I apply the gristle before the muscle. Robichaud does not remember with whom he was sitting or where, exactly. He claims the shock was too much and this has caused a loss of memory. Let us hope that it is temporary, eh? It would be a great calamity to us if we had to confine our fire marshal to the mental hospital at Bron!'

'And this Madame Gauthier?'

Good! 'Sizzled to bacon, my friend. *Bacon!* Pah! He was with his little bit of cunt and has abandoned her because he does not—I repeat not—want his wife to know about the affair!'

Ah *nom de Dieu*, Lyon and its politics! The couple would have met inside the cinema. 'Are you certain she was killed in the fire?'

'*Positive!* I make it my business to find out such things. There is another matter. Letters are starting to pour in. Anonymous, it's true. Always we get them now. One says that Madame Robichaud must have set the fire to get even—hey, it's been done before, eh? A lover lost. How many women go crazy after such a thing? But me, I'm not holding that one up like the gospel, though it's an interesting idea, is it not?'

One would have to keep the voice calm. 'Were there any other letters of interest?'

'Two. One points the finger directly at Monsieur Artel—that is only to be expected. A girl, I think. One who perhaps was interfered with and wishes to get even.'

'And the other?' It was coming now. Everything had been building up to this moment. *Merde!*

'Don't pretend to be so disinterested, Louis. This one claims Father Beaumont was breaking his vows with Mademoiselle

Aurelle in that flat above the cinema and that God became angry with him. As a measure of my good will, you may keep the letters for study but must return them when this is over, so that we will have a record of them in case they are needed.'

First the threats and now the warning, but the damaging evidence too! Clearly Guillemette expected him to inform the bishop of the allegations. This could only mean that they were true. 'And what about Herr Weidling?' asked St-Cyr cautiously. Talking with the préfet was like walking on broken glass in bare feet!

'What about his wife, Louis? Herr Weidling, like most men with young and very beautiful wives, must constantly keep up appearances and advance himself in her eyes so as to secure his position between her legs.'

'Ah *merde*, a young wife, an old fire chief and a need to always impress her,' muttered Louis. 'And Robichaud had a mistress who was lost in the fire!' It was a plea to that God of his for help.

Kohler grinned hugely as he joined them bearing the bishop's bottle of Calvados. Tapping the préfet solidly on the chest, he snorted and said, 'Madame Gauthier escaped the fire, *mon fin*. One of your crows has just died. Might I suggest you pick the buckshot out and attempt to sell the carcass on the black market? Try seven francs. That's the going rate in Paris. At least it was, the last time I was there.'

With barely controlled fury, Guillemette said, 'In Lyon we eat much better, *mein Kamerad*. What else did he confide in his alcoholic stupor?'

'Plenty but we'll leave it for now. Just see that he isn't bothered again. He's got enough on his plate without worrying about his back.'

'And yourselves?' asked the Préfet. Kohler . . . Kohler of the Kripo, the most ignored and insignificant of the Gestapo's subsections. Common crime.

"Right now we could use a place to eat and spend what's left of the night,' said Kohler blithely.

Without another word the préfet walked away into the deepest shadows of the basilica.

'It's all right, Hermann. Really it is. I think I have exactly the place. The address on this card our girl with the bicycle dropped in the place Terreaux.'

'What card?'

'A little yellow card.'

'You're full of surprises. Gabi won't like it but you can trust me, Louis. I won't breathe a word of it.'

'If you do, Giselle and Oona will be bound to hear of it. Me, I would not like to cause disruption in your little *ménage à trois*, especially when you're being sued for divorce!'

They shared the Calvados in crystal glasses Kohler had borrowed from the bishop's study. They wished each other a Happy Christmas, then asked, How can it be?

'The Salamander is out there, Hermann. Having given us the scare of our lives, he or she or they, for some reason, failed to strike the match.'

'Perhaps I scared them off?'

'Perhaps, but then ... ah, I do not know, Hermann. The cross leads us to the bishop and what do we find but everything in place for another major fire, a priest who messed about with spinsters, and a storeroom full of valuable paintings. It is a puzzle when puzzles are not needed.'

Louis always liked to take his time. The bugger *enjoyed* nothing better than a damned good case, murder especially!

'Three fires in the Reich, Louis. A pattern. Same method, same reason, eh?'

Good for Hermann. 'Yes, yes, and now that same reason again—is that so? The trigger for madness, the willingness to sacrifice so many perhaps all because of only one person.'

'Our priest?'

'Did the Salamander know him, Hermann, or better still, know of him?'

'Of that woman who was tied to her bed? The priest wouldn't have worn that cross if he was only going to fuck about with Mademoiselle Aurelle, Louis.'

'The priest received a telephone call of some urgency.'

'And that, then, caused him to wear the cross.'

'And attend the film.'

'Then he knew the Salamander, Louis, and was aware of what might well happen.'

'He had been warned but not by Mademoiselle Aurelle, by someone else.'

'But could not stop the fire and chose to die instead.'

Silently they toasted each other. Kohler refilled their glasses, draining the bottle and then tossing it over the edge to smash and tinkle and make its music somewhere below them.

'Our fire chief's no collaborator, Louis. The préfet's been having Robichaud tailed ever since friend Barbie came to town. Our Klaus suspects the *pompiers* of being in league with the *cheminots*, but Robichaud swears it isn't true. Not yet anyway.'

'Fireman and railwaymen, Communists and Resistants . . . That's a bad combination for the Occupier, Hermann.'

Kohler quietly confessed to everything he had found in the toilets at the cinema. He felt he had to do that. Things had become too rough as it was. 'I've got all the schedules and papers on me, Louis. I couldn't bring myself to burn them, and want to hang on to them for a bit. Okay? There's another thing. Klaus Barbie is a fanatic when it comes to hunting down Jews and terrorists. The bastard has a mistress, one of the locals, but visits the best houses as well. That's where he must have been heading after dinner, otherwise he'd have been here with the préfet.'

St-Cyr fingered the card the girl had dropped. 'Not at this house, Hermann. It's not one that is reserved for officers of the

Wehrmacht and now the SS. How things have changed, eh? The SS and the Army, who would have thought they would get together as they have? It's not Chez Blanchette or Chez Francine.'

'Since when was that ever a problem? All I'm saying is don't knock down any doors just in case. He might not like it.'

THE STREET WAS DAMP, FREEZING AND DAMNED unfriendly. Worse still, it stank of piss, mould, soot and dead fish. Not a streetlamp showed. Steps sounded behind. Steps stopped. Louis switched off his torch and they stood there listening.

At 3.35 a.m. Berlin time, the rue des Trois Maries sighed and creaked as its thin sheath of ice, made colder and harder by the depth of the night, tightened here and there to crack and split apart elsewhere.

The steps began again—again they hesitated. Two . . . were there two men following them?

'The bastards are learning,' breathed Kohler, exasperated that the préfet—it had to be him—was having them tailed. 'Louis, are you certain we've got the right place? This medieval street of sewers, it seems too . . . too unfashionable for a whorehouse with a name like La Belle Époque.'

St-Cyr kept silent. They were in one of the oldest parts of

Vieux Lyon, right below Fourvière Hill, right next to the quai Romain Rolland, the Saône and the bridge Alphonse Juin.

'Wait here, then. Let me handle this. *Don't* argue,' hissed Kohler.

'Of course.'

One seldom heard Hermann when he didn't want to be heard. His ability to tail or find a tail was uncanny.

Somewhere over in Perrache, perhaps, tyres squealed, an engine raced . . . Gestapo . . . Gestapo . . .

Otherwise the city was silent. Unearthly and eerie in the clutch of the Occupier.

Time didn't want to pass. It was so still. Then the scent of stale cigarette smoke came to St-Cyr, that of sweat, warm wool, urine and garlic.

The man was not two metres from him. Somehow he had slipped past Hermann and was now searching the Gothic entrances with their narrow sills.

Even as he watched the silhouette, dark against the deeper darkness of the opposite wall, he saw the man being rushed against the wall—heard the soft, sickening crush of flesh and bone, a smothered cry.

Smelled blood, then heard nothing more. Knew Hermann had dealt with the fellow.

Kohler cursed himself. He had let things get to him and had probably put the bastard in hospital for six months when a light tap would have sufficed! Now the bastard wouldn't talk because he couldn't, and the préfet would be in a rage.

Though he searched—went right back down the cramped and narrow street to stand among the tall stone columns of the austere and forbidding Palais de Justice, he could not find the other man.

He listened to the night. He tried to sort out its myriad odours and hear the heartbeat he knew must be near. The Salamander? he asked himself. Was it possible Préfet Guillemette had only sent one man to tail them, and the other was . . .

Perfume . . . was that perfume he was smelling?

La Belle Époque . . . ? he wondered. Mademoiselle Claudine Bertrand, age thirty-two, born 18 November 1910. Occupation: prostitute. Hair: black and long—most wore it short these days. Eyes: dark brown. Face: oval. Nose: normal—*i.e.*, not Jewish. Height: 173 centimetres.

A little taller than the usual Lyonnaise—but why had the one with the bicycle dropped this one's card? Surely the two were not one and the same. A wig? he asked and answered, The one with the bike was too young and far too timid.

Then why had she had the card in her hand?

The house was at the other end of the street. From there, the rue de la Baleine ran the short distance to the quai Romain Rolland and the Saône. There was a bell-pull. There were no lights.

They spoke in muffled tones. 'Louis, maybe we should come back another time.'

'Did you kill the other one?'

'No. No, I couldn't find him. The bitch got away.'

'The bitch . . . ? But . . .'

Kohler yanked savagely on the bell-pull. Jarred out of his wits, St-Cyr leapt and only realized then how pissed off Hermann must be.

Still no light showed. He switched on his torch. Instinctively ducking her face away, the woman who had answered the door tried to shield her eyes, then her flesh—her corset had slipped, the flimsy night-gown was open. It was freezing. Her long dark hair was everywhere. About fifty-five, if a day, and flushed . . . still flushed!

'Messieurs, the house . . . Please, I must insist. The curfew. It is forbidden to . . .'

'That does not matter,' said Louis grimly. 'We're detectives.'

'*Detectives?*' she shrilled. 'And have you brought the magistrate? Ah, you could not do so, could you, my fine messieurs, because that one, he is already here!'

'We knew he was,' snorted Kohler, impatiently pushing past her scented plumpness and into the foyer, into the warmth and the lively smells of wine, food and perfume, ah yes. Lots of it.

She closed the door and slid a bolt home. Louis switched off his light and crowded her.

'Please, messieurs, I beg you not to disturb the clients. We have had the *réveillon*, yes? The Christmas Eve feast. Ah it was such a meal but now they . . . why they are at the moments of their hearts' desires. Please, I am Madame Berthe Morel, the *sous-maîtresse* of this place. What is it you want?'

'Some coffee and a *marc*. A cigar,' breathed Kohler. 'And a little information.'

A Nazi, then. A fresh duelling scar, a bullet graze on the forehead . . . 'Please come this way. Come into the *grand salon*. Yes, yes, that would be best. It is a little untidy, you understand, but it will do. Madame will perhaps receive you there.' She gestured impatiently and spoke her thoughts aloud and only to herself as she turned away. 'It's her affair. She's the one who pays the sharks that come to feed in spite of the préfet's blessing. How could I have stopped such as these? *Les Allemands . . .*'

'I'm French,' hissed St-Cyr, not failing to notice her comment about the préfet.

She tossed her head and didn't look back over her shoulder. 'Well, that's not bad, your being French, but it's not good either. *Courage*, my little one. *Courage*. Each saint has his candle.'

Ah *merde*, a tough one! 'And to a good cat a good rat, eh, madame?' he snarled. 'Tit for tat, eh? Come, come, you insult an officer of the Sûreté, a chief inspector of detectives!'

'Very well, it's all right. It's just as you please, monsieur.'

Her corset slipped but she would not bother to pull it up or close the négligé. She would face them coldly with her two pistols and her hairy snatch! 'Wait here,' she said. 'Please do not move about the house until Madame has spoken to you.'

She was plump and round and curved in all places, and her

splayed feet with their bunions were as bare as the rest of her beneath the corset and the frilly, see-through thing she wore. The peignoir blew about like cheesecloth in a storm as she strode away, soon disappearing behind the little jungles of palm and fern and rubber plant, leaving them utterly alone in this jade-green and gold paradise.

'Don't let her bother you, Louis. Hey, me, I know you're a patriot.'

'Then perhaps you'd best tell me what happened in the street?'

'A woman, Louis. Perfume. Too damned good, that's all. I couldn't find her.'

St-Cyr nodded grimly and swept his eyes around the room. Ah *mon Dieu*, it lived and breathed *la belle époque*. Against a backdrop of gold and gold-tasselled drapes that fell from ceiling to floor, an immense chandelier glowed with lozenges of clear crystal and fountains of gold that rose and arched or twisted to white candles that could no longer be lit because they would drop wax on the carpet.

'It's magnificent, Hermann. Rosewood and ebony. Mahogany in the style of the Second Empire but updated a little. Yes, yes. Refined. Squared off—fluted and trimmed with gilding. Green baize-covered armchairs that are so wide and comfortable one could spend a whole day reading and never move. Wine-red morocco on the sofas and settees with throw-cushions of paisley in rich, dark blues, red and saffron.'

Two faience cockerels in their glory of peacock-hued glaze and gold crowed lustily from either side of the room. There were maidenhair ferns in porcelain pots on which storks flew. The walls were a wash of pastel water-lilies with naked nymphs lurking in the depths or riding frogs or lying asleep on beds of reeds or frolicking with male dragonflies.

Corsets and stockings—a garter that would have encircled a shapely leg just below a shapely knee . . .

A woman's ivory fan, a singularly tall dracaena with spiked

leaves that were slender and jade-green, a bamboo palm with long and elegant fronds. Jungles of plants everywhere. Oil paintings between the murals. Cigar butts in manly ashtrays beside deeply sunken armchairs. Empire table lamps in malachite and gold with parasol-shaped shades of pleated cream silk.

Everything was of that period from about 1890 until just prior to the Great War.

'I like it, Louis, but are we supposed to think one of those two women came from a place like this? The one I tried to follow in the street out there?'

'Was the girl with the bike leading us, eh?'

'Perhaps, but . . .' began Kohler like a parrot only to shut up.

The *sous-maîtresse* had come back. In defiance, her corset had not been yanked into place or used to draw in the fleshy waist and make it the stem of the hour-glass figure the fashionable women and *demi-mondes* of that era had so desired.

'Messieurs, if you will come this way, I will take you to Madame.'

'Louis, you handle it. I'll wait here.'

Madame Morel knew enough not to argue but even so the plump cheeks tightened and the dark eyes narrowed in warning. 'All our doors are locked, monsieur. Absolute discretion is our policy. To each in his own taste, the extended hour of privacy since all have paid for the night.'

There were butterfly palms and rhododendrons, fiddleleaf figs with deep green, papery leaves—did they wear them sometimes? thought Kohler as he waited. There were orange and lemon trees in fruit—none of the Occupation's horrible 'approximate' jam or marmalade for this place. Ah no. They grew their own fruit and would have plenty of sugar.

Two ornately carved, high-backed ebony armchairs with Gobelin tapestry coverings flanked the open doorway to which Louis and the woman headed. Beyond this doorway, beneath the raindrop cascades of another chandelier, a huge, dark green and flowered jar stood on bent golden legs holding the establishment's Christmas tree: a gorgeous kentia palm that had been simply and tastefully decorated with but a few small handfuls of golden pear-shaped ornaments.

'Wait here, please,' the woman said. Louis reached out to touch one of the pears. They were so light, so exquisite. Gilded Venetian glass and worth a small fortune because they were so old.

Ivy trailed over the lip of the pot. The carpet was an Aubusson. Crimson and mauve. Ah *mon Dieu*, the money in this place. The need, perhaps, to constantly replace things, thought St-Cyr.

'Monsieur, please state your business.'

The madam of the house was dark-eyed and dark-haired but here the similarity to the *sous-maîtresse* abruptly ended. The long, tight-bodiced dress of black silk that positively glowed was matched by swept-up hair, diamond pins and dangling ear-rings that glittered. Black silk gloves extended to her elbows. There was a choker of black velvet around her slender neck. Her skin was perfect and of a satiny lustre, the cheeks not rouged but red as if from frost. Had she only just come in from outside? Her perfume . . . it was so fresh. She was taller than himself—almost as tall as Gabrielle and slim, would have the figure of a goddess too, just like her.

'Madame,' he began. 'Please forgive the intrusion. One of your girls . . .'

The dark eyes in that finely boned, aristocratic face remained impassive.

'Mademoiselle Bertrand,' he said.

'Yes?'

'We would like a few words with her. Please, it is urgent.'

'She's not here, Inspector. She has a bad chest, a little crisis of the lungs—it's nothing. A cold, that's all. I told her not to come in until she was over it.'

Merde, why could God not have given them a break? 'Tell me about her, please.'

'There's nothing to tell. Claudine has been with me now for the past ten years. There has never been any trouble, Inspector. There never is with any of my girls.'

'Your name, madame?'

'Ange-Marie Céleste Rachline.'

Was he talking to a block of wood? Her lips were naturally red and beautiful but also cold, he thought. Yes, cold. Were they always that way, or is it because she really has only just come in from being outside? 'Age?' he asked sharply, not liking things one bit.

'Thirty-four. Inspector, what is it? Please, the house . . . these times. You do understand?'

'Husband?' he demanded.

'Am I under suspicion?'

'No. Not at present.'

'Then let us keep my husband out of this. We don't see each other, Inspector. He goes his way and I go mine as we have now for the past ten years.'

'Then Mademoiselle Bertrand has been with you from the start?' he asked. 'Yet there is nothing to tell?'

'Claudine cares for her bedridden mother who knows nothing of this place and thinks, in her confused state of mind, that her husband, who died in the invasion of 1914, still provides for her. They live alone here in Vieux Lyon, on the rue du Boeuf at Number Six.'

Not far away. 'She has no pimp?'

Madame Rachline shook her head slightly. 'None of my girls has one, Inspector. It's not permitted. It's a rule of the house that ensures each gets fair recompense for her services and there is no trouble.'

'And the doctor?' he asked. What was it about her that alarmed him in addition to the colour of her cheeks and lips?

'Dr Sévigny comes three times a week for their sake, Inspector, more than for that of the clients, though of course I am concerned on their behalf as well. My girls are good and I give them all the protection I can. It's a profession, isn't it? Therefore, let us put a little dignity into it. Each has money in a safe place but can draw on future earnings if necessary up to one-quarter of her annual take which is split fifty per cent for them, thirty for the owners, five for myself, and fifteen for the house.'

It was an amazingly fair relationship, almost unheard of. But if Madame Rachline had any further concerns about him, she hid them well. He asked if they might sit down. She did not hesitate but said, 'Would you prefer my bedroom, the *grand salon* or the dining-room?' He knew she had included the bedroom on purpose and he had to suggest it.

'Then follow me. It is the only bed that is not yet in use.'

'Were you outside in the street, madame?'

'Yes. Yes, as a matter of fact I was. I attended the midnight Mass at the Basilica.'

'And walked home alone in those clothes?'

'Yes.'

Ah *merde*.

Kohler helped himself to the *foie gras de canard*, the duck pâté with a mildewed crust that must be a good ten years old. He filled one of the ruby-rimmed, gilded Venetian goblets with Romanée-Conti, 1917—was it really that old?

Then he laid into the truffled veal sausage, had a finger-taste of the glazed fruit and then the Kirsch soufflé—all bits and pieces that still lay about the cluttered dining-room table with its tapestry cloth of deep red, green and white patterns beneath a chandelier of glass lozenges in shades of ruby, emerald, lapis and citrine.

He tried the oysters and then the *Portugaises vertes*—how had they come by them? A half-filled bottle of pepper vodka made him think of his two sons at Stalingrad. Were they saying it would be their last Christmas?

'*Salut!*' he said, pausing to spoon in the black Russian caviar.

'*Gott mit uns*, eh, Hans? Shit! Tell Jurgen you both should have listened to your papa and gone to Argentina like I said.'

Ah *merde*. *Merde!* This lousy war. He took another swill of vodka. Those two bitches in that tower, that one out on the street—had it really been a woman?

He downed a snipe that had been hung until it had dropped from the hook, then roasted on a cushion of toast smothered in a paste of brandy and its rotted innards.

A wealth of bone-white porcelain and old silver covered the table. There was a ceramic crèche as the centrepiece—elephants and tigers led by Nubian slaves with jewelled parasols to keep the sun off their masters as they made their way to Bethlehem. Decanters and bottles—strands of pearls and cut-glass beads, beeswax candles like he hadn't seen in years. Spirals and twists and fluted columns but plump, golden artichokes also, *and* bunches of grapes *and* fleurs-de-lis.

More caviar was swallowed, more vodka, pâté and soufflé. Some of the candles had gone out or had been pinched out by licentious fingers. He could almost hear the gaiety of their laughter. Fifteen couples had sat here, the cream of Lyon industrialists, bankers, lawyers and merchants, no doubt. Money, money and more of it because business was booming for them, ah yes.

The vodka was gone. He refilled his goblet. When alternated with the Romanée-Conti, it wasn't bad. A bit too peppery, but the Russians always had been driven to excess. Too emotional a people.

The braised goose had had all of its bones drawn out through its anus before being rammed with a forcemeat of *foie gras* and truffles. Small mushrooms lay like plump, ripe breasts among stoned ripe olives and small sausages that had first been fried in butter. All were mingled with a dark, rich sauce that had cooled and was now setting into a gel.

He spooned a bit, cut off a slice—tore away a larger piece—hell, there must have been a dozen geese scattered along the table. The potatoes were good. With the snipe and the pâté and the cold purée of leeks, a meal. Dessert too, and another shot of wine. He'd try the Clos de Vougeot this time or perhaps the Beaujolais Blanc.

'You must be hungry.'

For seven seconds he paused, then hesitated knowing gravy was drooling down his chin.

Her hair was as red as the sunset over Essen with the Krupp furnaces going full blast. Her eyes were a lively green, wide and full of innocence, the lashes long and a shade darker than the loosened mass that fell richly to delicious shoulders. *Nom de Jésus-Christ*, she was absolutely gorgeous. About twenty-three years of age.

Kohler swallowed tightly—he really hadn't realized how much he'd been missing his little Giselle back home in Paris, or Oona, his Dutch housekeeper. '*Bonsoir*,' he said. 'Pull up a chair. Here, let me fill you a glass. The Dom Pérignon, eh? Come on, I'll join you. Some of the pâté? A little of the caviar? Your client . . . ?' He arched his eyebrows. She smiled softly and her lips . . . Ah *nom de Dieu*, they were perfect! Paris . . . would she consider coming to Paris when this thing was over?

'My client, he is relieved of his little burden, monsieur, and will now sleep until it comes upon him again. Were you . . . ?'

'Waiting? Ah, sorry. I wish I was but know I haven't got the strength tonight. Maybe another time, eh? I'm Georges Chartrand from Dijon, here on business, and you?'

'Mademoiselle Renée Noirceau.' She pushed her hair back off her brow a little sleepily and pulled the blue silk wrap more tightly about her. 'Then why are you here, waiting, monsieur, and so hungry for the use of my body, one has hardly to look into your eyes but to see the depth of your lust?'

He gestured with the half-eaten chunk of goose. 'One of the house clients is an associate. He was supposed to put me up but his wife locked the door.'

She would give him a rapid little smile of disbelief and the shyness of a virgin's eyes. She would take some of the soufflé to keep herself busy, and have a sip of champagne. She would study this one from the Gestapo as one would a bull one wishes, perhaps, to castrate, should that be necessary to control him. 'Are you married?' she asked, not letting up.

Kohler grinned. 'How else does a man know best how to keep a woman happy?'

'And the woman? Does she learn best in the same way or by being with many men?'

He dabbed caviar on to a leftover snipe and handed it to her. 'Try this. I think you'll like the combination. It's interesting.'

She kissed his fingers, then the hand that held the snipe, its tiny head tucked under a wing, but demurely shook her head. 'I must get back. Monsieur Bertolette makes trucks for the Army of the Germans—lots and lots of them. Perhaps it is his conscience that causes him to be such a light sleeper. When he pays, he demands. I only came down for this.'

Another bottle of the Dom Pérignon, the 1908.

'Tell me about Mademoiselle Bertrand.'

Her eyebrows arched. 'Did your friend give you her name?'

'Instead of yours? Yes, he did. She's older, more . . .'

'Experienced?'

Gott im Himmel, she had a lovely accent! Refined, of the aristocracy of Lyon, the cream of the crop!

'Experienced?' she asked again, only to see him smile and hear him say, 'You tell me, Mademoiselle Noirceau. Is Mademoiselle Claudine Number One in this stable or Number Twenty?'

A stable . . . She would shrug at the insult. 'Perhaps it is, monsieur, that some women, they are good for many things and others are not. Is it that your tastes, they are . . . ?'

'Peculiar? No, no, I like my women *au naturel* and the usual way.'

'Not sometimes a little different? Over the arm of a chair,

perhaps, or up against the wall, the bureau, the armoire with its big mirrors or on the hands and knees like animals?'

Louis should have been with him! 'Does she go with women?'

The girl's throat tightened under her hand. Fear touched those lovely eyes only to vanish. 'Why do you ask such a thing?'

'Because it's possible.'

'Then you must ask Madame Rachline, monsieur. Me, I would not know since I service only those stallions with the proper equipment!'

Hot under the collar, eh, at the mention of lying naked with another woman? Kohler grabbed her by the arm and pulled her back, only to have her rake her nails across the back of his hand and grab a thumb that was already sore from the last investigation! He gripped her arm all the harder.

Ah *maudit*, he was so stubborn! A giant. Trembling, she let go of the thumb to touch the scar on his left cheek and then the wound on his forehead from which, hours ago perhaps, the bandage had fallen or been torn away.

'Claudine is special, monsieur, and that is why Madame keeps her on.'

Kohler collected two of the forgotten favours that were scattered about among the candles. The condoms were powder-blue or chartreuse, one took one's pick. Rolled up and ready with a gumdrop in each.

When he pressed them into her hand, she frowned and heaved a sigh. 'Monsieur Bertolette, my client for tonight, will not use these. Instead, he looks first to see if there is disease and then rides without the English riding coat. I'm pregnant, and now the sight of all this food is making my stomach turn.'

Bertolette was one of the old-style, union-smashing *patrons* who'd send his mother to the guillotine if necessary to further business. Trucks—he made them in plenty. His was the largest works in the country.

Kohler chucked her under a chin so soft and gently curved

he knew it had been raised on milk and that her family had been well off. '*Bon Noël*, Mademoiselle Renée. Don't shed tears. Just get rid of his bastard. Don't try to convince him to keep you.'

'For me, there are no illusions, monsieur. Madame has arranged everything but I cannot be free of my little burden until the New Year.'

'Does she go with any of the clients?'

'Madame? Ah no, of course not. She is our only defence in the times of crisis and must remain neutral.'

'Was she here for the supper?'

'Yes. Yes, of course.'

'Did she leave for a bit?'

'Ah, I . . . I would not know, monsieur. Me, I was kept busy.'

'Who owns this place?'

She had a way of shrugging that both pleased and puzzled. 'Others,' she said a little sadly. 'Oh *bien sûr*, we are the first to wonder, monsieur, and the last to know.'

I'll bet! 'This stuff,' he said. 'These things . . . this place and all that's in it? Hey, me, I've never seen a house like this. Who furnished it and keeps it going? Those dresses you all must wear? That robe? None of this stuff is being made any more, so where's it all coming from?'

'That I do not know, monsieur.'

The green of her eyes had darkened. Wary now, her eyelids flickered once under scrutiny, then she gripped her stomach, dropped the champagne bottle, and with a hand to her mouth, rushed from the room.

Fortunately the bottle didn't explode. Gingerly Kohler picked it up and followed her into the kitchen to wait while she emptied her guts, washed her face and tried to steady herself.

The stairwell was carpeted and grand, replete with staggered palms and ferns in porcelain buckets under gorgeous nudes on canvas. Renée Noirceau said nothing but led him up to her room on the first floor at the back.

'*Merci,*' she said demurely as he handed her the bottle.

Kohler let her open the door. Satiated, Bertolette lay face down among the scattered covers on an Empire bed. 'He snores,' she said, dismayed. 'Me, I think that men, they should not snore after they have made love to a woman.'

One stocking hung from the arm of a chair. Her corset, with all its metres of lacing undone, had been tossed aside.

As he watched, she pulled the tie from around her middle and let the robe fall to her feet. 'Goodbye, my dear detective. Me, I would perhaps prefer you to him, but really it's all the same once the eyes are closed, or is it?'

Ah *nom de Dieu!* How could a girl of good breeding become so wicked?

She touched her lips with a fingertip and smiled. 'Come, come, Inspector. Here on the floor. Let us experience the *grand frisson,* eh? the great shudder. Please, there is no need for you to shoot the stork in flight since the egg within its little nest has already been fertilized.'

Kohler kissed her on the lips and patted her gorgeous backside. 'Sleep tight. Good luck. We'll be back.'

'We . . . ?'

He touched her lips. 'My partner and I. He's downstairs with Madame.'

'Then it is a cold supper he will have, for that one opens her legs to no one.'

'Not even another woman?'

'Not even one of those.'

'I like your perfume. What's it called?'

'*Étranger.* It's Madame's. For tonight she has asked us all to wear it. A little gift.'

He closed the door. He stood there breathing in the last of it, said, Louis . . . Louis, I think I'm going to be sick.

Every moment in that tower came back, every second in the street. He saw the corpses in the ruins of the cinema, the young, the old, the not so old, and smelled the stench of their flesh.

*   *   *

Hesitantly St-Cyr strained to touch the chandelier in Madame Rachline's bedroom and heard the rippling, mocking laughter of its crystal lozenges as they brushed against each other only to fade as if in the distance like a far-off, fleeting embrace or whispered confidence. What had she in mind, and should he have let her go so easily?

Madame Rachline, having conducted him to her room, had left to go in search of one of her maids. Surely she must have known he would realize the room was unused and totally for show?

The walls were papered with pale green linen on which there was a white-rose motif in sprays and single flowers. This was matched by a quilted bedspread and curtained canopy which was draped from the ceiling over the head of an Empire-style four-poster of brass and ebony rods.

There was a brass peacock-fan screen in front of a grey marble fireplace on whose mantelpiece stood two flanking, pale green amphorae filled with white silk roses. One could imagine their scent. The same was true of the luminous poppies in a painting by Henri Fantin-Latour and in the older, and far richer spring flowers of van Dael.

The room was a museum. It felt like it—just as cold, just as remote and silent. All that was needed was a glass display case over the tall vase of pink silk lilies. Exquisite—yes, yes, and untouched. Yet now . . . why now she would try to suggest that it was used.

Even as he unstoppered a pale green bottle with entwining, swimming nudes, graceful, gorgeous things, he wondered if she had left him alone on a dare just to see how far he would go.

The scent was troubling. Bergamot and jasmine, rose absolute and petitgrain of lemon-tree. Orange flower, Clary sage and musk. Though it took him back to the belfry at the Basilica, it also took him back to his boyhood, for it called up with a suddenness that shocked, the faint-hearted trembling steps of a boy of ten who had found himself slipping guiltily away from his parents to search out and walk through the forbidden exhibits in the *Palais des Fils, Tissus et Vêtements*—thread, fabric and clothing—at the great Universal Exhibition in Paris, the year 1900.

There had been sweeping skirts and tiny, bejewelled or richly embroidered bolero jackets, smallish hats trimmed and veiled; frock coats, toppers and silk cravats for the men of substance. But deeper, deeper into the maze and to one side as if forbidden, there had been the lace and muslin over silk petticoats that had always rustled when *maman* or Aunt Sophie or any of his other aunts and older cousins had been angry or simply in a hurry and all too willing to box his ears.

Les Toilettes de la Collectivitée de la Couture it had been called, the first really public exhibit of *haute couture*. The chemises and corset-bodices—the whalebone and steel-shanked armour the women of those days had strapped themselves into. The camisoles, the white drawers that continued right down to their knees. The silk night-gowns that were so soft and sensual, all hand-sewn and monogrammed and edged with Cluny lace or Flounce of Argentan or any of the other antique laces and with pink or blue 'baby' ribbons inserted as if one would have to untie each of those tiny bows to get at what was within.

Black silk stockings of knee length and black shoes that were high and laced up the front, and more like boots with sharply pointed toes. Openwork muslin blouses of *broderie anglaise* that were deemed immodest yet allowed only the sight of a stiff white bodice that hid all cleavage beneath an armour of white lawn if one were decent and not up to mischief or really dressing up.

They'd shaken him savagely, both his mother and father. For days afterwards he had sweltered. His mother had refused to speak or acknowledge a delinquent son. The maid had accused him of secretly going through the laundry to find out things no boy should even think about!

And now? he asked a little sadly. Why now that boy knows far more of evil than that mother or father could ever have imagined.

He stared at the perfume bottle in his hand. The scent was earthy, not common and most certainly from forty to fifty years ago. It contained far too much musk for his liking—at least he thought so now, for it suddenly embarrassed him.

Madame Rachline had returned—she had caught him at her dressing table.

'Inspector, this is Michèle-Louise, one of my housemaids. Unfortunately one cannot retire without assistance. Please, we can talk while I . . .' She indicated the dressing screen, said nothing about the perfume vial that was still in his hand. Not even a hint of surprise or question. Clever . . . had she been clever?

The girl was sleepy-eyed, in plain white muslin that rose right up under her chin and was tied round the wrists, all but hiding her completely. About seventeen, he thought, with deep brown eyes, pale lips and thick brown hair that protruded in wisps and curls from beneath the night-cap. 'Good evening, monsieur,' she said, a shy whisper, the girl ducking briefly as if genuflecting.

The game began, Madame Rachline talking to him from behind the screen as the girl hung Madame's clothes over the top of it.

'La Belle Époque is a well-established house, Inspector, with an excellent clientele who pay in advance of each visit, in addition to a yearly membership. This ensures that they try to get the most out of each visit.'

'Is the préfet a client?' he asked, realizing she'd done this deliberately to avoid scrutiny.

A white cotton petticoat followed the dress. 'Am I forced to answer?'

'It would help.' Would she tell the préfet everything, or would she feel it best to say nothing of the visit?

Another shift or petticoat followed. More flounce to the skirts. 'La Belle can have no connection with that terrible fire, monsieur. How could it have?'

So much for the préfet being a member and having filled her in. 'Of course,' he said drily, 'but the fact is madame, this work card was dropped in the place Terreaux.'

'By whom?'

Again there was that coldness, that remoteness of tone. Utter blandness could mask so much. Would honesty be best? 'That we do not know as yet.'

There was a pause—perhaps she breathed a sigh of relief, perhaps it was only that a lace had been done up too tightly.

The girl gave a sharp cry. 'Ah, madame, I have broken a nail!'

'Then you must trim it, isn't that so?'

As he watched, Michèle-Louise came out from behind the screen and went over to the dressing table to find the clippers but, as the nail was on the right hand, she had difficulty with it. Swore under her breath. Did a bad job and decided to bite off the rest.

Was caught momentarily knowing the inspector was looking at her. Felt those eyes of his. Asked herself anxiously, Is he going to question me, too, about this place? and answered, Ah *merde*, I think he is!

Another petticoat was flung over the screen, silk this time. Again Madame Rachline spoke. She must have gestured impatiently—a first sign of emotion perhaps—for the screen rocked a little. 'That card is a forgery, Inspector. Someone's trying to *implicate* the house. It's . . .' She must have shrugged near-naked shoulders. 'It's the times, the hatred, the popularity of using anonymous letters that are sent to the police and now to the Gestapo at the Hotel Terminus.'

'Yes, yes, the times,' he said blandly. Quite obviously the letters had unsettled her and quite obviously the préfet, though he had told her of them, had failed to inform her of the contents.

'Is Monsieur Artel one of your clients? Please, I must insist on an answer, madame.'

'Is he under suspicion of burning his own cinema to the ground?'

Was it so impossible? He'd take out his pipe and tobacco pouch. He'd make her wait for a bit.

Angered at the lack of reply, she said, 'Yes, Monsieur Artel is a member in good standing but that one, he does not choose Claudine, monsieur, since he prefers the youngest of my girls and pays extra for them.'

'Michèle-Louise, eh, madame? Does he covet your little maid and is that why she shrinks under scrutiny?' he all but shouted.

'Michèle, undo my laces this instant!'

Grateful for the outburst and her refusal to answer for it said so much about Artel, he decided against the pipe but did not put it away. 'And his associates, madame, what of them?'

Insurance, banking and the law. 'They are all members, Inspector,' she said tightly, 'but why must you ask? None of them could have had anything to do with that fire.'

'But with Mademoiselle Claudine?' he demanded. 'Come, come, madame, let us not play at this any longer.'

She must have clenched her fists and stamped a foot, for the girl said, 'Madame, hold still, *please!*'

'Claudine, she is ... Ah, how should I say it, Inspector? In this world of such varied taste, Claudine is different. Very special.'

'In what way?' he hazarded. Ah *nom de Dieu*, what was it with her? The coldness of a face cream, the detachment of a

douche—this room, that girl, that child of a maid. The perfume . . . the scent of it now. Had the girl, unused to such
luxury, drenched herself? A gift . . . had it been a little gift to
open at the *réveillon* or had she been drenched on purpose?

Again he said, 'In what way, madame?' He waited. Perhaps
she smiled wanly in triumph, perhaps not at all.

'For that I think it best to let her tell you herself, Inspector.
I'm sure there is a very adequate reason for her work card
disappearing in some restaurant or café. Perhaps Claudine
simply took her gloves from a pocket and inadvertently the card
slipped out.'

'And someone else picked it up only to drop it in the place
Terreaux?' he demanded sharply.

'Yes. Yes, of course. That is how it must have been.'

A corset-bodice came free at last and was flung over the top of
the screen to hang there as if shot dead and rotted bare like
some strange sort of archaeopteryx skeleton. Then came a plain
white cotton shift, black silk stockings and white, knee-length
drawers.

It was warm in the house—too warm. In a land where coal
had become so scarce one received only enough to heat one
small room once a month for a few miserable hours, this place
had plenty for the furnace and boiler.

She was bathing behind the screen, and they spoke quietly
those two. Eventually the girl came demurely out to find
Madame a suitable night-gown and took from an armoire, a
grey-blue silk robe.

The game was almost over and clearly Madame Rachline
had been the winner, for he still could not tell what she was
thinking and he desperately needed to know this.

She sat at her dressing table while the girl unpinned the up-
swept hair and then began to comb it out before brushing it.
Only then did she realize that he had positioned himself so as to
meet her eyes in the mirrors.

He struck a match—struck another. 'These lousy matches

our government makes,' he said. And taking two, struck both together.

The flame burst. It was so sudden, so bright—flared up. Was sucked down into the bowl of his pipe, he gazing steadily at her through the smoke . . . the smoke, watching her . . . She mustn't look at the flame. She *mustn't*! she told herself. But had she for an instant? Had she? she wondered in despair.

St-Cyr nodded curtly at her reflection and said he'd show himself out.

Ah damn, he saw me looking at it, she said silently, and hesitantly touched a cheek.

It was only after he had left the room that she discovered he had taken the vial of perfume.

Downstairs, a heavy door closed. Slippered steps hurried along a parquet hall, their sound vanishing on the carpeted stairs. One flight, then two, then three . . . yes, yes, Madame Rachline, come to Hermann Kohler. It had to be her. He'd seen Louis come out of that same room.

The woman didn't pause but went straight to the end of the hall and had trouble unlocking its oak door. Was frantic. Dropped the key, threw a glance over a shoulder, tugged the sleeve of her robe up to get it out of the way.

The lock finally yielded and she closed the door behind herself. He waited. He followed and, nudging the door open a little, listened for her.

She was at the far end of the passage, trying to unlock yet another door. It was too dark for her. The key would not fit— was it the same key or a different one, he wondered? In her panic, had she confused them?

Again he drew in that scent, thought, *Étranger*, madame? and had very nearly reached her when she slipped away.

He heard her lock the door behind her, said, *Verdammt*, what have you been up to?

A light came on—he could see it clearly from one of the windows in the passage. She was now on the floor below him, but all too soon she had drawn the black-out curtains.

Snuffed out, the wall now appeared dark. Kohler held his breath. Once again every part of him was alert and tingling.

Slowly he picked out the degrees of darkness, distinguishing one from another.

The house, once the home of a wealthy Renaissance merchant perhaps, had been built in two quite distinct parts. Below this interconnecting passage there was a courtyard that had once been used for carriages. Stables, long since made over into rooms, would have given on to it. There could be spiral sets of outside stairs on either side leading to the floors above.

Two houses then, the one for La Belle Époque and the other perhaps a residence of some sort.

Louis was waiting in the foyer. Madame Morel, the *sous-maîtresse*, gave them the once-over as she let them out on to the street before bolting the door behind them as if for ever.

'Now what?' asked Kohler.

'The rue du Boeuf, Number Six,' said St-Cyr grimly. 'Let us hurry, *mon ami*. Madame Rachline was at the midnight Mass and says she *walked* home.'

'She couldn't have! She was at the *réveillon*.'

'Then she went outside just before we got here.'

'To see a prostitute, eh, Louis? To see Claudine Bertrand?'

Ah *merde*, were they too late?

At 5.00 a.m. the city had awakened to end the curfew. At 5.47 those who had to get to work were on the street, Christmas Day or not. Some pushed bicycles over the hard-frozen slush; others trod warily. There were few glimmers of light, no curses, little coughing and no talking. It was as if a throng of zombies had suddenly chosen to get up without their breakfast.

Lyon, like Paris and the rest of France, still could not get used to living on Berlin time. Two hours back in summer; one in winter, 5.47 becoming 4.47! There were no croissants, no butter! There was no real coffee except on the black market.

The rue du Boeuf was only two streets away and past the place de la Baleine. There were a few cafés, some of those little hole-in-the-wall places Lyon had been so famous for in pre-war days. Three or four tables at most. No lights showing. Hot muddy water and cold grey bread. A line-up at one place, a few stragglers at another. Tobacco smoke scenting the twenty degrees of frost but also those rude accents of the burning rubbish people tried to smoke these days. *Corn silk, camomile and oak leaves or kitchen herbs!* Sometimes a little peppermint would be added; sometimes they'd try dried lettuce, sometimes beet leaves. A nation of experimenters!

One woman was urinating in the gutter—caught short and no doubt uncaring since it was still pitch dark, or perhaps that did not matter to her. Only a sliver of light from a delinquent bicycle lamp caught her out. A tram-car clanged.

The concierge of Number Six sent one of his daughters to open the door, then came himself since the pounding was incessant.

The man's grizzled moon-face tightened. 'The flat is on the third floor, messieurs. The old woman ... Mademoiselle Bertrand's mother,' he managed, glancing anxiously at Hermann's Gestapo shield. 'We have not heard that one's constant complaining or moaning in the night. Not since this past day and night.'

He'd been worried. 'And before that?' asked Kohler, leaning on the half-opened door.

The man looked up and drew in a breath, said to himself, Ah such a slash on the face, the wound on the forehead ... 'The coughing of Mademoiselle Bertrand. The cold in the chest.' He patted his own flannel-shirted chest.

'But not since Wednesday evening when she returned?' asked St-Cyr, flicking the torch down a little more so as not to blind him.

'No. Not since then. Monsieur, has anything . . .'

Kohler took the ring of keys from him. 'Hey, we'll let you

know, eh? In the mean time don't leave the house. We may
need you. Put the coffee on. Sausages and eggs, bread and jam
will do.' He tapped the concierge solidly on the barrel chest.
'You look well fed, eh? So let us see a little of it and we won't
say a thing.'

Everyone knew the concierges of each city and town or village acted as black-market go-betweens. Soap from one, prunes
from another—cakes for special occasions and sugar too.

'Come on, Louis. I think he has to shit himself. You look
after your papa, eh?' he said to the girl of twelve. 'Make sure the
sausage is well done. We wouldn't want to make a Gestapo
sick.'

'What about him?' asked the child, nodding towards the
Sûreté who had crowded into the foyer behind the giant with
the slash.

'Oh, him,' retorted Kohler. 'He gets to taste everything first. If
it's poisoned, we lay a murder charge.'

'*Hermann, come on!*' seethed St-Cyr. 'Ah *nom de Dieu,* don't
be so hard on them. What would *you* do if you had six mouths
to feed and—'

'Eight, monsieur. Actually it is eight,' said the concierge.

'And my two cousins,' murmured the child. 'They are both
pregnant, but have gone to the early Mass.'

'*Lying,* Hermann! Do you not see what you Germans have
done to us? *Created* a nation of untruthful citizens whose children lie with equanimity!'

Somehow they got to the flat, gesticulating and shouting at
one another about the demerits or merits of the Occupation—
hiding from themselves what they most feared.

The flat was indeed too silent; freezing too. A small sitting-
room whose faded furniture was of thirty years ago, with a
threadbare carpet, no cat, canary or finch, and curtains that
were crooked.

A pantry-kitchen held a small, cold, cast-iron stove for
heating the flat and a two-burner gas ring. The kettle looked as

if it had been warmed to fill a hot-water bottle or a mug and then set aside.

The smell of friar's balsam was faint, the doors to both bedrooms closed.

'You or me?' asked Kohler, knowing it was his turn.

St-Cyr waited. In a whisper he said, 'The handkerchief, Hermann. How many times must I tell you? A clean one, *please*. The one you used in Saint-Denis put snot all over the fingerprints.'

That had been months ago. Months!

Madame Bertrand had died in her sleep, of a heart attack perhaps. She was probably only seventy-five but looked eighty, was thin and frail under her bonnet, had fortunately removed her false teeth, which rested in a foggy glass of water on the night table.

She'd been reading Proust—Kohler knew Louis would nod agreement at the astuteness of choice but would measure it against the reduced economic state of the occupants, a puzzle. One didn't need to look at the Frog any more to tell what he was thinking. One simply opened the mind to it.

'Anything out of place?' he asked, giving the grey-haired corpse the once-over. Getting old had always made him feel uncomfortable.

St-Cyr shook his head. 'Let's let the coroner decide. Touch nothing.'

'There's nothing to touch.'

'Meaning Mademoiselle Bertrand did not bring too much of her earnings home?' asked St-Cyr. He didn't need to look at Hermann to see him nod agreement.

They went into the other room but did not move far from the door. They let the hall light enter with them, throwing their shadows on the worn carpet and chair, the clothes that were not of La Belle Époque of course, but had been removed and left to lie. A red woollen dress, calf-length perhaps. A wide black belt of some sort of glossy ersatz leather with a silver-plated buckle as big as a fist—had it been aluminium-plated? Was that possible? Beige silk stockings, all but unheard of these days, a cream-coloured blouse and knitted cardigan, all pre-war. An overcoat in charcoal grey, a scarf, cloche and one high-heeled red patent leather shoe. Only one. Pre-war as well. Cherished no doubt.

Her garter belt and underwear pants had not quite made it to the chair. The brassiere had been dropped near the armoire from which she had taken her night-gown and robe and another, heavier sweater. The armoire's mirrored door was still open and in its reflections they saw her lying propped up by pillows in bed as if asleep. Her long black hair spilling over a freshly laundered white pillow slip. Her head tilted a little to one side as if she'd only just dropped off, was calm in repose and content.

'Louis . . .'

The sweet, resinous smell of friar's balsam was much stronger here. She'd been using a makeshift vaporizer, had had a towel over her head but had set these carefully aside on the night table before switching off the light.

'Baudelaire . . . She was reading *Les Fleurs du Mal*, Hermann. The Flowers of Evil,' said St-Cyr, his voice a hush.

Mademoiselle Claudine Bertrand had been an attractive woman, though now her lower jaw drooped and rigor had brought its stiffness to her. Still, there were suggestions of the child she'd once been. Fresh and alive, vivacious perhaps, full of fun and mischief.

'How can our lives go so wrong?' asked St-Cyr, carefully switching on the bedside lamp.

Louis always had to probe for that initial happening which had set life's train onto a track it should never have gone down. 'Are you going to stick the thermometer up her ass or do I have to?' asked Kohler grumpily.

'She's been dead since the fire, Hermann. One has only to look at her.'

'Murdered, Louis? Dead from breathing that crap?'

The vaporizer was simply a glazed pottery mixing bowl. There were perhaps two centimetres of water in the bottom and a thin scum left by the balsam.

On the surface, then, there was nothing out of the ordinary. Just a mother and daughter, one of whom had had a bad chest cold and the other who had been senile.

Greatly troubled by what they had found, Kohler parted the curtains to look south-east towards the rue des Trois Maries and the house of La Belle Époque, both still in darkness. 'Mueller's going to burn our asses, Louis, if we don't settle this thing fast. Boemelburg will make certain we suffer if there's another fire.' He tossed his head towards the bed. 'Was she the one who went up to see the projectionist?'

'Probably. There is only one red shoe, Hermann. Me, I cannot see . . .'

'*Ja, ja,* the other one! Louis, just how the hell did that girl with the bicycle come by this one's work card? Was it through a relative, a lover, a friend, or was she paying visits to that house? And did she know of this, eh? Did she?'

There were always questions, seldom ready answers. 'Patience, *mon vieux*. Patience, eh? It is the yeast that makes each investigation rise until the loaf, it is complete.'

'Piss off! I'm scared. That bitch in the street, Louis. I missed her. *Me*, who is always so good at finding and tailing someone in the dark, missed her and *that*, my fine Frog friend, says one hell of a lot about our Salamander as does this . . . this convenient death right after the fire!'

'When I talked to her, Madame Rachline had only just come in from the street, Hermann . . .'

'Yes, yes, but was it the madam who was tailing us?' he yelped. 'That perfume, Louis?'

'The perfume, ah yes. The last of it is on Mademoiselle Bertrand's bureau.'

So it was. A 250 cc bottle all but dry. '*Étranger*, Louis. The

Stranger,' muttered Kohler uncomfortably, for the name suggested someone as yet unknown. Shit!

'It's expensive, Hermann. Not common and probably hasn't been on the market for a good fifty years.'

'From *la belle époque*? Bought at auction, then, Louis?'

'And unless I am mistaken, shared with the others at the *réveillon* but worn by someone in that belfry at the Basilica and deliberately left for us to find.'

'Claudine Bertrand couldn't have been there, Louis. She'd have been dead by then.'

Hermann fell into such a silence St-Cyr had to ask him what was the matter. 'The shoes in that belfry, Louis. I . . . I forgot to take a look at them.'

'And so did I. Later, eh? Later. Hermann, Madame Rachline is fascinated by fire or very afraid of it. When I struck two matches, she tried to stop herself from looking at the flame and failed.'

'Ah *merde*, is that their fetish? As sure as that God of yours made little green apples, Louis, Claudine Bertrand catered to some particular perversion and unless I've completely lost my touch, she went with women as well as men.'

'The girl with the bicycle . . .' began St-Cyr, only to let the thought trail off into silence.

'Those paintings in that storeroom at the Basilica, Louis?'

'Yes, yes, the paintings, Hermann, and a whorehouse full of things of exceptional quality and expense. Things not easily come by.'

'Unless one has the *ausweis* to come and go, and the car also.'

At last they were getting some place. 'Auction houses, Hermann. Estate sales.'

'And classy whores whose madam runs from you to find someone in the other part of the house.'

'Pardon?' gasped the Sûreté, jerked from his bedside thoughts.

Kohler told him of the enclosed passage above the lane. 'She wasn't happy, Louis. Madame Rachline was damned scared and on the run.'

'And has known this one for at least the last ten years but can tell us virtually nothing about her.'

'A stranger, Louis. A Salamander and a visiting fire chief.'

'A pattern, Hermann. Three fires in the Reich in 1938 and now Lyon.'

'Why now? Why Lyon?'

'Why not, if for some reason there is a connection with the visit of Herr Weidling?'

Kohler glanced at his wrist-watch and swore. 'That bastard's going to get bitchy, Louis. We're late.'

'Then perhaps you should go and have a little talk with him, Hermann. Perhaps our visiting fire marshal's wife would be good enough to offer coffee and rolls?'

Instead of sausages and eggs courtesy of the concierge of this place. 'You certain you'll be okay?'

'Positive. Please cancel my breakfast on the way out. I need to concentrate and do not wish to be disturbed.'

Louis always liked to have his little tête-à-tête with the victim. In spite of knowing they were on the run, Kohler grinned 'Enjoy yourself, eh? Look for burns in those tenderest of places and ask her who caused them.'

**4** IN THE SILENCE OF MADEMOISELLE CLAUDINE'S bedroom all sounds were magnified. Each time someone came or went in the building, St-Cyr would hold his breath. The door to one of the other flats would open and then close. There would be steps on the stairs, a brief, muffled exchange with the concierge, eyes cast upwards to indicate the Sûreté's continued presence, then more steps and the outer door would open.

Sometimes people came in off the street to buy whatever the concierge had to offer, but these visits lasted so briefly, the caller hardly bothered to close the outer door. There were never any complaints. One took what one was offered and did not complain for to do so was to get nothing else. One didn't haggle and, as often as not, cigarettes were the floating currency. France had become a nation of beggars on the scrounge ruled by tobacco, collaborators and, still, that oligarchy of the wealthy and the well-to-do who had always taken care of themselves.

Claudine Bertrand had been a victim of that oligarchy, of

this he was now certain. In photo after photo he had seen her as a child in the gardens and rooms of a lovely house in the suburb of Les Brotteaux or on the beach at Concarneau along the Breton Coast, several times with the friend who was now Ange-Marie Céleste Rachline. Again and again the two of them as schoolgirls, then as students at the university here and then . . . the financial collapse of the Great Depression, this flat and La Belle Époque.

'*Claudine, she is . . . Ah, how should I say it, Inspector? In this world of such varied taste, Claudine is different. Very special.*'

He remembered the instant he had struck those matches and the look that had come into Madame Rachline's eyes. Had Claudine been just as fascinated or afraid of fire? Had those two children played with matches and found it a game neither could resist?

There were no photos beyond that point of lost fortune. The year would have been 1932, Claudine then twenty-two, Ange-Marie twenty-four.

He put the album back in the lower drawer of the bureau and covered it with sweaters as it had been. Then he stood up and began to study the perfume bottle. It wasn't one of Houbigant's or any of the other great perfumers. Lost to that world, he read the label and muttered, 'Joulbert. Perfumer to the Imperial Court of Russia.'

Right at the top of the label were the dates: 1785 on the far left, and 1900 on the right. At the bottom, the address was given as 17 rue du Faubourg St-Honoré, Paris. Joulbert had been classy, ah yes. Quite obviously the stuff had been very expensive even at the turn of the century.

In the illustration a bare-breasted, winsome girl of perhaps eighteen was seated with a peacock's rainbow of irises and tulips behind her. Masses of them. All the rest of her, except for the ankles and bare feet, was clothed in some sort of see-through webbed fabric, her look pensive as if assessing the object of her dreams and not in the least concerned about the spiders that might have woven her garment.

Unscrewing the cap, he brought it up to first one and then the other nostril. Yes, the scent was one of the 'Persian' types so popular at the turn of the century. Again he felt the musk too strong. Heavy and body-clinging and not at all suitable for the girl on its label. Perhaps some forgotten carton had come to light or perhaps the bottle had simply been from an estate sale. Perhaps the house had been given it by one of the clients and Madame Rachline had shared it out.

Then why, he asked, has Mademoiselle Claudine the dregs, unless it was she who had been given it and she was the sharer? Ah yes. Yes, of course.

There was nothing in the room to indicate it was Christmas. Going over to the bed, St-Cyr drew up a chair and began to study the woman earnestly, willing himself right into her skin. Alive, what were you hoping for? he asked. A return to those former days? Something better for your mother and yourself or release, Mademoiselle Bertrand, from filial duty?

It couldn't have been pleasant coming home to a place like this from La Belle Époque. Did you hide everything from that mother of yours? he asked. Were you afraid she'd find out? Or were you sick and tired of having to look after her and wanting only to get on with your life?

Had she had a child she wished to protect? he wondered. Is that why she brought so little of her income home? A child in a convent boarding school, a child who would know nothing of her mother's profession.

She had gone to the cinema in her red dress and high heels, of this he was now certain. She had not stayed out long, had come back and dressed for bed, then put the kettle on and had . . .

Swiftly he went into the kitchen and, lighting a match, checked the stove's draught. 'Excellent,' he breathed softly.

'The flue is not blocked. There can have been no poisonous fumes, no carbon monoxide to silently kill without the victim ever knowing.'

Returning to the chair, he leaned forward to ask those questions he had to ask. 'Did fire excite you sexually, mademoiselle? Did the men or women you went with like to tie you to the bed and then strike matches or burn candles over and around your naked body? Did you cry out for mercy until they had consummated their lust in an orgy of fire?

'Or were you the one to do the tying up? Did you brush their skin with flames as they tried to cry out through the gag you had stuffed in their mouths? Did you singe the hairs on the stomach, the groin, the face, eh, until, in ecstasy, they finally came?'

He gave her a moment, then asked, 'Did you go only with women, Mademoiselle Bertrand? Did you enjoy making them so afraid, that fear then heightened awareness until they shuddered with release at the touch of your tongue? Was that the only way they could ever attain sexual climax? The striving, mademoiselle, the straining for it until suddenly, the fire, the flames were too much for them and finally they yielded?'

Her expression of total innocence made him furious at his own inability to fathom this thing. Was there to be another, even more horrific fire?

'Who did you go to that cinema with, mademoiselle? Your childhood friend Madame Rachline? Come, come, I know you were there. You were sitting in that projection booth talking to the projectionist. When the cry of fire came, you lost a shoe, you dropped these . . .'

He tossed the bent and twisted cigarette case on her bed. The compact and lipstick tube followed, then the steel shank of that other shoe. He found the remains of the fountain pen and tossed it into the pile. He found the jewelled cross. 'Father Adrian Beaumont, mademoiselle,' he said so very quietly. 'Did you know of him? A Monsieur Henri Masson gave this cross to him.'

According to the bishop, Masson had died ten or twelve years ago. She'd have been twenty-two or twenty at the time. Had he been a former client of La Belle Époque? Had he been alive when Claudine first went to work for her childhood friend?

He took out the anonymous letters the préfet had given him.

My dear messieurs
As a concerned and loyal citizen I must tell you that Father Adrian Beaumont, secretary to Bishop Dufour, has been breaking his vows. Day after day I have seen Father Adrian enter Mademoiselle Madeleine Aurelle's building, sometimes right after her.

Always there is the long pause, the visit of two and sometimes three hours—once four hours. Always that one would return to the street like a thief, while Mlle Aurelle, the shameless harlot that she was, would gaze down upon the object of her lust, the vanishing figure of her confessor, from the bedroom window.

Once her night-dress, it was open and once she waved to him and he, caught by guilt, stood transfixed in the street unable to move.

I heard him whisper, 'Cover yourself, Mlle Madeleine. For God's sake, cover yourself,' and when he looked at me, aghast that I might have overheard, there was nothing but terror in his eyes.

There was no signature. Depressed that such letters had become all too common a means of getting back at others, St-Cyr ran his eyes over it again. The penmanship was excellent, the handwriting neat and small and precisely budgeted, the straightness of the lines perfect, the paper good but not overly expensive by pre-war standards—one always had to measure such things by those bygone days. Paper like this would no longer be readily available.

A woman? he asked. One didn't give much credence to such letters. Indeed, there was always distaste, yet one was forced to read them from time to time.

It must have come in early, just after the fire. Either it had been delivered to the Préfecture or Guillemette had got it from the Gestapo over at the Hotel Terminus.

He put the letter down on her bed and placed the cross with its chain on top of it.

Bishop Dufour had not given answers readily. There had been hesitation over Father Adrian but that would only have been natural. 'Ah *merde*,' he said of the letter, 'it's wrong of me to be trapped into paying any attention to this.'

The other two letters were equally condemning. Monsieur Artel had always 'talked of burning his cinema down to collect the insurance'. He had 'never treated his employees well'. He had 'cheated them of their wages and had done other things'. He had 'always kept the fire doors padlocked in spite of the regulations'.

The fire marshal's wife had 'known of her husband's love affair with Madame Élaine Gauthier'. She had been jealous and had 'sworn she would get the two of them'.

Madame Robichaud 'suffered from acute depression', was 'suicidal' and 'possessive'.

She had 'consulted the préfet on the matter and had asked for that one's help'.

She had been 'out' on the night of the fire. Her eldest daughter, who had been staying with her mother 'to calm her down', could give no 'adequate answer as to where her mother had gone that evening'.

Lined up in a row, the handwriting and the paper were as different as the other objects on the bed. The cheap and shoddy compact and cigarette case, the richness of the jewelled cross.

But, again, he found himself asking, Had a woman written each of them?

Three distinctly different women, one well-educated perhaps, another—that of the insurance letter—a disgruntled employee.

And that of the Madame Robichaud letter? he asked. The fire chief's concierge perhaps? The family would live in a reasonably good area, quite central probably and very middle class.

The writing was not so brutal or so refined but was something in between.

Clearly it was implied that the writer of the Madame Robichaud letter was a confidant of the woman, or knew some indiscreet person who was close to her. He was surprised the writer hadn't made derogatory remarks about the fire marshal, and he wondered then, in spite of telling himself he shouldn't, if it had not come from Robichaud's mistress, from Madame Élaine Gauthier.

The 'a's, though different, were the classic classroom 'a's of a schoolteacher. The 'l's were similar, the crossing of the 't's. Ah *nom de Dieu*, they had all come from the same hand. He was certain of it. Certain! But had that girl with the bicycle sent them? Had she dropped this one's work card on purpose?

Like Hermann, he found himself staring across the street in the direction of La Belle Époque. He could not see its chimneys, though he knew there would be smoke issuing from them even when there was little or none from most of the others.

Holidays were always the worst of times for such arsonists. A crowded café, a railway station, another church perhaps—yes, another cinema . . . any of the many blocks of flats. They were so old, they were just asking for a fire. The streets were often so narrow.

Lübeck, Heidelberg and Köln were all very old cities. Had those two women paid them each a visit or had they absolutely nothing to do with any of the fires?

And what of Madame Rachline and her continued evasiveness? The woman had lied about being at midnight Mass and walking home. But had she come here to see Claudine only to stand, perhaps, in the street below, gazing up at this very window in doubt and fear?

Yes, he said to himself. *Yes*, that is what she must have done. Then she does not yet know Claudine is dead, but only suspects there is something very wrong and is herself in danger.

In the kitchen he found an open bottle of friar's balsam. It was simply the usual alcoholic solution of benzoin, the balsamic resin from tropical trees of the genus Styrax, especially those from Java and Sumatra.

A spoonful or two into the hot water to clear the sinuses and chest by breathing the steam. A sweetly aromatic, quite resinous odour that strangely lasted long after inhalation. A clinging odour.

The Gare de Perrache was frozen in the pearly-grey light. At twenty degrees of frost, the swastika that flew above the central railway station hung as if in fright and wanting to disappear.

People came and went, all bundled up and grim about it. Just across the Cours de Verdun, at Number 12, two SS guards stood sentinel outside Gestapo HQ, the Hotel Terminus, a flag above them.

Four black cars—two Daimlers, a Citroën and an Opel—sat with their engines running, a bad sign. Swastika pennants were mounted on the right front fenders of the leading Daimlers and Kohler had to ask himself, Visiting royalty for Christmas? and said, Another bad sign.

The Bristol, all five storeys of staid respectability, was at Number 28. Leiter Weidling was pacing back and forth in front of a row of straight-backed chairs on which sat six . . . or was it seven ashen people. The harangue was loud and fast, the fist with its napkin clutched, the interpreter frantically trying to catch up.

Having breakfasted on rolls, plum jam and black coffee, Weidling had chosen to interview the prime witnesses collectively. He was all push and bad manners and not likely to get a hell of a lot out of any of them, a puzzle since he was experienced and must have had to do this sort of thing lots of times.

Fabien Artel sat with his knees together and fedora in hand. The usherette who'd seen the two women leave the cinema in a hurry, was pale and badly shaken. A kid of seventeen without her lipstick or anything much—she'd simply been dragged from some attic room in Croix Rousse, and had had her overcoat thrown at her. No boots! No time to even put them on.

Her bare toes were shy and they tried to cling to each other as the visiting fire marshal's words flayed the hide off her. 'Colour? Give me the *colour* of their eyes, you imbecile! The hair, *dummkopf*! Their clothing!'

He turned on the projectionist and shouted, 'You say no one was with you in that booth? No one? Then why did you not sound the alarm?'

The mouse-brown eyes in that pinched and angular face watered with alarm and deceit. Torn out of bed in the dark of night, the poor bastard had managed a robe and felt slippers that might have been all right fifty years ago but now looked downright shoddy.

Weidling clutched the napkin more tightly. A second usherette waited tensely but he passed her over to nail what must be the concierge of the flats at the cinema. He dropped his voice and stared the man in the face. 'You were responsible, *mein Herr*,' he said. 'You let him in.'

'Who?'

A tough one.

'The Salamander,' said Weidling. Quickly this was translated, the concierge seeming to chew on the name before saying, 'There are no such lizards in Lyon, monsieur. Please address the matter plainly.'

Ah *merde*, an arrogant imbecile! Kohler hissed in French,

'He'll have your balls on toast, idiot! Salamander is the code-name for the arsonist or arsonists.'

'Ah!' The man raised his bushy black eyebrows in acknowl-edgement of Germanic French that was at least passable. 'Then please tell this one, monsieur, that for me there can be no thought of such lizards. I let no one in but my tenants. There were no callers.'

This was all being rapidly translated. 'None?' blurted Kohler. 'What about the priest, Father Adrian Beaumont?'

'None, monsieur. Not Father Beaumont. Not anyone else. Of this I am positive.'

The bishop had got to him. The man didn't even throw a sideways glance at Artel for approval, was simply smug and steadfast about it. 'Loyal to the bitter end, eh?' snorted Kohler in French. 'Then perhaps, *mon fin*, you ought to know one of your tenants was murdered and that if you should lie, you'll be implicated.'

'Which tenant? Come, come, monsieur, you make accusa-tions. Is it that you can supply the proof of this . . . this murder?'

They'd get nothing from him. Weidling turned on the girl who sold the tickets and the thing went round again. First the questions—'Who did you sell tickets to? Surely you noticed something out of the ordinary? Lists . . . I must have a list of all who attended.'

Helpless, the kid burst into tears, and dragging up the heavy flannel night-gown between the open overcoat, began to wipe her eyes and blow her nose, disregarding entirely that she was quite visibly naked below the waist.

That put a momentary stop to things and a modicum of sense entered. Kohler sent the interpreter off for brandy and coffee, then suggested they use the bar as it would be more private and less formal. Weidling grunted approval. A last woman sat alone, having left an empty chair between herself and the girl that sold the tickets.

Her eyes were grey and she did not retreat from the puzzled frown Kohler gave her.

He took the gloved hand that was offered and knew at once that no matter what the boys in blue or black had shrieked at her, she had remained calm and had insisted on getting dressed.

'Madame Élaine Gauthier,' she said. 'Julien's mistress, Herr Kohler, and proud of it.'

Oh-oh. 'Does Robichaud know you're here?'

'I hope not but,' she gave a lovely shrug, 'I am prepared even for that.'

Ah *nom de Dieu*, Louis should have been here! She was an absolutely fine-looking woman in her early forties with a wide, clear brow and high, strong cheekbones. Her hair was ash blonde, short and waved, the nose aristocratic but not arrogant and the lips perfect.

A scar of about two centimetres in length cut across her chin just below the lower lip. It was something from childhood days he thought, and admired her for not trying to hide it.

Kohler took her by the arm to walk with her to the bar. 'This is not an arrest, so don't worry. Herr Weidling feels he has to prove to everyone he's on top of this thing and that he'll be the one who's responsible for solving it. Gestapo Mueller must have given him a blast.'

'And yourself?' she asked.

'My partner and I will just have to help him but we'll see what we can do for Robichaud.'

'Julien is very worried the Salamander will strike again. The ice on the streets, Herr Kohler. There is no sand to be had and the pumper trucks are having trouble getting around. We were in that cinema together, holding hands and kissing—yes, it must seem odd for a grown woman to say this, but where else can a couple secretly meet for a few moments of intimacy? When the fire started, Julien made me pull my coat over my head. He ran with me through the flames. He would not leave me. Then he told me to hurry home and tell no one I had been there.'

She had stopped him in the lobby and had held him with those eyes, a very straightforward, honest woman. She had made up her mind about him and had taken a chance.

'Herr Weidling is demanding that Julien be relieved of his duties and dismissed, Herr Kohler. In this he has the backing of the préfet and Obersturmführer Klaus Barbie. He will ruin a man France and this city have every right to be proud of.'

Kohler nodded grimly and took her into the bar. He felt there was more she could confide if convinced but this would have to await another time. He was glad she had trusted him. 'Does Barbie suspect Robichaud of being involved with the Resistance?'

The scar on her chin quivered. 'No. No, of course not. How could he think such a thing? What . . . What have they to do with that fire?'

Fear tightened all her features but she faced him bravely. 'Nothing,' he said. 'I'm only asking in case I have to have an answer ready.'

It was a warning—she knew this with an absoluteness that chilled. He had seen right through her. Had she been so transparent? 'Your partner, he is not coming here?' she managed.

He shook his head. 'Louis is busy elsewhere. One of the two women we believe left the cinema early is now dead.'

'Ah, no . . .' She turned swiftly away. Kohler hated to do it to her but she had to know exactly where she stood.

'Louis will sort it all out, madame. Louis is always good at such things. The best.'

'How did she die?'

'I don't know the cause yet. In her sleep and peacefully. She couldn't have felt a thing.'

The shards were conchoidal and of gilded glass and they had come from beneath the threadbare carpet beside Claudine

Bertrand's bed. Gingerly St-Cyr turned each of them over. He could hardly contain his excitement. A Christmas-tree orna-ment had been dropped and crushed under foot, he was certain of it. But the rest of the pieces had been carefully gathered and disposed of elsewhere.

Lost in thought, he looked up. Vasseur, long into retirement, had been called back to work because of the fire. An excellent coroner in his day, the old man was diligently bent over the body, searching for needle marks.

He seldom spoke but often ground his teeth and swallowed as if constantly thirsty. A man of some eighty-four years dressed in a black serge suit, vest and tie. There'd be elastics at his elbows when the jacket was removed. And suspenders. Men like Vasseur knew only too well that comfort's enemy was a leather belt no matter how loose.

'Monsieur the Chief Inspector,' said the coroner, straight-ening to ease his back. A legend of formality and correctness, he had been pleased to be called in. 'This one has allowed her pri-vate parts to be burned from time to time and most recently.'

He had said it with sadness and was still shaking his head. 'The labia, the vagina and the clitoris all bear the scars of ciga-rettes perhaps. The inner thighs also and no doubt the buttocks and the anus. Some are from a few days ago, others quite old. Some even from childhood perhaps. But there are no needle marks as yet.'

'Childbirth, Monsieur the Chief Coroner Vasseur?'

It was like old times. 'At least one difficult birth, perhaps two,' he indicated, tracing the marks with a forefinger. 'What sort of men would burn a woman like that? What sort of woman would willingly submit to it?'

These questions were always asked no matter how accus-tomed one became to the depravities of human existence. Care-fully St-Cyr folded the shards into a tiny packet and put them away. 'A *special* woman,' he said—one had to speak clearly even when wishing to do so quietly. The hearing, it was not so good any more but the eyes and mind still inspired confidence. The former were aided by spectacles. 'She was a prostitute, Monsieur the Chief Coroner Vasseur. I should have informed you of this but felt the préfet would have filled you in after my telephone call to him.'

'Monsieur the Préfet Guillemette is a busy man these days,' grumbled Vasseur testily. Saying no more, he went back to searching. Painstakingly notes were made and for the first time, St-Cyr had a twinge of doubt, for the handwriting was not as steady as it should have been were someone else required to read the notes.

'There was a powder, Monsieur the Chief Coroner Vasseur.'

The old man paused over a left breast whose nipple and aureole bore the scars of burns. 'What sort of powder? Come, come, Monsieur the Chief Inspector St-Cyr, you have said nothing of this powder and now ... now you tell me of it? Morphia?'

'No. Ah, no, monsieur. I think it is something else. It will need a chemical analysis.'

The teeth were ground. 'The little hairs of this aureole have recently been curled by the heat of a cigarette but the flesh nearest them, it has not been recently touched by fire. Did your woman do this to herself, Monsieur the Chief Inspector? Did she so enjoy the excitement, she willingly submitted herself to its threat?'

Vasseur was apologizing for the lecture about holding back on the powder. St-Cyr found its tiny packet and once more the coroner straightened up. Adjusting his glasses, he took hold of the proffered hand so firmly, St-Cyr was surprised and pleased by the strength.

The open packet was placed under the lamp. 'Sugar. Refined sugar,' said the coroner distastefully since the black market was implied.

'The granules are not cubic or nearly so, Chief Coroner. Their adamantine lustre is much less.'

Their eyes met. 'There is enough for an analysis,' said St-Cyr. 'You've divided it in half?'

'For security? Yes. Yes, I have.'

'Then let me have the other half, just in case. The préfet need not know until long after the fact, if that is your wish.'

A curt nod would suffice. 'We'll need a . . .'

'Yes, of course, the blood tests. It's not arsenic or cyanide. I will do the carbon monoxide test first since she bears every indication of having died that way. The rapid relaxation of the sphincters, the very pale pinkish cast to the skin—it would have been more noticeable at first. The collapsed state of the body. Vogel's test is still the most reliable for me.'

'Do it privately, then, and let only myself or Hermann Kohler know of the result.'

It could not be nice working under the Nazis but everyone had to do that these days. Vasseur patted St-Cyr's wrist and asked how he'd found the powder.

'Among the bristles of the broom in the kitchen. All the rest must have been disposed of elsewhere or washed down the drain.'

The old man was not above giving praise where it was due and sagely nodded. Again the room fell to silence as he hovered over the woman's right breast, noting two small bruises on its underside, three small and very recent burns and yet more singed hairs which could not have come from the cinema fire since the hairs on the head and the eyebrows had not been touched.

The old scars on the breast were deep and there were several of them, indicating again that she'd had a long history of submission to the exquisiteness of pain brought on by fire.

Patiently St-Cyr stood watching him. Carbon monoxide preferentially united in the lungs with the blood's haemoglobin preventing it from taking in the oxygen necessary for life. At one-twentieth of one per cent in air, giddiness resulted on exertion, if breathed for a half to two hours.

One-tenth of one per cent prevented walking. One-fifth of a per cent led to loss of consciousness and quite possibly death. Four-fifths of one per cent brought almost certain death within a very short time.

With one per cent, the victim became unconscious in but a few minutes, and this was followed quickly by death. There was no odour. The victim would never know the silent killer had done its work.

Uniting with the haemoglobin, the carbon monoxide formed a cherry-red carbonyl haemoglobin and it was this which, when the blood was diluted by 200 times its volume with distilled water, gave a decidedly pink solution not the yellowish-red of uncontaminated blood.

'I will do the test on the mother, Jean-Louis, and spend a little time with her at the morgue. It is best, is it not, for us to keep this one on ice? Now, please, if you will assist, let us turn her over. I am most interested in the back of her neck and ears, the knees and the base of the spine as these are often among a woman's most sensitive places. The shoulders too. Oh by the way, I believe she was wearing that perfume.'

St-Cyr nodded. Claudine Bertrand had allowed herself to be burned by cigarettes or some such object in all those places and in others and very recently, yet there were no rope-burns at her wrists or ankles.

Again he said she was special, but he said it to himself. Even the soles of her feet bore the scars. They were even between her toes.

Kohler leaned forward in his chair to let the words come carefully. 'What do you mean, Mademoiselle Bertrand was "interesting"?'

The projectionist's grin was small and short-lived and utterly revealing. Quickly he ducked his eyes away to hide the truth, settling them on the coffee table, the floor, the usherettes and then Madame Élaine Gauthier, before turning to Thérèse Moncontre, the young woman who had operated the ticket booth at the cinema. Fiercely she returned his gaze, colouring as she doubled her fists and held them defiantly against her thighs. Ah now, what was this? The expected? asked Kohler, inwardly patting himself on the back. All had not been well among the staff of Monsieur Artel's little nest of celluloid.

He exhaled softly. 'Your answer, eh, my friend?'

The man shrugged nonchalantly and muttered, 'The usual.'

His chin was forcibly tilted up so that their eyes had to meet. 'How usual?' asked the detective.

Flustered, the projectionist blurted angrily, 'Oh come now, monsieur. It's quite natural for a man to—'

'It's Inspector Kohler to you, *mon fin.* Sure I know that job must have been boring. Night after night the same film. You'd seen it all before, eh, so you had to have a woman in. What'd you get Mademoiselle Bertrand to do? Go down on her knees between your legs while the film rolled on?'

Ah *nom de Jésus-Christ,* the detective would stop at nothing! Suzie and Jacqueline were fidgeting. Thérèse was still staring at him—Well stare, you little bitch! Some day I'll have a knife at your pretty throat and your underpants in my fist, eh? Then we shall see how you beg for it!

Kohler read the bastard's mind. Hunting among the cigarette butts , he found one with lipstick and lit up. The shortages these days were always trouble. 'After you were done with her, Mademoiselle Bertrand asked you for the key to the toilets.'

'You have no proof, Inspector. I know my rights.'

'Do you? Hey, I thought I told you it was Inspector *Kohler?* Now don't forget or you'll find yourself on a train you'd rather not be on.'

A train to nowhere but the dark and brooding forests of Poland or the Reich.

Blonde, pale and quivering, the usherette Suzie Boudreau

blurted, 'It was *my* job to unlock the door to the toilets before each performance, Monsieur Martin, but you . . . you would not let me have the key that night. *Always* you are bothering us girls. *Always* you are wanting to get your filthy hands . . .'

Watching them impassively, Madame Gauthier calmly drew on her cigarette. Herr Weidling hesitated long enough in his interrogation of Artel to demand of his interpreter what had just been said.

The concierge kept to himself like a block of stone.

'Your filthy hands up their skirts?' asked Kohler. 'Hey, were you the one who tied Mademoiselle Aurelle to her bed for a little fun later on?'

One could have heard a pin drop. Frantically the projectionist looked for an out, then hissed, 'There was no easy way I could have done that, monsieur. I'd have had to go downstairs to the street to come in at the other door!'

'She was naked, and you could have played around with her all you wanted.'

It was Suzie who, brushing tears away, said bitterly, 'He has tried to take advantage of each of us, Inspector. First Jacqui because she is so young, then Thérèse whose husband is away in a prisoner-of-war camp in your country and then myself, but all three of us still.'

'And if you didn't yield, he'd bitch to the manager and you'd lose your jobs,' sighed Kohler. 'Hey, come to think of it, where is the manager?'

Weidling's interpreter tried to be helpful. 'Monsieur Thibault was not at his place of residence. The Gestapo, they . . . they are now searching for him.'

In brutal German the fire chief from Lübeck, et cetera, et cetera said, 'Herr Artel has sent that one into hiding, Herr Kohler.'

Artel shot to his feet, demanding legal counsel. Weidling

shouted at him to sit down. The interpreter tried to intercede . . . They'd be at each other's throats!

Kohler separated the two men, patting Weidling on the shoulder. 'Look, I know you want to solve this thing and get back home to your duties. If he's done as you think, I'll see that he hangs.'

He turned to Artel and translated everything but used the guillotine and the wicker basket instead of hanging. 'Cooperate, eh? Or else my partner and I will take you down to whichever river you choose and drown you.'

As he went back to his chair, Suzie blurted, 'We were all under their thumbs, Inspector. Monsieur Thibault, the manager, he . . . he was just as bad as this one only . . . only not so . . .'

'Sadistic?' breathed Kohler quietly.

She dropped her eyes and whispered, 'Yes.'

'So the washroom was locked and Mademoiselle Claudine went upstairs to get the key from Monsieur Martin?'

The girl nodded. Kohler gave her a moment. 'Did Mademoiselle Bertrand ask you for that key or did she know who would have it?'

'She . . . she has asked me for it, Monsieur the Inspector, and I . . . I have told her where it was.'

'And then?' he asked so gently she felt he might not blame her too much for what had happened.

'And then Mademoiselle Bertrand, she has come downstairs from the booth and has gone to open the door to the toilets.'

Kohler waited. Now it was as if there were only the two of them. 'She did not stay long, Inspector. Some others went into the toilets—three, four . . . I don't know how many. Men . . . women . . .'

The kid was desperate. 'Who locked them in, Suzie? Was it yourself?'

'Me? Ah *no! No!* I could not have done such a thing, monsieur. Their screams . . '

He gave her another moment. 'Look, just tell me the way you remember it.'

Her eyes pleaded with him for understanding. 'They went into the toilets. The key was in the lock. I went back to my station just inside the curtains across the aisle but when those patrons, they did not return, I went to see if . . . if everything was all right.'

'And the key was still in the lock?'

She knew he'd ask it of her. 'Yes. It's . . . it's not my job to stop such things. Sex in the toilets. I . . . I know I should have tried the door and . . . and checked for mischief, monsieur. *Mischief!* I know I should have taken the key and made certain the door remained unlocked, may God forgive me.'

The poor kid was still blaming herself for everything. 'What about the woman who came in with Mademoiselle Bertrand? The one who carried the bag woven out of rushes?'

'She . . . she was absent from her seat. Me, I have thought she must be in the toilets also, but . . . but I did not look, monsieur. I did not think to open that door and they . . . they . . .'

Kohler laid a hand on her forearm. 'Was the bag on the seat or still on the floor, or did she take it with her?'

'It . . . it was on the seat, so I . . . I knew she must be coming back. Don't you see, I *knew*, Inspector? I could so easily have taken that bag out into the foyer to look for her. An excuse . . . *anything*. But I . . . I did not do so.'

'Inspector . . .,' began Madame Gauthier only to see him hold up a silencing hand. Comforting the girl would have to come later.

'Two women, Suzie. Did this other one lock the door to the toilets?'

'Yes. Yes, I think she must have.'

'Then tell me what she looked like. Try to remember. I know it's painful. I know you hate yourself for not stopping them and for not unlocking that door, but . . . hey, you weren't to blame.'

His voice was so gentle and kind. She sniffed in and wiped

her nose with the back of a hand. 'I only saw her boots and stockings, Inspector. When I show people to their seats, I do not shine my light into their faces. The film was in progress and it was dark up at the back. Too dark. There is the balcony above or . . . or there was. *There was!*'

'Her boots and stockings then?' he asked, comforting her.

'Expensive. Black patent leather with full laces up the front and pointed toes. Perhaps well-fitted but perhaps a little too tight. 'Yes. Yes, this I think. Also, monsieur, that perhaps the boots, their style it is not worn so much any more. Except, of course, these days people will wear anything, isn't that so?'

La Belle Époque? he wondered. Madame Ange-Marie Rachline perhaps, in the shoes of the 1890s. 'And the stockings?' he asked gently. The kid was doing fine.

'Black silk and very expensive—lovely and with a very delicate pattern like antique lace. They . . . they made me envious, monsieur. Me, I have never had the money for such things.'

'Yes, yes, I quite understand. The woman?'

'Fairly tall, monsieur. A woman with very nice legs, I think, and a good figure. Not old. Ah no, not that one, but . . . but perhaps a little older than this . . . this Mademoiselle Bertrand that . . . that Monsieur Martin has . . .'

The girl blushed crimson and wiped her eyes. So much for French girls being forward, thought Kohler. Gruffly he told the projectionist to quit fidgeting and asked him, 'Did this other woman come up to see you?'

The man shook his head. 'I gave the key to Mademoiselle Bertrand. When she came back upstairs, she said she had given it to one of the usherettes. I thought no more of it, Inspector Kohler.'

'Too busy doing up your flies, were you?'

The smile was harshly triumphant. 'Too busy with the film, Inspector. A break had occurred and I had to repair it at once.'

The bastard! Left alone, he'd had long enough to think up an answer! His look said, Prove this was not so.

'Karl Johann . . . ?' Kohler swung round at the sound of another voice.

Verdammt! Leiter Weidling's young wife was stunning: tall, slim and leggy. One of the Master Race but with rich, dark auburn hair and dark grey-blue eyes that left nothing to chance.

She set the fur coat over the back of a chair and dropped her purse on to the seat as if fed up at the delay and expecting her husband to do something about it. Kohler let his eyes drift up over her: dark blue silk stockings, a dark blue skirt, smooth and tidy, nice calves, nice knees probably, and a wrap-around jacket in light beige with no collar and a V-neck that plunged to frame the throat above as if to say, You cannot look further.

'Karl Johann, have you forgotten we are to dine with Ober-sturmführer Barbie?'

'My dear . . .' stammered Weidling. 'This business . . . You must forgive me. Yes, of course, of course. Lunch.'

Gott im Himmel, she didn't even bat an eye! The clod had yet to catch on to the difference between *dine* and *lunch*!

Her brow was high and smooth, her face more narrow than full, the nose so fine and sharp and of the aristocracy he had to wonder which family she'd come from.

There were no rings, not even a wedding band, just bangles of gold and ebony, quite old, he thought. Ear-rings to match— delicate things, very finely carved and wrought. Nice, nice lips that pouted haughtily in his millisecond of undressing, then gave the quick, bland smile of, Well, Inspector, do you always look at women this way?

Through his interpreter, Weidling told everyone to wait for him. 'I am not finished with you. Perhaps your manager will turn up, Herr Artel, but until he does, please do not leave this place.'

Thérèse Moncontre, who sold the tickets, hadn't moved a hair but now the softness of her throat rippled tightly, and suddenly, in confusion and wanting to disappear, she dropped her deep brown eyes and kept them on the carpet at her feet.

Alarmed, Kohler glanced at Frau Weidling but she seemed not to have noticed. He gave it a moment, could hardly believe their luck. Clearly the girl had *sold* Frau Weidling a ticket! Ah *merde*. He could not ask her just yet. She'd deny it out of fear, and Frau Weidling would ask Barbie to get rid of her. He'd have to let the girl think her little secret was safe.

Madame Gauthier had, however, noticed the girl's reaction to Leiter Weidling's wife. Kohler met her eyes and he had to ask himself, Were you and Robichaud really holding hands in that back row, or had you come to the cinema for something quite different? A meeting with the Resistance?

Klaus Barbie was afraid the firemen would join forces with the railwaymen. Was Lyon, with its warren of old streets and passageways and its rail connections to everywhere, about to become the centre of active resistance?

He remembered the revolver he'd found among the frozen ashes. He remembered the railway schedules and the maps that had pinpointed the locations of switches and tunnels and flatbed cranes that would be so necessary to clear the tracks of wreckage . . .

He picked up the grey fox-fur coat that should have been sent to the Russian Front but had somehow missed Frau Weidling's patriotic duty. Without a word of thanks or acknowledgement, she turned her shapely back on him and let him drape it over her shoulders.

'That perfume . . . ,' he began, foolishly caught off guard. She paid no mind, picked up her gloves and purse and departed with her husband chasing after her. Nice ankles . . . yes, yes . . . dark blue high heels.

Étranger . . .

Kohler turned on the others and snapped, 'Wait here. If any of you leave, I'll have you dragged before a firing squad without a priest!'

Ah *mon Dieu*, Louis, what the hell have we got ourselves into this time? he asked himself. A wife who'll stop at nothing to build her husband's reputation? But why would a woman like that marry a pair of ancient rubber boots when she could have had something far, far better?

He told himself he'd have to ask the usherette Suzie Boudreau if either of those two women had worn that perfume. He would have to ask Frau Weidling how she had come by it and if she had enjoyed the little she could have seen of that film.

He'd have to ask her about those other fires. Lübeck, Heidelberg and Köln, and just exactly how long she and that husband of hers had been in Lyon to have some fun. Two weeks . . . had it been two weeks?

A Salamander.

The concierge at Number Six rue du Boeuf was wary. Trapped in his cage, he fussed with a newspaper that was ten days old and shooed the cat out into the corridor. 'Mademoiselle Bertrand said she had to drop into the pharmacy, Inspector St-Cyr. A cold in her chest, the phlegm like molten tar . . .'

'Yes, yes, spare me the medical details, eh? I've been with her now for far too long and do not want your words to cause me to catch whatever it was she had.'

'Then what would you have me say, Inspector?'

Ah *merde*, why must he be so difficult? 'She was dressed for an evening out, isn't that right, eh? Come, come, Monsieur Aubin, surely a woman like that does not wear red high heels on ice in fifteen degrees of frost just to find herself a little friar's balsam?'

'Was she murdered in my building? Is that what you're implying? Come, come yourself, Monsieur the Chief Inspector, let us have the truth of that!'

'*Nom de Jésus-Christ*, don't try my patience!'

The Sûreté . . . everybody knew what shits they were. And

corrupt! 'She was a prostitute, a public woman. Maybe she went to visit a client, maybe not, Inspector, but she would not have informed me of this. Ah no, monsieur,' he wagged a reproving finger. 'Not a family man such as myself whose daughters are generally visiting with their papa when he is not busy at his duties, or are likely to drop in on him at any time.'

St-Cyr took a deep breath and held it. Exhaling slowly, and more than exasperated, he said harshly, 'What did you pay her in exchange?' but did not wait for the answer. 'You agreed to look in on Madame Bertrand each evening, or one of your children did, or your wife perhaps. In exchange for this little service, Mademoiselle Bertrand was "friendly" towards you, eh? So, all right, there's no harm in that little arrangement if you can live with it and your wife is not infected. Now tell me when she left the building and when she came back?'

The concierge tried to roll a cigarette from the collected tobacco of several cigarette butts. It was no use. Papers and tobacco showered on to the carpet.

His grizzled moon-face lifted. 'She left at about seven in the evening—when she usually does. They came back at about nine thirty. Here, it is in the book.' He got up suddenly to push past and snatch up the ledger. 'Seven ten and nine fifty-seven. Mademoiselle Bertrand and Madame Rachline.'

'The two of them at both times?' blurted the Sûreté.

The man shook his head. 'Only when returning. You see, I have put the little tick beside Madame Rachline's name.'

There was a nod, but only just. 'And you're absolutely certain it was Madame Rachline?'

Théodore Aubin grunted, 'But of course, monsieur, I have seen her many times. The tall figure, the little cloche with the bit of veiling. The black overcoat also.'

'But did you see her face?'

Ah *nom de Jésus-Christ*, what was the cause of this suspicion?

'Well?' demanded the detective harshly. 'Yes or no?'

The fleshy throat was touched in uncertainty, the lower jaw gripped as if in cautious thought. 'Then no, Inspector. I did not see that one's face. Madame Rachline, she has walked past my cage, you understand, to tap the toes of her shoes or boots on the floor to warm the blood a little after coming in from such cold.'

'When did she leave the building?'

Be careful what you say, eh? Was that it? 'Me, I do not know, Monsieur the Inspector. One of the other tenants complained of a broken tap in the lavatory that is outside this building in the courtyard. I . . . I went with him to discover the trouble. A pipe had frozen.'

Had it been a chance bit of luck? wondered St-Cyr. Chance so often played havoc when something needed to be pinned down.

'Those pipes are always freezing in this weather, Monsieur the Inspector. Madame Rachline could not have stayed more than an hour at the most. During this time, I returned to get my tools and another light, since there is no electric light in the toilet. The tenants, they are always stealing the bulbs these days. I've left repeated warnings. What else could I do but remove all bulbs until the affair, it was over?'

'Did she come here often?' asked St-Cyr, ignoring the outburst.

Aubin shook his head. 'Once or twice a month, just to inquire as to how Mademoiselle Bertrand was if that one had been ill, which she often was—the chest, you understand. Sometimes to bring the mother a little soup or stew. That old woman didn't eat much, Inspector. I'm not surprised she died and only wonder which of them went first.'

'Oh? Why is that?' asked the detective.

The concierge displayed a humble nature. 'The mother, if she knew her daughter had died, would follow her, Inspector.

That is often the way of those who are totally dependent on another.'

St-Cyr dragged out a broken package of cigarettes and offered one. 'And if the mother had died first?' he asked.

'Then Mademoiselle Bertrand, she . . . she would have been relieved of a burden she has been forced to carry for far too long.'

The Sûreté struck a match and held it out. 'Did Madame Rachline know her friend was a prostitute?'

'That one? Ah no . . . no, Inspector. How could she? Madame Rachline is a mother with two children and no husband to support them. She takes in mending, is a seamstress, a fixer of dresses. A make-over artist to whom my wife and others go when the need is dire. A wedding, a funeral . . . ah, excuse me. A funeral, yes, yes of course. Another visit will be necessary, no doubt.'

Aubin looked up and shrugged at the added cost. Of course they would have to attend the funeral since who else would?

St-Cyr began to pack his pipe. 'Then this Madame Rachline lives nearby?' he asked non-committally.

The cigarette was budgeted with a sigh. 'She rents that part of the house behind La Belle Époque, on the rue des Trois Maries, Inspector. I think, but cannot be certain, you understand, that Mademoiselle Bertrand used to work in that place. Perhaps that is how they came to know one another? The dresses, the sheets, the seamstressing. Perhaps it is that Madame Rachline does a little work for the house. In any case, she is a lady who protects her children from all such things, of this you can be certain.'

'And her husband?' asked St-Cyr.

'Gone as I have said. Where, I do not know since she never speaks of him, nor do either of her children. A son of ten and a daughter of twelve.'

He put the tobacco pouch away. 'Did Mademoiselle Bertrand limp when she returned at nine fifty-seven?'

'Limp? But . . . ? Why . . . why, yes. Yes, she had lost a shoe.'

'Good!' St-Cyr crammed the pipe-stem between his teeth and lit up. Blowing smoke, he waved the match out and nodded sagely. 'Don't touch the rooms Let the police do their work. They will remove the bodies and dust for fingerprints and then they will seal everything until further notice.'

 GRIMLY ST-CYR DREW ON THE PIPE HE LONGED
to enjoy. It was Christmas Day, and for one brief
glimpse, the grey above cleared as church bells
pealed.

He reached the centre of the pont Alphonse Juin and leaned
on its carved stone parapet, gazing downriver at the Saône.
Sheet-ice had formed in places. Vapour rose above pools where
brown scums of sewage froth overflowed to stain that pristine
glacial sheath.

Two women, the one now dead, the other a 'seamstress',
the mother of two children, the madam of a very high-class
bordello.

Childhood friends, one of whom had been 'special'.

A convoy of Wehrmacht lorries began to cross the bridge,
startling him and scattering the *vélo-taxis*, vibrating the ancient
footings which seemed to cry out, For shame! How can you let
this happen to us?

The convoy was travelling at a march-past to impress the

populace and not suffer the indignity of skidding on the treacherous surface that had already spilled too many. Three motor
cycles were ahead of an open touring car. Klaus Barbie and
some woman . . .

The grey fox-fur coat rippled in the breeze. She laughed,
wore no hat and must be freezing but would not let on.
Flashing grey-blue eyes and dark auburn hair, not French, ah
no, definitely not. Frau Weidling . . . was it Frau Weidling?

The lorries threw their shadows over him and when the last
of them had passed, he heard the rudeness of a flatulent trombone and saw that it came from a concert band.

The convoy reached the far side and turned downstream
along the quai des Célestins. The sewage bubbled up from the
bottom of the river. The stains followed the lorries, flooding
over the ice as if unstoppable.

Two women, three fires in 1938 in the Reich and now
another and far worse fire in Lyon and an attempt that could so
easily have ended in disaster.

The shards of a gilded glass tree-ornament, an antique taken,
no doubt, from La Belle Époque so as to have a bit of decora-
tion, a little something to love and remind one of Christmases
past and childhood friends, the beach at Concarneau. Ah yes.

And a girl with a bicycle. One whose earnest brown eyes had
looked searchingly across place Terreaux towards the ruins of
the cinema.

A girl with short, light brown hair, no lipstick and no rouge. A
grey plaid skirt and dark grey woollen argyle kneesocks. Flat-
heeled brown leather walking shoes—was she English? Had she
once visited England and adopted that style of dress? Had
she been so agitated and distracted she had forgotten to wear
her winter boots?

Not beautiful, not plain either. About twenty-five or -six years
of age. A schoolteacher perhaps and therefore formerly a
student.

A priest who took advantage of lonely women. A jewelled cross and a wealthy benefactor who could well have been in the priest's debt: Monsieur Henri Masson.

La Belle Époque.

The girl had returned to the scene of the fire. She had been worried, had been struggling valiantly with her conscience. Why else the yellow work card of Mademoiselle Claudine Bertrand? Why else the one thing that would most easily lead them to the brothel and then to the prostitute's body?

Kohler warily let his eyes sift slowly over a pair of women's shoes that would come well above the ankles and were of black leather with lacing up the front and pointed toes. The shoes were on the floor at the back of the closet in which he had hidden for so long. But shoes they were and he knew that if presented with them, Suzie, the usherette who was still downstairs in the bar of the Hotel Bristol, would recognize them instantly as the 'boots' she had seen on one of those two women.

Frau Weidling and Claudine Bertrand must have sat side by side in that cinema. But two women had come in late, and he was almost certain Frau Weilding had come in alone.

Three women, then, had there been *three* of them? Frau Weidling first and sitting elsewhere, then the two who had come in late. Ah *merde*.

At last the chambermaids he had followed into the Prince Albert Suite departed and he was able to step out of the closet and take a look at the place. Room upon room opened before him, with ornately carved and gilded mirrors and Louis XVI furniture. There would be nothing like this back home at the Fire Protection Officers' School in Eberswald.

The bedroom was huge and with a canopied bed fit for a queen; another for Leiter Weidling elsewhere, of course, through a connecting door that was locked. Ah yes.

Kohler strode over to a magnificent commode. Opening drawer after drawer, he settled on the one with the lingerie.

Pinks and blues and white and lace like he'd never seen before. Airy and as soft as a summer's breeze beneath the moon, black and gold, silver and cinnamon—all colours. Silk ... nothing but the finest silk.

Frau Weidling liked it next to her skin and quite obviously wore nothing else in those parts no matter the climate.

There were six of each, with washdays on Sunday? he wondered acidly. Had she tried them all on before that husband of hers? He shook his head. She'd have shown them to him and let Leiter Weidling see what he had to earn.

The box was of ebony, about twenty centimetres wide by fifteen in depth and perhaps eight in thickness. There was much scrollwork at the inlaid corners and around the lock ... the lock, ah damn!

The box was heavy but when he shook it, there was no sound. She hadn't been wearing the key around her neck—he was certain of this.

It was hanging from one of the taps in the bathtub by a simple ribbon of cream silk.

Frau Weidling pleasured herself. Three ebony *godemiches* lay nestled in black velvet, one longer and much thicker than the others. Rings of silver formed little ridges to give that extra bit of shudder, the heads so penis-like he had to lift one out. Beautiful workmanship; polished as smooth as glass.

The French word for dildo came from the Latin *gaude mihi*, rejoice me. Lost in thought, he fingered them. To each her own, he said. By themselves they didn't mean a damn. Coupled with the presence of the boots, one had to wonder.

Closing the case, he put it back under the lingerie and swept the drawer for anything else. Was greatly troubled when he found a coil of sash cord and a pearl-handled pocket-knife. Ah *merde*, what now? he asked.

There were photographic prints, some twenty centimetres square, and they were not pleasant. When naked and very dead, the female form gave him no joy. Breasts that once might have been pleasing, sagged. Pubic hair that once might have drawn the eye, looked small and sordid, a clutch of nothing much. Wounds gaped but no longer bled.

The photos were all of sex crimes from the files of some criminal investigation branch—Lübeck, Heidelberg or Köln, which had it been and how had she come by them?

There was nothing on the plain brown envelope, not a stamp or signature, not a mention of any kind on the backs of any of the photographs.

Had the victims all been burnt in those most tenderest of places? he asked, wishing he'd time to study them—knowing now that time was precious and that the couple could come back at any moment.

The women's ages varied. Some were old, others young, heavy, thin, long hair, short hair, bound wrists and ankles—burned, yes, yes, that one—strangled, some; knifed, others—at least two had been shot in the forehead. Bullet wounds in corpses don't look nice.

Kohler slid the photographs away. Inadvertently, he saw himself in the mirrors, ashen, badly shaken and afraid. She'd be with Klaus Barbie. Louis and he couldn't withstand another run-in with the SS. Mueller would have them hanged with piano wire.

Sickened, he fled the room—could only spend a few minutes with Weidling's things. A briefcase tempted him and, in the end, he pulled out the files on the three fires and realized only then that the bastard had had them with him all the time.

Lübeck, Heidelberg and Köln. No need to contact anyone at home.

At the sound of laughter out in the corridor, he stopped breathing.

A light snow made greyer still the place Terreaux. Like a monument to loneliness, a single pumper truck sat near Bartholdi's fountain. Still in tall rubber boots, coveralls, cape and helmet, his gauntleted gloves thrown aside, Robichaud gripped a wounded right hand from which blood ran. Silently he cursed the twisted metal that must have done that to him. He looked utterly exhausted, like some ancient gladiator upon whom the lions would now feed.

The crowd, kept back behind the barricades, stared mutely at him but now there was definitely a mood of vengeance. They wanted a scapegoat and they had him.

Angrily the fire chief ripped the scarf from around his neck and bound his hand, then stood staring defiantly back at them.

St-Cyr searched the faces. Hats, raised coat collars, earmuffs and scarves made it difficult. The girl might have come and gone or might yet return. He had no other choice but to help the fire chief.

'There is a bottle in the cab,' gasped Robichaud when he saw who it was. 'Would you be so good as to get it for me. Quickly, I think, Inspector. Yes, the sooner the better.'

He didn't wait for the bottle to be uncorked but snatched it away and used his teeth. Flinging off the scarf, he exposed the eight centimetres of torn flesh to the crowd and poured brandy over the wound. 'Ahh ... !' he grimaced, clamping his eyes shut and dropping the bottle to grip the arm. 'Now another,' he gasped. '*Another!*' he shouted. 'In the Name of God, don't be weak. Just *do* it!'

St-Cyr got him bandaged and in the course of this, Robichaud saw the stitchmarks across the back of the detective's left hand. 'A knife in the night. Another case ... two, yes. Yes it was not the case before this one, but the one before that. A carousel.'

They agreed that life was seldom easy, and shared the remainder of the brandy. 'That gasoline at the Notre Dame came from the depot at the Delfosse Barracks in Perrache,' grunted Robichaud.

'So near Gestapo Headquarters?' blurted St-Cyr.

The broad shoulders lifted. The haggard eyes didn't waver.

'The bishop gets an extra allotment at Christmas, so nothing untoward was suspected. The three jerry cans were delivered to the Basilica that afternoon and left outside the caretaker's door.'

St-Cyr lit a cigarette for him. 'Was it usual to leave them there?'

'Ah no. No, of course not—not in these times, eh? But Auguste and Philomena—old Cadieux and that wife of his, the caretaker, you understand. He's difficult, so it's entirely understandable that one would leave the cans outside his door. He and the bishop are always quarrelling. It's a caretaker's right to defend his honour at all times, isn't that so? Those two exist on God's little piece of real estate only by being constantly at war. They act as though they've been married for years!'

He would ignore the allusion to Robichaud's own marriage. 'And the person who obtained the gasoline?'

The Sûreté had asked it so softly. Well, my friend from Paris, prepare yourself, thought Robichaud. 'He said he was the bishop's secretary, Father Adrian Beaumont. Look, Inspector, the caller knew all the ropes. He knew *exactly* who to contact and where to have that gasoline deposited.'

Ah *merde!* 'A man?'

Robichaud drew deeply on his cigarette then let it cling to his lower lip as he exhaled. 'Yes, Inspector, a man.'

'But . . . but it was two women at the cinema. We have the proof.'

'What proof? The word of a terrified usherette? That of a fire marshal who should have stayed inside to help others escape? Come, come, Inspector, we need more proof than that and even I, who was so certain, have been forced to admit I must have been mistaken.'

Still he could not believe it. 'A man . . . Surely he must have known we'd find out where the gasoline came from?'

Gruffly Robichaud gestured with his good hand and said, 'Ah, you detectives . . . Don't dodge the issue. Ask precisely *why* he wanted us to discover it was man, eh? Well, if you ask me,

Inspector, it's typical of an arsonist who wants others to know all about it. They offer help, they pose as authorities, they go for the jugular of another and . . .'

'Robichaud, what are you saying? That it was Herr Weidling who telephoned that depot and spoke in *French*?'

Frightened, a flock of pigeons rose into the light dust of snow. For a moment the fire marshal watched them, then admitted defeat. 'I must apologize, Inspector. How could it have been him but . . . but this business, it's got me afraid. Terrified, isn't that so? Hey, my friend, I know in my guts it's going to happen again. There is no sand for the roads. There are fifteen or twenty degrees of frost to plug the water mains. A crown fire . . . If there is a high wind, this will spread the flames from roof to roof and we'll never stop it.'

Someone had impersonated Father Beaumont who, by the time that telephone call had been made, was already dead.

A last cigarette was found and accepted with a curt nod and, 'What about yourself, Inspector?'

'I've had enough. The pipe . . . I prefer it but have, unfortunately, used up the last of my ration.'

'Then ask the préfet. That one has the right sort of friends. Anything you want. Just ask him.'

Ah *merde*! 'Go easy, eh? Watch what you say. Don't be a fool. I gather the caller spoke fluent French without trace of an accent?'

This was so, but someone could have been hired to make the call, someone who knew the ins and outs of the Basilica. 'In three days there is to be a concert at the Théâtre des Célestins, our most famous theatre, Inspector. The cream of Lyon will be there with their German friends but in addition, all the Wehrmacht's brass from the Army of the South. Oh for sure, I have tried to tell the mayor and the préfet that the concert must be cancelled but they will not do so. All the tickets have been sold. The money would have to be returned. It's a charity thing, an example of the good will that is supposed to exist between occupier and occupied. Hospitals, orphans, unwed mothers and warm clothing for the Russian Front. They will ask the Germans to—'

'Why not say the Boches? There are only the two of us.'

'Another patriot, is that what you want me to acknowledge, Inspector? Then forget it, my friend. These days each man must stand alone. The Germans, as I was saying. They will ask them for extra patrols in the immediate area of the theatre and they will have so many plain-clothes inside, this . . . this Salamander will not be able to strike a match. But they are fools. He and she, or those two women will outwit them because . . .'

Robichaud threw down his cigarette and purposely ground it out beneath a boot. 'Because, Inspector, it or they are the Salamander and elusive. *Elusive!*'

'Three days.'

'Tonight, tomorrow night and then the one after that.'

'Sunday evening.'

'Yes. But since the thing has been so well publicized, I have two of my men quietly searching the premises already. Please do not inform anyone of this.'

'And if I told you I thought one of your two women had been murdered?' asked St-Cyr, watching him closely.

Their eyes met. 'Then I would say to you that she had been silenced so as to make our task all the more difficult.'

Frau Weidling and Klaus Barbie were in the main sitting-room of the Prince Albert Suite. From where he stood hidden behind a door, Kohler could see the woman quite clearly but only a portion of Barbie.

She was sitting on the edge of a sofa, her long, shapely legs tightly together. Hands in her lap. No more teasing laughter now, no more thoughts of false flirtation. Only fear that perhaps Barbie had seen right through her and would refuse her request.

Barbie was standing not a metre from her. Hands in his

jacket pockets with the thumbs out, no doubt. 'My husban͏
the best, Herr Obersturmführer. If Johann is given halt a
chance, he'll find this Salamander and put a stop to the fires.'

He must have smirked, for she blanched and her fingertips
tightened their grip on the dark blue fabric of her skirt. 'And if I
do not want the fires to be stopped?' he asked quietly.

Verdammt!

'But . . . but Please, I do not understand, Herr Obersturmführer? Is it that you wish the fires to continue when Berlin and
Herr Mueller have demanded they be stopped?'

Kohler counted the seconds. Barbie must be stripping her
naked with his eyes, telling her not in so many words that he
knew all about her loves and hates, her private, private little
pleasures—hell, he'd have had the suite searched. He'd have
found everything.

Klaus Barbie: age twenty-nine, a bastard by birth, with an
abusive father who drank too much and died of a neck tumour
the very year Barbie graduated from grammar school. Latin and
Greek, 1933. A younger brother had died that same year.

Grandpapa had refused the bastard any of his rightful inheri-
tance even though the Barbies had married after the birth of
son Klaus.

Once a bastard, always a bastard under Germanic law,
snorted Kohler inwardly—he still couldn't see more than a
lower leg and an occasional hand. Barbie had wanted to go into
law or archaeology. Instead, the SS got him. Six months work
detail in the Arbeitsdienst to toughen the muscles and the spirit.
Then the Hitler Youth as a patrol leader, a Fahnenführer, to
prove he had leadership qualities and determination among
other things, ah yes. Then the SS in September 1935 and the
training school at Bernau near Berlin to put the polish on him.

An Iron Cross second-class from Holland, 1940, for bashing a
Jewish boy over the head with an ashtray and having him and
his partner shot dead for breaking the rules and selling ice-
cream. Of course it hadn't helped that those same boys had

resisted the attempts of Nazi-minded thugs to smash their little shop and beat them up . . .

A hand reached out to cup Frau Weidling's chin. Moisture must have collected in her lovely eyes for she blinked in apprehension and swallowed tightly.

'Of course, Gestapo Mueller wishes this Salamander to be stopped,' said Barbie. 'But at the time he sent your husband that telex, he had not received my report on the fire.'

She gave a half-smile and tilted back her head a little, causing her hair to fall loosely away from her neck and shoulders. 'All those railway workers . . .' she said. 'You are certain they were using that cinema as a meeting-place for the Resistance?'

Still there was that quietness to Barbie's voice. 'Not certain. Call it an educated guess, Frau Weidling. If we're wrong, nothing is lost. If we're right, then a great deal has been gained.'

'Yet Herr Robichaud still goes free?'

God, how sweet they were to each other! thought Kohler.

Barbie's hand fell. Her fingers having gripped her dress, lessened their hold, then gave it up and tensely smoothed the fabric over shapely thighs. She would be only too well aware of the Obersturmführer's reputation as a notorious womanizer. Was she wondering if he'd ask her to take off her clothes or was she hoping he wouldn't?

Infuriatingly, Barbie's leg with its regulation black shoe, and his hand disappeared from Kohler's view. 'Perhaps, Frau Weidling, we will let your husband destroy Herr Robichaud's credibility. Lyon's fire chief could then commit suicide.'

Her hands had come to a stop again, this time with the fingertips at the hem of her skirt and touching the meshed silk stockings of dark Prussian blue. 'And Robichaud's mistress?' she asked so quietly one had to strain to hear the coyness in her voice.

'A double suicide. Yes, yes, that would be nice.'

'Good.'

Ah *Gott im Himmel*, the bitch! What now? wondered Kohler.
Barbie was like a banker, a businessman—without the uniform
he'd pass totally unnoticed as a middle-class Frenchman in a
crowd. No problem. He spoke fluent French with only a faint
accent. Ah yes. Son of a bitch.

He wasn't tall, was really quite diminutive for the head of Section IV of the Lyon KDS, the Einsatzkommando under Lieu-
tenant-Colonel Werner Knab. Repression of political crimes *i.e.*,
Jews, Communists, escaped workers, counterespionage and all
those carrying false papers of any kind. An archive too, mustn't
forget that. All were under Barbie's command which was not
bad for a guy who really ought to have been allowed to go on to
the university if grandpapa had given humanity even the
blinking of an eye.

'You are attending the concert on Sunday evening.' It wasn't
a question but she answered Yes like a shy schoolgirl ready to
yield her honour, her little capital.

It was Barbie's turn to say Good and he did it in such a
clipped manner, she was startled and confused but only for a
split second.

Then recognition, perhaps, entered her pretty head. She smiled
knowingly and said again, with eagerness this time, 'Yes . . . yes,
I will be there. Is Johann to be in charge of security?'

He was. This pleased her so much she got up quickly and
went over to Barbie and out of sight, ah damn.

'A small fire is quite possible,' he said, 'but we will make certain there will be no panic except in those areas where we
might want it.'

Merde!

'Shall I inform my husband of this?' she asked, the schoolgirl
again.

'No. No, it would be best to leave it between ourselves.'

This time she must have reached out to take him eagerly by
the hand, for she gushed, 'I'm so grateful, Herr Obersturmführer.'

His heels crashed together in the little bow a bastard like that would give. 'Then consider it my Christmas present to you, Frau Weidling. Heil Hitler.'

She stopped him at the door. 'Why is it you think the Salamander a man? Please, is there something I should know? Johann, he is certain it is, but for myself, I . . . I have my doubts.'

I'll bet you do! snorted Kohler silently.

'And you'd like to know?' asked Barbie, teasing her now. Would he have sex with her right there on the floor?

'Yes. Yes, I would,' she answered demurely.

Kohler could feel her quivering. Ah *Gott im Himmel*, was the woman having an orgasm over it?

'Then read the profiles your husband has in his briefcase, Frau Weidling. The first is the most thorough and least speculative. It covers all three of those fires in the Reich in 1938 and suggests strongly that our Salamander is a man. A student at the time of those fires, perhaps, or the jealous lover of one.'

Though taller by far than Barbie, she leaned in close and down to brush her lips against his cheek and give him a tender whiff of perfume. Ah yes. Musk and civet and God knows what all else. Strong and earthy in any case. In heat but not wanting to rut.

Kohler heard her whispering that it was a pity Barbie couldn't stay longer. 'It gets so boring sometimes. Johann is always so busy.'

Barbie didn't spare her. 'Then perhaps it is, Frau Weidling, that you would enjoy sitting in on one of our interrogations? We have a woman in custody, a girl of twenty-two who refuses to answer my questions.'

'A woman?'

'Yes.'

That girl with the bicycle? demanded Kohler silently.

'If . . . if I can be of any service, Herr Obersturmführer, you . . . you have only to ask.'

'Good.'

The door closed and she stood there pilloried with her forehead pressed against it and her hand still clinging to the knob as she struggled with what Barbie had just implied about her. 'Enjoy,' she blurted. '*Enjoy*, ah damn!'

A minute passed. Another and another. Then she brutally locked the door and hurried through to Weidling's bedroom.

Knowing he'd best leave while he could, Kohler watched her in a sliver of mirror as she read the profiles. She was quick about it, flustering only when she came to the last of them.

Lips parted, she looked up and across the room. Her throat constricted. Her eyes watered 'Johann,' she croaked. 'Johann, how could you have done this to me?'

The profiles were returned and the briefcase taken with her. Kohler heard her undressing in her bedroom. Her clothes went underfoot and over a chair. A gorgeous figure. A round, high posterior with smooth, tight buttocks, good, slim hips and a long and supple back that gracefully and methodically bent as she undid each of her garters and smoothly rolled the stockings down.

Her breasts were not large but handsome, the nipples rosy and stiffening as, lost in thought, she touched them, then ran her fingers through the richness of her hair and dragged off the bracelets.

Lastly the ear-rings were removed, a hand running down her front to press flatly against her tummy, the dark auburn triangle of her pubes below.

'So, *gut*,' she said in throaty, brutal German. 'Yes, *gut*, Herr Obersturmführer. We shall see.'

A chanced look showed her soaking in the tub, smoking a cigarette and sipping cognac with the briefcase beside her on the floor. Self-satisfied and excited. Thrilled by what she had accomplished and by what the future might hold.

She blew on the end of the cigarette and gave that little laugh of a woman in heat knowing gratification was near. She looked at the embers but did not burn herself. She just liked the thought of it perhaps, the thought of pain in other women.

Now that the briefcase was out of reach, there was only one place he could find what was needed and that was in Klaus Barbie's office just down the street. Gestapo HQ Berlin wouldn't give it to him. Not after all the trouble Louis and he had caused the SS. They were dead fish, *verboten* and barely tolerated.

He'd have to manage it somehow.

Piling her hair up with a hand, she went under and for a moment he had only the sight of her cognac glass and the cigarette in its ashtray. Then ... then the sight of her posterior rising from the suds like some strange creature of the sea. Gorgeously round and sleek and draining water over a skin that glistened with bath oil, glistened with ... Were those the scars of welts? Had she been beaten, not once but several times and long ago?

Then the back ... beautifully melded to the hips and seat, but revealing more faint scars.

Ah *merde*! She'd been thrashed to Jesus.

Finally her head emerged as she gasped, drew in a breath and filled her lungs. Once, twice, three times—still bent over as if beaten and having only just dragged herself up on to her knees.

He could not understand why she had forced herself to stay under so long. It made him uncomfortable and afraid. Muttering, *nom de Dieu!* Louis, to himself he slipped away, still thinking of the scars.

She would remember she had put the lock on—he had no doubt of it. She went under again and he heard the silence grow as the little wavelets in the tub began to die. She stayed down so long, he turned in panic and was starting back towards her when she came up for air to suck it in and fill the suite with her choking!

Verdammt!

* * *

It was almost too much to hope the girl with the bicycle would come to the temporary morgue. As unobtrusively as possible, St-Cyr searched the queue only to find the hush made him increasingly uneasy.

Two abreast and looking shabby through the softly falling snow, the motley line stretched along the rue de la Bourse and around the corner on to the rue du Bât d'Argent, the street of the packsack of silver.

There were far too many French Gestapo plain-clothes in the line—one could spot them so easily from here for they stood in pairs with their snap-brims pulled down, trench coat collars up and cigarettes—yes, in a nation where tobacco was gold, they could afford to toss their butts away and light another.

But apart from them, there was not a whisper of the German presence. Instead, the préfet's men in dark blue kept order.

Klaus Barbie was using the queue to trap people. Once inside the doors, all papers would be examined and the names recorded to be later checked against the growing list of victims and those other lists: the badly burned who were still in hospital, the not-so-badly-burned who had been treated and released, that of the audience members who had escaped unscathed, and that of all others who in any way had been connected with the cinema of the Beautiful Celluloid.

Barbie had known that those whose sons or other loved ones had disappeared without leaving a forwarding address to avoid the forced labour or to go into hiding for any other reason, the maquis perhaps ... all would come in hopes their loved ones had not been found among the dead.

Only in the faces of the curious was there any sign of quickness but even they had had to succumb to the hush of the grieving.

The line crept forward. Occasionally someone would realize what was up and think to turn away, only to see that they dare not draw attention to themselves, that it was better to simply tough it out.

He wanted to shout, Go home. It's a trap! but could not do so, knowing only too well that like them, he, too, could be hustled away and into silence for ever.

When he found the girl, she was nearest the shop fronts, not far from the corner. And he realized then that she was using the windows to mirror the street and warn her if anyone had spotted her. The collar of the fawn-coloured, double-breasted overcoat was turned up. Muffled in a beige angora beret and scarf, she searched the glass as if looking at the window displays of suits made out of human hair or wood fibre and shoes with soles made out of wood or cork.

He let her believe she hadn't been spotted. Flashing his badge and holding up a cautioning hand to overcome objections, he slid into line four persons behind her. He hoped she would not panic when she discovered she would have to leave her name and address. He must not do anything that would give her away, must not let the préfet or the Gestapo get their hands on her or get any indication of whom he was after.

It took another hour but by then the girl had gone on to view the corpses amid the stench, wearing one of the regulation cloth masks and forcing herself to do so while the préfet confronted him.

'Well, Louis, is it that you are so brazen you would show your face to me, eh?'

A brawler, a tough in uniform, Guillemette clenched a fist and shook it threateningly. 'You and Kohler smashed up one of my best men in the rue des Trois Maries last night. Why have you done such a thing? He was there for your own safety, imbecile! Myself, I personally delegated him to watch over the two of you.'

How nice. 'But . . . but, Préfet, we thought he was a robber! There was no light. There was someone with him.'

'Who?'

'My partner and I never found out. We were forced to leave your man in the street and—'

'In the *gutter*, Jean-Louis! A broken nose that will take months to reset, four splintered teeth, twenty-six stitches about the face and five cracked ribs. No wallet or papers, no gun or knife or bracelets. Come, come my friend, what did you and Kohler do with them?'

No gun or knife or handcuffs ... the papers stolen ...? Ah *merde*—someone else had taken them! 'Préfet, those narrow streets are dangerous after curfew. The next time—if there should be a next time—please ask your men to identify themselves well beforehand.'

Guillemette grunted savagely. 'Don't play around with me, you little fart from Paris. What were you doing in the rue des Trois Maries?'

Madame Rachline could not have told him of their visit. 'Nothing, Préfet. We had simply lost our way in the dark.'

'*Bâtard*, I ought to have you run in! What address were you after and why?'

Some sort of answer was necessary but it was tempting to refuse absolutely. 'We were trying to find the pont Alphonse Juin so as to cross the Saône and make our way along the quai Saint Antoine to La Mère Aurora. Perhaps you know of it? A little place, of course, but the food, it is excellent. At least, it was before the Defeat of 1940.'

'*Maudit salaud*, you were up to something and should not have been in that street!'

'Then perhaps the one who followed your man should not have been there either, Préfet, nor should she have taken his gun among other things.'

'She?' Ah what was this?

St-Cyr nodded curtly.

'One of the two women?' demanded Guillemette swiftly.

'Perhaps, but then ... ah, then, Préfet,' he shrugged, 'perhaps my partner and I were mistaken.'

'A woman.'

Guillemette was no fool. He'd put two and two together and

come up with La Belle Époque but . . . ah, why not tell him a little? 'A woman, yes. Perhaps.'

'What's that supposed to mean?'

It would be best to shrug.

As the préfet turned angrily away in thought, St-Cyr looked down and a name leapt from among the lists on the desk. 'Martine Charlebois, Apt. 3, Number 12 allée des Villas.' A flat overlooking the Parc de la Tête d'Or in one of the most fashionable parts of town.

'Louis . . . Louis, why are you here?'

'To see Herr Weidling, Préfet, and to meet with Robichaud.'

'And Kohler? Where is that one?'

'Doing his job, Préfet. Keeping himself busy.'

In mirror after mirror Kohler saw himself as he paused in panic among the elegant corridors of the Hotel Terminus. Things never stopped, not even for Christmas. Gestapo Lyon occupied sixty rooms in the fine old hotel. The grey mice and the troops seemed to be everywhere. The bitches from home hammered on their typewriters and teleprinter machines with military precision. Their skirts were hitched up, their backs ramrod stiff, blonde braids pinned into diadems or coiled into buns, and bosoms straining behind grey tunics two sizes too small. *Merde*, what was he to do? There had been absolutely no chance to get into Klaus Barbie's office even though the door to that suite of rooms had been open.

Torture was on the third floor and he didn't want to go up there, not after what he'd seen on that last case. A typewriter stopped. A voice said, 'Are you looking for someone?'

'No. No. Just on my way out, fräulein.'

'Then it is the other direction you want, *mein Herr*.'

Ducking into a lavatory, he glanced madly about. Grey woollen underpants encircled thick ankles draping themselves over black brogues with heavy laces . . .

On the third floor it was quiet, a surprise, and when he opened a door, the room he entered held only a plain wooden table, two kitchen chairs and a copper bathtub with a sturdy rod of oak across it.

Uncomfortably he flicked his eyes around the room as he breathed in the mingled stench of excrement, vomit, blood, soap and disinfectant.

There was a poster from home nailed to the beautifully carved panelling, one of those brash *soldaten* things with Rhineland maidens gazing raptly at the helmeted men of their dreams and the Führer beaming benevolently from among the clouds like God without His Messerschmitt. *'Morgens Grusse ich dem Führer. Und abends danke ich dem Führer.'* In the morning I greet my Führer. And in the evening I thank him. For this? he wondered sadly. Even the rugs had had to be removed.

Several newspapers were scattered in a corner. *Der Stuermer*, the *Berliner Tageblatt*, the *Voelkischer Beobachter* ... Hitler's own flagship and his magazine, *Signal*. All light reading while waiting for a prisoner to come round.

Oak planks, a metre long, had been used to knock sense into the recalcitrant. After all, the 'reinforced' interrogations were done up here, those in which the prisoner had shown signs of withholding information. One of Barbie's two German shepherds had defecated among the slats.

'All right,' he said. 'Louis, it's this or nothing.'

When the blaze was going, Kohler added the chairs and then the table but drained the bathtub and made certain the ropes would not plug the hole.

He was downstairs in the toilets when the cry of fire came; he was inside Barbie's office staring dumbly at the bastard's bullwhip when the alarm bells began to ring.

Of plaited rawhide, the bullwhip lay coiled on top of a dossier that was clearly marked Frau Kaethe Weidling yet he could not touch the dossier without moving the whip! He felt the panic rising inside himself, a mad, totally uncontrollable watery sickness. He heard the crack of the whip as it snapped back, saw it flash forward to rip his chest open from the right shoulder to the left hip. Ahh . . .

Then it tore open his left cheek and all of that moment came back and he saw the hot flood of urine growing around his left shoe. *Verdammt!* He had pissed himself again! Son of a bitch, what was he to do?

Barbie had learned of the incident and had left this little reminder for him.

The alarm bells were still ringing. Determinedly he put the lock on the inner door, fought down the nausea to move the whip, and read:

'Frau Kaethe Weidling née Voelker, born Schwering 21 April 1913. Father, the banker Karl Ernst Voelker (suicide by shooting, 1921); mother, Gretta Inge, only child of the Kapitän Guenther Horst Ungerfeld, one of the Count Felix von Luckner's raiders.' A stern old Prussian no doubt.

'Married Leiter Karl Johann Weidling 4 September 1938 . . .' Right after the Köln fire. Ah *nom de Dieu!*

The second page gave a full frontal photograph of her as she was today, standing in the nude leaning nonchalantly against a wall. She was holding a small pear, an ornament of some kind, in the cage of her hands and was staring at the viewer as if to say, So, *mein Herr*, what else is new, except that he did not think she went with men.

The third page was a montage of female victims, and he realized right away that Barbie had had it made from the photographs she had in her bedroom at the Hotel Bristol, and again he could not understand how she had come by them.

The fourth page revealed her holding a lighted match to the breast of Claudine Bertrand. Both women were naked. Claudine was not tied in any way to the ornate iron headboard of the bed, but who had taken the photograph? Who? It could not have been done with their knowledge Both were far too

involved with each other. Claudine had a hand between Frau
Weidling's legs . . .

Gestapo Lyon, he wondered, or someone else, someone with
access to that whorehouse or Madame Rachline herself?

There was talk of matches, of a child so fascinated by fire she
would masturbate among lighted candles and brush flame
across her skin to heighten sexual awareness.

There was talk of fires, of 'accidents' in which 'no positive
proof could be found'. Talk of whippings by a grandfather of the
old school, ah yes. Talk of her later searching out other females
of a like mind to gratify her unnatural urges, of her visiting
whorehouses . . . but she'd never been a prostitute, had come
from too good a family.

Leiter Weidling, a widower, had followed her to Köln. He
had personally handled all three investigations and out of
fighting those fires had come not only the medals for bravery
and the prestige of citations, but also a new and very beautiful
young wife.

Had he trapped her into marrying him so as to gain her help,
or had she realized that when one wants desperately to hide,
one seeks a position of utmost security? What better than the
cold arms of an old fire chief, especially if he'd known you had
been present at all three of those fires?

The couple had been in Lyon since 10 December. The
tenth!

There was no time to go through all the pages. The *pompiers*
were arriving in the Cours de Verdun to put an end to the fire,
Christ!

Reluctantly Kohler closed the dossier but could not
remember which way the bullwhip had been coiled.

The pastis was not alcoholic but a vile concoction of anise
and liquorice that was lime-green and yellow and stayed that
way even when a half-pitcher of water was added!

The beer was home-brew, made right in the kitchen sink

where they washed the dishes and the pots. Little things swam among too many bubbles. The cheese was not cheese but something of sawdust, powdered milk and synthetic rubber, perhaps; the bread grey and full of asbestos. 'Louis . . .' began Kohler.

They'd been arguing constantly. Both were bitchy, both on the run and in need of a damned good lay and a bit of comforting, not a prolonged spell on the Russian Front courtesy Gestapo Lyon. Shit! 'Louis, listen to me. Frau Weidling gets a kick out of sadism and is fascinated by fire. Hubby brings her here and she knows a friend from the past, from Lübeck, Heidelberg and Köln. Claudine, *mon vieux*. Claudine Bertrand.'

'Yes, yes, but—'

'Shut up! They have a little fun. They want a little more. And every time Frau Weidling lights a fire, hubby gains in stature and no one thinks to question her.'

'But . . . but Claudine was upstairs with the projectionist, is that not correct?'

It was. 'And Frau Weidling came in alone,' said Kohler lamely, the steam having suddenly gone out of him.

'Then there were three women, Hermann. Not two as we have been led to believe. Frau Weidling, Claudine and someone else.'

'Someone special Claudine had brought along for Frau Weidling to meet. Ah *Gott im Himmel*, Louis, have we finally hit on it? Gestapo Lyon know all about Frau Weidling and that husband of hers and want to keep on using her but they do not know the identity of this other woman. They think, like Weidling, that it must be a man. Hell, hoisting heavy jerry cans up into that belfry proves it to them, but we both know two determined women can do as much or more than any man.'

Louis nodded curtly and brushed non-existent crumbs from the table. 'Claudine enters with this other woman but leaves her seat to find the key to the toilets and goes upstairs to the projectionist for it. She then comes downstairs and opens the door but does not stay long. Instead, she returns upstairs for a little visit. Others go into the toilets for a meeting of their own, but leave the key in the lock. Those others don't return to their seats and the usherette goes to see what is the matter and finds the key but does not check to see what is going on or even if the door is locked.'

Kohler heaved a sigh. 'When Suzie gets back to her station, the woman who came in with Claudine is now absent from her seat but the rush bag they brought is still there.'

'Yes, yes. Presumably this other woman went out to meet Frau Weidling.'

There was a terse grunt of acknowledgement. 'And not finding her in the toilets where expected, Louis, this third woman then locks the door to the toilets, perhaps pouting in anger at having been stood up. We may never know.'

'Or perhaps she thought Frau Weidling *was* in the toilets, Hermann.'

'Pardon?'

'Trapped, Hermann. Ready to be caught in the fire.'

'Ah *merde* . . .'

'Claudine is upstairs,' continued St-Cyr. 'She remains with the projectionist until after the fire starts. She panics, she loses a shoe—she realizes what has happened, Hermann, and is far more terrified at first because she knows who did it.'

Again there was a sigh. 'And that, my fine Frog friend, is why she had to be killed, but how the hell was it done?'

St-Cyr gave a massive shrug. 'Time . . . Time is what we need. The white powder from Mademoiselle Claudine's kitchen floor is being analysed. Vasseur will track us down. A careful murder, Hermann, and one that must have been planned well in advance, since she could so easily have been killed in that fire had more gasoline been splashed across the stairs to the balcony.'

'Perhaps our Salamander ran out of gasoline?'

'Perhaps it wanted Claudine to die in bed, Hermann, and could not bring itself to have her burnt to death.'

'Then it knew Claudine well, Louis, and had some feeling for her as a person.'

Hermann hunted for a fag and, finding none in any of his pockets, looked desperate. Their coffee came but he shoved it aside, planning no doubt to dump everything on the floor as they left. 'So why share the perfume, Louis, and give Frau Weidling a sample?'

'Because it was Claudine who insisted Madame Rachline distribute the perfume yet not give its source, and because she may well have been told to do so by our third "woman".'

'Who was *not* Madame Rachline?'

'Perhaps, but then we are dealing with a Salamander, Hermann. One so slippery it can murder with confidence and present us with all sorts of hints. An expert, Hermann. One who is so sure of itself, it relishes the dare and thrives on the meal.'

'Was it Frau Weidling who came back with Claudine to the flat at Number Six, or was it Madame Rachline as the concierge maintains?'

'That concierge was absent from his cage, Hermann. A matter of some plumbing in the courtyard lavatory. It is possible Claudine's murderer could have gained entry while Madame Rachline, if it really was her, was still upstairs with her friend.'

'Our third woman, then.'

'Or man.'

'And our girl with the bicycle, Louis?'

'Ah yes, Mademoiselle Martine Charlebois. I must pay her a little visit while you occupy yourself with Madame Philomena Cadieux, I think, the caretakeress of the Basilica.'

'Those shoes . . . Ah *merde*.'

'Yes, Hermann, those shoes and a little more perhaps about the gasoline and Father Adrian.'

'And the bishop, Louis. The bishop.'

FROM THE PLACE TERREAUX TO THE PONT
Morand it was not far to the Parc de la Tête d'Or
and the allée des Villas which overlooked it.

St-Cyr paid off the *vélo-taxi*, wondering if he oughtn't to tell
the man to wait, since the streets had been so difficult. He
searched the identical grey-stone façades whose precise ele-
gance of tall French windows and Louis XVI iron railings was
matched only by the view across the park.

The wind had died, the snow had stopped and in the soft
blue blush of the closing day, the solitary trees, long walks, distant woods, lake and iron-and-glass dome of the arboretum were
sharply defined.

There were a few cross-country skiers, a few walkers, some
with their dogs, one throwing a stick. Children, of course. Children always loved the magic of a park like this.

There were a few Germans, two black Mercedes, a general in
one with a motor-cycle escort, but these were both too distant to
matter and no one seemed to pay them any mind.

He searched the changing light, sought out each tonal variation and what it delineated, breathed in deeply, thought of the Loire, of Gabrielle and her son, then returned to duty with regret.

There were only two apartments on each floor at Number Twelve, and the central staircase, with the warm, dark amber of its polished banisters, made a rectangular spiral above him. Tall mahogany doors—good, solid things—led into each apartment. The concierge, if there was one, was not about and probably lived in a couple of rooms at the back, looking out on to the central courtyard. That's where the girl would have left her bicycle, but had she been the one to leave the lock off the outer door?

Unbuttoning his overcoat and loosening the scarf his mother had knitted for him thirty years ago, he rang the bell.

The bolt was undone, the door yanked open, the girl's, 'Henri . . . Oh, pardon,' was caught in the air and held until it was too late for the shock to be hidden.

'Monsieur . . . ?' Ah no. It was him!—and he could see this written in the anguish of her expression. 'My brother,' she said, running a worried hand through her light brown hair. 'I . . . I was expecting him, monsieur.'

Her brother. She was every bit the school mistress he had settled on. Affably St-Cyr motioned with his trilby. 'Permit me to introduce myself, Mademoiselle . . . ?'

'Charlebois.'

'Mademoiselle, I am Chief Inspector Jean-Louis St-Cyr of the Sûreté Nationale from Paris Central, but please do not be alarmed.'

'My brother . . . You have found his body among the deceased. Ah no. *No!*'

She buried her face in her hands and broke into tears. He tried to comfort her but she turned her back on him, making him feel terrible. Always there was this time bomb of the Sûreté introduction. One used it often but one never quite knew how it would be taken. 'Mademoiselle, I did not come to tell you your brother was among the dead but merely to return this.'

'*What?*' She would blow her nose and wipe her eyes—yes, yes, that would be best so as to distract him—and she would pray to God and the Blessed Virgin for assistance in this moment of crisis. 'What?' she asked, her back still turned to him, her head bowed, the shoulders thin.

St-Cyr closed the door behind him. 'The yellow work card of a woman who is now dead, Mademoiselle Charlebois. *Dead!*'

'Ah no! *No!* Dead? But . . . but how can this be?'

He tried to be kind as he spoke to her back. 'A few small questions, mademoiselle. Nothing troublesome, I assure you. Please, why not sit down? It . . . it would be better, would it not? You're worried. You've had a terrible shock. Come, come, let us go into the salon. Ah! I will remove the shoes and you will for-give the holes that have developed in my socks since I last washed them.'

She wasn't having any of it. 'Why have you come? I hardly knew Mademoiselle Claudine. She was not a friend of mine, not even an acquaintance.'

Her eyes were smarting. Tears glistened in them making greener still their greeny-brown. There were freckles over the bridge of her nose and on the pale cheeks and chin but these served only to heighten a gentle handsomeness that was really quite attractive were she not so distressed and wary, and touching her pearls as though grasping for a lifeline.

St-Cyr indicated his overcoat and hat, and reluctantly she allowed him to put them on a chair. 'This way, then, Inspector. My brother and I live alone. He's away a lot and I . . . Well, I have thought a fire like that . . . We're both great lovers of the cinema. It's our only form of relaxation these days. I have thought . . . well, you know . . . The worst, of course.'

'And the work card of Mademoiselle Bertrand?'

It was no use. 'She came to see me on the day of the fire, in the afternoon. I . . . I said that . . . that I didn't think my brother could help her any more, but that when he returned I would ask.'

'And the card?' he asked again. 'How did you come by it?' Her back was still to him.

'It . . . it must have fallen from her purse. I . . . I have found it on the sofa between the cushions.'

For now that was enough and he would not push the matter yet for fear of upsetting her too much. 'Your brother, mademoiselle, what does he do?'

'Henri . . . ? Henri runs the shop of our grandfather, Inspector. *The* Henri Masson of Lyon. Fine antiques and estate sales. Jewellery, rare and old books, porcelains, crystal and paintings. Silver too, of course. It's . . . it's on the rue Auguste Comte near place Bellecour. Henri was always there with our grandfather and when the old monsieur died, why he left the shop to my brother. And . . . and the one in Dijon, of course, though Henri, he has a manager for that—well, two of them. One for the Lyon shop and one for Dijon.'

Through the awkward silence that developed between them came the sound of a finch and then that of a canary. 'Excuse me, please, a moment,' she said, giving a brief, shy smile while wiping her eyes. 'My family, Inspector. My little friends. I have been so worried about the tragedy, I have forgotten to give them seed and water.'

He knew she needed a moment to herself and gave it to her. He could not believe their luck. A *brother*. Estate sales and fine antiques. A link at last to the jewelled cross and Father Adrian. Ah *nom de Dieu*, had they struck so close?

Everywhere the eye settled it fell on a gorgeous clutter of exquisite pieces. A Buddha, fourteenth-century at least, in a lime-green glaze, complemented the satin damask that covered the walls with soft green and gold floral patterns. There were paintings in richly gilded frames—oils that impressed. A bouquet of roses, tulips, peonies and lilacs by Jan Frans van Dael, a vase of lilacs by Pierre-Joseph Redouté. A Gobelin tapestry of

Africa with chattering monkeys and parrots. A chinoiserie cabinet in a deep-red lacquer that glowed. Art deco vases with etched patterns, the colours sea-green, amber-rose and turquoise from the Daum-Brothers' glassworks—not old, probably 1925, but totally in keeping with all the rest. Another glass vase from that same period was by Maurice Marinot. An almost Gauginesque nude in a wash of pale citrine mended a net against a background of dimpled, frosted glass, the lines so simple yet masterfully evoking the rhythm of life for which Marinot was justly famous.

A sixteenth-century portrait of a lady reading an illuminated breviary. Savonnerie carpets, a fluted white marble chimney-piece, a large gilt-framed mirror and a Louis XVI clock with flanking elephants in silver. Louis XVI armchairs whose velvet upholstery had been faded not so much by use as time, yet venerated throughout those years.

A far more modern sofa and comfortable armchairs were in an off-cream and flowered silk velveteen. There were apricot-coloured taffeta drop-curtains with tassels and fringes, bits of statuary, bronzes from the sixteenth and seventeenth centuries—Italian, he thought. Eighteenth-century leather-bound books, bibelots, snuffboxes, jewel cases, bits of crystal and ivory, a sapphire bracelet ... Ah *nom de Dieu*, three chains of superbly matched dark blue beads, each with a tiny clear-white diamond and diamond-encrusted clasp. It was just lying there on the secretaire as if cast off in despair.

'As you can see, Inspector, my brother is a collector whose fancy does not always run to things that are very old. That bracelet is from Cartier in New York, not twelve years ago. Ah no, it was thirteen years. Yes, the stock market crash on Wall Street. A suicide in the family and the wife on holiday in France and forced to part with it at once. Henri bought it from the estate of the aunt to whom she had sold it for a pittance, believing the old lady would then leave it to her in her will.'

'And the icons?' he asked. They were centuries old.

'Purchased from German soldiers on holiday from the Russian Front. Oh they're stolen, of course—everyone knows this including Henri, but saving them from the ravages of such careless hands is better than having them destroyed through misadventure.'

The soft yellow mohair cardigan, strand of pearls and plain beige skirt suited her but she stood as if condemned. 'And yourself, mademoiselle?' he asked gently. 'What do you do besides keep house for your brother?'

She was still some distance from him, she thought, and he would not see the pain she felt, revealed as it must be in her eyes. 'Me? I am a teacher, an assistant professor at the Lycée du Parc. Germanic studies and French literature.'

'Then you must speak German very well.'

'Of course. It is essential, is it not? Otherwise the students would become bored with their studies and do quite badly.'

To avoid any further awkwardness, she decided to break with tradition and offer coffee. 'It . . . it is already made, Inspector, and just needs warming up. Henri . . . it is my brother's and my custom to always share our day's events over coffee at this hour of the apéritif. Neither of us take alcohol, not even wine. Henri says that it destroys the brain cells and in this I am forced to agree, though at times, of course, one longs for a little taste.'

Had she once been under the empire of alcohol? he wondered. She didn't look the type, but then with those it was often so hard to tell. Shattered dreams, a love affair never consummated . . . There were any of a thousand reasons.

The ersatz coffee would be fine and when she brought it on an antique silver tray, the complete service was a deep Prussian blue and jewelled Sèvres porcelain with beaded white and gold rims and a jade-green, rose-red, white and turquoise floral pattern. Ah *mon Dieu*, it would be like sipping vinegar out of a fortune among kings and princes.

'Your brother has exceptionally good taste, mademoiselle.'

She would lift her chin and proudly say it. Yes . . . yes, that would be best. 'We both had an excellent teacher in our grandfather, Inspector. When one has access to such fine things, it elevates the soul to use them now and then in the fashion for which they were originally intended.'

He would give her several moments of silence and deliberately let them grow into uncomfortableness. He wished he could take out his pipe and begin to pack it—always that tended to set people off and was most useful, but the shortages . . . that last crumb of tobacco had already been used.

She thought she had best say something, but she would do so demurely since he had not grimaced at the taste of the acorn-and-barley water. A disgrace, of course, to sully such pieces with such mud. 'My brother specializes in breaking up estates whose owners have died and left them to heirs who do not care to keep them, Inspector. This salon—indeed, the whole of the flat—changes its décor often as pieces come and go. One mustn't become attached to anything.'

'And the shop in Dijon?' he asked, taking out his notebook to unsettle her more.

Flustered, she pressed her knees together and tried to shrink from things. 'On the boul de Sévigné, of course, near the place d'Arcy. Inspector, why are you writing this down? Is Henri suspected of something?'

Of *what*, mademoiselle? his look said, but he shook his head. 'Ah no. No, of course not. A mere ritual, I assure you. One becomes so accustomed to interrogating people, one automatically takes out the little notebook.'

He had known she'd been worried, then, and was pleased about it. He did not put the notebook away but set it to one side on the coffee table whose patterns of sandalwood, gum and cherry splintered their designs around it as if shattered.

Again he let the silence grow until she wished he would say something. Anything! 'How did Mademoiselle Claudine die, Inspector? Was it her chest? She . . . she came to ask again for money. She was not well. This time pneumonia once more, I

think. I . . .' She shrugged helplessly but could not bring herself
to face him. 'I did give her our bottle of friar's balsam. I told her
how best to use it, Inspector. For myself, I am sorry to hear that
she has passed away.'

Their bottle of friar's balsam . . . He would favour his moustache in thought. He would ask the question she would not
want him to ask. 'How is it, please, that your brother knew
Mademoiselle Claudine Bertrand, a woman of the night,
Mademoiselle Charlebois, a woman of joy, a known prostitute?'

There was a quiver, a loss of colour though there had been
little enough of that. 'Henri knew Claudine from the years
before her descent into the night, Inspector. When he was very
young and I was much, much younger of course, our parents
and grandparents on our mother's side always took us to the seaside for the holidays. Claudine's family knew our parents.'

It was all he could do not to breathe, Good! That's good!

The front door opened. They heard a voice. She cried out,
'Henri, is that you, *chéri*?' and bolted from the room. Throwing
herself into her brother's arms, she touched his face, his hair
and kissed his cheek, saying, 'Where have you been? I've been
looking everywhere. I was so worried. *Terrified*, Henri. *Desperate* that we had been parted again, this time for ever.'

Sobbing, she clung to her brother and shook so hard he
had to hold her tightly until he noticed, ah yes, that they had a
visitor.

From a rat-hole shack outside the stone-and-iron fence of the
Basilica, the old woman who was the caretaker's wife sold black-
market candles and other religious nick-nacks in the plunging
darkness. Kohler let her serve the frozen customers she seldom
greeted with anything more than a grunt of distaste or a
scathing remark. Though not blind, she could have done as
well, for she knew the feel of each bill and coin. 'Another, monsieur,' she said to one, sucking on her cheeks. Age had made
her small and bent and when he stood before her in the dark-

ness, she tossed her shawled head back as if struck by the size of him. 'Monsieur . . . ?'

'Madame Philomena Cadieux?'

Hastily she crossed herself but said nothing and said it defiantly. 'Look, Madame Cadieux, I'm like Jesus. I come in peace. eh? Here's five hundred francs to prove it.'

'The Christ Child would have come with more,' she said doggedly. 'An old woman whose bladder is full but frozen. A bishop who hoards his silver on this day of giving and takes not the half as agreed these past countless years, but three-quarters.'

Ah *merde*, a family feud! 'Then here's another and another, eh, to warm the bones and the heart.'

'What is it you want?' Suspicion was in every particle of her and he had to grin, had to say to himself, What a delight it was to deal with the French.

'Why not let me help you close up. Here, let me buy the rest of your stock and we'll leave it right here for another time.'

The Germans were fools, but God had made them that way and who was she to question Him? 'Five thousand then, and I will allow you to close down the front shutter. It's too heavy for me but my husband will not listen.'

There was no thought of her inviting him into the two rooms she begrudgingly shared with that husband. This little stucco building was at the front and just to the right of the Basilica's entrance—joined to the main body as if a growth of accident, the builders having realized at the last that there had to be some place to dump the caretaker.

'It's too cold in there,' she said. 'Come with me. Come into the bishop's study. Let that one's fire take the ice from us even though he will be furious and will say it is the last straw, that that useless husband of mine and my good self have been dismissed!'

So much for the bishop and the husband. Kohler found her the half of another bottle of Calvados and wished her a happy Christmas. Her button eyes were fierce and full of rheum. Both nostrils ran. She sipped, wiped and wiped again with fingerless black woollen gloves that were frayed.

'Tell me about the gasoline,' he said. He would not grin. She was freezing and could hardly keep her fingers still enough to clutch the glass with both hands.

'The gasoline ...' She clucked her tongue. 'Yes. Yes, I warned Auguste not to leave it where he did but that one never listens. You should have let this Salamander torch the place, monsieur. Rats ... mice ... vermin ... lice and fleas ... You've no idea. It takes forever to wash that floor in there and I'm the only one who does it.'

She had to pee, and he had to turn his back while she used the bishop's best potted begonia and felt good about it.

'The gasoline was not taken by a woman, monsieur, but by a man. I have seen the footprints in the snow myself but no one has bothered to consult me. He was wearing Father Adrian's shoes, the ones with the cracked soles but it could not have been that one, could it, since he was already dead.'

Kohler tossed back his Calvados. 'Then who knew Father Adrian well enough to have taken his shoes and gained access to where he lived—where is that, by the way?'

'In two rooms, not far from the bishop's quarters in the manse that is next door. Oh yes, I have thought he may well have borrowed a cassock too.'

'And this person?'

She would let him have it, since to have a crumb was not to have the loaf but only a taste. 'Someone who knew Father Adrian had oiled his way among the women, though may God forgive me for saying it.'

'Was Mademoiselle Aurelle one of those women?' he asked.

The slut had been tied to her bed, thought Madame Cadieux, but there was no need to remind this one of it. 'And others, monsieur. Oh *mais certainement*, the good father had the Church in mind when he visited them and asked for donations and did whatever else he did to encourage them in the

Blessed Sacrament, but me, I have seen the evidence no priest should ever have in his rooms.'

Jesus! 'What evidence? Here, your glass is empty.'

And you are eager for another few crumbs, said the woman to herself. This time she would drink it all. She would drain the fine glass of the bishop who knew only too well what his secretary had been up to but had turned a blind eye. 'Oil, in a small bottle. Perfumed.'

'Condoms?'

She would duck her head aside to indicate a speck of modesty. 'The *capotes anglaises*, monsieur. I have counted them and noted when some were missing.'

The English bonnets, hoods, greatcoats or 'riding' coats. 'Who knew Father Adrian so well that person was aware the priest would be visiting Mademoiselle Aurelle the night of the fire?'

'But ... but Father Adrian was not supposed to visit her, monsieur, ah not on such a busy night.'

'He received a call?'

'Oh but of course, from one of his women. Madame Béatrice, that slut of a housekeeper for the bishop, that one says it was Mademoiselle Aurelle who telephoned Father Adrian in urgency for a visit, yes? But me, I do not personally think it was Mademoiselle Aurelle at all. I think it was someone else who only said she was Mademoiselle Aurelle.'

'Are there two telephones?' She was making him feel totally out of his depth.

'There are three, monsieur. Extensions here in the study and two in the manse.'

'And you listened in.'

She held out her glass. 'At about five thirty the new time, the German time.'

'And it wasn't Mademoiselle Aurelle?'

He was so eager for the crumbs. 'That one always called in tears, monsieur. There were none. Indeed, for myself, I felt the voice too educated.' There, she had said it and may God forgive her.

Too educated ... 'And Father Adrian, did you see him before he left?'

'How was he—is this what you wish?' She would wet her lips and stare at the bottom of her glass, and she would give him a last crumb and hope he would find the loaf. 'Agitated.'

Kohler looked away to the book-lined shelves and gave his thoughts aloud and with a sigh. 'Then he really did know what was up and that's why he took the cross with him.'

The cross was lying on the coffee table between herself and her brother, thought Martine Charlebois. Diamonds and rubies and sapphires and Henri looking so distressed. Tall and thin, and sitting up stiffly, for his back was bothering him again. Wan and almost jaundiced-looking now that the cold had left his cheeks, poor darling. Tired from working so hard—the train from Dijon had been late, held up by another of the interminable delays. And now this, a detective from the Sûreté with the cross from the Family Rouleau once more in this room.

The same light that was thrown back by the diamonds was absorbed by the rubies until they glowed with fire and the sapphires were warm.

As always, when there were others present, Henri did the talking.

'Our grandfather came across it years ago, Inspector. A very wealthy family with land-holdings in the Rhône Valley to the south of here. Five farms in excess of a total of two hundred hectares. Vineyards and orchards, cattle, sheep and pigs. I was with him when he broke up the estate and we found the cross tucked away in the back of a kitchen drawer.'

'Did he declare it to the owners?' asked the detective quietly. No doubt one of the kitchen help had been about to steal it.

'Of course he declared it, Inspector. Our grandfather had a reputation for being the most honest of men. How else could he have become *the* Henri Masson? Everyone trusted him absolutely. There was never any suggestion of impropriety. How could there have been?'

A saint—one could see this pass through the detective's mind, causing nothing but jaded doubt, even though the cross had been purchased from the owners for more than its value. The big ox-eyes lost themselves in studying Henri. They observed the delicate chiselling of the face, the fine and aristocratic nose, high cheekbones, dark brush of the eyebrows and long curve of the lashes. The lips that were not wide and coarse but soft and lovely, though they hardly ever smiled and were now so serious their expression matched the darkness of his eyes. The hair, jet black and fastidiously trimmed because Henri was such a tidy person. Tidy about his life and hers—everything was to have its proper place. Tidy about the affairs of business because one had to be so tidy there and grandfather, he had been so tidy himself. Ah yes.

'Tell me about Father Adrian Beaumont, please, Monsieur Charlebois. Your relationship to him, last contact—anything that might be of use no matter how seemingly insignificant.'

It would not go well, and she knew this now. Henri was so tense and irritated by the unpleasant surprise of finding a detective in the house and his little sister entertaining him.

'There is not much to tell, Inspector. We attend Mass at the Basilica, as our parents and grandparents did. Father Adrian was known to us, of course. Any dealings with the bishop went through him. We met a few times recently but only to discuss some of the paintings that are stored in the church. I was adamant that they be moved to more suitable quarters—drier, you understand. The constant humidity of these parts plays havoc with old masters. Father Adrian would not hear of it and in this, I am afraid, Bishop Dufour concurred.'

The detective would note all Henri's little mannerisms, the way he nervously rubbed the back of his left hand, the way he used his seriousness to force home a point, the way, when pressed, he would touch his left cheek and let the fingertips linger until they trailed down to the lower jaw, his mind still deep in thought. Every word so carefully debated before escaping from his lips.

'Your sister thought you might have gone to see *La Bête humaine?*'

Henri shook his head with that rapid little motion of firmness he always used on such occasions. 'I distinctly told Madame Doucette, the senior secretary at the Lycée du Parc, that she was to tell Mademoiselle Charlebois I had been summoned to Dijon.'

'Why?'

Ah, such an expression of sympathy and concern had entered Henri's eyes. It showed exactly how clearly he had been worried about her but his use of 'Mademoiselle Charlebois', not Martine—why must he always use her formal name when dealing with others?

The detective asked again why he had gone to Dijon.

'The shop had been broken into and some things taken, Inspector,' said Henri firmly. 'An icon, four canvases that were cut from their frames, some silver and a few small pieces of jewellery. Good pieces. In all, about seven hundred and fifty thousand francs.'

The detective's expression became grave at the size of the loss. 'When . . . when did this happen, monsieur, and when did you leave Lyon and return?'

Henri gave the brief, tight little smile he always saved for such grim moments of relish. 'Last Tuesday night, the twenty-second. I've only just returned, Inspector. There are several who will gladly tell you I took the train on the afternoon of the twenty-third at four o'clock and that, as is my custom always, I stayed in Dijon at its Hotel Terminus, room seventeen. You may ask the manager, the desk clerk, the maître d' and the maids if you like. All will swear to my being there from the evening of the twenty-third until today at two o'clock.'

'I did not ask for the precision of an alibi, monsieur. Is it that you felt the need to give me one?'

Ah *merde*, Henri . . .

'Why else, then, are you here, Inspector, troubling my sister?'

The detective ducked his head to signify that this might or might not have been the reason for his visit. 'Tell me about Claudine Bertrand,' he said, knowing that she had had no chance to warn Henri whether anything untoward had already been said.

St-Cyr was troubled. They looked at each other, this brother and sister, the one perhaps thirty-six years of age and the other not more than twenty-six. Alarm in Monsieur Charlebois's eyes but carefully masked by concern; nothing but concern in hers. Ah *maudit*, what were the two of them up to behind closed doors?

'Claudine was a childhood friend, Inspector. From time to time I tried to help her a little. I once gave her a job in the Dijon shop but she was unhappy away from Lyon and unsuited to the work.'

'And Madame Ange-Marie Rachline?' he asked, his voice so quiet the question startled them both.

'What does she have to do with this?' asked Henri.

There was still that hostility when questioned about Ange-Marie, even after so many years. Henri, she wanted to say. Henri, be careful. He would not look at her, he would not see the tears collecting so rapidly she was forced to excuse herself and go into the kitchen to stand before the sink with head bowed, gripping the edge of the basin.

'Henri . . . Henri . . . Dear God, please guide his tongue,' she whispered and heard:

'My sister and Ange-Marie have never seen eye to eye, Inspector. Mademoiselle Charlebois blames Ange-Marie for the situation Claudine found herself in.'

'And yourself, monsieur?'

'I did not judge. Both had been childhood friends. One

retains that special sense of loyalty. One does what one can to help and leaves judgement to God.'

'You gave Mademoiselle Claudine a supplier's bottle of perfume.'

'*Étranger*, yes. From an estate sale, It pleased her and it pleased me that it did, though I must confess I had little liking for the scent. It was much too strong. There was far too much musk and civet.'

'When did you give it to her and where?'

Ah how guarded their questions and answers were!

'In the shop on the morning of that fire. Claudine came to see me. She wanted help—financial help—to start a new life somewhere else. She was insistent but . . .'

Henri's expression was pained. The back of the left hand was touched and then the top button of his jacket . . . He could not know that Claudine had come to see her that very same afternoon. Ah no . . .

'But I had given so much in the past, Inspector, I could not give any more—there was the robbery too, you understand, and the cash that would be needed to carry on. Claudine owed me . . . A moment, please. I have the account book.'

'A moment yourself, monsieur. Please,' cautioned the detective with an upraised finger. 'A new life some place else?' he asked.

Henri gave that shrug she knew so well, that reassuring smile. 'Claudine was always short of money, Inspector, and always wanting to leave Lyon. It was nothing new, I assure you. She keeps two daughters in a convent school in Orléans. She was always saying she wanted to live closer to them but of course, with the Occupation, that was impossible. Virtually all her earnings went to them and now I shall have to take care of it for her.'

Two daughters. 'Who is the father, monsieur?'

'That . . . that I do not know nor . . . nor did I ever ask.'

Henri went over to the secretaire to pause briefly as if struck by the sight of the bracelet just lying there—how could his little sister have been so careless? Is that what he was thinking, the poor darling? wondered Martine.

Quickly he opened a drawer and found the red, morocco-bound booklet that was no bigger than one for listing telephone numbers.

The detective accepted the proffered evidence. He would note the precision of the penmanship and that, in each entry, the sum was the same. Ah yes. 'Two thousand francs to the total of one hundred and sixty-eight thousand?' he said.

'Over the past ten years, Inspector. Ever since my grandfather died and Claudine went to work for Ange-Marie at La Belle Époque.'

'She would have been twenty-two at the time; Ange-Marie twenty-four and yourself, monsieur?'

'Twenty-six but it's of no consequence.'

Though the detective kept his thoughts to himself, he would not leave things so simply defined. Ah no, he was too persistent, too dedicated, thought Martine. 'Perhaps,' he said, 'but then . . . ah then, Monsieur Charlebois, age so often has its meaning. One is older, another is much younger, and one is in between.'

Had it been wise to tell him of the money, of loans that could never be repaid?

Henri said nothing. What could he have said about those days when the three of them were young and so much had happened?

An interruption at the door brought the impasse to its close. She would let Henri do the answering. Yes, yes, it would be best to get him away from the detective.

It was Jean-Pierre and Fernand and Lorraine, her three *zazous* in dark glasses, and they had come with a little gift for their teacher. Henri was irritated and upset on seeing them at his door. He did not like their grins or constantly erratic motion. He did not value the attentions they paid his little sister and thought such an extracurricular association undignified and unprofessional of her. Yet he could be very nice to them when he wanted. Had they startled him for some other reason? she wondered. Had their presence alarmed him? He was afraid.

With difficulty and muttered apologies, he allowed them to come in and called her from the kitchen.

She would throw on an apron and seize a tea towel—would pretend to wipe her hands as she went toward them. Each removed the dark glasses and the huge cock-hats, the earmuffs of gold and orange and livid green. Ear-rings on the boys no shirts this evening but leather jackets open to the navel in spite of the freezing cold. *And* pegged trousers that exposed bare ankles and sockless feet that were tucked into laceless shoes which had not a trace of polish. Lorraine was opening the umbrella that was always carried closed in the rain to infuriate passing adults who had none. There was long, greasy hair on all three of them. Lorraine's pleated skirt was so short her shapely thighs half exposed their pinkish blush of frost. They'd all get pneumonia. They were rebellious youth unleashed and wanting to show the Occupiers and everyone else exactly what they thought of them. But ah *mon Dieu, mon Dieu,* they were so lovely! Her two heroes and her little heroine.

St-Cyr watched the greetings of the sister with interest. While the brother remained aloof and uncomfortable, the sister hugged each of them, kissed their cheeks and made a fuss.

'Come in . . . come into the kitchen and warm yourselves. A little gift . . . Ah, you shouldn't have. What is it?' And so the chatter went until the three of them clutched mugs of herbal tea that had been sweetened with a purée of chestnuts.

'Inspector . . .' began Charlebois, hoping to get him back into the salon.

'Ah no, monsieur. For me, the kitchen is fine.'

The teenagers were ebullient. They threw themselves around in states of sloppiness but were grateful for their teacher's warmth and admiration. 'A detective,' said the one called Jean-

Pierre with awe. 'Paris . . . Monsieur, permit me, please, to ask are we . . .'

'Are we like the *zazous* of the clubs on the Champs-Élysées? The Ledoyen?' asked Lorraine with a seriousness one found disconcerting.

He would take them all in with a sweeping glance. He would exercise caution and preach patience to himself. 'Very,' he said, finding the will to grin. 'Exactly as those I've seen at the Colisée, the Bar Select and other places.'

This set them to talking rapidly amongst themselves while their teacher basked in the praise and fluttered around with ersatz biscuits of some sort. Fig perhaps.

Fernand, a pimply-faced youth of fifteen, produced Swiss chocolate with a flourish. Jean-Pierre ignored the loot and offered real coffee and cigarettes.

Lorraine had several tubes of lipstick to display. All the items were offered for sale and this was quietly understood.

'Inspector . . .' began Mademoiselle Charlebois. 'It's Christmas Day. Please do not be too hard on them. These are little things, isn't that so? Lyon, it . . . it is not under your . . . your . . . well, you know. The préfet, he . . .'

'My jurisdiction, is that what you mean, mademoiselle?'

'Martine, how could you?'

'Henri, the coffee was to be for you, the chocolate also.'

'And the lipstick?' asked the brother sharply. 'You know how much I hate the sight of your wearing such things. It cheapens you.'

'And the present?' asked the Sûreté, for it still lay on the table. Clearly the students were working the 'System D'*, making do and taking care of themselves by playing the black market. Every lycée had its System Ds and the *zazous* were a part of it. A chicken for the pot, a roast of veal perhaps or packet of salt—clothes, the leather jackets, the girl's skirt . . . all were products of the system.

*from the verb *se débrouiller*, to manage

'The present . . . ?' he said again, seeing them look questioningly at each other while the brother watched them with alarm.

'Open it, please,' breathed the detective, 'or would you prefer I did?'

It was the girl who kept her eyes focused on the thing while Monsieur Charlebois stood across the table from her, frantically trying to get her to give him a hint as to what it contained. She refused to raise her lovely blue eyes to meet his gaze but whispered, 'Mademoiselle Charlebois, our Assistant Professor of Germanic studies, must open it, Monsieur the Detective from Paris. It is just a little something. It is nothing much.'

'Henri, you open it,' said his sister but the brother refused and went into the other room saying, 'You should be ashamed. They should not have come here.'

Upset by his words, her pale lips quivered, and her fingers shook as she undid the wrapping and tried not to damage the paper.

There was a small cardboard box and, inside this in tissue, a ring of keys that made her gasp and burst into tears of relief and gratitude. 'My keys!' she blurted, fondly touching each of her students and hugging them. 'The keys to the Lycée du Parc, Inspector. I dropped them some place. I never lose a thing—I've never lost anything until . . . Ah, I was so upset and distracted—the examinations, their grades. My Director, le Docteur Taillander, he . . . he would have dismissed me, had he known of my carelessness.'

She clutched the keys in her left hand, held them to her lips and, shutting her eyes with relief, bowed her head to steady herself.

The *zazous* reached out to her comfortingly. They were distressed and embarrassed at the depths of her relief. Perhaps they had not known she would have been dismissed. Perhaps one of them had taken the keys and now all three were united in the shame of returning them.

It would be some moments before she recovered. St-Cyr signalled to them to leave and went with them to the front door. 'Who found the keys and where?' he asked. 'When were they lost and when was their absence first discovered? Come, come, answer truthfully.'

It was Jean-Pierre who reluctantly confessed. 'I found the keys last Tuesday, Inspector, beside the lake in the park. There is a pavilion which is used for the band concerts. It . . .'

'It is one of our meeting-places, Inspector,' said Lorraine, not looking up. 'The keys were lying in the snow below the railing.'

Ah *mon Dieu*, what had they been up to? 'Tuesday the twenty-second and you have let her suffer all this time? When did she lose them and for how long has she had to live in fear their loss would be discovered?'

'A week prior to that Tuesday,' offered the boy Fernand. 'We searched everywhere, Inspector.'

A week! The fifteenth . . . 'And yet you kept the keys a further three days knowing how distressed she was?'

'Only to make the present more suitable,' said Jean-Pierre.

'Pah! If I were your father, I would soon straighten you out! Wearing rubbish like that. Dealing on the black market. Now get out of here. Be home and indoors well before curfew.'

'It was only a set of keys, Inspector,' said the girl.

He stepped out into the hall after them and closed the door behind him. He knew he was edgy and unreasonable—that he'd defied authority himself as a boy and had paid dearly for it, but this . . . this was something else, something so deliberate it hurt. 'One hundred and eighty-three are dead, my little birds. Three others also. Some sixty are still in hospital, some so badly burned they will be horribly disfigured for the rest of their lives. At present, I do not know if the keys have even the slightest importance, but if they have, you had best tell me everything and do so immediately.'

They objected. They said the keys could have nothing to do with the fire, that he must be crazy.

They begged him not to tell their teacher. They said she must have set them on the pavilion's railing and that she'd been upset and distracted for days prior to their being lost.

Days prior to the fifteenth. The Weidlings had arrived on the tenth. Claudine had had to get away . . .

When he returned to the flat, the sister had excused herself and gone to her room, the brother held his coat, scarf and hat at the ready.

The desire to ask where Charlebois had been on that Tuesday of the lost keys, and from then until the finding of them on the twenty-second was there, but for now had best be left. 'Monsieur, if it would not be too much trouble, could I ask that you drive me to Number Six, rue du Boeuf? I must take another look at the flat of your childhood friend and link up with my partner, Hermann Kohler of the Gestapo.'

'Is this necessary?'

Ah *mon Dieu*, the guarded anger. 'Absolutely, monsieur. Lyon is a city in fear and we must put a stop to it before there is another fire.'

'Don't the Sûreté and the Gestapo grant their detectives transport?'

'Not since some gangsters shot my Citroën all to pieces in Montmartre. It's still under repair.'

'Then I will drive you to Claudine's and answer any further questions you might have of me.' Ah damn, the Sûreté had found out about the car.

'Just the ride to save time, monsieur. Perhaps if you could wait in the street outside Number Six, then the lift over to the temporary morgue? We can talk on the way. You can fill me in on Mademoiselle Bertrand and the cross of Father Adrian, I think, and then a little more about your sister, the Lycée du Parc and her studies to become an assistant professor. Yes, that would be excellent!'

Questions, there were always questions, thought St-Cyr. The streets were treacherous and the cold could easily cause the car to stall. Left alone inside, the two of them would talk as the windows iced up. Ah yes. Already the cinematographer's cameras were rolling but there would be no floodlights, only darkness in the rue du Boeuf outside the house where a friend had been killed to keep her silent.

'Oh by the way, Monsieur Charlebois. My compliments to your sister for the tastefully simple way she has decorated the fir tree in your salon. Those gilded glass pears are exquisite and must be very old. Venetian, I believe.'

Bishop Frédéric Dufour was not happy. A busy man on this busiest of days, he threw off his vestments, tossing hat, robe and dangling scarf—was it called a scarf?—into a chair. 'That vile old woman, Inspector Kohler. May God have mercy on her. Saint Peter will have to cut out her tongue if the Devil doesn't get her.'

He spotted the dregs of Calvados and one dirty glass. The detective still held the other.

Snatching up the scrubwoman's glass, he threw it into the fire. 'The bitch!' he swore. 'I'll show her. This is the last time, absolutely, that she violates the sanctity of my study! Vermin . . . did she tell you my church was full of lice, eh? Well, she's the one who is carrying them!'

'Hey, calm down, eh? She was only doing what I asked.'

Dufour clenched a fist then dropped it, realizing that Philomena Cadieux would never change. 'Father Adrian was a good man, Inspector, a true servant of Christ. Please don't let the scandals of a wicked imagination sully a character that was without blemish.'

Kohler removed his scruffy shoes from the desk and helped himself to the last of the Calvados. He would give the bishop a moment to clear the cobwebs of religion.

'Inspector, what is it you want?'

That was better. He'd let him sit down behind his desk, would take in the florid, frost-burned cheeks and carefully brushed iron-grey hair, the red nose and horn-rimmed glasses. The crinkly smile, the open-handed gesture of . . .

'So, what is a little misunderstanding among friends, eh, Inspector? Mademoiselle Aurelle . . . that one believed the spirit of the devil was within her flesh and that her body had to be purged. Mademoiselle Bertrand . . . Ah with a woman like that, what is one to do? Father Adrian administered to his little flock, that is all.'

Son of a bitch, Mademoiselle Claudine Bertrand had been among them! 'What about Mademoiselle Martine Charlebois, Bishop? Was Father Adrian also her confessor?'

Ah *merde*! 'What . . . what has she to do with this, my son?'

Kohler flicked his empty glass over the bishop's left shoulder. As it shattered among the flames, Dufour leapt, then settled down. 'You tell me, Bishop. My partner found her name on the list at the temporary morgue. Did Father Adrian hear her confessions, too, and is that perhaps why he died?'

'Monsieur . . . Monsieur, what is it you are saying?'

Dufour looked positively ill. 'It's Inspector, Bishop. Gestapo HQ, Paris Central.'

'Yes, yes, *Inspector*, as you wish. Father Adrian was confessor to several. Mademoiselle Martine Charlebois was among them but her brother, Henri, he came to me.'

'Good. Then start by telling me about him. We'll work from there. Did he know Claudine Bertrand, Bishop? Claudine is also dead.'

'Lost in the fire?'

Perplexed about it, was he? Kohler hunted among the clutter for the bishop's cigarette box and relieved it of its contents. 'Not in the fire, Bishop.'

The bushy, dark eyebrows lifted questioningly behind the horn rims. 'Ah, not in the fire,' *Maudit*, what was one to do? wondered Dufour. 'Er . . . how . . . how did she die, monsieur?'

'Inspector.'

'Inspector, how did she die?'

'First tell me if Henri Charlebois knew Claudine?'

'Yes, yes, he knew her from a long time ago. Now, please, how did she die?'

'Silently and without a struggle. I just had a call on your line and the other two, Bishop, so Madame Charlady may have listened in. Vasseur, the coroner, says that I am to tell my partner Claudine Bertrand died of carbon monoxide poisoning. Trouble is, it wasn't an accident. When she breathed in what she thought were the steaming vapours of friar's balsam, she took in enough CO to drop a horse.'

'Murder?'

Kohler lit up and sat there drawing on the cigarette, watching the bishop closely.

Dufour silently cursed the unmitigated arrogance of the Germans. Oh for sure, he could claim the sanctity of the confessional, but this one, ah he wouldn't listen. Too much had happened, too many had already died but Henri ...? Henri Charlebois could have had nothing to do with it. Absolutely nothing. 'Philomena is not always correct in what she invariably states so emphatically, Inspector. It's true that someone other than Mademoiselle Aurelle might—I say might—have telephoned Father Adrian in the twilight of that terrible day. But it could not have been Mademoiselle Claudine Bertrand or even Mademoiselle Martine Charlebois since neither of them would have known of her desires for Father Adrian's person.'

'Yet someone did, Bishop. Father Adrian knew very well what was about to happen to that cinema. It's my belief, though I can't yet prove it, that he found Mademoiselle Aurelle already naked and tied to her bed. He saw for the first time perhaps that others knew only too well what he'd been up to with her, and he went downstairs and into the cinema hoping to find his accuser and beg forgiveness, only to burn in hell.'

'The anonymous letters ... the préfet has given them to your friend but they ... they can mean nothing, Inspector. Nothing! Merely the poison of the unforgiving.'

Dufour's swarthy hands favoured the edge of his desk, caressing thoughts too deep and sad to reveal. He heard, in snatches, the mumbled, secretive words of a young woman who had brushed her body with flames while thinking thoughts no girl of such a tender age should think. He knew that spying on another's confession was paramount among ecclesiastical sins and he begged God to forgive him. He had had to discover what hold Father Adrian had over those women—there'd been too many whispers, too many visits outside the duties of a bishop's secretary . . .

'Who knew him well enough to borrow a spare pair of his shoes, Bishop?'

Irritated by the interruption, Dufour left off touching the desk. 'Yes, yes, Philomena made me aware of the footprints but they could just as easily have been from the day before. She's no detective, whatever else that old bag of bones and lice might claim.'

'Tell me about the cross. Why was he given it? What favour was exacted in return?'

Mademoiselle Claudine was dead. The image of her at the age of seven came and then at the age of ten and then, alas, at the age of eighteen in the flower of her beauty. 'Monsieur Henri Masson gave it to him as I have already informed your associate, Inspector.'

'Yes, but why did he give it to him?'

The Gestapo lit another cigarette, pinching out the butt of the first and pocketing it for later use. The laws of the Church said to remain silent; the laws of humanity said that all must be revealed, that that same Claudine Bertrand, that same child had been tormented by and terrified of the beast within her. That she could not understand why God had made her the way she was and Ange-Marie and young Henri had . . . had revealed her to herself. 'Henri Masson gave the cross to Father Adrian in return for his promise to ... to watch over his ... his only grandson.'

Henri Charlebois. Ah *merde*. 'And not the boy's sister?'

'No, not the sister.'

'Was he given it to keep silent?'

'About what?'

'Bishop, you know damned well what I mean! Don't fuck about with me.'

'Then God must answer you, Inspector. When he was presented with the cross, Father Adrian did not tell me the reason for such a gift. It was Monsieur Henri Masson who felt it necessary to ask in return that I keep Father Adrian on here as my secretary.'

'Would the grandson and/or his sister have known the workings of this place?'

'Of course, but so would others. People come and go all the time. Both Father Adrian and myself and my other clerics have had many visitors in the past. Once a month we dine with close friends at the manse; others come for an apéritif or cup of tea or coffee in the afternoon. It's natural when one is at the centre of a city's religious life.'

'Tell me about the grandson, then, and his sister, Mademoiselle Martine Charlebois.'

'There's nothing to tell. Both are above reproach and I happen to know the young Monsieur Henri was not even in the city at the time of the fire.'

St-Cyr switched off the lights in Claudine Bertrand's bedroom and, parting the curtains, looked down into the darkness of the rue du Boeuf as a cold-hearted cinematographer might have done.

Henri Charlebois sat in his car waiting for him, the engine running in spite of the extreme shortage of gasoline. They'd been stopped twice on the icy streets by German patrols and, each time Charlebois had handed over his papers, the Feld-webel had noted the pass.

The antique dealer was free to come and go as he pleased long after curfew. Though he didn't offer any explanation, it was obvious he had an in with the German authorities and probably supplied some of them with antiques and works of art.

Though he had grown up with Ange-Marie Rachline and Claudine Bertrand, there was not one photograph of him in the album. Had they all been carefully sorted through on the night of Claudine's murder and all trace of her killer's past removed?

Charlebois was too close with his information, too uptight and wary and yet . . . and yet, the arrogance and the aloofness were only too typical of the well-to-do and those accustomed to dealing with them.

He should have asked him to come up here to look at those empty beds and the bowl and towel that had been used as a vaporizer. He was certain Claudine and her mother had been murdered, certain too, that her killer had been cleverer than most. Hermann might now have the answer.

Things were not right between the brother and sister. Their relationship suggested a naiveté no assistant professor should possess. Clearly the woman needed the affectionate adoration of her *zazous*, failing completely to realize they would be only too willing to use it against her.

She had spoken of her, 'family', her 'little friends', a finch and a canary. Devoted to her brother she might be, but was the relationship one of suppression and fear?

Hermann had been so certain it had been a woman in that belfry. He'd been certain, too, of a woman in the rue des Trois Maries last night, the scent of *Étranger* in his nostrils. Was it yourself, Monsieur Charlebois? he asked and said, You are finely boned, tall and thin . . . yes, yes, monsieur. The long dark eyelashes, the lack of hair on the backs of your hands—is that why you touch the left one when nervous? Do you like imper-sonating women?

Given kohl and powder, rouge and lipstick, a dress, coat, gloves, scarf and hat with its bit of veil, would the concierge here not think you Madame Rachline, or is it that you came in afterwards when he was busy elsewhere?

The Dijon alibi—would they have time to punch holes in it? Probably not, and Charlebois probably knew it too.

Then I will take him to the morgue and make him view Claudine's body, said St-Cyr silently. A positive identification, monsieur. Yes, yes, cruel though that might be. Vasseur's incision right from beneath the chin down to the sexual organs. We will look at the lungs, the heart, the stomach.

He would take him to the Lycée Ampère and make him walk among the corpses. He would break him if he could just as Charlebois, if it had been him, had inadvertently stepped on the Christmas-tree ornament Claudine must have had in her left hand before slipping off into oblivion. An ornament that had either come from his own apartment or from La Belle Époque, but also one, perhaps, that Frau Weidling had been photographed with while naked and holding it in the cup of her hands. Ah yes.

Could Charlebois have been so cruel as to have planned it all so carefully? Two women, then three, then one, a man. A Salamander.

Claudine had needed money to leave Lyon and start a new life. She had either known exactly what must happen, or had been convinced that only a meeting with Frau Weidling was planned for that cinema.

Someone had called Father Adrian to summon him. Had it been Claudine or Martine Charlebois, or Ange-Marie Rachline?

The high-heeled shoes that had been left in the belfry were of dark blue alligator, pre-war and handmade in Italy for the firm of Stadelmier und Blechner on the Leipziger Strasse. Good goods and probably the best pre-war shopping street in Berlin.

Kohler was impressed. Which Cinderella had the Salamander chosen to target by leaving the shoes up there or had she left them herself? Madame Rachline—were her feet that small? One of her girls at La Belle Époque? Claudine perhaps? Frau Kaethe Weidling née Voelker, or Mademoiselle Martine Charlebois, the girl with the bicycle?

The shoes had hardly been worn. Indeed, though they were well kept, he had the thought they'd not been worn since those other fires in 1938. They'd been bought on impulse perhaps and then hidden away. Had she been ashamed of them and what they'd shown her of herself, or had the joy of such pretty things been taken from her by those fires?

Madame Philomena Cadieux didn't want to give them up but he told her she'd better. 'You'd look ridiculous in them at your age. Right? Besides, I have to find the feet they shod.'

Oxalic acid, Louis, he said to himself as he went out into the night. A white, crystalline powder looking not unlike granulated sugar. Used as a cleaning agent and as a bleach. *When combined with sulphuric acid, it produces carbon monoxide* AND *carbon dioxide.*

Deadly if breathed in concentrations of one per cent CO, which would have been the least case, and not a hint of what was happening, poor thing.

Whoever had fed Claudine the vapours of friar's balsam had made damn certain she'd die. So, too, her mother.

But Louis would not yet know of this. 'Ah *merde*, be careful, *mon vieux*. Don't take anything for granted.'

7 'MADAME RACHLINE, IT IS ABSOLUTELY ESSENTIAL that you accompany me to the central morgue. I regret the necessity but . . .'

'But business is business, Inspector St-Cyr. Is that it?'

Ah *nom de Dieu*, had he struck a sensitive chord at last? 'Madame, a childhood friend and employee is dead. Please, I must insist. I've a car waiting.'

A car . . . 'Did she die in peace?'

What was the woman thinking? 'Yes. She would not have known.'

'Then what is the concern? For years Claudine has wanted release, Inspector. If she died in her sleep, then her soul is at rest.'

He would have to be firmer. 'Madame, murder is suspected. A positive identification is necessary of both Mademoiselle Bertrand and her mother. The law requires that you accompany me. If you refuse, then I will ask the magistrate to issue you with a summons and the préfet to provide you with the necessary escort!'

Murder . . . 'The préfet, of course. Shall I ring for him?'

The bitch!

'Or shall I come peacefully, Inspector, without further discussion?'

'Peacefully, I think. Bring an extra wrap and boots for it is very cold and will be equally so in the morgue.'

'These will have to do.' The shoes were from that other time, from the *belle époque*, of black patent leather, laced up the front and well above the ankles. Once again her jet-black hair was swept up and pinned with diamonds to match those that dangled from her ears and fastened the black velvet choker about her slender neck. A tall and splendidly elegant woman in a tight-bodiced dress of black silk crêpe that shimmered.

A girl, a maid he had never seen before, brought a hat with a bit of black veil and a ribbon. A lace scarf went over the hat and was tied beneath the chin. Then the black overcoat with its Persian lamb collar, scarf and gloves were added until she looked exactly like a painting of Tissot's.

They went out to the car and he held the front door open for her saying, 'I believe you know our driver, madame.'

There was no light with which to see her reaction, only the silhouettes of two people who had spent their summers on the beach at Concarneau with Claudine Bertrand.

St-Cyr left her to close the door while he got into the back seat. That way at least he would catch their first words.

'Ange-Marie . . .' began Charlebois. 'Forgive me. I had no other choice.'

'Nor I, Henri.'

What was it between the two of them? wondered St-Cyr. Would they drive in total silence, cold to each other, frozen to the heart?

They came to the quai Roman Rolland and the Saône. Scant blue-washed lamps, staggered at irregular intervals in the frosty darkness, revealed the pont Alphonse Juin. Once across it, Charlebois headed upriver along the quai Saint Antoine.

St-Cyr studied their silhouettes, trying to fathom what was going through their minds. They both sat so stiffly, the bad back of the one perhaps, the rigid control of the other. Had they once been lovers, had they come to hate each other, or were they united in this, a Salamander? There was a terrible strain between them that could not help but permeate the car just as the faint scent of her perfume did, although the perfume was not *Étranger*, not tonight.

'Madame Rachline, the concierge at Number Six rue du Boeuf claims he saw you return with Claudine at about ten on the night your friend died.'

Ah *merde* ... 'Is he positive, monsieur?' she asked, not turning to look at him.

'As positive as a concierge can be. You were apparently an infrequent visitor. He has said that you—'

'She was ill. I had told her to take a few nights off, Inspector, but then there she was at my door. I ... I took her home and put her to bed. What harm is there in that?'

Then Claudine had gone to her house and not to La Belle Époque ... 'None.'

'Inspector, surely Madame Rachline is not under any suspicion?'

Was it a crack in their collective armour at last? 'Everyone who had any connection with her is under suspicion, monsieur, until the deaths of Mademoiselle Claudine and her mother are cleared up and the arsonist is apprehended.'

'But ... but surely there is no connection?' said Charlebois. 'Surely Claudine had nothing to do with that fire—how could she have, if she had gone to La Belle Époque to see Madame Rachline?'

'Of course. It is a question that plagues me, monsieur. So,

madame, you took her home and put her to bed. How was her mother?'

Only pinpricks from the headlamps gave light to the road ahead. There was ice everywhere, and everywhere it was bumpy and cut by ruts. 'Her mother, like all old ladies who suffer from dementia and do not know why they are where they are or why God has put them there, was asleep.'

'Would Madame Bertrand have welcomed release, do you think?'

How carefully he had chosen his words and lowered his voice. 'From dementia, yes, Inspector. From life, no. Madame Bertrand . . . you would have to have known her from before her husband was killed in the last war. Even though I was very young, I can still remember her smile and the graceful way in which she moved. There . . . there was always a quiet dignity to her, Inspector, a . . . a . . .'

'A radiance that encompassed everyone who came within her presence.'

'Yes. Yes, Henri is correct, monsieur. A radiance. Thank you for saying it, Henri.'

Saying it at last—was that it? Frost clouded the windscreen and iced up the side windows. Though there was a heater in the Ford sedan, it was not of much use. Charlebois was forced to lean forward over the steering wheel, gripping it tightly. This allowed her to study him without turning her head.

Again St-Cyr found himself trying to fathom what was going through their minds. Had she stretched out a foot to warn Charlebois of the danger—Be careful what you say, Henri. The detective may know more than he is letting on—or to signal something else, something far more direct?

'Madame, the friar's balsam . . . Did your friend find it gave relief?'

They were on the quai Saint Vincent now, right at the foot of Croix Rousse, whose steep beehive of tenements, narrow streets and *traboules* the inspector would know well enough to realize their potential for escape. The road was treacherous. One simple mistake and Henri would skid off to the left and go through the railing and down over the bank into the river. An accident ... an accident ... They'd be at the morgue soon. Would she be able to keep control of her emotions? she wondered.

The detective asked again about the balsam, ah *merde*! 'Yes. Yes, a minor relief, Inspector. Claudine's chest was very bad. If it didn't improve I was going to have to get her into hospital. There was the problem of her mother but someone could be hired to sit with Madame Bertrand during the days. I . . . I had worked it all out in my mind, and of course, I should have seen it coming.'

Death, but not of the two of them, was that it? 'When you took her home from La Belle Époque, madame, did you stop anywhere along the way?'

Had the detective not realized Claudine had come to see her at the house, and not at La Belle? Was it too much to hope for?

'A pharmacy?' asked Henri, suddenly straightening to ease his back and causing her to look sharply at him.

'A pharmacy,' muttered St-Cyr, angered by the intrusion for it had warned her of the trap.

'Yes. We went along to the pharmacy just before it closed. Monsieur Roy will remember. A bottle of the balsam and . . . and two aspirins—I begged him for more, but he insisted on the ration tickets and a doctor's certificate of illness, and I . . . I had no wish to take Claudine back to La Belle for the aspirins I had in my . . . my room. She was coughing terribly and had lost a shoe.'

There was no sign of Louis at the city's central morgue. *Verdammt!* Where the hell was he?

Kohler yanked open the door of the bishop's black Citroën sedan, and, fuming, got in behind the wheel again. He'd been positive Louis would show up here. Louis would want to know what had caused the deaths of Claudine and her mother. Louis wouldn't leave a thing like that alone. Perhaps he had telephoned Vasseur and already had the news.

There was no comfort in the thought! 'I know you, Louis. *Gott im Himmel*, imbecile! You were on your way here to find out but something's happened to you!'

Merde! What was he to do? Go to Barbie for help and confess to setting that little fire, or go to the temporary morgue again or back to La Belle Époque?

Lighting yet another of the bishop's cigarettes, he leaned on the steering wheel and stared through the half-moon of frostless glass. Claudine Bertrand had been gutted and stitched. Blood caught in her crotch though she'd been hosed down. Clots of it under her arms among the thick black hairs. Cigarette burns all over her body, some old, some new and others far too recent for comfort. She'd had a child, at least one, had had her appendix out, an old scar.

The shoes from the belfry could not possibly have fitted her. God, he hated having to look at corpses, especially those of young women. The shoes had been far too expensive in any case.

Impatiently he glanced at his wrist-watch. Christmas Night and now nearly a quarter to nine Berlin time and still no Louis and no supper. He'd call the Hotel Bristol and find out if Louis was there. Maybe Leiter Weidling would know something, maybe that wife of his if she wasn't too busy pleasuring herself.

He'd call the Préfecture and the temporary morgue. He'd call around but had the feeling it wasn't going to be of any use.

Leiter Weidling had 'not returned since this morning early. What are we to do with all the people he ordered to stay in the bar?'

'Feed and water them—drinks on the house, understand? Then send them home in a taxi or else.'

'Frau Weidling went out several hours ago—about 4 p.m. perhaps and has not returned.'

Four p.m. . . . 'Don't tell her I called. Just say it was Klaus. She'll know who you mean.'

Louis wasn't at the temporary morgue and 'hasn't been seen here since this afternoon.'

Kohler got back into the bishop's car. Nine damned o'clock and no sign of the Frog! *Gott im Himmel*, what had happened to him?

Spinning the tyres, he pivoted the car and shot out to the quai Joseph Gillet, skidding as he turned downstream. Then he paused to rip the black-out tape from the headlamps. There, that was better. No sand on the roads—a skating rink! but no traffic either, so that was okay.

When he reached the quai Saint Vincent, he slowed to a crawl, then brought the car to a gently skidding stop at a bend in the river just below the Fort Saint-Jean Barracks. There were four work-horses on the road ahead and each of them pulled at a black and ugly length of logging chain. A car had almost reached the top of the embankment. A four-door, dark blue Ford sedan.

'Louis . . . ?'

There was no one inside.

The place Terreaux was dark and all but deserted but some snow fell and there was contrast. Beyond Bartholdi's fountain, the gaping roof of the cinema cried out to the ghostly pallor of the sky, and the stench of wet plaster, ashes and death was everywhere.

Kohler stood alone beside the bishop's car. There were scavengers rooting among the ruins, now that all the bodies had been removed. In anger, he drew his gun but at a shout, turned suddenly away.

Again the shout came, and then again from near the Hôtel de Ville. People were gathering. Someone was pointing. Distant— far distant on the cold, hard air came the wild clanging of pumper trucks. He began to run toward the crowd. He slipped and fell and nearly lost his gun, got up and carried on. The sky glowed. In a pillar of fire somewhere on the hillside of Croix Rousse, flames leapt. Shit!

'The passage Mermet!' cried someone, pointing madly. "The rue Pouteau . . . No, no, the montée de la Grande Côte!'

'The montée du Perron,' shouted another. 'The Théâtre des Clochards Célestes.' The Theatre of the Celestial Beggars.

A pumper truck raced by, heading for the quais. Another and another followed. All points were converging on the fire but the hill was steep, the roads sheet ice and narrow—some merely sets of stairs or worse still, tunnels, passageways . . .

Again he ran. Again he fell and, when he got to the bishop's car, he thought he'd never reach the fire in time. Louis . . . had Louis been caught in the flames? Louis trapped. Louis roasted. Louis crying out, H . . . E . . . R . . . M . . . A . . . NN! Why have you not covered for me?

When he left the car at the foot of the rue Pouteau, Kohler left it against an iron light standard, leaking antifreeze all over the place and hissing steam.

Everything was bathed in a warm glow and he felt it against his face long before he reached the flames. 'Louis . . . ?' he gasped. 'Louis . . . '

St-Cyr distrustfully watched his two charges as they gazed at the uncovered corpse of Claudine Bertrand in the cold, damp silence of the Institut Médico-Légal where all sounds echoed. Ange-Marie Rachline was impassive, the blush of frost deep against the natural pallor, for he had forced them both to walk through the night from the scene of the accident—had it really been an accident? He was all but certain one or both of them had put the car into the railing and over the embankment but not before, may God be thanked, they had managed to scramble out.

Like her, Charlebois could not take his eyes from their childhood friend, but unlike her, he sought each detail and repeatedly passed uncertain eyes from head to toe and back again.
Breathing quietly, thinking what? That it was all over, Claudine? That there would never be a time such as they had had at
Concarneau, never another fire? Was he making her that
promise as he searched her naked body and did not shrink
from it?

Was he the Salamander or was Ange-Marie, or were both
of them?

At last Charlebois spoke. 'May I touch her?' he asked in a
whisper.

'Henri . . . ?' gasped Ange-Marie in alarm. 'Leave her in
peace. She's suffered enough.'

'But . . .'

Ah *mon Dieu*, thought St-Cyr, such anguish in the eyes, the
hand faltering then dropping uselessly to the side. A former
lover? he wondered.

The marble on which she lay was blue and cold and sloped
at her feet to an ugly drain. It was all too evident that she bore
the scars of innumerable liaisons. She had been touched again
and again by fire. The smell of sweat, urine, vaginal secretions
and perfume would have mingled with that of male or female
tobacco smoke, candlewax and searing flesh. The biting back as
fear raced to the exquisiteness of orgasm.

He would ask it softly. 'What really happened on the beaches
at Concarneau? Did one of you hold her down while the other
burnt her, or did she beg you both to do it and did you then find
pleasure in it?'

'How *dare* you? She's dead!'

A reaction at last, a shattering of Madame Rachline's impassive emptiness. Colour racing to join that of the frost, her dark
eyes blazing fiercely.

'Inspector, is this really necessary?' asked Charlebois. 'It's

Claudine. We've identified her and her mother. Now will you kindly let us go on our separate ways?'

'Please do not be so polite, monsieur. I only want to know which of you killed her. Was it you, Madame Rachline, or was it yourself, Monsieur Charlebois, or the two of you together?'

It was Ange-Marie who smirked and said sarcastically, 'Or neither of us?'

'Madame, you were the last to see her alive. The concierge will swear to it!'

'She died in her sleep, Inspector,' said the antique dealer. 'You've no proof she was murdered. No proof whatsoever that either of us was involved.'

Ah *nom de Jésus-Christ*, how could Charlebois remain so aloof and calm? 'Then tell me, monsieur, exactly how it was at Concarneau and why, please, your grandfather thought it necessary to leave such a valuable thing as this to Father Adrian Beaumont?'

Ah, damn him! The detective dangled the cross of the Family Rouleau above Claudine's middle. He was deliberately trying to unsettle them, thought Charlebois.

'She . . . she was . . .' began Ange-Marie.

'Special?' asked the detective, tossing his head back a little in agreement. 'She was your friend, Madame Rachline. Since when does one treat one's friend in such a fashion?'

'Ange-Marie, we don't need to stay here. I was in *Dijon*, Inspector!'

He would let them think about it. He would take out his pipe and begin to pack it. Yes, yes, that would be . . . ah *merde*! No tobacco when most needed!

They watched as he self-consciously tucked pipe and pouch away. They stood at the foot of the slab, at each corner, brother and sister perhaps. The resemblance was uncanny but, had he not seen them like this, doubt would most certainly have crossed his mind. The same dark eyes, the same finely boned features. Both tall and thin, both with essentially the same build and the same jet-black hair.

'Inspector . . . ?' began Madame Rachline.

Reluctantly he had to say it. 'Yes, yes, you may go for now. Please do not leave the city.'

Outside the morgue they could not fail to notice the orange-red glow in the sky above Croix Rousse nor the billowing plumes of smoke and sparks. Both held their breath and let their pulses race. Both were fascinated—mesmerized—yet deeply troubled and uncertain.

It was Charlebois who started off toward the fire though it must be nearly two kilometres away. It was Madame Rachline who said, 'Now are you satisfied?'

'Of what?' demanded St-Cyr hotly.

'Of his innocence, Inspector. His innocence.'

The building was tall and narrow and sandwiched between others. Five storeys high and a raging inferno. No trucks could get close enough to use their turntable ladders so hand-ladders had had to be used. There were men on the roof-tops, men half-way up the front of the building pouring the water in and trying to contain the fire or climbing higher and higher. Some on the staircase at the back, some inside in the smoke-filled corridors. People being rescued, some still ready to jump. A child was dropped, the little bundle falling . . . falling . . . Kohler began to run. He didn't think, he just ran and slipped and ran and slipped and threw out his arms yelling, 'Please, God. Please, God,' in German at the top of his lungs.

The kid hit him in a smothering cloud of flannelette and he went down hard hugging it to himself only to hear it crying.

Stunned, he got up, drenched and cold and tripping over the hoses. A canvas tarpaulin was being stretched but would the parents jump?

Bathed in the terrible light, he held the baby up to them and watched as the woman squeezed out of the attic window to plummet like a stone, her night-dress billowing above her head to leave her naked until she missed the net. Ah damn.

Then the husband leapt. His legs and arms seemed so useless, the hairy scrotum and bare ass almost comic. He took no time at all and he, too, missed the net.

Kohler touched the kid's forehead. The little tyke seemed only to wonder what all the noise and excitement was about. 'Monsieur . . . Monsieur,' said a young woman, 'please let me have him. I knew them a little, yes? Both were not from these parts, you understand, but from Belgium, from Brugge, I think.'

He understood and nodded sadly. Ah *merde*, to have come all this way through the blitzkrieg of 1940 only to die like that. 'Look after him, eh? Here, wait. No, no, I insist.'

He thrust a roll of bills into her hand and would not take no for an answer. Then he went back to the fire to help with one of the hoses. Louis . . . There was no sign of Louis.

Later, and with a roar, the roof of the tenement caved in and everyone turned in shocked surprise to back away, for the men up there in the floodlights had disappeared to the muffled gasp of the crowd.

Robichaud coughed blood and vomited. Down on his hands and knees near one of the pumper trucks, he doubled up to drag in a breath. Flashbulbs popped as he pitched over. His mouth opened and closed in agony. He was wallowing on ice, desperately trying to get up, desperately trying to breathe.

Again there was a cough, a ragged drawing in of the chest as he lay among the hoses, two of which had sprung leaks and now pissed streams across him. One of his men pushed through the black leather trench coats and jackboots of the Propaganda Staffel to sit him up. Another tore at his things and got his chest and shoulders free of the heavy garments.

He looked at them once, his eyes drifting numbly up into the flashbulbs before he passed out.

Then the flames began gradually to die as those who were left refused to leave their stations. Sweat sharpened the tension in their faces, etching the streaks of soot, grease, ashes and tears. One man had broken his right hand which was now useless to him, the hose tucked under that arm. Another had received a gash on the forehead. There was blood in his eyes and it kept blinding him. Two were burned by hot coals under their gauntlets and threw these off to seize the nozzles with bare hands. No one had had time to remove the bodies of the child's parents or to cover them.

Water rushed away and down the street, cascading over stone steps to freeze elsewhere, carrying charred wood and plaster, feathers, too, and straw ticking that had failed to ignite until caught in the updraught and charred to settle slowly among the constant rain of ash.

Mirrored in the water were the flames and the moving shadows. And when he lifted his head to look uphill again, Kohler first saw the drain down the centre of the street, then the stone stairs going up to the next level, the crowd, some in blankets huddled against the walls, then the rest of it, a shell.

His view was momentarily blocked and he saw Frau Weidling staring raptly at the blaze. He knew she loved it, knew it so clearly it angered him and he began to move toward her only to be held back.

It was Louis.

'A moment, Hermann. Please, *mon vieux*. It gratifies me to find you alive.'

'Me? But I thought you were—'

'Later, eh? For now let us observe.'

Bundled in her fur coat, hands in the pockets, Frau Weidling stood apart, the rich, dark auburn hair free of any hat, the dark grey-blue eyes alive with intense excitement. Quick to follow every detail, she searched the roof-tops where men with hoses clung precariously. She held her breath at a shout as one of them slipped—gasped in awe along with the crowd as he dangled over the edge, hanging by the thread of a slack hose.

As the man was pulled to safety, she gave another gasp, more of a sigh perhaps and hunched her shoulders, hands pressed against her thighs, hugging herself.

Then she made her way through the gap in the crowd until she stood in front of it to watch her husband at work.

Leiter Weidling basked in the flashbulbs of the Propaganda Staffel. They caught him pointing up at an adjacent roof and motioning the men to direct their hoses more steeply downwards. They had him holding brandy to the lips of an exhausted Robichaud who looked like a drunk that had been rolled in the gutter, blood running from his injured hand. They caught him with his beautiful wife and then they dragged Kohler into the limelight and thrust the child back into his arms.

Baffled and looking like a vagrant on the run, Hermann stood stupidly beside the still-collapsed form of Robichaud. Not satisfied, the Propaganda Staffel had him risk life and limb to stand with the kid between the bodies of its parents.

Another and another photograph. 'Now crouch, please. *Ja, ja*, that is good, Herr . . . What's his name? Make sure you get it down.'

Then one of the hero with Frau Weidling and her husband, and a final shot of the detective with the child he had just 'adopted'.

'Is it a boy or a girl, Hermann?' asked St-Cyr.

'Piss off or you're its uncle, eh? The Hotel Bristol, Louis. Weidling insists. An emergency meeting. They're taking Robichaud with them for the fireworks. Frau Dazzle's car is at the foot of the street near where I left the bishop's.'

Hermann thrust the child into the arms of the woman who had wanted it and said he was sorry the *flics* had roughed her up and stolen the money. 'Hey, I'll get it back for you, okay?' he shouted, but by then she had turned away to vanish into the crowd.

Eighteen had died. Eighteen. At 4.10 a.m., the grand salon of the Prince Albert Suite was in an uproar. Perhaps twenty of the powers that be in Lyon had been called to the meeting. Waiters came and went while she, Frau Kaethe Weidling, stood with her seat pressed against the door between times, stood in a deeply V'd, long-sleeved dress of black silk Charmeuse that was covered with black sequins.

Like bantam cockerels or little boys whose play had erupted into battle, they cursed each other finding blame where there was none. They shook their fists, gesticulated violently, got very red in the face as only middle-aged and older men will do. Spilled drink, dropped half-eaten sausage on the carpet. Squashed olives, bread, oysters, pâté, cake and anchovies underfoot without caring in clouds of tobacco smoke.

And all the time she watched them, one or another would flick a glance doubtfully her way to see her trapped with her hands pressed flatly against the door on either side of her. They'd see the cleavage of her dress open to them. Lust and consternation in their startled glimpses, the bumbling fools. Johann's wife, yes, yes, my little men. Leiter Weidling's beautiful young wife!

Johann, in his dark blue uniform with all its ribbons and medals, was right in the midst of them. Johann was not going to back down one millimetre, so good—yes, that is good, my *liebling*. Fight for what is only right and best for the both of us. The interpreter was to one side of him; Herr Kohler, showered and draped in a blanket, was to the other, looking very sleepy now. A hero of the moment, soon to be forgotten once the newspapers had gone on to other things. Would Berlin want him home on a visit, to cheering crowds and an adoring wife?

Herr Kohler of the Benzedrine tablets whose wall-eyed gaze from too much cognac had demonstrated extreme exhaustion as he had tried to take the tablets from her bedside table where she had shaken them out of the bottle he had had in his jacket pocket. Had had among other things, yes, such as those he had taken from the cinema fire, those the Obersturmführer Barbie would be most certainly interested in. Incriminating papers. Railway schedules, the locations of tunnels ... Resistance papers.

Kohler had been naked and hadn't cared if she saw the long red welt from a rawhide whip, the shrapnel scars and old bullet wounds or the thumb that had recently been bitten and stitched. He'd known she couldn't have cared less about his nakedness, that for her it had meant nothing.

His friend, St-Cyr, had removed the pills and had refused to let him take any more of them. It was only as St-Cyr had brushed past her that she had realized he'd been in Johann's room all along, looking among her husband's things. And now? she asked. Why now he studied everyone, herself especially, with an intensity that frightened. What was he really thinking? That she had caused the fires, that she could only attain sexual arousal and orgasm through fire?

There was a sudden lull in the uproar. Fragments of talk were broken off and then ... 'You're dismissed! *Dismissed!*' shouted the mayor, furiously wiping his moustache as the translator gave it all loudly to Johann. 'Incompetent! Another fire and then another, eh? Ah yes, Robichaud, me, I say it to your face. You are *out!*'

The blanket slipped from Herr Robichaud's shoulders as he leapt from his chair past Johann to shake a wounded hand in the mayor's face, and she didn't know whether to laugh out loud or clap. '*Always* you side with Guillemette, Antoine. *Always* you are in the pocket of someone. Well, to hell with you both! That fire was not the same. It had too hot a start. How many times must I tell you?'

Too hot a start ...

'Hot or cold,' shouted the mayor, 'what is the difference? You have not stopped the Salamander.' This, too, was translated.

'Me? *Me?*' shouted Robichaud, using both hands to indicate himself as the blanket slipped completely away to reveal the

barrel chest, chunky hips and stalwart stance. 'Hey, my fine collabos, it's my job to put the fires out!'

'And to prevent them,' snorted the préfet, smirking viciously
at such a stupid, stupid burst of patriotic idiocy. 'Collabos,
Julien? Come, come, we have invaluable assistance at hand.
Let us use it.'

Several grunted agreement. '*Never!*' shouted Robichaud.
'Not while I draw breath!'

'Then stop breathing,' shouted Charette, a councillor from
the Croix Rousse.

'*Yes!*' shouted another. 'Leave the room and let us get on with
things!'

His muscles rippling, Robichaud pushed his way through
them and when he reached the man, the buttocks and thighs
tightened as the feet were planted. He didn't hesitate but flat-
tened him with a fist.

Then he turned on them all, a naked savage in a rage, blood
running freely down his arm. 'Bastards!' he shouted. 'You want
a scapegoat, eh? Then begin by asking why that fire began *after*
the concierge had checked the building for the night? Did the
Salamander hide inside and then leave or was a starter planted
that would do the job?'

'Wasn't there gasoline?' shouted someone derisively.

Robichaud ignored him. 'The fire began in the attic, in an
unused room that had been let to a young woman the day after
the cinema fire.'

A young woman . . .

'And the gasoline?' asked Johann through the interpreter—
she could see how determined he was to let Robichaud hang
himself just like the ridiculous fruit of a flaccid little penis that
dangled between the marble-hard thighs of the Frenchman.

'There was gasoline, perhaps,' grunted the savage begrudgingly. 'Ah, it's too early to say. When morning comes, we'll have
a look.'

'I will,' said Johann. 'For now, I think you've said enough.'

The look was swift and dark as this was translated, the reaction fast. 'Three of my best men have died, monsieur,' seethed Robichaud, so near to tears she had to smile. 'Fathers all of them. A dozen mouths that will have to be provided for, now that their dear papas are no longer with us.'

'They were doing their duty. The Fatherland will take care of them,' said Johann tersely.

'And their wives?' shouted Robichaud. 'Hey, my friend with the interpreter, me, I have yet to tell their wives they no longer have husbands.'

'Then get dressed and do so.'

Ah *nom de Jésus-Christ*! They'd kill each other, thought St-Cyr.

Robichaud clenched his fists in utter frustration but never in defeat. 'You were right behind the first of my pumper trucks, monsieur. How is this, please?'

Weidling stood right up to him. 'I was at the Préfecture going through the records of known arsonists when I heard the alarm.'

'And that wife of yours?' demanded the savage hotly.

'Dining with the Obersturmführer Barbie and friends.'

'And did you find anything among the préfet's records?'

'Don't be so mule-headed, Herr Robichaud. If you had acted properly, the deaths in the cinema fire would have been far less.'

The bastard! thought St-Cyr.

'And this most recent fire, monsieur?' demanded Robichaud. 'Is it that I did not act properly? Well, come, come, monsieur. Answer me, please. You're the expert.'

'You acted properly but I must question your methods.'

Ah *merde*! thought St-Cyr.

Robichaud pointed a forefinger at all of them then stabbed it repeatedly in Weidling's direction before wagging it bitterly. 'Then understand this, my friends. That one doesn't know the city as I do nor does he have the loyalty of the men. Nor can he ask them to risk their lives or be with them when their own lan-

guage is needed most. Or is it, Herr Weidling, that you intend
to take along an interpreter?'

St-Cyr attempted to hand the fire chief the blanket but it was
brushed aside.

'You think that I am with the Resistance,' said Robichaud to
the préfet, 'that that is why Élaine and I were in the cinema
on the night of the fire. You think that, to save the city and
pacify the Occupier, a sacrifice should be made. All of you ache
for blood. Then let me tell you—no, no, Monsieur Barrault,
please do not interrupt. The Théâtre des Célestins is in
Presqu'île, in your very own district. Listen carefully, my friend.
A hot start means an igniter that burns with a very high temperature. Any rubbish that is nearby also flashes into flame
because the heat of the starter raises it well beyond the ignition
temperature. Oh for sure, trailers of gasoline may well have
been used, and perhaps one ran down the central staircase from
the attic, all of which implies, my friends, that the Salamander
must have gained entry to the building twice or maybe even
three times.'

Someone at the back of the room demanded that Robichaud
explain. Johann was going to give Herr Robichaud every opportunity to make a fool of himself. Suicide . . . would Klaus Barbie
really organize such a thing to silence the savage for ever? she
wondered.

'First,' said Robichaud fiercely, 'a room is rented and the
device then put in place, either on that day or subsequently.
Another visit, perhaps at nine thirty or ten in the evening, is
used to activate the starter and then lay down the trailer. Gasoline was smelled by more than one of the tenants but for myself,
I know only too well how confused and terrified victims can be.
Our very mention of gasoline during the preliminary ques-
tioning could easily have caused them to believe they had
smelled it.'

Lost in thought, Johann reached for his glass but decided

abruptly not to touch it. 'Phosphorus?' he grunted—only that one word. She held a breath.

The interpreter translated but there was no need. Robichaud agreed with hesitation, revealing doubt, but then more strongly, as if now convinced he'd best be firm, he said, 'Yes, it is my belief that phosphorus was used as the starter. This very quickly burned through the old floorboards and then the fire was able to race along between the joists and up the inside of the walls. It got a good start, my friends, because it was out of sight until it was too late to save the building. For me, though I know you will not listen, this indicates that gasoline was not used.'

Begrudgingly Johann nodded agreement and she couldn't understand why he would do so and was hurt by this. 'One places the phosphorus in a small bag of water and hangs it up,' he said. 'So long as the phosphorus is under water, the air cannot get at it and there is no problem in storing it safely. The arsonist then punctures the bag with a needle and lets the water drip slowly out while he or she leaves the building and is soon far away before the fire starts.'

This was translated but she could not take her eyes from Johann or stop the tears from forming. Why had he said it? Why had he done this to her?

'Air then comes in contact with the phosphorus,' said Robichaud sadly. 'It flashes to a flame that is so hot, the presence of a little water on the combustibles is of no consequence.'

'Then what are we to do?' asked someone in fluent German—Kohler, had it been Kohler? she wondered.

'Has he such starters in several places?' asked another, also in German. Had it been St-Cyr?

'It was not a man who rented that attic room,' said Robichaud, looking her way. 'It was a woman.'

'Only one woman?' asked someone in German—St-Cyr again?

'Ah yes, only one and young,' said Robichaud. 'Not two as in the cinema fire. A strong German accent also, it is thought, but this must be checked. Now am I to be dismissed or am I to carry on?'

It was the préfet who, making a big show of brotherly love, praised Herr Robichaud for his tireless efforts and then turned things over to the mayor. 'Take a rest, Julien,' said that one. 'You've been on your feet for several days and nights, isn't this so? A long sleep will do you the world of good. We shall see how things go once the Salamander is caught.'

They were leaving it up to Johann.

St-Cyr opened Frau Weidling's purse and removed the papers she'd taken from Hermann's jacket. Rummaging, he found a key he could not explain and then three Wehrmacht-issue rubber condoms. Phosphorus was not easy to obtain at any time, never mind in wartime unless one dealt with incendiary explosives and their manufacture, but could she have gotten some?

Wooden matches, cigarettes, elastic bands and two twists of heavy white string followed and then a worn slip of folded paper with the address of La Belle Époque and a name: Claudine Bertrand.

Another and much newer slip of paper yielded the address of an antique shop: M Henri Masson, rue Auguste Comte, not all that far from the hotel.

A silk handkerchief smelled of the perfume *Étranger* and he had to ask, Why had they all been wearing it, if not to confuse Hermann and himself?

There were two tickets to the concert at the Théâtre des Célestins on Sunday evening. A small bottle held fluid for a cigarette lighter, but he could not find the lighter—had she lost it in the cinema? Now a magnifying glass . . . ah *merde*! What had she been planning? The use of the sun's rays in wintertime? In Lyon of all places?

Lipstick, a compact, rouge and eye shadow followed, then nail clippers and a nail file. Some Occupation marks—about ten thousand, he thought—and about twenty thousand francs. A first-class ticket for the Lyon—Paris express on the morning after the concert, at 6 a.m. Had she taken the Lyon—Dijon express on Tuesday, the twenty-second, to rob a certain shop so as to get Henri Charlebois out of the way or to provide an alibi for him?

There were books of ration tickets just in case she felt hungry and had to eat as the natives did. And four 7.65 millimetre bullets. A Beretta? he wondered.

As he closed the purse, he was momentarily lost in thought and was not conscious of her standing in the doorway to her bedroom. She grabbed the sides of the doorway to stop herself from shouting at him, and when he struck a match, she did not say a thing as he held it to the papers she had taken from Hermann.

Then he turned to look up at her as he held them over an ashtray, coning the flame upwards so as to contain the embers.

At last he said in German that was really very good for a Frenchman, 'In the morning, Frau Weidling, you will accompany me to the Lycée Ampère, then to Number Six rue du Boeuf, and then to the Croix Rousse to talk to the concierge of that tenement.'

'And if I refuse?'

'Then we will go to the Préfecture.'

'I've friends.'

'That is understood.'

Kohler tried to keep his eyes open long enough to focus on the profiles he had dug out of Leiter Weidling's briefcase. Louis was still with the woman in the other bedroom.

'Profile One: male in mid-to-late 30s. Well-educated, sophisticated ...' *ja, ja* ... 'able to move freely among established society and the leading hierarchy ...' Come on, cut the drivel, get to the meat of the thing ... 'sees fire as a means of purging the evil within himself. Is fascinated by it but does not display the usual pyromaniac . . .' Did they have to use such big words in Berlin? And here he'd thought all they understood was Heil Hitler and *Raus! Raus!* Get out! Get out! Halt or we'll shoot!

The usual firebug traits of hanging around the scene of the fire, offering help, condolences . . .' et cetera, et cetera . . . 'Prefers to read about it in the newspapers and to sustain excitement in this manner. Will most probably have kept a record of every fire he has caused.'

Ah *merde*, a library. His head dropped as he thought about it, and for perhaps ten seconds he slipped away only to awaken with a start.

'Profile Two: male'—here the age range was very broad but grouped: '18–26; 30–45; 50–70 . . .' Seventy? Again there was a lot of psychological drivel . . .' uncomfortable in established society who consider themselves his betters. Intelligent, well-educated even if at tradesman level, may speak several foreign languages fluently, a leader . . .' *ja, ja* . . . 'Ambitious, conceited, not above destroying others to get ahead, nor using others to gain position. Views himself as a hero and strives always to demonstrate this. Is totally without conscience . . . very knowledgeable in the ways of arson and clever . . . Likes to confuse and torment investigators and to demonstrate that he is far superior to them. Sexually very attracted to women who see fire as a means of sexual arousal . . .' Arousal . . .

Kohler nodded off. Flames leapt before him. The papers began to slip away. A woman was coming toward him through the flames. Rich, dark auburn hair and stunningly dark grey-blue eyes. She was . . . was rubbing her . . . her . . . 'Ah, *mon Dieu. Verdammt*, idiot! Wake up!'

Arousal . . . 'Jealousy may motivate the urge to arson, fire being used as the supreme act of revenge on a partner's illicit lover or to purge the couple, killing both of them. May often return to the scene of the fire. Plans fires well in advance, often staging them in groups of three at widely diverse points so as to further confuse and elude investigators. Favours gasoline for its shock factor, since everyone understands its explosive nature, but likes to use other means to demonstrate the fullness of his knowledge. May be sexually infatuated with an unobtainable woman or actively engaged in the sexual suppression of another such as a close relative.'

Incest? Ah *merde*. And no time to close his eyes.

Louis and Frau Weidling must have gone into the salon. Surely Louis wouldn't leave him here alone?

'Profile Three: female, age 26 to 34. Uses fire as a fetish to attain sexual gratification and climax. Returns repeatedly to the scenes of her fires. Either has a troubled conscience and is constantly tormented by what she has done, or has no conscience whatsoever and thinks only of orgasm.

'Enjoys masturbating when in the presence of fire so that she may see flames and feel their heat but never let them touch her naked body. Hence, the flames are seen here to take the place of the male erection which she totally rejects. Has strong lesbian tendencies but avoids any lasting relationship and enjoys arousal through the sight of pain in others. To this end, collects images of female murder victims.' Shit!

It was really furnace stuff. Naked, as a child, and whipped by her grandfather to cleanse her of unclean thoughts, the file he'd found in Klaus Barbie's office had indicated. Sodomized by the old bastard because it was safer to shoot the stork up there and female buttocks . . . Well, at the age of fifteen, what could one say of Prussian sea captains who'd seen it all?

A door closed at a soft word. A light in the hall went out. The blanket slipped from his shoulders as he stuffed the papers back into the briefcase and tried to close the lock . . . the lock . . .

'Johann . . . Johann, darling, is that you? I . . . I thought you had gone with the others?'

Kohler switched off the lamp and held his breath. 'Johann . . . ? Johann, St-Cyr thinks it's me.'

The door was nudged open and, though he tried to see her, his eyes were not so good. They kept on closing.

'Johann . . . Johann . . . ?'

Her perfume enveloped him. He remembered the belfry, remembered a street some place and a whorehouse with palms and lights and ostrich plumes. Corsets too.

'Johann . . . ?'

She would have a gun, a little pistol. She would find him naked and that would be it. Kohler of the Kripo shot for the attempted rape of a fire chief's young wife. Ah *merde*, Louis . . . Louis, where the fuck are you when needed most?

The saucer of saccharine was filthy. Dead flies from August were one thing, cigarette ashes from then on, another. And the muck they called coffee in the Café de la Gare was about as tasteless as the water from a pugmill in a brickyard.

Zombies, in from the cold, coughed, hawked phlegm and blew out each nostril with a knuckle pressed to the other. They shuffled as if in giant boots, their breath steaming. Like a dunghill just before the frost had crucified its inhabitants, the Gare de Perrache was crawling with people. Trains to here, trains to there with long waits in between and no one seeming to care that pride, self-respect and *joie de vivre* had once been hallmarks of civilization.

Four German soldiers sought a table in between trains but found none. Their rifles were slung over greatcoat shoulders that no longer bore unit insignia for fear such information might be fed to England via clandestine wireless or courier.

Posters decried waste. USE THE WATER FROM YOUR NOODLES TO MAKE A NOURISHING SOUP. SAVE THREAD. UNRAVEL WORN-OUT SOCKS TO MAKE NEW ONES. OPEN YOUR CURTAINS TO LET IN THE SUNLIGHT. DON'T FORGET THAT IT IS A SOURCE OF HEAT. In winter? In Lyon?

WHEN BOILED, BONES RELEASE MUCH PROTEIN AND NOURISH-MENT. NEVER THROW THEM OUT BUT ALWAYS THINK OF REUSING THEM THEN SAVE AS A LAST RESORT FOR MAKING SOAP OR POUNDING INTO FERTILIZER.

Make jam without sugar—oh, he knew it well. Do the washing in cold water. It was like a catechism. Use sand for the difficult stains, never mind the fabric! MAKE SALAD OIL OUT OF WHITE LICHEN, A LITRE OF WATER AND A CRUST OF BREAD—what bread? TO TAKE AWAY THE CHEMICAL ODOUR AND TASTE, PURIFY THROUGH POULTICE MUSLIN—in wartime, with all of it confiscated for wounds on the Russian Front? Ah *maudit*! CONSUME THE OIL WITHIN 48 HOURS TO PREVENT IT FROM GOING RANCID. *Rancid!*

TWO HUNDRED GRAMS OF MUSHROOMS ARE EQUIVALENT TO ONE SERVING OF BEEFSTEAK!

Starved for tobacco, St-Cyr searched the saucer of saccharine for a cigarette butt to no avail. Hermann was taking forever. What could have kept him? Surely he hadn't forgotten they had agreed to meet here?

When a young man in a brand-new suit and open overcoat hesitantly put down a cardboard suitcase to sit opposite him, he wondered apprehensively how long the fellow could possibly remain at large and asked himself if he could not help in some little way.

'Monsieur,' said the traveller, indicating the chair. 'May I?'

The schoolboy French was not too bad. 'Ah, but of course, of course. Going far?' he asked pleasantly.

The boy shook his head and took to studying a grimy pre-war railway schedule that had somehow remained stuck to the wall. 'Paris,' he mumbled. 'I've friends.'

'*Tobacco?*' hissed St-Cyr.

'What?' yelped the boy in English. His face fell. 'What?' he asked lamely in French.

St-Cyr told him. 'I must do some thinking while there is still time, monsieur, but unfortunately with the rationing, I seem to have run out.'

Was he Gestapo? wondered the boy. He looked like a cop . . .

'I *am* a cop, a detective, monsieur. A chief inspector.'

The pouch contained a coarse-grained mixture of Vichyblended pipe tobacco that, given the circumstances, was quite acceptable. '*Merci*. Have your coffee ... no, no, please do not worry. For the moment, the three Gestapo who were watching this place have gone after other fish. Try to stay close to those soldiers—strike up a conversation in broken French. Be quite loose about it, not rigid, so that they can grasp a little. And when you get to the barrier, they will walk on ahead but you will shout *auf Wiedersehen* to them as you hand your papers over. The Swiss border is a good day's journey and it will be closely watched. Have you a friend, a contact—no, please don't give me a name or password. Just nod.'

'Is it that easy to spot me?'

'Try to relax a little, eh? Ditch the suitcase and steal another that is not nearly so new. Keep the overcoat buttoned up. Everyone despises suits like that, even the Nazis and especially their Gestapo. Use common sense. It's always best.'

'The ... the woman I stayed with thought it would be best if I were dressed properly.'

'Forget you ever saw her. Just concentrate on looking like one of the crowd. Don't hesitate when you come into a place like this. Walk right up to the counter as if you know it well and are only intent on going some place else that is equally known to you.'

'I—'

St-Cyr held up a cautioning finger and shook his head. 'Enough. I'm a perfect stranger and such people seldom talk to others. We've discussed the weather and now will brood over our coffee in silence. You're a gunner or a pilot that has been shot down, monsieur, but I know nothing of such things or would, of course, most certainly have to turn you in for the reward.'

The detective took forever to pack his pipe and when he lit it, he gazed off into space with moisture in his eyes, and one knew that he was saying thanks for having come over, that this war could not last forever.

One by one pieces kept coming from his pockets with a disgruntledness that said he was angry with himself for having been such a fool as to have even said a thing. The spiked iron shank of a woman's high-heeled shoe troubled him. A bent and twisted compact and charred cigarette case were then firmly laid beside it as if he knew to whom they had belonged. A little slip of paper with a name . . .

The boy left the tobacco pouch on the table and his coffee only half drunk. In the fashion of the times, and to cover himself in case anyone was watching, St-Cyr swept up the tobacco and emptied the coffee into his own no matter what germs it might contain. He'd damned well drink it in a toast to freedom!

Three women had gone into that cinema. Claudine and another had arrived late, and she had then left her seat to find the washroom key and spend her time with the projectionist. Frau Weidling had also been in the audience—she'd been recognized by the ticket-booth operator. And while Claudine was upstairs, her companion left the rush bag on the seat and went in search of someone else perhaps, and/or to lock the door to the toilets in anger, perhaps, at not finding her there but finding several others. Everything pointed to Frau Weidling being the person to be met, but had they both returned to those seats to start the fire?

Madame Rachline had said she and Claudine had been to the pharmacy, but Mademoiselle Martine Charlebois said she herself had given Claudine a bottle of friar's balsam that very afternoon.

He drew on his pipe in earnest contemplation. The trip to the pharmacy could simply have been cover for the cinema they had left in such haste, but had it really been Ange-Marie who had returned to the flat with her friend as the concierge maintained, or had it been Frau Weidling or someone else? The other woman? The later absence of the concierge must also be considered as a factor in getting into and leaving the flat.

Oxalic and sulphuric acids release carbon dioxide and carbon monoxide in equal volumes when mixed and warmed a little. Both gases will kill, but the carbon monoxide was, of course, much faster and far deadlier. Depending on its concentration, the sulphuric acid might fume when poured out, and such fumes would have had to be cleared away lest they warn the victim. The balsam would give a strong enough and pleasantly sweet aroma. The residue could then be disposed of without a trace by simply washing it down the drain. Death by natural causes then. Pneumonia in wartime under the Occupation and who would care? She had been a prostitute anyway.

But how had the Salamander come by such things, and the phosphorus, if indeed it had been used to start the tenement fire?

Henri Charlebois would not have used oxalic acid to clean metal antiques. Ange-Marie Rachline could not have had such a working knowledge of chemistry.

Leiter Weidling would know only too well the reputation of the silent killer and perhaps, too, the making of those gases in the laboratory. His wife had had Claudine's name in her purse and that of La Belle Époque, but would she have understood the intricacies of mixing the two acids and of warming them? Had he taught her how to do it? Were the two of them working together?

Henri Charlebois had been in Dijon. His sister had lost her keys . . .

For a woman to understand chemistry so well, and to have access to such things, she would have had to be a chemist, a metallurgist—ah, there were so few females trained in the sciences—a teacher . . .

Ah *merde*, a teacher of course. A chemistry laboratory . . .

Sweeping everything into his pockets, he grabbed his hat and made for the front desk of the Hotel Bristol.

'The Inspector Kohler has left the hotel, monsieur, with Frau Weidling and the Gestapo agents she asked me to summon. I believe the five of them went straight to the Hotel Terminus but I cannot be certain of this.'

'The five of them . . . ?'

'Yes. Herr Kohler was under arrest.'

'*Arrest?*'

'Naked and struggling, monsieur.'

Maudit! It had happened again. The Gestapo had taken one of their own. Hermann!

8 RUEFULLY KOHLER LOOKED AROUND AT THE damage he had caused to Gestapo HQ Lyon. The windows of the third-floor room were broken and splintered, the walls, floor and ceiling scorched—stained by water and flame-retardant too. In the rush to extinguish the fire, the copper bathtub had been dented but the dents had been hammered out and the tub refilled so that it was brimming. *Verdammt!* Were they going to drown the three of them? He was freezing and could not stop shivering at the sight of the water and the memory of Frau Weidling ducking her head and holding it under. She would want to see the real thing. She would want to get her kicks out of it.

'So now it begins,' snorted Robichaud. 'The final descent into hell. Élaine, forgive me.'

Tied to chairs, they had been left to think things over.

'It's nothing, Julien. It does not matter. We're together. That's what counts.'

'To think we could have agreed to meet at any other cinema, that all we ever wanted was to be together.'

'Yes but . . . but now we are, *chéri*, and for me, ah, I no longer care who knows about us. My husband, my children . . . May God forgive me but I could not stay another moment in that house. When we were together, Julien, those were the best times of my life.'

'Mine also.'

Good *Gott im Himmel*, they were trying so hard! They knew the room would be bugged! 'Look, I'll do what I can,' grumbled Kohler. 'Barbie must want something from me. Otherwise it doesn't make a damned bit of sense my being here!'

They looked at each other and said nothing—after all, he was Gestapo too, and he couldn't expect much else from them. Élaine Gauthier had spent the night in the cellars; Robichaud had, of course, been at the tenement fire and had not known she'd been picked up. Nor would he know what she'd said during the hours of interrogation that had left her gaunt and haggard.

Kohler remembered their meeting in the lobby of the Hotel Bristol and feeling that she had had more to say. Was the truth now to be forced out of her, and himself to be witness to it? A lesson for him perhaps?

She would not look at the bathtub. Robichaud could not help but do so or look up at the meat-hooks that hung above her. 'I love you, Élaine,' he said, and then again, 'Forgive me.'

'For involving her?' shouted Kohler angrily. 'Ah *nom de Jésus-Christ, dummkopf*, come clean and they'll go easy on her. You were at that cinema to meet with Resistance people among the railway workers. You bastards want to unite throughout France. Every fire-fighting unit in every city and town; every railway worker on every train and in every marshalling yard and repair shop. *That's* what Obersturmführer Barbie believes and nothing you or I say to the contrary will ever change this. Can't you see what he'll do to her? He'll have her stripped naked in front of us. Then he'll question her, and if she doesn't speak up, they'll shove her head under in that thing and hold her down until her lungs all but burst!' He dragged in a breath and clenched his fists. 'Then they'll do it all over again,' he added sadly, 'and they'll keep on doing it.'

The couple said nothing. They gazed steadily at each other. Kohler pleaded with them even though he knew Barbie would be listening in and that everything he said would be written down and used against him if not today, then later on.

In desperation, he said, 'Leiter Weidling doesn't stand a fart's chance in a windstorm of stopping the next fire with you out of the way, Robichaud, but the blame for it is going to rest solidly on the Obersturmführer's shoulders. Right about now my partner will be filing our interim report with Sturmbannführer Boemelburg in Paris, who will then call Gestapo Mueller in Berlin. Hey, they're old friends. They're in this together, right? That report will place full responsibility for this fiasco on Herr Barbie but the sap just doesn't know his balls are for the skillet!'

'And myself?' asked Robichaud steadily.

The fire chief had realized there could be no escape for him. 'You have no other choice but to tell them what they want to hear. Look, I'm sorry but that's the way of it. No matter how hard you both deny it, this will only reinforce what he wants to believe. But what he doesn't see is that he could accomplish everything he wants *and* earn himself an Iron Cross First-Class into the bargain. All he needs is to keep Madame Gauthier in custody. She's insurance enough you won't try to escape. Gestapo Mueller wants the Salamander stopped and to do so, my partner and I need you.'

It was Madame Gauthier who said distantly, 'The Salamander knows the city so well. Without Julien's help, the Théâtre des Célestins will be child's play.'

'Phosphorus?' asked Kohler sharply so that the boys in the next room could hear.

'Perhaps,' said Robichaud gravely. 'Only a little is needed

and, of course, one can hide it in several places. That theatre . . . beautiful and ornate as it is, why . . . Ah, I've been telling them for years that something must be done to improve the fire exits and the extinguisher syst—'

The door opened and Barbie's two German shepherds came in to get acquainted. Shit! Excited by the prospects ahead, Frau Weidling darted her eyes from the woman to the bathtub, then to the larger of the dogs and back again to Madame Gauthier who could now no longer look at any of them.

The dogs . . . Kohler could hear her saying. The dogs . . .

Not a month after he'd arrived in Lyon, Barbie had earned himself a reputation for the baseness of his cruelty towards the women he interrogated, never mind the men. Though he knew he mustn't shout, Kohler raged at Frau Weidling and tried to stall them. 'What'd you do to get those photographs, eh? Prostitute yourself to some zero-brained detective in Lübeck? Hey, my sweet little bit from Schwerin, is Lübeck where they came from? Throats slit, breasts cut open, vaginas . . . *Ja, ja*, Frau Fire Chief, the Lübeck cop-shop and you with your bare ass on some bastard's desk even though you didn't want him to dip his wick into you. He knew you were responsible for those fires. He *knew* you would try it again and again and . . . Ah *Gott im Himmel*, I'm an idiot! It was that husband of yours. He'd followed you from fire to fire. That's why you married him. The bastard found you out and forced you to—'

There was no denying she was beautiful when angry. She fingered his scrotum and said quietly, 'You should not have touched a thing in my room, Herr Kohler.'

'It's Inspector to you.' Barbie was smirking. Shit!

'I was nowhere near Lübeck or Heidelberg or Köln at the time of those other fires. I was in Paris.'

She had the whitest teeth. 'You're lying. That husband of yours knows all about you. Hey, I think you and Claudine Bertrand were once lovers—a casual little affair that was remembered, eh? So, here we have a chance to come to Lyon and by

God, love again. But Claudine promised to bring along a
friend, someone really special, another woman. Did you want
to hold a lighted cigarette between that one's toes, or were you
more interested in the other parts? Flames when you masturbate. A grandfather who—'

Her features sharpened. Excruciating pain shot through him,
stiffening every muscle as she squeezed his scrotum until he
could not help but scream in anguish and gasp.

Then she hit him until there was blood in his eyes, and in a
blind, numb way he understood this was her only means of con-
vincing Barbie of her usefulness.

Boemelburg had a filthy cold. 'The line is scratchy, Walter.
No . . . ah no, there is no need to shout!' pleaded St-Cyr.

The Head of SIPO-SD Section IV, the Gestapo in France, had
no patience for an old acquaintance from before the war. 'Louis,
what has Kohler been up to this time? Come, come, you know
very well that *dummkopf* should have telephoned me himself.
Another fire, eh? Yes, yes, Gestapo Mueller has just been on the
line demanding . . . *demanding!* . . . to know what is going on.'

Hermann's Chief hawked up lumpy custard and let it erupt
into a handkerchief perhaps. St-Cyr anxiously wiped the receiver
on a sleeve just in case the lines carried more than words.
'Walter, we are almost positive we know who the Salamander
is but I absolutely must have Hermann's help. Klaus Barbie
has him.'

A difficult gob was swallowed. 'The Obersturmführer . . .
but . . . but why is this?'

They were speaking deutsch, though Boemelburg was fluent
in French. 'A small misunderstanding,' confessed St-Cyr.

'Has he been arrested?'

'Yes, Herr Sturmbann—'

'*Gott im Himmel*, Louis, why was he arrested?' Kohler . . .
Kohler . . . oh *mein Gott*, not again!

It would be best to tell him just a little. More rubbish was swallowed. St-Cyr filled him in and then said, 'Herr Robichaud knows nothing of the Resistance, Walter. The man was simply in the cinema to meet up with his girlfriend, a married woman who has a family, that is all. French—yes, yes, Walter, they're both French and the Pope will castigate them for their infidelity.' Ah *merde*! 'I swear they had nothing to do with those people who were locked in the toilets. We need Robichaud for a little while. Just until the concert is over.'

'Concert? What concert is this? Don't tell me you're all fucking the dog down there?'

'Walter, Walter, *please*! It's a benefit. Something to gather money and clothing for the Russian Front.'

'Then that is good. Yes, good. When is it to be held?'

Was he thinking of coming himself? 'Tomorrow evening. It starts early and ends well before curfew. At least, I think it does. I imagine it does. I . . .' Have said too much?

'Phosphorus, Louis? Oxalic and sulphuric acids? Our arsonist is a chemist, a metallurgist, an engineer, teacher or professor perhaps. Yes, someone with access to such things and the knowledge to use them.'

They talked for a little longer and then that was it. Short of setting fire to the place himself, there was little else he could do. Exhausted by the conversation, St-Cyr put down the telephone which rang immediately. Orders flew. An SS corporal raced for the stairs. Another leaned on the bell-push of the lift.

Impressed, the Feldwebel on the desk gave the Frenchman the once-over.

St-Cyr let him have it. 'Get these clothes and a pot of coffee up to Inspector Kohler immediately. See that he receives the following message. He is to bring Frau Weidling and the others to the temporary morgue at the Lycée Ampère, and he is to wait there with them until I return.'

The hotel's frescos were mirrored in its lobby doors as he

turned swiftly away. Oozing sentiment, they blissfully portrayed life in the Rhône Valley and in Renaissance times. Joyous faces among the peasants. No rain or snow or twenty degrees of frost and Gestapo torture rooms.

He would not take a *vélo-taxi*. He would catch a tram-car to the place Terreaux and use the ruins of the cinema to cover his tracks before continuing. Yes, yes, that would be best. There was no sense in leading Gestapo Lyon to the quarry. Martine Charlebois might simply have been duped, but she'd lost her keys and someone had found them.

When he got there, the Parc de la Tête d'Or appeared gripped in the fierceness of a polar waste, devoid of all sign of human life, dog, bird or cat. Down by the lake, the iron-and-glass cupola of the bandshell was hung with jagged icicles and at first he didn't see her.

She was standing alone, gazing out over the ice-covered lake toward the Île des Tamaris, the nearer of the two islands. Lost in thought, she was totally oblivious to the wind and the cold. Worried . . . ah so concerned with the turmoil of her thoughts, the brow beneath the knitted, dark brown toque would be well furrowed.

Now and then the gloved fingers of her right hand rubbed the railing as if, though still undecided, she had to agree it must have happened. When, finally, he cleared his throat and stepped up on to the platform, she awoke to him and gasped, then held a hand to her mouth to stop herself from saying anything. Trapped . . . Oh *mon Dieu*, she was terrified. Sick and looking away from him, panicking . . .

'Mademoiselle Charlebois, it is one thing to have lost your keys and to have had them returned, it is another to still agonize over how you could possibly have lost them and why, of all places, here. Is that not so?'

Dear Jesus help her. There was no one else with him but why had he come? *Why?* That latest fire, that tenement . . . did he know the truth of it? 'I . . . I was daydreaming, Inspector

Thinking about . . . about how I loved this old bandshell as a child. Pirates and castaways . . . oh, it was so many things for me. A ship, an island . . .'

She threw up suddenly, and he waited for her sickness to pass as she leaned over the railing in tears.

'Mademoiselle, if you dropped your keys here, why was it that you had them in your hand? Surely you would have kept them in a safe place? Your purse, your briefcase, a drawer at home perhaps . . . ah, it is a puzzle unless . . .'

Unless *what*? she wanted to shriek at him. Unless she was lending them to someone? Was that what he thought? 'I . . . I was trying to remember, Inspector, while . . . while thinking of my childhood. I . . . I can't understand why I had them out but I must have, mustn't I?'

Ten days ago at least! 'Mademoiselle Charlebois, why, please, did you have the keys at all? Is it not customary for the concierge of the school to open and lock all doors?'

He had not yet mentioned the tenement fire but would he ask her where she was last night? *Would he?* 'M . . . Monsieur Legrange, our custodian, has been quite ill. We all like him so much, we did not wish to seek a replacement so the staff agreed to take turns. I . . . I had not yet passed my keys on to Madame the Professor Calmette, my superior.'

'But if the keys were lost and it was your duty to lock up, who did this for you?'

He was *trying* to unsettle her with all this talk of the keys . . . the *keys*! 'Monsieur the Assistant Professor Paul. He . . . he has the other set. Usually we alternated. Every other day one of us would do it but he . . . he said he would cover for me until I . . . I found my keys.'

He would make her think he was suddenly fed up with her evasiveness. He would grip the railing and stare across the lake. 'Were you alone when you lost them?' he asked. 'Come, come, mademoiselle. Was it your three *zazous* you met here ten days ago or your Monsieur Paul?'

'My Monsieur Pa ... ul? He ... he is too old for me, Inspector. He is ... he is fifty-six. I am only twenty-six!'

He'd be gruff about it. 'Fifty-six is not so old, not these days when most of our young men are away in POW camps or in the grave.'

When she didn't respond, he said, 'You were meeting Jean-Pierre. He's the oldest of your little tribe. Seventeen, is he, or eighteen?'

'I ... I don't know what you're implying. Me? Having an affair with Jean-Pierre? One of my students? It ... it is just not possible for me to love another, Inspector. I once did but ... but soon learned my lesson. Oh yes I did! Jean-Pierre had managed to get me a capon. I ... I must have taken the keys out of my pocket when I found the money for him.'

She had once had a lover—a fiancé? he wondered. 'So you set them on the railing here and then ... what then, mademoiselle? Did you turn to look back toward your house in fear your brother might have seen you together with that boy? Did your elbow then knock the forgotten keys to the ground where they lay hidden for so long? You were distracted for days prior to their loss—that's what your three *zazous* told me. Yes, yes, mademoiselle, you needn't look so betrayed. What had been troubling you? The thought that your clandestine meetings here had been discovered and misinterpreted by your brother or had he really misinterpreted them?'

Dear Jesus help her to stop quivering. The detective was *not* going to leave her alone. 'Henri, he ... he understands that Jean-Pierre is ... is just a friend, Inspector. A helper—doesn't one need such helpers these days if one is to survive?'

She was crying again but had not realized it. 'Then was it worry over your brother's relationship with Claudine Bertrand, mademoiselle? Please, the time for truth is upon us.'

Her eyes and nose were wiped, her head was bowed. 'I ... I have told you I ... I hardly knew her.'

'Yes, but when she couldn't get money from your brother,

she came straight to you. Therefore, mademoiselle, she knew you well enough!'

Ah no. 'She . . . she was a terrible woman, Inspector. Morally bankrupt. I have told Henri many times to have nothing more to do with her, but . . . but he . . . he never listens to his little sister.'

'All right then, did he go with her? Did he visit her at La Belle Époque?'

She would have to face him and pray there were no more tears. 'My . . . my brother is not like that, monsieur. Henri . . . Henri knew everything there was to know about Claudine. What she thought, how she would react to . . . to things. Her moods, her hopes, her little . . . Well, you know. And so did Ange-Marie.'

He could not let her off the hook. 'Where is the husband of Madame Rachline?'

'The father of her children?' She would shrug—yes, yes! 'No one knows. They didn't get on. One day he was there, the next he . . . he has left her for another, perhaps, and she has found her bed cold and herself as mistress of that place. Henri . . .'

'Has kept the house furnished in the décor of the times.'

Must he be so cruel? 'Is there harm in that, Inspector? Our grandfather . . .'

'Owned the house. Am I correct?'

She bit her lower lip and felt her cheeks colouring rapidly. 'Yes, damn you! Henri sold shares to several Lyonnais. The préfet, the magistrate—oh *bien sûr* my brother is a business-man, Inspector. *Very* successful, *very* determined to carry on the name of the shop and "other" things. He thought it best to see that Ange-Marie had as little trouble as possible. It was to be *business* as usual, right from the day our grandfather died and Henri caught the madam of that place cheating!'

So much for Monsieur Henri Masson's respectability! 'Have you ever been there?'

'Have I ever prostituted myself? *No!* of course not. I . . . I was once very much in love but . . . but my fiancé was killed in . . .'

He was not going to leave it now! 'In Köln, in . . . in a fire, a terrible fire.'

Ah *merde*! He must go easy. 'Tell me about it, mademoiselle.
Tell me everything.'

A coldness came to her. He was not a priest, not Father
Adrian. 'There is nothing to tell. We met in Lübeck, went to
Heidelberg and finally to Köln. I was a student on an exchange
programme the Nazis . . . the Boches . . . ah, please forgive me,
the Germans had offered. He was a student also, but German.
The . . . the son of a prominent lawyer.'

'And your brother knew of this romance?'

He would think the worst, though his voice had softened.
'Yes. Yes, Henri knew of it.'

She had not been able to hide her bitterness. Had she been
sleeping with the boy? Had the brother then found out? 'And
now, mademoiselle? This Monsieur Paul? Did he attend the
cinema on the night of the fire?'

Ah good! Yes, good! The detective had overextended himself
at last! 'Monsieur Paul thinks film beneath anyone educated
enough to read Molière and the others, so I did not worry about
him in that regard. Only Henri. Always Henri. My brother and I
are very close, Inspector. Like two doves that mate for ever, we
worry about each other when one is away.'

Two doves that mate for ever . . . 'Have you still got the keys?'
he asked.

She shook her head. 'This morning I took them to my superior, Madame Calmette.'

He'd be firm with her though he knew she was distraught.
'Are you certain of this, mademoiselle? We shall have to ask
Madame . . .'

Everything had slipped from her—everything! In defeat, she
would have to answer. 'As it is the holiday, the keys are in my
briefcase at home.'

'Good! Then together we will pay the Lycée du Parc a little visit. Since the custodian is ill, we should have the school to ourselves.'

'I know my rights, Inspector. I do not have to do this.'

'It would be best, but if you wish me to get the magistrate's approval, I will.'

The couple had been selected for 'special treatment' using 'reinforced interrogation', all of it 'legalized' by the SD's Berlin decree of 12 July 1942.

Poor Louis had thought Boemelburg would put a temporary stop to it. All Barbie had had to say to the chief was that he had good reasons to suspect Robichaud and Élaine Gauthier had connections with the Resistance. Never mind the Salamander, never mind the threat of another fire.

For now, work on the woman and keep the man no matter how much he shouts or rages—that's what Boemelburg would have said. Unleash the terror. Ensure that the Occupier would be hated as never before and eventually driven out, ah yes. In his heart of hearts, Kohler knew it to be the absolute truth.

On 28 November a Wehrmacht soldier had been shot and wounded by two young men on bicycles in the place Bellecour. It was Barbie's task to put a stop to it and the son of a bitch would use any method he could.

Kohler didn't know what to do. They had stripped Madame Gauthier and had forced her to her knees beside the tub. They had bound her wrists so tightly she could not move them. The dogs were restless and kept going up to her . . .

Somehow he found his voice. 'Frau Weidling really was in that cinema on the night of the fire, Herr Obersturmführer. She was absent from her hotel at 4 p.m. and was in Croix Rousse to watch the tenement fire. Why not ask her to tell you about those other fires? Lübeck, eh, Frau Weidling? A Salamander and Claudine Bertrand . . .'

It was Barbie who unexpectedly said, 'Perhaps a few answers are in order, Frau Weidling.'

'I . . . I don't know what you mean, Herr Obersturmführer?'

'I think you do,' he said, not sparing her.

She stiffened. 'Then yes—yes, I was at the cinema but *not* to meet anyone! Johann was busy. I thought to take in a film but soon realized there were no subtitles. Besides, it was a stupid film. I left almost as soon as I got there.'

'I'll bet you did,' breathed Kohler, 'and in one hell of a hurry.'

Barbie watched her closely. Her fingers shook as she tried to find a cigarette in the package beside his cap. Irritably flicking the lighter several times, she finally got it going.

Exhaling through her nostrils, she tried to steady herself, tried to think. 'I didn't do it. I swear I didn't.'

Barbie nodded curtly toward Madame Gauthier but abruptly Frau Weidling set the cigarette aside and reached for her fur coat. 'I must go now, Herr Obersturmführer. Johann will be wondering where I am.'

'Do it,' said Barbie quietly.

She was desperate. 'I . . . I can't. It's . . . It's not the same. Johann would . . .'

'Disown you?' asked Barbie.

Why was he doing this to her? *Why?* 'Yes. Yes, that is so.'

Barbie wasn't about to leave it. 'But why would he do such a thing?'

She could no longer look at any of them. 'Because he . . . he would feel that I had betrayed him.'

'That's interesting. Was Leiter Weidling in the audience at that cinema, Frau Weidling?' asked Barbie.

When she didn't answer, he shrieked it at her and she said, 'Johann is . . . is an extremely jealous man, Herr Obersturmführer. My driver went to tell him where I was. They . . . they were waiting with the car in the place Terreaux when . . . when I came out of the cinema. There was no problem, no fire. We started back to the hotel, but when we reached place Bellecour, Johann heard the alarm and . . . and we returned to find the cinema in flames.'

'And where were you last night?'

'At the hotel in my room until . . . until the fire. I had gone out earlier but . . . but came back because . . . because I wanted to be alone.'

'Then do it,' said Barbie. 'You have nothing to be afraid of.'

'I . . . I can't. I *mustn't!*'

'*Do it!*' he shrieked. She leapt. The fur coat fell. The cigarette was snatched up and . . . and . . .

When the scream came from Madame Gauthier, it filled the room and set the dogs to barking viciously. 'Tell them,' wept Kohler. 'Ah *nom de Jésus-Christ*, Robichaud, don't be so stubborn! Do it for her sake.'

'There is nothing to tell and I have nothing to say.'

They were alone in the Lycée du Parc, just the two of them, the detective and herself. Was it the last time she would ever walk these endless corridors and hear her own steps amid the maze of classrooms? wondered Martine Charlebois. Up some stairs, down others, the skirting boards of darkly stained, vertical tongue-and-groove scuffed and dented by the shoes and boots of boys who so often thought they were prisoners. Elsewhere, in another part entirely, the coveys of jabbering girls rushing along to a destiny they knew not. The smell of them so different from that of the boys. No lipstick, no varnish on her nails, the girls assessing her with the harsh cruelty of their tender years; the boys also but in such a different way and, if a skirt was accidentally raised above the knee when sitting, or a button of a blouse had come undone, or sweat dampened the underarms, they would laugh silently and rut with her in their minds or talk openly about it to the others in whispers. Ah yes, but she did not dislike them doing this or the way they stared at her breasts.

Indeed, these incidents brought their little pleasures for at least then she knew she was still attractive.

They came to an intersection and she turned left, saying meekly, 'It is this way now, Inspector. Only a little more.'

St-Cyr flicked the beam of his torch over the sickly yellow plaster above the panelling. To think that lycées had grown so much. It was like a huge warren of *traboules*. It made him feel old and lost—passed by. Baffled at the change in an educational system none had thought would ever change.

The decided smell of formaldehyde in which the zoology professors kept their specimens signalled that they had all but reached their goal. Then the faint mingling of burnt sulphur, the sharpness of acid and above it all, the high note and faint trace of mustard gas that lingered from some experiment to warn all future generations of its horror.

Unaware that he was doing so, St-Cyr suddenly crossed himself at the memory of past battlefields and kissed his fingertips— realized at last that she was waiting for him. And when he shone the torch up, it revealed the stark black letters on a door— CHEMISTRY FOUR—and the lines in her face, the worry and the strain.

'Please shine the light on the lock, Inspector. I cannot see which key to use.'

A hardness had entered the voice of one so timid.

There were rows of black-topped workbenches with tall stools upended on each. Cold Bunsen burners with retort stands, sinks, taps, beakers and racks of test-tubes, blackboards on three sides and no windows.

'It is vented by fans in the roof,' she said as if reading his thoughts. 'The storeroom is over there past the professor's desk. In the corner there is another door which is kept locked when he is not present.'

'The keys, mademoiselle.' He snapped his fingers to unsettle her. 'Please wait here in the dark. I will take a look myself.'

So that she could not know if it were true? Was he so cruel?

He would know exactly how much she would agonize over the delay. He would use her fear as a weapon to send its barbed shaft into her. He would rape her as no man had ever raped but it would not be of sex or of the body, ah no, not with him. Humiliated by not knowing, she would break down and confess everything as she had to Father Adrian, and this one, why he would realize this and would soon know it all. She could not allow him to do that to her. She mustn't!

The tops of the desks were smooth but pitted where acids had touched them. The drawers below did not move easily and when, at last, one became unstuck, glassware rattled and she straightened up silently, seeing only in her mind's eye the shadows cast as his torch beam passed furtively over the rows of bottles behind the windows of the cabinet doors.

Phosphorus, Inspector? she asked silently. It is grey-white and non-metallic though it looks like a metal. Very light, very soft and unctuous and in cubes that are about one-and-a-half centimetres square which cut like butter. Kept under water in brown glass jars, it looks like some strange sort of condiment, a pickled Turkish Delight perhaps because when you open the top, there is a whitish crust on each cube as on a Camembert, but when burned there is a garlic odour which is very strong, and a pungently choking white smoke—a great deal of this smoke—and a very, very hot flame into which the phosphorus suddenly bursts on exposure to air.

Still he had not come out of the storeroom. Still he had not called out to her with, Ah, it is not here, mademoiselle. Two rings of dust. Two jars taken. It was not much used apparently. It was kept well to the back of the cupboard on the top shelf. Yes, yes, Mademoiselle Charlebois, the phosphorus, it has been taken.

Trembling, she felt renewed tears. She did not know what to do, knew only that he had to be stopped. *Stopped! Stopped!*

The gas was on. A little miracle Father Adrian would have

praised. It hissed too loudly but when the valve was opened wide, the sound lessened substantially.

One after another she opened all of the bench-top valves, then closed the outer door. Hunting—moving quickly now— she searched frantically for one of the igniters. They were at every bench. They were very simple things of wire, with a flint striker that was pushed across a platelet of sharply ribbed steel. One squeezed the igniter, bending the wire handle in on itself and springing the striker.

He did not come until she had it in her hand. He did not understand what was happening. 'Mademoiselle . . . ?' he said, surprised—yes, yes! 'Mademoiselle Charlebois, what are you doing?'

The smell of gas was everywhere in the classroom. Feverishly she gripped the igniter and struggled frantically to kill them both. St-Cyr ran. He moved among the workbenches hearing the rush of gas as it poured from each nozzle. Again she tried to blow them up. *Again!*

Dizzy, sick at his stomach, he tried to shout at her to stop. The beam of the light danced away. He pulled it back—shone it at her. Willed it to blind her.

With a ragged sob, she flung the igniter at him and raced for the door. Was pulling at the collar of her coat. Air . . . She had to have air . . .

Must close the valves, he shouted at himself as he ran from bench to bench. No time, no time. *No time!*

He reached the last of them. Vomiting—dragging in a breath—St-Cyr pitched out into the corridor, flinging the light from himself, tearing at his collar just as she had done.

The light was out. Where . . . where had he thrown it? Ah *merde!* 'Mademoiselle,' he managed weakly. He had no voice. Air . . . he must still need air. 'Mademoiselle Charlebois, you are under arrest for trying to kill a police officer.'

There wasn't a sound. He knew she was standing in some doorway, lost in the darkness, her heart racing.

When she vomited, he knew she was just as ill as himself, but when he reached the place where she had been hiding, she was no longer there. '*Mademoiselle*, why did you set that tenement on fire? Eighteen dead, mademoiselle. *Eighteen* on Christmas Night!'

He would never find her where she was going. He must never find her, she said to herself.

'Did Jean-Pierre steal the phosphorus for you?' he shouted. There was so much rage in his voice, she trembled. He would beat her. He would drag her down and hit her . . .

The detective stopped. Still dizzy and throwing up, he tried to steady himself.

'Mademoiselle, did he tell you how to kill Claudine? It was perfect, wasn't it? Just a little balsam around the lip of the bowl to give the proper smell and not a trace afterwards of what you had done.'

Again St-Cyr listened for her, hearing only silence. *Maudit!* 'But you were nervous,' he called out. 'As you opened the bottle of oxalic acid some of the granules spilled. You swept them up—of course you did. You even took them away or washed them down the drain but you forgot to tap the broom against the floor.'

She had sought refuge in a very large room, an auditorium, he thought. Immediately there were changes: a deeper darkness, a greater coldness, sounds echoing upwards. The smell of beeswax, chalk dust and sweat. A gymnasium.

Kohler tossed off the cognac and held the glass out to Barbie for more. 'Now that she's left us, Herr Obersturmführer, I can tell you Frau Weidling lied. She was nowhere near that hotel of hers last night when the tenement caught fire. Her husband told us she was dining with you.'

'And the night of the cinema fire?'

'There wasn't enough time between when she went in and when the fire started. She could have got there earlier and been waiting long enough, but I don't think so. That driver of hers had to find Leiter Weidling, who then had to extricate himself from whatever he was doing. Then they had to drive back to place Terreaux *and* then back to place Bellecour before turning around to find out where the pumper trucks were heading.'

'Leiter Weidling is above reproach. He has very good references, the best of security clearances.'

Kohler sighed inwardly at the futility of dealing with Berlin. 'Was he keeping tabs on that wife of his, Herr Obersturm-führer? Was he using her to set it all up, eh? A Salamander who was just a bit too smart for him.'

Boemelburg had said that if anyone could stop the Sala-mander it would be Kohler and St-Cyr. 'It was Leiter Weidling who gave us the dossier on his wife.'

'Like a good Nazi should? Well, listen then, Herr Obersturm-führer. If that bastard isn't bird-dogging his wife at her games then how is it he came to marry a woman like that? Either she knows something about him he doesn't want anyone else to hear, or he's in it with her and the two of them are making monkeys out of us all. Hey, you've given them exactly the set-up they need, so what's it to be?'

Kohler would never learn that to swear allegiance to the Führer and the Party was to obey its dictums. 'Robichaud will be released into your custody. The Gauthier woman stays here until I am satisfied the Salamander is no longer of any use or a threat.'

'And then?'

'Then we shall see.'

Gingerly St-Cyr began to walk out on to the floor. There would be ropes for climbing, mats for tumbling, a box-horse and parallel bars . . . Wax? Had there been a dance? Ah no, of course not. Only in the most progressive of schools perhaps, but not here, he thought.

Ah *merde*! She was sprinkling wax on the floor behind herself. She was laying down a trail of it in hopes he would run and slip!

He stepped to one side. 'Was Mademoiselle Bertrand blackmailing your brother, mademoiselle?' he asked suddenly, his words echoing. 'She wanted out, didn't she? And fast! She knew Frau Weidling had suddenly turned up in Lyon and wanted to play—that's why she needed money to escape. She knew that the cinema fire might happen and when it did, you had to kill Claudine to protect your brother.'

The canister of wax hit the floor and rolled away into a distant corner, and he knew she had thrown it as far as she could to fool him.

He started for her. When he had taken several steps, he stopped suddenly and she shrilled, *'Henri was in Dijon! Are you mad? Insane?* He . . . he had nothing to do with that fire. How could he have?'

She gave another ragged sob but did not move—at least he did not think she had. Ah *merde*! 'Father Adrian had to die, mademoiselle. Did you telephone the Basilica using the name of Mademoiselle Aurelle? Did you get him to come to her flat where he found her naked and tied to her bed? You wrote the anonymous letters denouncing not only him but also Monsieur Artel, the owner of that cinema, and Madame Robichaud. How often did you watch for Robichaud and Mademoiselle Gauthier at that cinema? How often did you watch for Father Adrian and stand in the street outside looking up at Mademoiselle Aurelle's bedroom window?'

She had moved away from him. He was forced to turn back. When he spoke resignedly it was as if something had gone out of him and a great sadness had entered. 'How many times did you bare your soul to Father Adrian? You told him everything. How as a child you had secretly watched your brother and his friends, Claudine and Ange-Marie. Father Adrian encouraged you, didn't he? Well, answer me. *Answer!'*

'He . . . he made me take off my clothes. He said that . . . that God would not punish me and that . . . that I would begin to forget myself, my troubles.'

Ah no . . . 'Where . . . where did this happen?'

'At . . . at the house. Henri . . . Henri was always away. Dijon . . . Paris . . . out in the countryside some place. I knew it was wrong, that he was a priest and that Henri would find out. But I was so very lonely, Inspector, and so very worried. I . . . I could not stop myself, I could not stop Father Adrian. When I knelt before him, he . . . he would put his hands on my head, then pass them slowly down over my shoulders and under my blouse, my sweater, whatever . . . "Sin," he would say. "Sin, my child, so that God will see that you are normal." *Normal!'*

'He knew about the fires, didn't he? The ones in Lübeck, Heidelberg and Köln.'

'Yes . . . Yes, he knew of them. *He was my confessor, damn you!'*

She ran. She slipped and cried out—fell and rolled sideways.

He heard her scramble up and bang into something—the wall perhaps. He heard her frantically searching for the door.

When he gripped her by the arm, she leapt and stiffened. When he let go of her, her back was pressed to the wall and she knew then that he had trapped her, that he would force her to tell him everything. *Everything* about those days at Concarneau on the beach among the dunes and in the woods. *Everything* about Henri and Ange-Marie and how Henri had touched Claudine between the legs and brought the flame close . . . close. A scream and then . . . then the sound of her crying out in rapture.

Everything about Claudine and Lübeck and how Henri had sent Claudine to find his little sister with her fiancé naked in bed, sweating—copulating! Crying out to God in joy. *Everything.*

'Is your brother intimate with you in a sexual way, Mademoiselle Charlebois?'

Ah no. *No!* '*How dare you say that to me?* How could you? Henri . . . *Me?* What is it that makes you think such a horrible thing?'

'Mademoiselle, is it true?'

'No. *No!* Of course it is not true!'

'Then why, please, did your grandfather give Father Adrian that cross? Come, come, Mademoiselle Charlebois, Henri Masson would not have done so had he not exacted a promise from that priest.'

Promise . . . a *promise*. Why had the gas not exploded and killed them both? Why had it not burst suddenly into flame to burn the hair and melt the flesh? It would have been best that way. Flames, Henri. Flames. Your little sister, your little 'Mademoiselle Charlebois'.

Throwing herself at the detective, she pushed him in the face and ran—ran—said, Must get away. Must not let him stop me. Not now. Never now. Run . . . run . . . A door . . . door . . . the hall . . . the hall . . . Hurry, hurry . . . *Stop!*

Listen.

He was searching for light switches. She was outside one of the toilets. There were windows high up in the far wall . . .

Easing the door open, she slipped inside and quickly crossed to the grey light of day that came in through wire-meshed, frosted glass. He must not find her. She must not go home. Not yet. Perhaps not ever. Henri . . .

Kohler's spirits sank. Though he had no time for such things, the Théâtre des Célestins was magnificent. It offered up its magic in ornate gilding everywhere and in plush, wine-red velvet on rows of seats too many to count.

Up on stage, and lit by floodlights, the outer curtain hung in folds of ruby-red that were held aside as by a woman's hand to reveal the flame-red of her petticoats through which shafts of yellow shot upwards.

Clearly the wealth of Lyon and the *belle époque* had been

poured into the theatre and just as clearly there were far too many places for the Salamander to hide both starter and trailer— up on the lighting bridges that were so cleverly hidden from the audience, up in the high recesses of ventilation and heating shafts.

Down in one of the many wicker hampers of costumes that would be piled in the storage rooms and closets.

There was a boiler room, somewhere below him. There were dressing rooms, practice rooms, offices, workshops, paint rooms, wig rooms, a millinery and fitting room, dye shop, laundry, unloading bay—fly galleries above the stage and out of sight to drop and lift panels of scenery—a lighting board, sound panel and control room, prompter's box, stage doorman's office, call system of speaking tubes from the old days, now updated by an intercom but still keeping the bells and clocks of those former days. *La belle époque* all right, ah yes. Everywhere he looked there was evidence of that period of refinement when life was supposed to have been at its best and whores were told to bare a breast to the naked embers of a cigarette or cigar. Male or female.

Staircases were lost in the background. At either side of the stage there were private boxes for the wealthy and the establishment. Klaus Barbie and his boss, the SS-Obersturmbannführer Werner Knab, General Niehoff who had just arrived as commander-in-chief of the *France-Sud* military region, i.e. what had formerly been the Free Zone. The bishop of Lyon, too, of course, the préfet and the magistrate, et cetera, et cetera.

Perhaps the theatre would seat a thousand, perhaps twelve hundred. There were fluted columns with globes of light above them, cherubs, maidens and turbanned boys with open arms who offered up the conjured magic of the place. All gilded like some fantastic *gâteau d'anniversaire* just waiting to be torched!

Robichaud handed him the programme for the concert of 27 December. 'If it is all right by you, Inspector, I will begin a preliminary reconnaisance just to refresh my mind, since my men did not find anything before.'

'You sure you don't want something to eat?' asked Kohler.

'Ah no. No, Inspector. I couldn't. Not after ... Not knowing ...' He left it unsaid and soon vanished into the warren behind the stage.

The soup in the aluminium canister was good and when that was done, Kohler had the omelette and then a piece of fish and afterwards the baked vegetables in sauce lyonnaise, then coffee and thick slices of gingerbread, the *pavé de sante** of Dijon, the least expensive cut but most delicious.

Exhausted by the morning and the night before it and the days and nights prior to these, he had a cigarette and began to study the programme.

Was it to be a menu for disaster?

The concert began with the *Horst-Wessel Lied* in chorus with full kettledrum rolls and male voices in German, of course. 'Raise high the flags! Stand rank on rank together. Storm-troopers march with steady, quiet tread ...' *Quiet?* Ah *Gott im Himmel*, the idiots!

Horst Wessel had been a pimp and a pal of Himmler's in the Berlin of the 1920s. Both of them had lived on the avails of prostitution. Herr Himmler's girl had been seven years his senior and they'd fought like hell all the time. Early in 1920 he had suddenly disappeared. Her body was discovered. Arrested on 4 July 1920, in Munich, the future Head of the SS and its Gestapo had got off for lack of evidence, the lucky bastard. Then on 23 February 1930, Horst Wessel, who had put his song to the stolen tune of an old naval ballad, was killed by another pimp in a dispute over another prostitute yet the song lived on as the anthem of the Party.

Immediately after it, the orchestra would plunge into bits from Wagner's *Tannhäuser* and lift to the *Weiner Blut* of Johann Strauss Jr., the *Vienna Blood Waltz*.

*the pavement or cobblestone of good health

Kohler remained unimpressed by the stultifying thunder of Nazi-minded klutzes. Mendelssohn, a good German Jew, was next. *Fingal's Cave* and a bit from the Fourth Symphony, Opus 90.

And how the hell had the Propaganda Staffel missed it? A Jew?

Bach beat the Jesus out of Herr Mendelssohn's memory with the Brandenburg Concerto after which came selections from Handel's *Water Music* to give prelude to the rush to the bar and the toilets.

Oh *mein Gott*, what son of a bitch had set this up? A member of the Resistance?

Haydn's 'Surprise' Symphony led off the second half then Liszt with selections from *Dante* and Beethoven's Third Symphony in E flat, Opus 55, the second movement done with *Marcia funebre*—a funeral march, eh?

Mozart, a good Austrian, offered *The Magic Flute* to brighten things up and suggest that, though the Occupation and the war were long and hard, there was magic on the way. Ah *merde*!

Wagner came back in for a little more pounding in *The Ring of the Nibelung*, after which Brahms gave that tasty little morsel, *A German Requiem*.

For an encore there was Bach's Fugue in C minor to cheer everyone up and if that didn't work, there was always that old favourite, *Deutschland Über Alles*.

From the lycée to the house was not far. Slogging it hard, St-Cyr grimaced constantly at the turn of events. He'd trusted the girl to wait for him in that laboratory. He had been completely taken in by her timidity!

When he reached the concierge's room off the inner courtyard, he was furious with himself and adamant. 'Monsieur, I have no other choice but to ask that you allow me access to their flat. Mademoiselle Charlebois is wanted for the attempted murder of a police officer, myself.'

One should ask for the magistrate's order, one should demand to see it! 'You've no right, Inspector. Monsieur Henri is absent from the premises. Mademoiselle Charlebois—'

'Has not come back from her walk in the park, monsieur, and will not unless she wishes arrest. Now, please, I know absolutely the duty of every concierge is to protect the sanctity of the tenants, but if there are complications—another tragic fire perhaps . . .'

'The fires . . . ? But . . . but what has Mademoiselle Charlebois to do with them?'

St-Cyr told him. Tears leapt into the old man's eyes. He used the back of a forefinger to self-consciously tidy a superb handlebar moustache. 'She was worried about her brother, Monsieur the Chief Inspector. Mademoiselle Charlebois is a kind and gentle soul. It . . . Ah no, no, it's impossible what you say. Oh for sure they might quarrel—what brother and sister don't, and he's much older, she's never married. But for her to have set such fires and caused so many deaths . . . ? No. No, monsieur, it is just not possible. A mouse . . . she wouldn't let me kill a mouse but made me release it in the park.'

'Where is her brother?'

'Monsieur Henri . . . ? At his shop. Always that one works. Always he comes and goes. There are so many people dying these days, so many of the old estates being broken up. She's the anchor, the lamp behind the black-out curtain, the one who keeps house for him.'

'And teaches school.'

'Yes, yes, of course.' The concierge, a throwback to the days of yesteryear, hesitated. One could see him struggling with things from the past—little incidents—and things from the present. 'How long will you be, Inspector?' he asked, defeated at last by some remembered incident.

'Not long. Now tell me what made you change your mind? Come, come, monsieur, time is something we do not have.'

The chin was gripped and favoured in doubt. Loyalty . . . the years of service flicked past on the screen of memory. 'Mademoiselle Charlebois came to ask about her brother, monsieur. The car was not here, you see, and she . . . she wondered where he had gone so late in the day. His supper . . . she had yet to get it ready, had not had time. She was frantic and could not understand why he would leave without telling her.'

'When . . . when was this?' breathed the Sûreté.

'Why . . . why the day she lost her keys. She thought she might have left them in the car. She had searched everywhere and thought her brother might have taken them by mistake.'

On Tuesday night, 15 December.

'The car had to go in for repairs and did not return until the following Thursday. Me, I have heard Monsieur Henri drive in in the small hours, but when she came to search the car in her night-gown and slippers, Mademoiselle Charlebois could not find the keys and was most distressed.'

Thursday the twenty-fourth, the day after the cinema fire, the day Hermann and himself had arrived. 'She did not ask her brother?'

The concierge shook his head. 'Monsieur Henri did not go up to the flat. He would not have wished to disturb her at such an early hour.'

Had it even been Henri Charlebois? 'There was a robbery at the Dijon shop, on the night of Tuesday the twenty-second,' said St-Cyr gruffly. 'Monsieur Henri left here on the morning of Wednesday, the twenty-third, and did not return until Christmas Day in the afternoon.'

'But the car . . . ? I know it returned here on Thursday, Monsieur the Chief Inspector. Everything is recorded. Everyone hears cars these days because there are so few of them, isn't that so?'

'Then perhaps you would let me examine your register,' breathed St-Cyr.

The car had been clocked in at 3.37 a.m. No Salamander

would have been so careless unless desperate or absolutely sure of himself.

'The flat,' said St-Cyr.

Concern leapt into the concierge's eyes. 'You will touch nothing?'

'Only what is necessary.'

'Then come this way. Please remove the shoes. No one will steal them.'

'All the same, I will take them with me and put them on the mat Monsieur Charlebois keeps just inside his door. Please do not attempt to telephone him, monsieur. It would be best for you if he did not know I was here.'

AT THREE THIRTY IN THE AFTERNOON, A LONE Daimler was parked outside the shop of Henri Masson, and the street that ran past it, ran straight from place Bellecour to place Carnot, the Hotel Terminus and the Hotel Bristol.

Frost had built up inside the windscreen of the Daimler and on the side windows. Lots of it, so the wait had been long and the driver frozen.

Kohler stood a moment in the rapidly fading light. Henri Charlebois's name, and that of the shop, had been among the list of concert patrons, automatically guaranteeing the antique dealer a handful of complimentary seats.

Bundled against the cold and fighting the ice underfoot, people hurried along the narrow street, oblivious to the shop windows, to fine china, crystal, furniture and paintings most could never have afforded even in pre-war days. Jewellery too, and walking-sticks of all things—watches, silks and bits of sculpture.

A few *vélos*, tragic in the freezing cold and likely to split apart, struggled to master the ice but could only do so with speed.

He crossed the road, pausing in the middle as a girl shouted, 'Monsieur, a moment, please!' The grey mouse in the back of the *vélo* didn't like the look of him. Plump and stuffed into uniform at the age of forty, the silly bitch had at last realized her true station in life and was proud of it.

He resisted the temptation to grab the *vélo* and wreak havoc. He wanted to tell her, Watch out, fräulein. One of these days some disgruntled bastard will drop a grenade into your lap and give you something to think about.

Instead, he strode purposefully into the shop, into an Aladdin's cave of glitter and warmth, the hush of talk over *objets d'art*, with but momentary glances his way from the clerks. A generaloberst with a monocle browsed, a generalmajor, a hauptmann—a few Frenchmen and their wives, a few very fine-looking Frenchwomen. All talking, all foraging, some pausing to pass fingers over a nice bit of porcelain or a bronze Pegasus or a truncated bit of Roman statuary with testicles just waiting to be fondled to soft, teasing laughter. '*Don't* squeeze them,' he warned one pretty thing. 'It hurts like hell and is still hurting.'

There were three floors, with a broad, spiralling staircase rising right in the middle to a huge chandelier of Baccarat crystal just waiting for a bomb to fall. No sign of Frau Weidling yet or of Henri Charlebois. Old friends? he wondered. Old lovers?

There were clocks, clocks and more of them. There were paintings big and small, tapestries long and short—weavings of silk and embroideries . . .

'Monsieur, is there something I can do for you?' sniffed someone.

The little squirt gave him the once-over from shoes to fedora. 'Gestapo,' breathed Kohler. 'To see the boss and the woman who is with him.'

The clerk started up the stairs. Kohler grabbed him and said, 'Don't. It's a surprise.'

'Then . . . then they are with the fabrics and the estate lingerie, monsieur. The shoes and dresses. It is on the third floor, at . . . at the back. There are three rooms. The Monsieur, he . . . he has said they . . . they were not to be disturbed.'

'Good.'

Martine Charlebois had got to the flat first. There were droplets of water near the mat just inside the door. Gingerly St-Cyr set his shoes down and drew the Lebel. Should he call out her name? She must have heard the concierge unlocking the door for him, must have heard them talking in the hall. Ah *merde*, where was she?

Not in the salon, not in the dining-room or kitchen, not in the brother's bedroom or her own . . . Had she killed herself? Had there been enough time? Yes, there had, idiot!

He hit the door to the bathroom and burst inside to find it empty. The lavatory? he shouted at himself, racing for it.

She'd been and gone and he did not know if she had taken the phosphorus. Two jars . . . two of them in a woven rush handbag, perhaps wrapped in a towel for safety.

And with bottles of gasoline? he asked and shuddered at the thought, smelling the garlic odour and seeing on the cinematographer's screen of his mind in black and white, with no fooling about in colour, the phosphorus bursting instantly into flame and giving off dense clouds of white smoke. The girl naked and on her knees in front of that priest who then had knelt facing the flames of retribution. The girl so desperate, she would defy all logic to come back here . . .

Like a cold, hard wind he went furiously through the flat. It was all so tidy it made him angry. Assistant professors of lycées had virtually no time, yet to have kept a house like this without help, she must have worked herself to the bone.

Even the superb Louis XV desk, with its regimented stacks of exercise books, was tidy.

It was a Hitlerian tidiness he could not understand. Sweating, he dragged off his overcoat, letting it fall where it would with a clunk, reminding himself to empty its pockets.

He tossed his fedora onto one of the Louis XVI armchairs whose gilt and pistachio-green trim was flaking. The scarf, he reminded himself, removing it. Ah *merde*, the place was like a mausoleum and a museum in which life had passed and the history of its artefacts had been jumbled. Royalty might once have slept in her bed, a superb *lit à la duchesse* with sumptuous drapery in gold and pale green brocade. Certainly it had come from well before the Revolution.

There was a magnificent, gilt-framed eighteenth-century Venetian mirror that reflected almost the whole of the room. And though he saw himself, shabby and diffident and lost among such refinement, he saw her too, naked and kneeling on the sumptuous Savonnerie carpet, saw her reflected in the mirror. Had Father Adrian made her watch herself as he had had sex with her?

The brass of an antique cage held a finch that sang, startling him for it must have been singing all along.

The canary was quiet. Soft and as golden yellow as a canary he remembered from another case, it lay on its side with the little door open.

She had had only enough time to kill the one. It being winter, she would not have released them, but would she have thought of this? Would she, in all her haste?

Trembling, he could not keep his hand still enough to get it inside the cage and had to calm himself. The canary felt cold but, then, little birds that die lose their body heat very rapidly.

No drawer had been untouched by himself, no door to either of the two magnificent armoires, and he knew then that he had been so frantic to find the phosphorus, his mind hadn't bothered to record if any of them had been partially closed.

There were condoms in a lowermost drawer of her dressing table—a loose handful, thrown down perhaps. In the wastebasket there was a pessary that, when held to the light, revealed the sabotage of a pin. Not once but several times.

Sadly he recalled another case, long distant from this lousy war. A girl in tears. A pessary with similar holes and a brother who had done the damage to a sister who had loved another.

A pair of forgotten ballet shoes in pink satin hung from the back of her door. Only a pair of shoes. Only their reminder of the dance, of hope and prayers and things one would like to be.

There were scent bottles on her dressing table and among them one containing *Étranger*. Gorgeous bits of glass and gold and silver. The photograph of a young man. 'Max.' Nothing else. Not, From Max, with all my love, my *liebchen*, or anything else. A German boy.

Though he must not feel sympathy for her, a sudden sadness would not leave him.

There was no sign of the sapphire bracelet he'd seen in the salon the other night. He was certain it had been a gift from the brother; certain, too, that it had been rejected by her. Pins and ear-rings and brooches—one superb pink topaz necklace with a rope of silver and a diamond-encrusted clasp from which finely braided tassels of silver hung. An emerald ring, an opal, a cameo—all of it was from the *belle époque*, that age of refinement before the guns of war had come.

The sister had known only too well that life is to be lived on borrowed time with borrowed things. Even the contents of her jewel case would come and go as circumstance dictated.

Gaps in the leather-bound books on her shelves revealed a missing Baudelaire and a volume of Proust. Had Claudine Bertrand given her that vial of perfume in exchange for the loan of the books? Probably.

She played the cello and this, a fine old instrument from

some estate sale, leaned against a chair in a far corner beside a music stand. Handel's *Water Music*, Mozart's *The Magic Flute*—she wasn't among the first cellists but among the seconds. Notations, in a tight, neat hand, were marked on the scores. 'Andante, Martine; fortissimo, *chérie*. Don't be so nervous here. It's all right. You'll do it.'

Flipping through one of the exercise books on her desk, he compared the handwriting. She'd done them both and had probably written the anonymous letters the préfet had given him. Yes, yes, she had.

Henri Charlebois's bedroom was every bit as immaculate. Two very fine Empire-style beds, with beautiful mahogany head- and footboards and inlaid ebony posts, had been pushed together. A single antique spread of pure white damask covered them. There were pillows enough for two. A superb Renaissance tapestry hung on the wall above the bed. A cathedral, a wedding ... Beside it, and to the right, there was a large painting of a young woman who modestly covered her eyes with the crook of an upthrown arm while the viewer ravaged her splendid breasts and wished the flimsy skirt of transparent gauze would slip from the soft swell of her hips.

It was of the *belle époque* and joyously marvellous, but a skylight in the painting, behind and to the left of the woman, let in the only light and this set her off starkly, as if to say, This is what you will get, monsieur, when you pay the price a young virgin commands.

In the bottom of an armoire he found the ledgers. They dated back to that period of time. La Belle Époque had done very nicely over the years. Had Henri Charlebois been afraid to own it completely or merely astute in selling shares to others? Astute. He had to grant him that.

Claudine Bertrand had indeed come to work there ten years ago, when the handwriting changed dramatically to a more martial stiffness that indicated Ange-Marie Rachline had first fought with her new employment.

But had Claudine not had a history prior to this and had not Ange-Marie Rachline and Henri Charlebois known of it?

There was a cold purity to the room he could not understand. Certainly things would come and go, and the brother had an eye for interior decorating as well as for his purchases. And certainly the semi-nude was suggestive of carnal thoughts, but had there really been any? Had the brother really coveted his sister?

The sterility of the twin beds suggested each kept to their own room as was befitting. But was that same coldness not their best defence against discovery of the forbidden?

Only Ange-Marie Rachline could answer him. The sister would never confess it to another now. The brother would never confide it even to the bishop.

Henri Charlebois was too astute, too knowing of his position in life. Both servant and master to the needs of others, to their desires for beautiful things and for all the sins of the flesh.

When he lifted the pillows, he found a pair of plain white cotton underpants with excellent needlework. They were not of today but of the past. They were those of a girl of ten or twelve perhaps but not, he thought, those of the sister.

Though he could not prove it, and perhaps would never be able to, intuitively he understood they had once been Claudine Bertrand's. He heard the sea in his imagination; he felt the wind among the dunes as it blew the grains of sand and made them silently roll. He saw a young girl spying on her brother and two others; saw a pair of underpants lying cast aside and forgotten.

The cotton was not harsh but soft from frequent laundering. Had the sister recently put them here to remind the brother of those days and what he'd done, or had he kept them all that time?

She had put them here, as a last gesture. He knew she had.

* * *

Frau Weidling had not, in so far as Kohler could determine, known Henri Charlebois from before, from Lübeck, Heidelberg and Köln.

The woman didn't even seem to know of him in any other context than that of a shopkeeper of antiques, period costumes, shoes, boots, fine fabrics and ebony *godemiches*. Ah yes.

Puzzled, Kohler held his breath. Frau Weidling was being fitted for a shimmering sky-blue silk dress, something old, something from an estate. Charlebois was methodically fixing pins around the hem. The shoes . . . the 'boots' she would wear were the same as those he'd seen before.

When the hem was done, and she faced one of the dressing mirrors, Charlebois adjusted the puffed shoulders, took a tuck in each of the long sleeves and then one in the back to tighten things up a little.

She passed a smoothing hand over her bosom, lifting a breast and then proudly tilting up her chin. 'Yes. Yes,' she murmured softly in German. 'That is good.'

'It ought to be. It's eight thousand, seven hundred francs with the alterations.'

Charlebois's German was really very good, thought Kohler and heard him saying, 'You can take it off now, I think.'

She did so, stepping out of it to stand in a white undershift beneath the corset that was laced up the front in the French style and hung with garters. He took the dress from her without a second glance at that statuesque bit of pulchritude which was bulging out of the top of the corset.

'Tomorrow,' he said, folding the thing once over on a cutting table. 'I will personally see that it is delivered to your hotel by noontime.'

She shook out her auburn hair, showed no desire to dress— fingered fabrics like a schoolgirl in a candy shop. There were shelves and shelves of them, all colours, all patterns against the highly polished spiralling support posts of mahogany. Fantastic prints in silk and satin, cotton and linen too, a fortune these days. There was a dressmaker's dummy in the corner nearest her—a cage of wicker over which only a blouse had been stretched so that the skirt of rods appeared as one of birch switches and obscene.

'The petticoats will not cause a problem?' she asked suddenly.

He didn't object. 'Frau Weidling, if you wish to try them on with the dress, please do. I've allowed for them. You can trust me.'

'All the same, I would like to,' she said demurely. Did she get a kick out of him helping her dress? wondered Kohler, still hidden from them but not, he felt, from the mirrors. Ah *merde*!

A shift-blouse was found—no neck or arms or buttons, just pretty bows of pink ribbon at the shoulders and lots of lace through which the corset could be seen to give that extra thrill.

The petticoats were of deeply pleated silk taffeta that rustled as she stepped into each of them. Not since he'd been a boy had Kohler seen a woman get dressed in such things, and then only in brief glimpses which had been ruthlessly punished.

'This one has a sateen dust ruffle.' Charlebois was all business. Nothing interfered, not even the nearness of her.

'I like the feel of them,' she said, smoothing her hands over hips and thighs to touch the pleats. 'They are like a young woman's skin, a girl's, is that not right?' He didn't answer. For just a split second he stiffened. 'So now, the dress again, Herr Charlebois, and then the hat,' she said. 'I must see it all once more.'

Ah *nom de Dieu*, what the hell were they up to?

'Then you had best put on the stockings and the shoes,' said the shopkeeper.

'And the necklace,' she answered.

Kohler saw him kneel to help her with the stockings. Was he going to stick his mitts up under all that stuff to fish about for garters and not get a hard-on?

'The underwear pants . . . ?' she said. 'Where are they?'

She got her hands up under everything and pulled her briefs off. He held drawers of silk trimmed with lace, into which she stepped. Perhaps he got them to her knees, perhaps a little farther before she took over. Did she have him in the palm of her hand? Was that it?

Would he kill her? Was he so cold and detached he was planning it even as he helped her, or had they been working together all along, yet she still did not know his true identity? A Salamander . . .

The stockings were of dark blue mesh and when he smoothed them over her calves, she let him. 'Hook them,' she said, and he saw Charlebois hesitate.

'I will get Mademoiselle Découglis, my shopgirl.'

'Don't be silly. There is no time. Besides, what harm could you possibly do me?'

He didn't like it. As he stuck his hands up there, she held him by the back of the head. Charlebois stiffened. Her fingers began to rub firmly up and down the nape of his neck. 'You will be at the concert?' she asked.

'Yes, of course. Mademoiselle Charlebois is in the orchestra.'

'Your little sister.' Had she tasted the saying of it, had Claudine primed her?

'Yes. Yes, my sister. She is always nervous before a concert.'

Frau Weidling didn't let go of him. He was on the left leg now, at the back. 'Isn't she afraid the Salamander will strike again? My Johann says that the theatre is a perfect location and that, once started, such a fire would be very hard to stop.'

Ah *merde*!

Charlebois found the shoes for her but did not lace them all the way up. Straightening, he removed her hand from the back of his neck. 'There will be no fire. The Salamander—if such a one even exists—would be foolish to try it, Frau Weidling. Your husband will be very thorough. I happen also to know that the men under the Obersturmführer Barbie's command have already placed the theatre under the strictest surveillance. Now, please, the necklace, I think, and then the hat.'

They were like two puppets going through their separate dances. Teasing, flirting in their desperate ways but numb to each other.

The hat matched the stockings and was like a small mush-room trimmed with rows of fluted braid and ribbons of satin taffeta into which three cock pheasant quills had been thrust. The height of fashion forty or fifty years ago, and as sure as that God of Louis's had made little green apples, she'd been fucking around with Claudine in La Belle Époque and wanted to play dress-up herself!

The necklace was of dark blue sapphires and diamonds, and when it was placed around her slender neck, she stood before the mirrors tilting her chin up this way and that, saying, 'It's per-fect. It's just as I imagined it, and just as you said it would be. This little concert first, so that the General Niehoff and the Obersturmbannführer Knab will notice my husband and me together as the lights are dimmed. Then the New Year's Eve concert at the Vienna Opera House with the Führer and the Reichsmarschall Goering who will both have heard of the Hero of Lyon and will see that my Johann becomes not just a pro-fessor at the Fire Protection School in Eberswald, but Gener-aloberst der Feuerschutzpolizei for the Reich.'

Verdammt!

'There are droplet ear-rings in my safe. I think you should consider them,' said the shopkeeper.

Christ!

'And the bracelet. Yes, it will not be too much.'

Every high-ranking Nazi in *France-Sud* must be attending the Lyon concert. A small fire just to keep them all happy, a handsome couple, a hero.

She was like a schoolgirl before her first ball; dressed like that, she was exactly like one of Madame Rachline's girls. Was Charlebois merely the servant, the decorator of this little

Christmas tree? Or had he another golden pear for her to hold in her hands when she was naked so that he could secretly photograph her and anonymously drop the print into Gestapo Lyon's lap?

'Johann says that Herr Robichaud has been placed in custody,' she confided, turning sideways to examine herself.

'That's a mistake I would wish them not to to make, Frau Weidling. Over the years, Herr Robichaud has worked very closely with the theatre committee.'

'Of which you are a member?' she asked coyly. She could have knocked him over with a fan.

'As was my grandfather before me,' came the answer stiffly. 'Julien knows the theatre intimately and could be of immense help. He and I and the other members of the committee have been over the building hundreds of times. If . . . if it is not impertinent of me, Frau Weidling, might I suggest you urge your husband to have him released?'

'Does the theatre mean so much to you?'

'It was my grandfather's pride and joy.'

'Then I shall ask Johann to request that the Obersturmführer Barbie release him, and I shall do so in return for this.' Delighted with the dress, she swirled around and grinned happily. 'But I will pay you in cash, have no fear.'

Had they been feeling each other out? Had she everything to do with the fires or absolutely nothing?

And what of Charlebois? What really was his game, if anything?

It was dark now, and the wash of dim blue light inside the crowded tram-car made it hard to concentrate, though St-Cyr knew he must. Bathed in this horrible light, the passengers appeared sickly and from another, quite alien world. Suspicious of him, accusative—Why cannot you solve this thing, monsieur? they seemed to ask with silent lips and furtive looks. Beaten, yes. Afraid, yes. A Salamander, monsieur. A Salamander . . .

Henri Charlebois, Claudine and Ange-Marie had experienced something so profound among the sands at Concarneau, it had come back to haunt them but would Madame Rachline tell him?

The car rumbled on toward another stop as though blind, for all the windows had been painted blue to shut in the light. Concentrating hard, he tried to stay awake. Concarneau, he said and heard the wind in from the sea.

Again he dozed off. Again he was awakened—ah *maudit*! The chasing around in that school, the warmth of the Charlebois apartment . . . When a seat became available, he threw himself into it and slept. Dreamed of flames and of their warmth, of Gabrielle and a few days of holiday, then of the fires and only then of Hermann, whom he saw from high up in the second balcony of the Théâtre des Célestins. Hermann was dwarfed by the magnificent vault of the ceiling and the glow from the stage curtains. Alone among the rows of empty plush-red seats the Gestapo's Bavarian nuisance was slumped dead centre in a front-row seat. Snoring up into the gods, melodiously and uncaring, his long legs stretched out so as to ease himself in the crotch. That left testicle . . . ah *merde*, was it bothering him again? During the last war Hermann had caught a cold in that most unfortunate of places and had ever since been proud of it as one would an appendix scar or a torn ligament!

The snoring continued. The house lights were dimmed. From high in the flies, Frau Kaethe Weidling watched with Martine Charlebois and her brother . . . her brother . . . and the ghost of Claudine Bertrand. Ange-Marie Rachline was there also, and Leiter Weidling—yes, yes, even Robichaud and his Élaine, and someone else, someone wearing the finery of La Belle Époque perhaps. Someone into whose face those of all the others dissolved until the mask was empty, the Salamander had disappeared again, and the house lights had been extinguished.

When the tram-car reached Perrache and the end of its loop, he was rudely awakened and told to get off.

'The rue Grenette,' he muttered, digging into a pocket for the notecase his mother had given him so many years ago, it was seedy and all but falling apart at the seams and had been mended many times with fishing line. 'I must cross the pont Alphonse Juin and make my way to a seamstress off the rue de la Baleine,' he said, still half asleep.

The conductor snorted as he took the fare. 'A seamstress ... he talks of seamstresses, Arthur,' the man shouted to the driver. 'He's not drunk on methylated spirits, perfume or shaving lotion.'

'Then let him sleep if he pays.'

'Until curfew?' asked the conductor, thinking the worst, that they'd have a corpse on their hands, dead from the cold.

'Ah no, not until then,' said the detective. 'Please awaken me when we get to my stop.'

A tip of five francs was handed over. Another was demanded. 'For the driver. He's the one who has to strain the eyes to watch for ice build-up on the tracks. Me, I am the one who must chop it out.'

'Then take two more and be sure to awaken me unless you want the city to burn. I'm a Chief Inspector from the Sûreté who has not slept in over two days.'

'Without transport?'

Ah *nom de Jésus-Christ*! were they to argue? Numbly he shook his head. 'With adequate transport suitable to the condition of your streets. Please see that you do as I have asked and please do not stop suddenly. Let the baby sleep or I will personally fire all six rounds from my revolver into your rheostat and call it self-defence.'

Having returned to the Théâtre des Céletins and nodded off, Kohler awoke to find the house lights out. *Verdammt*, what was the trouble now?

Easing himself upright in the pitch darkness, he listened hard. Weidling and Robichaud had been arguing off in some distant room. Fists raised like their voices. Something about there not being enough extinguisher globes—the lightbulb-shaped glass globes filled with red-coloured retardant that were to be tossed like hand grenades at the base of a fire-front. Weidling had wanted more of them mounted on the corridor walls and in the stairwells, no matter if they spoiled the décor and to hell with consulting the theatre committee; Robichaud had maintained that the globes would not be of much use anyway, because if the fire became that bad, then God help them.

But now there was not a sound. Seven fifteen p.m. and about two and a half hours of sleep.

Yawning, he got to his feet and tried to get his bearings. He was at the front of the theatre, right in the middle and just before the orchestra pit. Exits at the corners led to the stairwells and around to the foyer and backstage areas. Robichaud? he asked again, not liking the thought. Had someone got to the fire chief? They'd never stop the Salamander in this place without him. Ah *merde*!

Feeling his way, he made it to the exit in the far right corner and slipped behind and through its hidden entrance. Now there were the stairs up to the balconies but these would still be some distance ahead of him.

When he came to the corridor that led backstage, he went along it, feeling his way. Then down the long ramp deep into the cellars, to a warren of storerooms and dressing rooms, to smells of greasepaint, face powder, mothballs, sweat, laundry soap, stale tobacco smoke and stale perfume.

He struck a match. Oh *mein Gott*, the corridor had narrowed to a tunnel. The ceiling was now so low, his head all but touched it. Waving out the match, he struck another and another—cursed the French for their lousy matches—said, Robichaud, where are you? but said it silently. Did not look for a light switch, not yet. Ah no. There was something ... a feeling. A sixth sense that troubled.

The dressing room had a toilet in a far corner, no privacy wall or screen and Turkish, a hole in the floor with a pan around it. Shadows were flung about from the flame of the match in his hand.

There was a narrow counter with a mirror and an inadequate sink, walls that were scratched with the graffiti of lesser artists. Playbills that advertised *Das Rheingold, Tristan und Isolde, Madam Butterfly, Tannhäuser, Falstaff, Carmen, Die Meistersinger, Don Giovanni, Faust, Salome, La Traviata* and others. Faded, curled-up photographs of the singers, all of the greats he supposed, though he could not think of any but Caruso and envisioned that great tenor squatting in the far corner before racing up on stage to sing an aria from Puccini.

Notices advertised rooms to let, with and without meals. One in large block letters, read: DON'T TRY TO FLUSH THE TOILET UNLESS YOU'RE READY TO RUN!

There was greasepaint on the wire cage of the gas mantle that was used to heat it and probably to fry eggs or melt cheese if needed. There was a buzzer nearby. There were coathooks on one wall, a few cheap, wooden chairs, a steamer trunk with a broken lock, everywhere the calling cards of barbers, hairdressers, dressmakers, wigmakers, boarding houses, whorehouses and economical wine merchants.

There was not a sign of Robichaud in this or in any of the dressing rooms and he knew now, positively, that the main electrical switches had been pulled and that he'd run out of matches.

It was a bitch having to get about the city on foot when transport was so desperately needed. Breathless and half-frozen, St-Cyr banged on the door of the house behind La Belle Époque. Not a light showed. Like a tomb, the passage to the courtyard closed in on him and he wondered if he'd been right to come here, if he was not already too late.

Again the pounding echoed. 'Ah *nom de Jésus-Christ*, my

fist!' he shouted. 'Open up at once. Gestapo! *Raus! Raus!*' Get out! Get out!

No light showed even when the door was opened, but this was usual these days so one must not panic.

'Monsieur, what is it you desire?' came a hesitant voice, young, so young, a boy of ten perhaps.

Ah *merde*, the children, of course! 'A word with your mother, but please do not be alarmed. The vestibule, eh? Permit me to step inside a moment. This weather ... I feel as if I've just crossed the Mer de Glace without decent boots or brandy.'

Uncertain of what to do, the boy waited, forcing him to add, 'Please tell her Monsieur Jean-Louis St-Cyr is here from Paris.'

The attempt to hide his true identity and cushion the shock failed. 'You're a detective,' bristled the boy. 'Did you think we would not recognize such a one? You've come about the fires.'

'And about the murders of Mademoiselle Claudine and her mother,' said a girl sadly. 'Do not deny it, Monsieur the Chief Inspector of the Sûreté Nationale whose specialty is murder. The préfet himself has been here and has informed *maman* of the details.'

'The préfet ... Yes, yes.' Ah damn it, the young ... so tender of age. Had they relatives to take them in if necessary? 'Your mother?' he reminded them.

'*She didn't do it!*' shrilled the boy, trying to shut the door in his face. 'Our mother only tried to *help* Mademoiselle Claudine!'

'Yes, yes, I understand,' he said, pushing firmly on the door. 'Could you ... ? Would you please tell her I'm here.'

'She's *busy!*' hissed the girl fiercely. 'She has important work to finish and must not be disturbed!'

'A German lady,' piped the boy, still shoving manfully on the door. 'A dress for the concert.'

His foot was slipping! 'Now listen, eh? Lives are in danger. Time is very short. Take me to her at once!'

He heaved on the door and reluctantly they gave up but now,

in the light, he found himself subjected to such a hurtful scrutiny, it was unsettling. The boy was the image of the mother; the girl, taller and two years older, bore only touches of her. 'Our mother isn't here,' confessed the girl. 'Mademoiselle Charlebois . . .'

'Our aunt,' said the boy.

'She's *not* our aunt, René. She's only a . . . We only call her that because . . .'

St-Cyr let his shoulders relax a little. He took off his hat and heaved a sigh. 'Then Mademoiselle Charlebois came to see your mother as I suspected. Where have they gone? Come, come, it's important.'

'Our mother wouldn't let her stay here with us,' confessed the boy. 'They argued. Aunt Martine, she . . . she has shed the fountain of tears, monsieur, and cried to God for mercy.'

'She tried to kill me. She was distraught,' said St-Cyr sadly. 'I think she did something she need never have done and, fearing the worst, then attempted to take her own life and that of myself so as to protect her brother.'

'Uncle Henri?' asked the boy, startled.

The detective nodded gravely. He said that he did not yet understand everything, but felt a great mistake had been made. 'Where did they go?' he asked and one could see how weary he was both in the body and the spirit. 'To the shop of Mademoiselle Charlebois's brother?' he said and then, urging, 'Come, come, I must have answers.'

'We don't know,' said the girl, 'but could you not use the telephone, Inspector?'

The telephone . . . Would Hermann have gone to the shop? Suddenly it all seemed so futile, this chasing around without adequate transport. It was as if the préfet and Gestapo Lyon *wanted* the Salamander to succeed! 'If I telephone, I will only warn them,' he said. There was a chair in the vestibule, and though it was chilly here by the door, he slumped into it. 'Christmas,' he said. 'This is how a detective must spend his holiday, my little friends. Don't ever forget it; don't ever consider the life. Now, please, don't push a man who is exhausted. Tell me what they said to each other. They argued. Mademoiselle Charlebois said things your mother would not have wanted you to hear, is that not correct?'

Their silence told him this was so. 'Mademoiselle Charlebois has always come to your mother for help when she felt there was trouble with . . .'

The detective waited for them both to say it. He was searching them with the eyes of a priest . . .

Paulette Rachline swallowed with difficulty and dropped her gaze to the floor. 'When . . . when there was trouble between her and her brother, Inspector. Yes, that is so. You are correct.'

'What sort of trouble?' he asked, but one could hardly hear him, his voice was so gentle. 'The fires,' he said, softly again. 'Lübeck, Heidelberg and finally Köln. Now the cinema of the Beautiful Celluloid.'

'But not the tenement?' asked the girl, suddenly looking up at him with the clarity of truth betrayed.

'No, not the tenement,' he said, 'but then . . . ah then perhaps it is yet too early to say.'

They were quiet for a moment. They knew there were things they should tell him but knew also they must not do so.

'Tell me about the dress,' he said, catching them off guard. Suspicion rose in the girl's expression, doubt more slowly in the boy's.

'The dress . . . ?' said the girl. 'It's upstairs in mother's work room, Inspector.'

'Good. Take me to it.'

Frugal snippings of fabric littered the floor along with tiny bits of thread, lace and elastic and the trimmings from paper patterns. There was a sewing machine, a lamp over the work table—remnant bolts of cloth to the ceiling on shelves. Dressmaker's dummies—a half-finished blouse, being made over from another—several pairs of lady's bloomers, slips, suit jackets, skirts, dresses, overcoats and boxes of buttons and spools of thread, a measuring tape . . . The work was everywhere and so much, he had to wonder how Ange-Marie Rachline could possibly have found the time, then realized she must have delegated virtually everything at La Belle Époque to her *sous-maîtresse*, thus hiding the truth from her children and others.

The dress was magnificent and when told again that the owner was a German lady, a Madame Weidling, he thought he understood what was planned.

'Our mother didn't want to do the alterations, Inspector,' said the boy, plucking at the fabric. 'Uncle Henri, he . . .'

'He, *what?* Come, come, young man. To protect your mother is admirable, but to deny an officer of the police information vital to a case is to reject all that society has struggled through the centuries to accomplish. Like your mother and Mademoiselle Charlebois, they also argued, is that not correct?'

It was. 'Mother . . . mother already has far too much work, Monsieur the Inspector,' said the girl, 'She cannot simply set aside everything else, even for a German lady.'

'She . . . she has said it was unwise, monsieur.'

'Very dangerous?'

'Very stupid—foolish. That . . .'

'René, shut your mouth! We must let *maman* tell him. It is *not* up to us!'

'But it is, because in your hands rests the fate of the city,' said St-Cyr. 'With this weather, the waterlines may freeze. Once a major fire gets out of hand, it spreads from roof to roof until it cannot be stopped and the wind is drawn in so that the sparks and the flames rush up, up and up to silence the screams of all those who are trapped within.'

They shuddered. The girl said bleakly, 'Uncle Henri has told *maman* he will dismiss her if she doesn't do exactly as he says, Inspector. And . . . and that we . . . we will be thrown out of our house.'

'Had they argued like this before?'

'Yes. Yes, often—well, not so often, but yes, it was not the first time.'

'Think back. On the night of the cinema fire, did your mother go there with Mademoiselle Claudine Bertrand?'

'Mademoiselle Claudine had a bad chest,' said the boy. 'When she came to our door that night, *maman* was upset with her for being out in such terrible weather.'

'She took her home,' said the girl.

'Yes, yes, but did they go to the cinema first?'

'The cinema?' asked the boy. 'But why, monsieur? It was too late. It was already nine thirty or ten and Mademoiselle Claudine had lost a shoe.'

'Then did your mother know Mademoiselle Claudine had been to that cinema?'

They glanced at each other and kept silent. 'Look, you've already said you overheard the préfet telling your mother Mademoiselle Claudine and Madame Bertrand had been murdered. Your mother was the last to see them alive, but me, I do not think she killed them.'

'Then she could not have been the last to see them alive,' said the girl with wisdom beyond her years.

St-Cyr curtly nodded agreement. 'Someone must have followed them and gained entry when the concierge was absent.'

'Absent . . .' muttered the boy, hunting for something on the work table. 'Paulette, the big shears, they . . . they are gone.'

'The shears?'

'Yes,' said the girl. 'Mother was up here when Aunt Martine came to see her. It was here that they argued.'

Ah *merde*! A pair of shears with blades perhaps twenty centimetres in length. 'Take me to the telephone at once,' he said. 'Hurry!'

From somewhere distant in the darkness of the theatre, the sound of a telephone came. His pulse hammering, Kohler listened for it. *Ja, ja*, it was up over there at the back, beyond the first balcony, in the manager's office probably. No, no, it was in front here, down below him along the corridor to the dressing rooms in a little booth whose door must now be closed. Extensions? he asked.

Gott im Himmel, he was getting too old for this! The telephone rang and rang—jangling forlornly until suddenly it was answered at the half-ring and listened to.

Shit! Retreating, he found the stairs quite by chance and almost fell down them—had to grab the curtains to steady himself. Oops! *Verdammt!*

Counterweights would be swinging somewhere. Ropes wound around belaying pins would be straining.

There had been no sign of Robichaud or of Leiter Weidling for that matter or of any of Barbie's Gestapo watchers.

Keeping to one side, he went down the steps and when he came to the wig room, he ducked in there. Felt again the dyed horsehair under the hand, the stiffness of it, then that of a human. Much softer, much silkier . . . Perfume . . . was that perfume?

The head was round . . . Bald—was it bald beneath the wig?

It sat so still and at first he thought—ah, what did he think? That . . . that whoever it was had been sitting there for some time. A woman . . .

Plaster met his fingers as they explored the featureless face and neck of the wigmaker's dummy. *Étranger?* he asked. The scent was so strong now.

From chair to chair he went, feeling always—always ready to dodge aside, drop down, feint to the left or right.

Robichaud was not here—indeed, there was no one else but himself, but had there been someone?

Hesitating, he finally decided to go back up on stage and walk loudly across it just for spite. At once there were the curtains, heavy, cloying and, opposite them, why nothing but the floor— backdrops over there, then. Yes, yes, and directly ahead of him, the electrical switchboard and the pin-rails with their coiled ropes and belaying pins for lowering and raising scenery flies from the gridiron above the stage.

The smell of the place, of chalk dust and mould, greasepaint and powder, sour wine, old garlic and scenery paint. Mice probably and rats—that fetid, close smell of their dens, sour with their urine.

In the darkness, he could not touch the switchboard for fear of electrocuting himself. Everything in him wanted to cry out, *I'm here, damn you!* Yet there'd been no sign of Robichaud, and the fire chief was his responsibility. Ah *merde*.

Something moved. Stiffening, Kohler heard it again and then again, a gentle see-sawing. When he looked up into the inky blackness, he felt a droplet hit him on the forehead.

Crouching, he ran his fingers delicately over the floorboards, tracing out the gaps between them as he did so.

Again he heard the see-sawing high above him and when he found the pin-rails with their ropes, he found one rope that was much tighter than the others.

Unwinding it, he eased the heavy object down and down and down until it touched the stage. Then he let it collapse, and he waited.

Her perfume was stronger now and at first he thought she was standing so near he could but reach out to touch her. He remembered the belfry of the Basilica, the shoes that had been left for him to find, the gasoline. He remembered standing among the columns of the Palais de Justice and in the rue des Trois Maries.

Louis, he said. Louis, we're in trouble. He knew it was a body he'd lowered, knew that if he crouched over it, the killer might well strike again. But had the Salamander any need now, having removed the one man they needed most?

He did not need to touch the body to know that it was Robichaud. A sadness entered. Élaine Gauthier would never leave the Hotel Terminus alive, he knew that now. The couple had gone to the cinema to meet with Resistance leaders among the railway workers, or simply to see a film, *La Bête humaine*, and to be with each other. She wouldn't be able to tell Barbie much. Robichaud would have made certain of that for her own safety.

There was no knife or other sharp instrument sticking out of the throat or chest, yet there was blood, lots of blood and it soaked the sweater and had seeped right down to fill the shoes.

Kohler wiped his fingers on a trouserleg. He wished he'd been able to find the weapon but knew only that it had been removed.

Multiple stab-wounds then, an act of frenzy or one so clever, it had been made to look like that.

A Salamander . . .

Listening hard, he cautiously straightened up and waited, willing his mind to reach out into the darkness, but to where . . . where . . . ?

Close . . . so close, he could feel the distance between them and yet . . . and yet . . .

'*Shears* . . . a pair of dressmaker's shears, idiots!' shouted St-Cyr desperately in German to the Gestapo watchers sitting warm and cosy in their car. 'Can you *not* get it into your thick skulls that the Salamander is *already* inside that theatre? My partner . . .'

He gave up. Furious with them, he banged a fist against the roof of the car and stared futilely at the blue wash of paint which all but hid the lamplight and gave the vague outline of the place des Célestins.

Somewhere high over the city a lone aircraft had lost its way perhaps. From the corner of the rue André came the tramp of the patrol which constantly circled the theatre.

'Please, I . . . oh for sure I know I'm begging, my friends, and that you have no orders to enter the theatre with me, but . . .' He shrugged expansively, throwing his hands out in futility towards the frost-covered windows, one of which had been rolled down a centimetre. Dark . . . it was so dark within the car, except for the glow of their cigarettes. 'But I have tried everywhere else. Leiter Weidling left the theatre some time ago. Hermann—'

'Robichaud and Kohler have not yet come out,' grunted their driver.

'Yes! At last you being to under—'

'No one else has gone inside. No one could have got past us. Everything's locked up tighter than a termite's ass.'

Ah *merde*, the idiots! Had they not thought others might have keys? 'Then have you a key to one of the entrances?' he asked.

They had, and this was dangled through a gap of no more than ten centimetres. 'Enjoy yourself.'

'Enjoy myself . . . ? But—'

'Obersturmführer Barbie says that if you want so badly to find out where your partner is, you had better go in there yourself.'

'Does he *not* want to stop the Salamander?'

'Not until tomorrow night.'

The key was to the stage door and they let him find this out too. As he felt his way gingerly along a corridor, images kept flashing through his mind of theatres past and murders past, of an actress who had been hanged in the full costume of a lady-in-waiting but had had a bad job done of it, for the pipe above her had broken under her weight and had showered her corpse with effluent; of a promoter who had been shot for a failure, not by a disgruntled backer but by a young actor whose brilliant career had come to an abrupt end and justly so, according to the notices. He saw the furtive, crowded liaisons of urgent lovers both of whom had had jealous mates who would savagely kill them; he heard the gossip, the insidious backbiting, the carping and the cajoling, the commotion that always went on behind stage and beneath it during a performance.

There was no one in the wig room, no one in any of the

dressing rooms, but Hermann was very good at this, and Hermann would have checked them all out.

Martine Charlebois and Ange-Marie Rachline would have gone to the brother's shop on the rue Auguste Comte, which was not all that far from the theatre if one cut diagonally across place Bellecour. Perhaps the shop had been closed when they got there, perhaps not. Frankly, he had no way of knowing. Henri Charlebois could just as easily have been out at his supper with Frau Weidling perhaps, for Leiter Weidling had said only that his wife was dining elsewhere . . .

When he heard a pair of shears close, he knew he was in a large yet crowded room. The costumes were everywhere, some half finished, others complete; some hanging in bunches from hooks on the walls, others from wires that dangled from the ceiling. Still others on the dummies, both male and female.

He ran a hand lightly over one. Ruffled satin and silk velvet with pompon buttons. A clown, a harlequin?

Again the shears closed tightly, quickly, and in his mind's eye he saw a cutting table long and cluttered, was taken right back to Ange-Marie Rachline's house and those two children.

Cocking the Lebel, he pointed it at where the sound had been and waited.

When nothing further happened, he knew that whoever had closed the shears had left the room, or had they?

The scent of *Étranger* rushed at him only to dissipate, and for a time there was silence.

'Louis . . . Louis, it's me. You wouldn't happen to have a match, would you? I seem to have run out.'

The savagery of the killing suggested a torment that had gone beyond the bounds of sanity. In thrust after thrust the shears had been plunged into the fire chief's chest, the heart, the lungs, and then the throat, cutting the jugular. Then again in a last desperate embrace that had seen the shears pulled out by his killer and dropped on the stage only to be picked up later and . . . what wondered St-Cyr? Washed and dried, taken back to Madame Rachline's work room, hidden among those here, or thrown into the Saône on departure?

They would have to search outside. Surely there would be a thin trail of blood, surely a bloodstained overcoat, sweater or blouse? And why hadn't Hermann heard a thing?

He had been too far away perhaps, but had the killer known the theatre so well as to be aware of this?

Robichaud had come up on stage to see about the lights, but had his killer known this was what he'd do, that Hermann could not possibly have found the main switch? The fire chief had not been wearing his overcoat and hat—these had been left in the manager's office, upstairs at the back of the theatre. He'd been digging into every nook and cranny, but had he been killed because of what he'd found or simply as insurance against the future?

Everywhere there were Gestapo agents supposedly trained to search out hidden documents, et cetera, et cetera, now looking for the phosphorus. They were thorough, of course. Certainly they'd look in all the logical places but were they dealing with logic?

When Hermann came up to him, the Bavarian was shaking his head. 'Are we supposed to think it was the sister, Louis, or did she really do it? The first wound was to the heart—I'm almost certain of it. But would the kid have had the strength or knowledge to hang him up like that, or did she have help?'

'Are we being played for a pair of fools, Hermann? Is the third fire even to be here?'

Hermann imagined he could see the flames and hear the screams, he could see himself straining to reach yet another fire-starter even as the smoke enveloped him. 'Patience, *mon ami*. Patience,' cautioned St-Cyr. 'If there is to be another fire, then the sequence is not the same as in 1938. It took fires in Lübeck, Heidelberg and finally Köln to do away with Martine Charlebois's lover.'

'But this time round, if indeed Father Adrian ever touched her—'

'Oh he did. That priest most certainly did and several times.'

'Then there need only have been one fire, that of the cinema.'

'Precisely! And that is the sadness with which we must deal, Hermann, for now we have a Salamander who must strike again in order to hide the truth about another person.'

'Or else it's Leiter Weidling and that wife of his. Claudine set her up, Louis. As sure as we're standing here, Frau Weidling was there to have some fun. If you ask me, that husband of hers was using her as bait.'

'And the Salamander, Hermann?'

'Knew all about it and made use of them.'

They would meet up here on the terrace in front of the Basilica, said St-Cyr grimly to himself with satisfaction. They would look out over the darkened city as he was doing to see where so much went on behind closed doors yet was seldom admitted beyond a secretive whisper or nod. Guillemette, the préfet, would come first with Madame Rachline. She couldn't refuse the chief of police and part owner of her house. The bishop would bring Henri Charlebois who would have come to him for succour in his hour of need. Lastly, Klaus Barbie would find and bring Frau Weidling and her husband, if for no other reason than sadistic curiosity.

Within that select group lay all the answers they would need, but had it been wise to summon them at the same time?

Hermann hadn't liked the idea. It offered too many outs; darkness alone would shield escape.

Yet in darkness was there truth, for without light, the voice tended to betray the deeply hidden thoughts. And the silence of the city was an asset, for it allowed each inflection to be magnified.

Alone and desperately afraid, Martine Charlebois would hide

or roam the city until both the cold and the curfew drove her to seek refuge.

Not at her home, ah no, poor thing, nor up here under the bishop's wing. With her *zazous* perhaps, but he did not think so — she was fundamentally too kind to want to involve them any more. Not with Ange-Marie Rachline either, or at La Belle Époque which she hated with a passion.

A room ... would she have taken a room in one of the tenements as she had before only to hang herself this time?

He shook his head over such a thing and sadly said to himself, She will not attempt to do so until after the concert.

At the sound of steps, he turned.

'Louis, if this doesn't work, we're going to have to have transport. Let's take the préfet's car and say to hell with the consequences.'

'Why not Klaus Barbie's?'

'Are you crazy?'

'Unless I am very much mistaken, Hermann, the Obersturm-führer will be only too glad to allow us the use of his car.'

'Louis, we're dealing with a Salamander that can change its colour any time it wants.'

'But usually when warmed, Hermann, by the heat of the sun or a fire.'

'Thanks! *Gott im Himmel,* I wish you'd tell me what you've got in mind for this little conference of yours! I *can't* watch all the exits by myself.'

'That's why we need the car, and that's why the Obersturm-führer will let us have it.'

Ah *merde*, he might have known! 'Because if we fail, the blame for what happens will be ours.'

'And we *must* force the Salamander into making a move now, Hermann, before it's too late.'

Kohler told himself to give it a moment. He'd take a deep breath. 'We needed Robichaud, Louis. We should have had him with us.'

'And Madame Élaine Gauthier, Hermann? What of her?'

Did he have to ask it like that? 'Dead—she threw herself out of a fourth-floor window at the Hotel Terminus. Went right through the glass before the bastards could stop her.'

It would be best not to sigh. 'Then that's all the more reason for the Obersturmführer to allow us the use of his car and the full co-operation of Gestapo Lyon should we need it.'

'*Never*, Louis. *Never!* I'd rather shoot myself.'

Ah no. 'Please don't say things like that, Hermann. You can't tell who might be listening. Besides, we've a date to go fishing after this war is over.'

Louis hardly ever had the last word but this time he'd let him. It'd be freezing at Stalingrad. The boys would be hunkered down behind some pile of rubble trying to keep their Schmeissers warm enough to prevent the gun-oil from freezing and seizing them up. They'd be trying not to think of home.

And Gerda? he asked. Ah *nom de Jésus-Christ*, was it not a form of poetic justice to have her wrapped in the arms of a French labourer and suing himself for a divorce?

He thought of Oona and of his little Giselle in Paris. He thought of all the cases Louis and he had been through, of sleep needed but denied to the point of overexhaustion.

He thought of Frau Weidling and of the cartridges Louis had found in that woman's purse, and he said so quietly to himself alone, You're mine.

10 KOHLER HUNCHED HIS SHOULDERS AGAINST THE cold and pulled his collar up more tightly. The little buggers were going to kill themselves. Instead of the silence Louis had depended on, the kids and teenagers were whooping it up on their bobsleighs, and oh *mein Gott*, what a wizard of a run! Right down Fourvière Hill and through Vieux Lyon to place Bellecour or place *Terreaux*! Right down the snaking climb of the jardin du Rosaire past the Stations of the Cross . . . zip! What Cross? Then straight on down the montée des Chazeaux, hitting each section of steps. Bump, bump, rumble, rumble . . . Forty . . . fifty . . . sixty kilometres an hour—would they hit such a speed? *Maudit*, they had the guts and the wild abandon of their youth!

And wasn't it nice to hear them having such a good time, forgetting all about the fires and the threat of others, forgetting everything about this lousy war?

It had been years since he'd been on a bobsleigh. Years! He'd led the pack—there'd been no one to catch him, and Gerda . . .

why Gerda had been there too, sometimes on the sleigh, *ja, ja,* as light as a feather in those days. Sometimes by the old iron kettle of hot cider, cocoa or mulled wine if they could steal it, and always ready for a roll in the hay. Always ready with water for the runners.

Ah *merde,* sentiment had no place in a detective's life. Louis was having trouble. The noise was constantly distracting him. Once a father, always one, the poor Frog would leap in alarm at each gap in the rumbling, each pause that might signal a cliff, an imminent head-on collision with a stone wall or tree, then he'd try to recover only to catch an impatient breath as the next bit of quiet suggested its ugly possibilities.

'Monsieur Charlebois, don't be so evasive, eh? A tragedy, my friend. Your sister . . .'

Rumble, rumble . . .

'Mademoiselle Charlebois telephoned me here, Inspector. I assure you she could not possibly have tried to kill you,' said the brother stiffly.

'*And* herself!' shouted Louis nervously.

'No, no,' grunted Bishop Dufour. 'It's just not possible in one so tender.'

'*Tender?* Is that how your secretary found her, Bishop? Ah, must I throw the two of you to the Obersturmführer Barbie? That girl is out there, my friends. Does she have the phosphorus? Is she going to torch another crowded tenement?'

'Inspector, what is this?' demanded the antique dealer. 'Are you suggesting Mademoiselle Charlebois is the Salamander?'

That was better, thought St-Cyr. He would take out his pipe now and begin to pack it and they would know he was doing so, because he would offer them some tobacco. Resistance tobacco!

An uncanny silence closed in on the hill, and for a moment all the bobsleighs had gathered for a rest or had departed, or perhaps it was the riders were simply hauling them back?

Louis waved out the match. 'No, monsieur, I am not suggesting your sister is the Salamander.'

'Then *what* are you suggesting?' demanded Charlebois nervously.

'Monsieur, if she telephoned you here, tell me, please, how she knew you'd be with Bishop Dufour? It's a Saturday night. You cannot have seen her in some time or is it, monsieur, that you saw her at your shop at around seven this evening and that what she said then drove you to seek an audience with the bishop?'

'Henri, let me,' began Dufour. The Sûreté had no business being so high-handed! 'Monsieur Charlebois and I had a meeting, Inspector, to discuss the final details for the concert. This meeting had been arranged for some time and was conducted over supper in the manse. Martine Charlebois would have known of it. She is also a member of our symphony orchestra.'

Ah *nom de Dieu*, had he to contend with them both? 'The cello ... yes, yes, Bishop. But the girl did try to kill me and herself...'

'Surely not. The gas is often turned off by our German friends out of necessity, is that not so? Perhaps the main valve at the school was left open, the others also?' said Dufour.

All right then! 'Did you give Monsieur Charlebois absolution this evening, Bishop?'

'If I did, Inspector, that is a matter between God, myself, Monsieur Charlebois and no other.'

The bastard!

'Inspector,' said the antique dealer, 'I have a great deal of work to do tomorrow. There is an important sale in Paris on Monday afternoon and evening. The Reichsmarschall Goering will be there. Due to the robbery at my shop in Dijon, I must place a number of pieces up for auction and must have them ready to leave with me on the first train.'

How convenient! At 6 a.m. Berlin time, and with Frau Weidling, was that it? 'Paris . . . yes. Yes, I understand, monsieur, but what of your sister? Surely you have a thought for her? A little concern, perhaps?'

'Mademoiselle Charlebois will be at home where she belongs. Bishop Dufour will attest to the fact that I told her she had nothing to fear, Inspector, and that she was to go home and wait for me there.'

'And then, monsieur?' asked Louis, drawing on his pipe. God, but the city was quiet!

'Then I will sort it all out, Inspector. I promise you there's been nothing untoward. It's all a misunderstanding.'

'Yes, yes, a misunderstanding,' echoed Dufour.

'Bishop, we have the deaths of so many to consider, that of Father Adrian also, and now that of Monsieur Robichaud.'

'Julien . . . but . . . but . . .'

Were they both so taken aback? wondered St-Cyr. Ah, it was not possible to tell, and now . . . why now the shouting grew again as the boys and girls struggled back up to the heights with their sleighs.

'Inspector, surely Julien was not murdered? An accident . . .' said the bishop, aghast at what had happened.

Louis was brutal. 'No accident, Bishop, and now the city is at the mercy of the Salamander. Yes, my friends. With Robichaud out of the way, the Salamander has a clear field unless . . .'

Damned if Louis didn't pause to tap out the pipe and begin to repack it!

'Unless *what*, Inspector?' asked Charlebois impatiently.

More shouting came from well off to the left. 'Hey, Cécile, over here, my sweet little rocket. Let us have the challenge match!'

'Together, Cécile, a marriage of our racers, with no holds barred.'

'Marie, he wants to contest his little bit of sandpaper with our goddess of the ice!'

'Every year it is the same,' grumbled the bishop. 'Shut up, you bunch!' he shouted violently. 'You are to leave the hill at once!'

Dead silence followed, then giggles, after which came laughter and a few catcalls. 'A *meeting!*' shouted Dufour angrily. 'An important conference is in progress. The . . . the fate of the city . . .'

Rumble, rumble . . . bump . . . bump! Rumble, rumble . . . Ah *merde*, the first bend in the Stations of the Cross . . . A shriek! A cry . . .

Then cheers as the racers flew past others in the darkness.

'Unless we have the truth, Bishop. The truth!' leapt the Sûreté. 'Mademoiselle Charlebois made a tragic mistake. Once committed, she had no other choice but to follow through.'

'What mistake?' demanded Charlebois.

Stung, Louis turned on him. 'Please do not interrupt a police officer in the exercise of his duties, monsieur. A mistake compounded by a history of your abuse! Now I *must* have answers from you both!'

'What abuse?' asked Dufour, his suspicion all too clear.

Others had arrived. 'Not physical, but mental,' said Madame Rachline. 'Admit it, Henri. You have always wanted Martine for yourself and to protect her purity. Oh not to love in a sexual way, Inspector—she would never have agreed to that—but to keep from others who would only violate her.'

'Hermann . . . ?'

'Louis, I'm over here.'

'Good! Préfet, this man is to be placed under arrest.'

'Now wait a moment, Louis. Monsieur Charlebois . . . ? Pah! It's impossible. You must be out of your mind. You expect me to put the bracelets on him for what, please?'

Guillemette had always been difficult.

'For the murder of Robichaud?' snorted Charlebois.

The antique dealer was breathing quickly, but was it the moment to pounce? 'Three people were involved in the cinema fire, monsieur . . .'

'*Three*, Louis?' demanded Guillemette. 'Don't tell me our Salamander is three *women* and if so, hah! how does that explain your inclusion of Monsieur Charlebois?'

Hermann had best be working the shadows. If only the bobsleighs would cease their torment again. 'Madame Rachline, did you go to that cinema with Claudine Bertrand?'

It was all coming back to haunt them. Concarneau and the beach, Henri and his little sister. 'I did not, Inspector. There are several who were at La Belle the night of the fire. Any or all of them, if necessary, will tell you I was at the house over the supper hour and left it to cross into my own house at about 9 p.m. to be with my children.'

'Good. Then please tell us, madame, when Claudine came to your door, having lost one of her shoes, did she come in tears? Was she distraught?'

'She's dead, Inspector. It cannot matter,' came a woman's voice in German.

'Ah, Frau Weidling, I am glad you are here at last. Leiter Weidling, Obersturmführer . . . we are all now gathered before a city in darkness and fear,' said Louis in German. 'Was she distraught, Madame Rachline?' he asked in French, only to translate so as to bring it home to the others.

The time had come, and she had known all along that it would. 'Yes. Claudine was in very bad shape, Inspector. She had been scared out of her wits but more than this, was terrified she'd be killed.'

Rumble, rumble . . . bump, bump . . . *bump*! Rumble . . . rumble . . .

'She was certain Frau Weidling had been involved in the fire, Inspector, and that the woman would . . . would see to it that she . . .'

'Ange-Marie, be careful what you say.'

'Henri, why should I, with two police officers beside me?'

Klaus Barbie would be translating for the Weidlings.

Charlebois waited. Perhaps he held his breath in impatience, perhaps he was figuring out what to do.

Louis told Madame Rachline to continue. Klaus Barbie said in French, 'Yes, please do. I've a prior engagement I must attend.'

Another visit to the favourite brothel, eh? snorted Kohler, hugging the deeper darkness of the Basilica.

'Yes, please continue,' said Frau Weidling in brittle German. 'Am I a suspect, Inspector? Johann, ask him if I am.'

'You most definitely are, Frau Weidling, as I believe you are only too aware. You were at those other fires in 1938. In each, it would not surprise me if you—'

'Ah no, of course,' said Madame Rachline. 'Why could I not have seen it before? Another cinema, a crowded lecture hall . . .'

Was she being clever, wondered Kohler, or honestly blaming herself?

Again the bobsleighs took to the ice. Again there was the rapidly dwindling rumble of their runners, the bump, bump, bump as they went down over steps, then the awful gaps in sound, the sudden pauses as the sleighs took wing . .

'Herr Obersturmführer, this is preposterous. I must insist that we return to the hotel. My wife is very tired and I must go back to the theatre if I am to search it thoroughly,' said Weidling.

'Your wife,' said Louis. 'Herr Weidling, tell us how the two of you met.'

'That's none of your business nor does it concern us here.'

'Is it that you wish me to tell them?' demanded Louis. 'Come, come, Leiter Weidling. She was a prime suspect in the Lübeck fire. From there, you followed her to Heidelberg—is that not right?—and then to Köln. She was in those cities as were Martine Charlebois and her lover.'

'Her fiancé . . .' said Madame Rachline. 'And . . . and Claudine, Inspector. Claudine asked for some time and I gave it to her. A little holiday, she said, a few addresses we all knew about, *oh bien sûr*. Martine was in the Reich on a student exchange. Claudine said that Henri wanted her to . . . to check up on his little sister, that Martine had . . . had found herself a lover.'

'Louis . . . ? Louis, one of them has left the terrace.'

'Hermann! Why did you not stop him?'

He'd been there and then he'd not been there, but was he still close and was he really the Salamander?

Rumble, rumble, rumble . . . bump, bump, bump . . . 'Johann . . . Johann, do not leave me now! Please, my *liebling*, I beg it of you.'

St-Cyr grabbed the préfet and told him to make certain Frau Weidling was not let out of sight. Then he shouted to Hermann and began to run, to slip and slide and almost end up on his ear! Ah *merde*, the ice! 'Hermann, where are you?'

'Over here, Louis. Here!'

A small incline, nothing much—the grand slide perhaps. Silhouettes standing around, objecting. Hermann shouting, 'Gestapo. This sleigh has been requisitioned!' Teenagers . . . teenagers . . . Ah no.

'Get on, Louis. That's an order.'

'But . . . but . . .'

'The girl, idiot! The *sister*. She must be hiding at the shop!'

Rumble, rumble . . . Rumble, rumble . . .

'Push, Louis! *Heave!* Ah *Gott im Himmel*, idiot. Give it a run and leap on or stay behind!'

They bolted down the hill. They took the bends, shot out over something. Hit the ground only to lift again. Ah *mon Dieu, mon Dieu* . . .

Hurtling through space, the sleigh crashed on to a street, crossed over, bashed sideways into a wall . . . the hands . . . the hands . . . 'Hermann!'

'Hang on, Louis!'

Bump, bump, bump—rumble, rumble, rumble . . . Ah no, the montée des Chazeaux . . .

Streaking past a foot patrol, they turned onto the rue de la Bombarde, shot past the Palais de Justice and downstream along the quais, across the pont Bonaparte and across place Bellecour.

Coasting to a stop, they ended up in front of the shop of Henri Masson, Fine Antiques.

'Are you still there, Louis?' asked the captain doubtfully.

'Yes, I am still alive. Me, I am continually being surprised by your talents. Please enter the shop, find the girl and arrest her before the brother arrives.'

'I take it we don't need the magistrate's order?'

'No. Not if you are from the Gestapo.'

'Then wait here and stop him when he comes along.'

'Of course. It will be my pleasure.'

Verdammt, but that had been one hell of a run! Walking nimbly up to the door, Kohler fired two shots into the lock and yanked on the wires to silence the alarm. Then he vanished inside, leaving his partner and friend to gradually still the shaking that was in him.

St-Cyr considered things. The sleigh had best be moved, the street allowed to return to itself.

When, after twenty minutes perhaps, he had heard nothing, he crossed the road and hesitantly entered the shop, saying silently, Hermann . . . Hermann, what has happened?

The girl was on her knees. Bathed in the glow from a single candle stub set on the floor in front of her, she trembled as she waited for them to apprehend her. And the trembling was such that the nubby end of the needle-pointed dagger at her breast quivered in the light, throwing little flashes of ruby.

Kohler sucked in a breath. Ah *merde*, what was he to do? All around her were the trappings of the shop—fine antiques, exquisite gold and glass, marble and oils. The pickings of a scavenger who fed on the deaths of others. The bones of the centuries.

They were on the second floor of the shop, behind so many things—tucked away in a far corner beside a case of weapons. And all about them, the warm air stirred as the draught from the open door below let in the frost.

'*Don't come any closer!*' she shrilled at last. There wasn't a hint of hesitation about the dagger now. '*Have you taken my brother?*'

When no answer came, she shrieked the question at him and he saw then that the pale cheeks were stained by tears.

'Look, I . . . We . . . My partner and I won't harm you, Mademoiselle Charlebois. I swear it.'

She didn't listen. With one hand, she ripped the white cotton blouse open—tore at it until brassiere and flesh were exposed and he could see that blood was trickling.

Again the hilt was firmly clasped with both hands. 'Okay, okay. You win, eh? Here, let me put my pistol on the floor where you can see it.'

A warning sounded in him but the detective paid no attention to it, and in any case, no matter what she said, he would not understand, would not care because everyone would blame her. 'I didn't want to do it. You have *forced* me to, monsieur! You have *raped* my mind until I had to do it to save him.'

Had Louis come upstairs? Had she seen him? 'Now look, crimes of passion are always dealt with less severely. If there are extenuating circumstances, the courts will be lenient.'

She gave the half-smile of tragedy. 'Eighteen, monsieur? *Eighteen?* Were you not the one to catch the child that fell from it's mother's arms?'

'The tenement fire . . . You lit it to take the heat off your brother.'

'A *Salamander*, monsieur! A creature of mythology. One that lives in fire and basks in its warm embrace as naked lovers do in the act of their union. A scaleless, slippery animal whose skin is *soft*! A creature that can change its colour when trapped! A *chameleon*, monsieur—that would have been a far better code-name for you people to have used. A lizard that can *vanish*!'

'Will he torch the theatre?'

'As he torched the cinema of the Beautiful Celluloid?'

Again there was that half-smile both cruel at what life had dealt her and yet bemused. 'Another fire for which there is no need, monsieur? You see, I didn't know. Until that fire at the cinema, I never thought for a moment that my brother might have been responsible for those other fires. He was my saviour. He was the one person to whom I could run for shelter. And in any case, he could not have done the cinema fire alone, could he? Oh *mais certainement* he must have had help before, but had he had it this time? I hesitated to approach the ruins. I was so afraid Henri would have been trapped inside. Burnt to a crisp. Ashes ... nothing but ashes. But the memories kept crowding me and I saw my Max in flames. I saw his face begin to melt, I heard his screams. Now I know Henri must have found us together just as he discovered Father Adrian with me.'

Ah *Gott im Himmel*, the kid was going to kill herself!

'My brother has always been fascinated by fire, monsieur, and has always wanted me. Henri used to watch me when I was naked as a child. He would strike matches and hold them up, and I would not understand the intensity of his gaze. Oh for sure he would never bring them too close to me and I knew this yet was always afraid. He used to bathe me, did you know this? He used to worship his little sister whom he called "perfection".'

She became more matter of fact. 'You see, monsieur, Henri would play a game with Claudine and Ange-Marie, a game in which fire was discovered to cause arousal. Really it was fear, I guess. Oh *mon Dieu*, who's to say? But Ange-Marie knows all about it. You'll have to ask her.'

'And Claudine? What about her, mademoiselle? What about the keys to your school?'

He wanted the phosphorus. He *wanted* to keep her talking so as to still death's sweet moment for as long as possible. 'Claudine had to be killed, isn't that so? She could not be allowed to live knowing what she did. She had made a telephone call for Henri that had summoned Father Adrian to his death, she had agreed to meet with a certain woman in a certain cinema. The white sugar of oxalic acid was placed in the bowl, then the concentrated sulphuric allowed to drain slowly down the inside to cover the oxalic which immediately began to fizz.'

'Yes, but who did it?'

'Claudine would never know. You see, she feared another— isn't that correct? A German lady. Beautiful, wanton, eager to touch Claudine's breasts with fire as a lover would. Naked and alone but secretly watched by another who would take photographs of them. Photographs that would then anonymously fall into the hands of the Gestapo thus pointing the finger of suspicion at the two of them. Me, I have found the negatives and destroyed them.'

The girl took a breath. Perhaps she wanted to quickly brush the hair back from her left cheek, perhaps she simply wanted to swallow, thought Kohler.

'Carbon dioxide gas is heavier than the more deadlier carbon monoxide, monsieur. Both are released in equal quantities and they tend to displace the air that is in the bowl above the mixture but . . .' Again there was that smile. 'But it really doesn't matter, does it? Once the gases are breathed, the blood absorbs the poison and the mind slips into unconsciousness. Then death comes quickly to steal the soul and silence the tongue for ever.'

'Did you kill her?'

He would not believe her but she would tell him anyway. 'No, I did not. Jean-Pierre, my beautiful *zazou*, told me how it must have been done. He found it in one of his father's chemistry texts.'

'Did Ange-Marie Rachline do it?'

'For you I have no more answers, monsieur. I have sinned and the futility of my sin is that I wished only to protect the brother whom I loved and admired and tried so hard to understand.'

'Don't do it, *please*. The phosphorus . . . Two bottles, Mademoiselle Charlebois. At least five hundred grams in . . . ah, God alone knows how many cubes.'

The phosphorus . . . 'Kept under water, it bursts instantly into flame on exposure to air . . .'

'Please tell us where it is,' begged the detective and she saw that he, too, had gone down on his knees before the flame and that there were tears running down his time-ravaged cheeks. 'Must more be killed?' he asked. 'Robichaud, mademoiselle? Did you have to silence him? Leiter Weidling will not be a good enough match for your brother.'

'The German fire chief, he questioned Max and me many times after the Lübeck fire and then again after the one in Heidelberg and then . . . why then only myself after the fire in Köln. The flames that took my lover from me, monsieur, and now have broken my heart completely because Henri, he was there and I did not know it at the time, nor did anyone else except a certain butterfly who helped him so much and did his every bidding because she was afraid of him.'

Claudine . . .

From behind the ordered clutter of *objects d'art*, St-Cyr watched the two of them. Hermann was trying his best to pry every last thing he could out of the girl. She, in turn, was holding back even now but . . . but were they alone? Was the brother not watching too?

'Leiter Weidling understands only too well what it's all about, monsieur. The fire chief from Lübeck won many awards on the backs of my brother's fires and now will do so again because he is not only ruthlessly ambitious but swift as a fox. When I saw him in the place Terreaux that day after the cinema fire, my heart stopped. Oh for sure I knew he was in our city, and I had been terribly worried about this because Henri had been so upset. But why had Leiter Weidling come like a vulture to feed on the roast of carrion unless he had known who was to blame?'

She paused, then said, 'His wife, she is very beautiful but like the Salamander, must be able to change her skin when threatened or trapped.'

Louis was behind him—Kohler felt it strongly. 'Did she know your brother would be in that cinema, mademoiselle?'

'Was she there to meet him? Was Father Adrian? Ask . . . ask what you will, but not of me.'

'Ah no, don't. *Don't!*' Kohler leapt. The dagger was savagely driven into her breast. In shock, her eyes widened and her mouth opened. For a moment she clung desperately to life, wanting to tell him more . . . more . . . She *must* tell him about Concarneau. She must! The sea . . . the sound of the sea, the warmth of the sun in the heat of the sands, burning . . . burning. A pair of white underpants she would later steal to remind Henri of it all some day. Voices . . . secret voices . . . Whispers, a shrill scream . . . 'Ange-Marie . . . Ange . . . Ma . . . rie is . . . is the . . . the . . .'

She toppled over, knocking the candle stub so that it rolled on to its side with the flame flickering in her hair. Now a touch, now a curling of the hairs as they were singed.

Awakened by the stench, Kohler picked up the candle. 'Louis . . . Louis . . . ?'

Pale blue and ethereal in a night of frost, a tram-car clanged from the far side of the place Bellecour. Like marionettes in a play of shadows, the dark silhouettes began to run, and St-Cyr knew he could not hope to keep track of Henri Charlebois in the rush.

Some slipped and threw out their arms as they fell. Some cried to God in despair, while others laughed insanely until the clanging became unbearable.

'Ah no, *wait*! Please wait for me,' cried a girl, only to hit the ice with a fist and add dejectedly, 'The last car, messieurs. Positively the last! Have you no heart? The curfew! It's Christmas! Well, it is the day after but why should I have to spend the next months in Montluc among the convicts without a toothbrush?'

Punished by the frost, those who had missed the car stood sentinel or in little clusters, grumbling as such will do. Cursing openly or silently the miserable bastards of the Public Transport, the high wages such imbeciles were paid, the security of their precious pensions . . .

He had heard it all so many times before. Breathless, he let his gaze search everywhere. Charlebois was taller than most. Charlebois was thin. He had lost his hat, had fallen once. Perhaps he had sprained an ankle or wrist?

As St-Cyr hunted for him, he heard the girl who had fallen say, '*Merci*, monsieur. It is very kind of you to help me up.'

'Are you all right? There is nothing broken, I trust?' asked the helper.

He was tall and his hands, they were without gloves, thought the girl, for she had had her mittens stolen only yesterday and had not been able to get others.

'No. No, I'm fine,' she said. 'It . . . it is just that . . . that I live so far away, monsieur. Over in Saint-Jean on the rue des Antonins.'

Almost at the foot of the montée des Chazeaux.

'Well, that's good. I'm going that way myself. We'll walk together.'

He took her by the arm and she was not so sure she liked this. Ah, it was so hard to tell with some these days. The grip of the French Gestapo, monsieur? she wondered apprehensively. He had about him an urgency that made her feel uncomfortable, but perhaps it was just the nearness of the curfew and the need to be indoors.

They walked in silence, blending in with others so that perhaps she would feel more at ease with him, thought St-Cyr. 'Were you at the cinema?' asked the man. '*La Grande Illusion.* Did you enjoy it as much as I did?'

To go alone to the cinema was to admit that one lived alone, she felt. To make up stories about a boyfriend who lived across the Rhône in Part Dieu or La Guillotière would do no good with this one. 'Yes . . . yes, I have enjoyed the film very much, monsieur.'

'Even though we have had such terrible fires?'

'I . . . I have prayed that it would not happen to me, monsieur. Evidently others did the same, for the cinema was packed, was it not?'

The girl should not have said that, thought St-Cyr ruefully. Ah *merde*, was he to step in now in hopes she would not be killed?

Charlebois's chuckle was polite. As they crossed the rue de la Barre, he again used the girl as a shield and mingled quickly with others, chiding her gently. 'Don't we both wish that had been the case, mademoiselle? There were so few brave souls in that cinema, it did not pay the owners to open the doors.'

Embarrassed to have been caught out so easily, the girl must have sweltered under the rebuke. But then, determined to be certain of him once and for all, she foolishly began to ask specifics. 'Who played the part of the French officer, de Boeldieu, monsieur?'

Several people now separated St-Cyr from the couple. He dodged round them, only to be blocked by others. Ah damn . . . Must God do this to him? Must He mock a poor detective on the run? That film had been released in 1937. Hitler had banned it in the Reich and later the Nazis had banned it in Paris . . .

'Erich von Stroheim was magnificent as the German von Rauffenstein, mademoiselle. Pierre Fresnay did an excellent job of de Boeldieu. Why not ask me about the British officers in that prisoner-of-war camp of theirs? Why not tell me how they dressed up for the variety night to amuse their French counterparts?'

'As women,' she blurted. She would not be able to trip him up with anything. She knew this now, yet still was not certain of him. Ah, it was his grip on her arm. Yes, yes. It was as if he not only would not let her go, but could not. Had he a *need* of her, but why?

'Your name, monsieur?' she asked sharply.

Momentarily St-Cyr lost sight of them again. 'Christian Matras,' said the Salamander, a little test of his own.

They had stopped in the middle of the pavement. They were facing each other now but others were still passing them. 'That . . . that is the name of the photographer who has made the film,' she said, trembling, for he had not released his grip on her arm.

'Jean-Pierre Rouleau at your service, mademoiselle. Shopkeeper and widower, hence my presence at the film.'

'Forgive me. It's just that . . . Ah, one never knows, does one?'

His grip relaxed. They hurried along. When they came to the river, Monsieur 'Rouleau' felt it best to use the quais and the footbridge, as these would bring them more quickly to the Palais de Justice and her street.

Reluctantly she agreed. Ah *merde*, how easily women were taken in, thought St-Cyr. First they are afraid, then not afraid, then suddenly afraid again.

She asked what kind of shop he kept and for a time they were lost in a crowd that quickly vanished. *Maudit*, where had they gone? The infrequency of dim blue streetlamps gave futile guidance. Against the night sky, St-Cyr made out the stumpy branches of the trees that lined the quai des Célestins on the river side. There would be benches, places to hide—steps down to the water's edge where the ice had now gathered.

Lovers were caught in frozen embrace. Somewhere across the river, a car started up and he watched, as all others would, for the glow of the headlamps. And when it came along the quai Romain Rolland, he, too, saw that it was a German staff car.

But then it disappeared up the rue de la Bombarde and for a moment, anyway, the city dropped back into its silence and he heard the stirrings of the river as it flowed beneath the ice.

Another couple kissed, and at first he thought he'd found them, but then this girl whispered, 'Albert, I love you. Albert, I *must* go home! Until tomorrow, then?'

The boy swore he'd see her at church and they parted, he to hurry one way and the girl another. Teenagers . . .

Left alone and to the river, St-Cyr searched the half-light and the deeper darkness. Night was seldom so dark things could not be seen. With ice and snow on the ground, it was much lighter still. Out over the river, threatening dark stretches of water lapped razor-thin ice near upwelling pools of sewage. Along the bank, the ice tended to thicken except right at the sewer outlets. In these places gaps were kept open and vapour rose thickly from them.

Had Charlebois already killed the girl? Had he left her body for him to find?

When a shrill scream came, he began to run. When she shrieked and fought and cried, 'No! No, *please! I cannot swim!*' he saw her spinning drunkenly out across the ice, throwing her hands this way and that as she tried to stop herself. She went down hard. She went right through but did not cry for help. Ah *merde*!

He pitched down the frozen steps to the water's edge. As he raced out over the ice, he tried to fling off his overcoat.

A fleeting glimpse revealed Charlebois etched against the night sky, standing in the middle of the footbridge.

She bobbed up like a cork just beyond the edge of the ice, only to disappear suddenly. Where . . . where was she? 'Mademoiselle,' shouted the Sûreté. 'I'm a police officer. No, no, please do not give up. Here, I am coming to help you.'

'Louis, I'm right behind you!'

'Hermann? Ah *grâce à Dieu*, thank goodness you are here. The current is too fast for her.'

'She's downstream against the ice. She's trying to smash her way in but will never make it.'

They ran. Louis slid himself flat on the ice and worked his way out to her. He grabbed and grabbed again and again, but each time she slipped away.

'You or me?' shouted Kohler desperately.

'I must be wetter than you,' said the Sûreté's little Frog. 'Hang on to my ankles this time.'

The ice broke and it nearly took the two of them. When Louis grabbed the girl, she cried out and tried to fight him. Now both of them were yelling and spluttering. Kohler ran. Working his way downstream, he hunted for a place where he could get out to them and use his overcoat as a lifeline. Louis threw up a hand but missed it. '*Verdammt!* Must I jump in there too? Hang on. Don't let go of her!'

A sleeve was caught, then a wrist. '*Pull!*' shouted Kohler. He grabbed the girl by the scruff and hauled her out, was now soaking wet and freezing rapidly.

'Louis . . . ? *Louis, where the hell are you?*' Downstream . . . downstream.

His head was just above water. He was swimming in a pool some fifteen metres away.

Leaving the girl, Kohler crawled out on the ice. Thin . . . it was so thin. He felt it give, heard it crack and sigh and crack again. Ah *merde* . . .

They touched hands, and he managed to get Louis out. With fifteen degrees of frost, they had but a few minutes and they knew it. Dragging the girl, they forced themselves to run. They made it across the footbridge and past the Palais de Justice, were slowed to a crawl in the rue des Trois Maries and could barely pound on the door of La Belle Époque.

In rosewood, ebony and gold, the green baize-covered armchairs and peacock-hued faience cockerels began to change their places, thought St-Cyr. And the maidenhair ferns flew languidly with the storks on their pots, while the water-lilies on the walls kept trying to go round and round.

Vaguely he was aware of many hands tearing at his clothes, of corseted and uncorseted bosoms, lace, perfume, much flesh, powder, eye shadow and rouge. Of black-meshed silk stockings, garters and urgent voices that demanded rum and blankets and hot water. 'Blue . . . they are so blue, madame,' cried a girl with sunset hair that spilled over bare and gracefully moving shoulders. 'She's more frozen than those two,' said another, rubbing the arms of the girl they had rescued. 'The bath, madame. Upstairs. Quickly! Quickly!'

Four of them pushed and heaved him up the stairs. His legs, they wouldn't work. Ah *merde*, what was the matter with him?

Hands were everywhere, with sponges. Earnest faces drew close, only to dissolve as they receded.

Gradually warmth returned. The tub was huge and there were at least five of them in it. Hermann's eyes were closed. The girl they had rescued was being turned on to her stomach so that her seat and back could be sponged and rubbed. One of the others was holding the girl's head and shoulders just above the water.

A last glimpse revealed Madame Rachline with three glasses and a decanter of dark rum. Rum . . . rum . . . Mustn't touch it . . . mustn't touch it. He shut his eyes and, giving himself up to the ministrations of her girls, allowed himself a momentary lapse into sleep and warmth . . much warmth . . .

'Drink,' urged someone sternly. 'Ah *nom de Dieu*, come on, Inspector. Open the mouth like a little bird in orgasm. Swallow!'

The rum burned his throat. Like liquid fire, it spread its warmth to his loins and he knew he was slipping off into oblivion, knew that he could no longer stop himself.

'Don't drown them,' said someone harshly. 'Put them to bed and keep an eye on them.'

Grey-white, and with a crust like Brie, the phosphorus shone in the brilliant glare of the torch but it had not yet burst instantly into flame. A forest of undressed, upright timbers no more than a metre high separated him from it. The posts were stubby, had splintered surfaces that were coated with coal dust and webbed by spiders. Absolutely bone dry and excellent fodder . . . fodder . . . And the space between the floor above and that below was crammed with the rubbish of a theatre. Stage props and steamer trunks on their sides, suitcases left in haste or arrears ten, twenty—fifty years ago. Was there no end to the space, no end to the distance between him and the phosphorus?

Frantically St-Cyr scrambled among the timbers, ducking under bracing cross-timbers, banging his head on the floor joists above. An arm was caught, an ankle . . . Savagely he yanked them free and cried out in pain, snarled at God. Said, Why can You *not* stop mocking Your little detective just this once, eh?

Probing anxiously in the pitch darkness, the torch beam picked out only more and more of the same. Then he saw it in a far corner. A bag of some sort hanging from one of the joists by a bit of string. It was dripping water . . . water . . . slowly, steadily. Would there be time to reach it before all the water was gone? Was he now too late . . . too late? He must try. He must!

The bag was plump and soft and smelled mildly of garlic, and where the water seeped out to gather into each droplet, there was a small protuberance, stiff and with an aureole of little bumps around it.

Gingerly he caught hold of the bag with both hands. He must not squeeze it. Somehow he must stop it from dripping. He must not let air reach the phosphorus. Air, he said. Air.

Awkwardly he ducked his head under and turned to face upwards. A pin-hole . . . yes, yes. A droplet hit him in the eye. Another fell on his forehead. A third on his cheek . . . Stop it. You must stop it from sweating, he shouted at himself and demanded, How . . . ? How?

He closed his lips about the protuberance and put the tip of his tongue against it, but the bag moved and gave a sigh, and when he looked up, it was into a pair of stunning green eyes that silently watched him with animated curiosity. Ah *merde*! 'What time is it?' he asked, his throat dry.

She sat up. 'Exactly three in the afternoon, Inspector.'

Sunday? Ah no . . . 'Where is Hermann?' he asked. '*Hermann*, mademoiselle? My partner.'

She frowned. She very nearly burst into tears. 'Well?' he asked, only to hear her blurt, 'Next door, monsieur. Next door.'

'Were we drugged or was it simply exhaustion?' he demanded bitterly. 'Come, come mademoiselle, I must have the truth.'

Tears flooded from her, making her shoulders and breasts shake. 'Madame has gone after the Salamander, monsieur. The *Salamander*! Your friend, he is—'

'My clothes. Ah *nom de Jésus-Christ*, mademoiselle, where the hell are they?'

'The kitchen. They have been cleaned and . . . and ironed. You must stop madame, monsieur. You must stop her before it is too late. Already it is hours since she has left the premises. *Hours!*'

He ran. He stumbled and fell. When he reached the door, he grabbed it to steady himself and catch a breath. 'The girl that was with us, mademoiselle?' he managed, tossing a look her way. Ah, he was still so dizzy . . .

'Here. Here with me, asleep. Hurry, Inspector. Hurry!'

Hermann was next door in Madame Rachline's work room. He was with the children, over by the big work table, and he was not happy. 'Louis, Gestapo Lyon will now be after him. I've just filed our report with Boemelburg and the Chief's definitely worried. Apparently Knab and the other bigwigs really are going to attend the concert. Also, the shears, if they were returned to this room, have now been taken again.'

Maudit! 'But to where, Hermann. *Where?*'

Though dressed, Louis was still shaky. 'The house on the park. That's what the children say but me, ah, I don't think so. The dress she was working on is gone, Louis. Did she deliver it to the Hotel Bristol? The kids don't know why she'd have done a thing like that, given what's happened, but me, I think it's possible. There's also a spill of Cs on the floor over there. A box from next door was ripped open and a few handfuls taken.'

'Cs?'

'Riding coats,' blurted the boy, hastily wiping his eyes only to release more tears. 'Did you think we would not know what has been going on next door for nearly all our lives? A whorehouse, Paulette! A brothel! Our mother!'

Condoms, ah *merde!* He got down on his knees before the children and took their hands in his. 'Now listen, your mother was forced into this. I cannot tell you why because we do not have the time, eh? We must know where your Uncle Henri might have gone. She will know of it. That is why the shears have been taken again.'

The shears . . . the scissors!

The girl screwed up her face in tears and doubt. 'The . . . the Marché aux Puces, then. In Villeurbanne, monsieur. Uncle . . . Uncle Henri, he . . . he always goes there on Sunday afternoons to hunt for things.'

'He . . . he has a warehouse,' blurted the boy. 'It is the one with . . . with the bust of Nero above the door.'

'Caesar, René. It is the head and shoulders of Caesar Augustus but . . . but there are many of these and . . . and all of them, they look much the same.'

St-Cyr's heart sank at the prospect of what might lie ahead.

'The flea market, Hermann. It is on the Rhône well to the other side of the Parc de la Tête d'Or.'

They managed to hire a *fiacre* but it was drawn by a bronchial horse and would not go fast enough. Out on the pont Alphonse Juin, they commandeered a *gazogène*, a farm lorry laden with produce for black-market restaurants, only to have Hermann leap from behind the wheel to tell the driver of the *fiacre* to steam his horse and use some friar's balsam. 'Here . . . here, take this bottle my partner had in his pocket. Use a bucket of hot water and a sack over the head, and do it or I'll come back to give you the full treatment myself.'

'Me?' asked the terrified old man. The driver of the lorry was starting to sit up in the road.

'You, you son of a bitch!' snarled the Gestapo's Bavarian protector. 'That mare of yours has a bad chest. A cold, eh?' With the ham of his good hand, Hermann shoved the poor bastard's nose up into the air and slapped him soundly. 'Gestapo,' he breathed. 'Don't forget it!

'You *French*!' he cursed as he got back behind the wheel. 'How can you people treat animals like that? It's no wonder you lose all the wars you drag other people into!'

Ah *nom de Dieu*, what was one to say? At the height of a crisis, the doctoring of a horse!

The *gazogène* crawled by the streets, the *vélos* had plenty of time to get out of the way when the horn was honked. The ice lay in treacherous sheets that sometimes helped and sometimes didn't. And when they got to the park, Hermann didn't bother with the roads any more but drove straight overland. Ah *merde*! *Merde!* 'Not across the lake, Hermann! The ice, it will not be—'

'Hang on, Louis. We'll go round it.' Bump . . . bump . . . bump . . .

The Marché aux Puces looked like a medieval fairground. Replete with heraldry and bunting, it was at a bend where the Canal de Jonage met the Rhône. There were *gazogènes* and *vélo-taxis*, *fiacres*, wagons, sleighs and tram-cars, those vehicles of the Germans too, for several in uniform could be seen. Tents and marquees, kiosks and more permanent structures in rows, and people . . . people everywhere. Crowds of them. All colours of clothing. All sorts of faces. Perhaps four . . . maybe five or even six hectares and, rising right in the middle of it, the blue-washed, glass-and-iron cupola of the main building. *Verdammt!* 'Let's stick together, Louis,' said Hermann, exasperated by what lay before them. 'We'd better this time. Barbie won't have had time yet to get the troops out in force. Charlebois . . .'

'Will be dressed as a woman?' asked the Sûreté.

'A woman?'

'Yes. It is what I think must have happened at the cinema on the night of the fire.'

'And at those other fires in the Reich?'

Only the barest nod was given as the crowd was surveyed. 'Claudine Bertrand would be bringing a special friend for Frau Weidling to play with.'

'A Salamander,' grunted Hermann, checking the Walther P38 that was still miraculously with him in spite of the dunking in the river. 'Louis, hand me your Lebel.'

'Is it that your weapon is all gummed up, Hermann, and you have need of mine before the shooting starts?'

'No, but I'm going to have to strip it down and oil it later on.'

'Good! My Lebel is in the river. Me, I am sorry for the loss but still have my bracelets.'

'Then let's get going. I'll cover you.'

'Hours, Hermann. It has been hours since we came so close to the Salamander and last saw Madame Rachline.'

Was it a warning of some kind? 'And in about another hour this place is going to be swarming with Gestapo and it'll be dark.'

'He'll have friends.'

'Associates.'

'Those who might offer help in exchange for a little something.'

'Enemies too.'

And then from Hermann also, as they got out of the lorry, 'Frau Weidling, Louis?'

It was one of those times when the soul had to be searched. The Sûreté's little Frog cast a doubtful glance up to that God of his for assistance, only to see that the sky was grey and threatening snow.

'Yes. Ah yes, Hermann, the Salamander could well have called Frau Weidling to him since she did not die in the cinema fire as planned.'

'Locked in the toilets?'

'Yes!'

Above the constant murmur of the crowd came the shouts of the various vendors. Above these, the sounds of an accordion, a child who played a tambourine and another, the violin. Then in the distance somewhere there was a steam calliope.

It was a madhouse. No one would understand the urgency because they were all here to enjoy themselves and it was the holiday.

There were wicker baskets of used cutlery, stacks of old china—cups, saucers, tureens and platters in some of the booths, old glass, old pots, butter churns no one could possibly want these days, bits of tinware . . . ah, so many things. The images flashed by as Louis shouldered through the crowd and finally shouted, 'Sûreté, Sûreté!' and blew his whistle—stopped suddenly right in the middle of the Alley of the Old Maid's Most Precious Possessions and gave it another blast.

The shrill sound of the police whistle was met with a stunned silence that gradually extended outwards from them as each person halted to look apprehensively his way.

'Good! Now step aside,' he shouted.

Ah, *Gott im Himmel*, another Bismarck! 'Louis, why not ask where the Alley of the Caesars is?'

'Because I already know where it is. On the other side of that.'

The main building.

The warehouses were down along the canal. They were not big. Indeed, they varied in size according to the needs of their owners, yet before each of them was a scavenged marble statue, a bust, a headless figure, all Roman, all of Caesars perhaps, it was hard to tell.

'They remind me of Provence, Louis, of walking through the ruins of that hill fort,' grumbled Kohler uncomfortably.

'There were no statues that I recall. The Saracens must have taken care of them.'

Louis *would* toss in a bit of history! 'There wasn't anyone else around but our archer and here there isn't anyone either!'

Ah yes, it was quite quiet. All the activity was behind them.

Henri Masson had accepted stone busts that could seldom find a buyer. They were of the kings and queens of France and their children, of generals and politicians, great thinkers and great artists, musicians and writers. And he had gathered them on tiers of benches in a separate chamber that was lined with stone beyond the stacks of old furniture, paintings, packing cases and other things. It was cold and there was a smell that was most distinct. Ah no . . .

Hanging from a string, attached to the lamp high in the arch of the vault, were the collapsed remains of at least three scorched condoms.

'Louis . . .'

As yet they could not see much else. Only those stone faces that sat as in final judgement, silent and all staring down at the person on the floor between them.

A bare foot, a cast-off shoe . . . some scattered female clothing and, in a heap, the sky-blue dress with all its underthings.

Ange-Marie Rachline was huddled in an armchair, off to one side of them. Hermann threw an anxious glance her way. The woman wasn't moving. She was just staring at them as those busts were staring at someone else.

He stepped away. 'Ah *merde*, Louis, look.'

Leiter Weidling's wife was naked and lying face up—spread-eagled beneath the condoms with her wrists and ankles securely tied to the stone legs of the benches. And the water that had dripped out of the condoms above had fallen on her skin to remind her of the phosphorus, and when this had burned its way through the thin rubber, it, too, had fallen on her.

She'd been gagged and must have arched her back as she stiffened. The burns were horrible. The flesh had been eaten away until the blood had finally put out the flames or the phosphorus had been consumed. There was little left but a cavity between her breasts, nothing but entrails where her navel had been . . .

'Cover her, Hermann. There are some rugs. Let me have a moment with Madame Rachline.'

'That one didn't get here soon enough, Louis. The shears are still in her hands. He must have done it late last night or early this morning.'

She'd have killed Charlebois if she could have. The child-hood friend from the seaside at Concarneau was bitter.

'Look, Inspector, I really didn't think he had had anything to do with the fires. That was all past. Martine . . . ah, that one detested me. I thought she was *crazy* saying the things she did. Dragging it all up. I . . . Would I honestly have helped him in the slightest, knowing I had two children to care for?'

'You knew Frau Weidling had been with Claudine at La Belle Époque not once but several times since coming to Lyon.'

'Yes, I knew.'

'You knew that Henri Charlebois secretly watched them. Come, come, madame, you could not have been unaware of this.'

Vomit rose in her throat, and she turned away suddenly as she swallowed hard. Burning, it made her eyes smart. 'I swear I didn't, Inspector. Henri . . . he has always had his own set of keys. I . . . I never thought of his doing this. Surely one of the others would have seen him?'

'A Salamander, madame? A man who could stand over you while you slept?'

Dear Jesus forgive her. Henri in the house, Henri with the children . . .

'Madame, what has happened to your husband, please?'

'Émile? What . . . what the hell has he to do with this?'

St-Cyr gave her a moment. He would draw up an armchair, a thing with the stuffing sticking out of it. 'The past always pre-conditions the present, madame. Your husband left you desti-tute. Henri Charlebois remembered his childhood friend.'

'Henri was never my lover, Inspector. He could not possibly be the father of my children.'

He tossed the hand of dismissal. 'Ah no, of course not, but he knew who the father was, madame, and on the death of his grandfather, he imparted this little bit of knowledge to your husband.'

Ah damn him! 'Henri . . . Henri Masson . . .'

'Did not just take advantage of Claudine, but yourself also.'

She did not look away but into the past so deeply he could hear the sound of the waves on the beach of memory. 'Clau-dine was the youngest, Henri the oldest. She was anxious to be friends, so submitted to things she might not otherwise have done. We . . . we discovered that fire sexually aroused her and that Henri liked to watch her. He would . . . would bring the flame up to her skin again and again as he . . . he brought her to orgasm. It became a compulsion with him—she was only nine when it started, twelve when it ended and it . . . it was a sickness in which I shared in the desperation of my own loneli-ness, but . . . but I could not stand to be burned. For me, the nearness of the flame only made me scream.'

'But when brought close to another, madame, did it sexually excite you also?'

Vehemently she shook her head—could not help but look toward the alcove of the stone busts. 'It *fascinated* me to watch them both! *That's* why I let him do it to her!'

'When . . . when, exactly, was it that Henri Masson, Senior, discovered his grandson playing with matches?'

The children would have to be told. They'd hear things—the girls at La Belle Époque would be bound to say something. 'After . . . after several fires had been mysteriously lit. A pavilion, a boat-shed, a trawler, a barn, a house in the country in which five people perished. Monsieur Henri, Senior, found us among the dunes. They were not big dunes. They were just little hills and we ought to have known better. Claudine was lying on the ground and I was letting her hold me by the hands while Henri . . . Henri caressed her naked body with the flame.'

'And then, madame?' he asked so quietly she blinked.

'He beat us savagely. Claudine most of all but myself also, over his knee with my . . . my underpants around my ankles and my dress pushed up over my head. After this, we stopped going to Concarneau for the summers. Later . . . later she became his mistress but Monsieur Henri, Senior, was never satisfied, Inspector, and took me as well.'

So much for the quiet undercurrents beneath the veneer of Lyonnaise respectability. 'Was Martine Charlebois the one to tell him about the three of you?'

Again his voice . . . ah, it was so gentle. 'Yes. She was only six at the time and did not understand what was going on. Much later, and just before the old man died, he made Father Adrian swear to watch over Henri. No one could have foreseen that Father Adrian would take advantage of Martine and others, Inspector, but Henri found out about it and now . . . now so many have died, I must blame myself for not having stopped him.'

'She knew her brother had caused the fires that eventually killed her fiancé.'

'Yes. Claudine went to Lübeck first, but I did not even think Henri had also done so. He's away so much of the time.'

'Did you kill Robichaud with those?'

The shears. 'Robichaud . . . ah no. No, of course not. Nor did Martine. Henri saw his little sister with them when we went to the shop. He . . . he must have . . .'

'And now, madame? What will he do?'

She shrugged. She tried not to meet his eyes and failed. 'He will kill himself and perhaps others. He's lost her—don't you see? For him, Martine was everything I could no longer be, and the irony of it is, Inspector, that Henri Charlebois is my half-brother.'

'Pardon?'

'Look, I wouldn't have known as a child, would I? Oh for sure I saw the similarities—you've only to look at my son and me. But my mother, whom I adored, never gave me so much as a hint.'

'And your father?' he asked.

Must he push until he had all the answers? 'Was never happy with me and always suspected me of something I could not possibly have known anything about.'

'Louis . . .' The Bavarian had come to join them. The two detectives looked at each other. Grimly the one called Kohler nodded. So, the job was done and the body covered. 'We'd best get going, Louis. We haven't much time.'

They would have to be told. 'You'll never stop him, Inspectors. Henri knows the theatre too well. He'll play games with you and you'll never know which game he intends to use until it is too late.'

'And if he finds you there, madame?' asked Chief Inspector St-Cyr. Quite obviously he hated himself for having asked, yet had known he must.

She would give him the shy half-smile of the child she had once been before the fires had ever started. 'Then Henri will kill me, Inspector, and the *ménage à trois* of Concarneau will be complete. Claudine, myself also, and Henri, your Salamander.'

They were running now, and the sound of the orchestra was coming to them through the closed doors of the upper balcony. A Strauss waltz ... yes, yes, thought Madame Rachline. The German fire chief had met them in the foyer below. No sign of Henri. No way he could possibly have got through security. Everything safe ... safe ... His wife ... The German did not yet know about her and still wondered where she was.

St-Cyr had said nothing, only hurried on. Kohler had said, 'Idiot, you're crazy! Charlebois must be inside!' and had run after them.

All along the corridor there was carpeting. Red globes of fire-retardant hung on the walls near gas lights that were so subdued, the laughter and the good times of the past came as if in the present on the soaring strains of the waltz and it was mad ... mad ... crazy, yes! Henri would be hiding some place. Henri would also hear the waltz, a favourite. Was it that the detectives did not know he had chosen the pieces? Would it make any difference?

'In here,' hissed the one called Kohler. 'You first, madame. Louis, you take the far aisle. Search the faces. He'll have timed the release of all those bloody bits of phosphorus!'

'What about the elevator shafts?'

'The shafts?'

'Yes. Wind tunnels, Hermann. The belfry, remember?'

Verdammt! 'Later. Let's look for him first.'

The theatre was packed. The music soared and with it came the glitter, the sumptuousness of black ties and dinner jackets, silk and satin evening dresses, bare shoulders, plunging necklines, swept-up hair, droplet ear-rings, bracelets and necklaces.

Everywhere he looked, Kohler saw that the audience, finding the furnaces on, had shed their overcoats and wraps. And oh *mein Gott* but there must be half the fucking Army of the South in attendance, scattered about among the élite of Lyon. The bishop in his box, the mayor, the préfet, the Obersturmbann-führer Werner Knab and Klaus Barbie with two gorgeous women in another, General Niehoff and his party in yet another.

Over one hundred musicians were onstage, arranged in tiers with kettledrums and bass viols to the back. Trombones and trumpets next, with French horns to one side and violas. Then to the left, the violins in front, woodwinds dead centre, and the first and second cellos to the right . . . the right . . .

Maudit! There was an empty chair among all the sawing, a naked cello leaning against a stand and not lying on the floor waiting to be picked up by its owner. A music stand on which the sheets had been spread . . . spread . . . 'Louis . . . ?' he said, searching desperately along the far aisle for a sight of him as the waltz swirled upwards to fill the hall.

Kohler heard Madame Rachline sharply suck in a breath and say, 'Martine's cello . . .'

'What about the cello?'

'Henri . . .' she began, but could not bring herself to continue.

Again he hunted for Louis. Again he found there was no sign of him. Ah *merde*, where had he gone?

Kohler shook her hard and at last she blurted. 'Henri . . he . . . he must have got past the guards by carrying that in.'

A cello. 'Dressed as a woman?' demanded Kohler.

Her nod was quick, and she fought to tell him about the stage door. 'So, the game has begun, Inspector, and now you and your partner must find him among all these people.'

The swirling, soaring richness of Strauss was suddenly all about them. Loud and full and magnificent. Violins gave ques-tions; cellos answered, then trumpets signalled change and flutes and oboes came in to join the violins and violas.

Plucking . . . there were strings being plucked in a counter-melody. The cellos . . . yes, yes, he said, anxiously looking down over the crowd below, now here, now there . . . Barbie using his field glasses to find them . . . Knab asking what the trouble was . . . Ah *Gott im Himmel*, Louis, where the hell are you?

Exasperated, St-Cyr breathed in. There'd been a minor alter-cation with Gestapo Lyon at the door to the balcony. The bas-tard had insisted on seeing his ID, and unfortunately the Sûreté had broken a Gestapo nose on the *belle époque* ashtray stand. One could not please everyone these days. Such things were hopeless.

From the balcony railing he scanned the faces row by row. Charlebois could be anywhere Dark black hair—a wig perhaps, if as a woman, but short hair if as a man. Long lashes, short lashes, lipstick, rouge and eye shadow or none.

No, it was impossible. They'd never find him this way. Besides, people were beginning to take notice. Ah *merde*.

He turned and he, too, saw the cello alone among the others as the music fell only to lift again and he, too, was tempted to listen, to fill his mind and soul with it, for the *Vienna Blood* was perhaps the most stirring of Strauss's waltzes.

A cello . . . an empty chair, a tribute to a sister who had died in vain, but did that instrument have some other purpose? Did it?

Hermann nudged his arm with a pair of borrowed opera glasses. 'You take the left down there, Louis. I'll take the right. He's not up here.'

'Or is he, eh, my friend? Come, come, how can you be so sure?'

The sound of violins filled the theatre. 'She'd have recog-nized him even if he's dressed as a woman.'

'Who would have?'

'Madame Rachline, idiot! She's right here with . . Ah *nom de Jésus-Christ*, Louis, she's vanished!'

'So we look for her and we find him, Hermann. Is that the way it is to be?'

'And we ask, will he also use gasoline?'

The elevator shaft went up to a drum hoist on the roof and down to a well in the cellar. Hermann hated lifts. Old ones, new ones, it did not matter. They seldom worked properly. Life too often hung by a thread when least expected. There was pork grease on the cable, not petroleum grease, a bad sign. Strands of wire had become frayed and some had parted.

The grease was pale whitish grey and glistened in the beam of the torch as they gingerly stood on top of the cage and the fucking thing rocked in its housing.

Which of them saw it first, they'd never know. Gasoline was trickling down the cable in a little river of its own. Already it had formed a puddle in a corner of the roof, and from there, had seeped down the outside of the cage until droplets were released to hit the floor far below them.

Hermann looked questioningly up into the darkness of the shaft above. 'You know I don't like heights, Louis.'

'*Time*, Hermann. Is there time? Let us use the stairs and not the ladder.'

'Leiter Weidling will have checked the drive house. It must be between here and there.'

A different droplet fell and then, after an indeterminate pause, another. 'Louis ...' Again the torch beam probed the darkness but Occupation batteries were subject to failure. 'Water, Louis,' he muttered. 'It's dripping on my head.'

'Water?'

'Yes.'

The cold and impersonal iron ladder beckoned. It went up one side of the timbered shaft but neither of them had thought to tell anyone the lift must not be used while they were up there.

When the hoist drum began to turn, it filled the shaft with its sound and through this came the muted strains of Mendelssohn's

Fourth Symphony, Opus 90, the second movement, ah yes. The whirring soon filled the shaft and then the clunking of the stops as the cage descended to leave them stranded.

Mendelssohn . . . If one tried, one could almost see the cellos as they carried the countermelody. Lovely . . . it was lovely. Did Charlebois know his music so well?

Half-way to the hoist there was a cable guide and stop, and it was here that the Salamander had tied a jerry can of gasoline. They could just pick it out in the feeble beam of light.

Again there was dripping water, and again Hermann felt it, this time on an outstretched hand. With almost haunting, terri-fying progression, the music reached them. They thought of heating and ventilating ducts, they thought of all the places Charlebois might hide and never be found.

'A condom,' grunted Louis. 'It's hanging from a bit of wire, Hermann. It bulges with water like a woman's breast with the milk of my dreams.'

'Milk? Dreams? Can you get it? Don't drop it.'

'The cube of phosphorus will be in the centre at the bottom, Hermann, just above the pin-hole of the nipple.'

'Nipple?'

'You're taller,' said Louis, straining. 'Your arms, Hermann, they are longer than mine. Please, I am sorry for the inconve-nience but if I were to climb down and you were to climb up . . .'

The torch fell away, and they listened for it until it was heard.

'Hang on, Louis! Ah *Gott im Himmel*, idiot! Give me some room.'

'My foot! You are standing on my foot!'

Hermann paused as the echoes chased their words. 'Maybe you'd better find us a bucket of water, Louis. Just in case.'

'Shall I stand on the cage and hope to catch the condom in the dark, eh? Get up there, my friend. That's what they pay you for. Please don't piss on me.'

Hermann unbent the wire in the darkness—he was really very good at such things, having once been a demolitions expert.

Gingerly the bag was passed from hand to hand. 'Easy, Louis. Easy. You're right. It's like a pregnant woman's tit just before the kid comes.'

'Is he trying to tell us something, Hermann? Is this nothing but a decoy?'

'No phosphorus, is that what you mean?'

'We will have to see, once we get it under water.'

Grey-white and looking just as Martine Charlebois had said it would, the phosphorus appeared harmless as the flaccid rubber of the cut-open condom, stirred by some hidden current, drifted silently away only to cling to the side of the galvanized bucket like a manta ray in a distant ocean.

'Now are you satisfied there is a threat, Herr Weidling? And you, Herr Obersturmführer Barbie? Will you not now empty the theatre in an orderly fashion before chaos descends on us?' asked the Frog. *Verdammt*, but he looked worried sick. Proud though he was, at any moment Louis would go down on his knees to them. A patriot.

It was Barbie who said, 'It is not necessary. He will be found and stopped.'

There was a cube of phosphorus safe under water in one of the toilets, a reminder. There was another in a condom, hanging from the nozzle of the only showerbath to service the dressing rooms.

The French horns were very regal, very stirring as they reached high into the heavens of the first Brandenburg Concerto, in F, the third movement. They sounded as if greeting a royal coach that came at full gallop. They were very distracting.

Leiter Weidling was grey with fatigue and sweating. Anxiety tore at him for he knew he must now face their questions. The three of them were alone for the moment in the manager's office on the second floor.

'My wife did not know the identity of the Salamander. I swear it,' he said gruffly even though they hadn't asked. 'Oh yes, my Kaethe went to meet someone special in Lübeck and those other places, and here in the cinema also, but,' he raised the stump of a reproving finger, 'she did not know him and expected another woman, a friend of the one she had been . . . well, you know.'

'Fucking,' said Hermann, to clarify things.

'Claudine Bertrand set her up,' said Louis quietly. 'In each fire a scapegoat was needed, someone upon whom suspicion would fall until, finally, Martine Charlebois's fiancé was killed. Then the fires stopped.'

Weidling removed his cap and ran a hand wearily over his thinning hair, touching the bald spot she had ridiculed. 'Two "women", and my future wife, gentlemen. *Ja, ja,* Herr Kohler, I knew perfectly well what she had been up to. I needed her. How else could I find the Salamander? But she was not the cause of the fires and took no part in them, of this I was certain. She was the bait I used and watched and finally trapped into a confession and . . . and marriage.'

'You knew Claudine had come from Lyon,' said Louis. 'Did you trace Martine Charlebois here as well?'

The French. Always they were a nuisance. 'I had no time. I was kept far too busy. My superiors chose not to let me continue the investigation and go after the Salamander for fear of antagonizing France at such a critical time.'

'The war came, then the Occupation and finally a chance to visit Lyon and reopen the case,' breathed Hermann. 'Gestapo Mueller gave the okay and you brought your wife along, thinking to use her to flush the bastard out, but he got wind of it and now you're going to have to bury her.'

Weidling reached for his cap to put it on. 'And the man she sought but understood to be a woman like herself, Herr Kohler, until the two of them finally met. We must concentrate on the stage. I am almost certain that is where the Salamander will have planned his little surprise. The audience, yes? In full view of everyone.'

'A surprise?' blurted Hermann, dragging a piece of paper from a pocket. 'Haydn, Louis. Right after the intermission.'

'He can't time things that closely, Hermann, not unless he intends to be there.'

Weidling took a pistol from his jacket pocket. 'My wife's,' he said. 'Sadly I neglected to tell her I had taken it from her purse. When the call came to go to the warehouse at the flea market, she must have forgotten to look for it. A Beretta I intend to use.'

'Then let us hope you do,' swore Hermann. 'This place will go up like a torch.'

The lobby was crowded. People were streaming out through the doors. Drinks on the house as a gesture of good will. Champagne and darting looks. Stares and bolder stares.

They went back to work but found nothing further. Absolutely nothing!

Haydn's 'Surprise' Symphony contained the simple melody of the child that should be in everyone. Again the cellos were being worked hard. Always one was waiting for something new to happen. Always there was this overwhelming sense of expectation and the excitement of it. A childlike innocence if one would but listen, yet very, very deliberate a seduction and very, very sophisticated.

From the upper balcony, Louis could not help but wonder at Charlebois's choice of pieces. Had he chosen those passages which raised the spirits beyond all else to subvert the alertness of those who sought him, or had he done so out of a genuine love of beauty?

A strange man, one governed by an obsession. One who became so desperate after the cinema fire, he would, in hopes of pointing the finger at someone else, plant in the Basilica's belfry the frivolous shoes of the sister he loved.

Using the opera glasses, St-Cyr searched the faces of the audience. Four rows in from the unused orchestra pit in front of the stage there had been two empty seats side by side and next to the aisle. Seats that Leiter Weidling and his young wife would have used.

Ange-Marie Rachline had taken the farthest one from the aisle. Pensive, and with hands clasped in her lap, she waited for Charlebois to join her. From where she sat, she could not possibly see the sister's cello yet he was certain she looked that way.

The melody was repeated. It was so like something that would accompany a nursery rhyme or a child's game of hopscotch perhaps. Again St-Cyr found himself listening to it, again he waited expectantly for it to change. A surprise . . .

She had taken off her overcoat so that Charlebois might see her better. He knew she would have stood to search the faces of the crowd, hoping to be found. Had she still the scissors in her purse? Would she still try to kill her childhood friend or had she, like Father Adrian, resigned herself to a death by fire?

Following the line of her gaze, he paused at the prompter's box which was inset into the floor of the stage right at the front and low enough so as to be unobtrusive. He let the glasses search its mat black hood as he remembered the dream, the nightmare and asked, Had anyone thought to look immediately beneath the stage? Surely someone must have.

The cello . . . Hermann was standing at the far side of the stage out of sight of the audience. He did not look happy.

The cello . . . Ah *mon Dieu*, what was there about it? A beautiful glow to the wood, warm, so warm The sound holes, yes Yes, of course. A string   . Ah no.

Around the strings near the bridge there was a thin piece of gut and this stretched until it disappeared into the farthest sound hole

'Hermann . . .' he began. 'Hermann . . .'

Kohler saw Louis turn on his heel so swiftly he knew there was not a moment to lose. He started out across the stage. He knew he'd never stop the Salamander, not now. Never now. Ah *merde!* A music stand . . . He grabbed the thing as it fell, and flashed a grin as he straightened it. Then he was leaning into the conductor's ear. 'Keep playing this piece over and over. Don't stop unless you want the fucking place to burn!'

Threading nimbly among the first cellos and along past the seconds—ah *Gott im Himmel* it was a squeeze—he reached for the instrument only to see the gut around its strings and hear the music all around him, the rising, joyously mischievous sound of cellos playing *Zaddle-zaw, taw, daw, dah. Zaddle-zaw, tah* . . .

Verdammt! The son of a bitch had run another line from the foot of the cello under the platform on which some of the second cellos sat.

Now what was he to do? Aghast, Kohler looked up. Everyone would be watching him. Everyone! Ange-Marie Rachline was coming toward the stage . . . the stage . . .

Somehow he got down on his hands and knees between the instruments, the chairs, the legs of the musicians and the music stands. Somehow he got out the wooden-handled trooper's knife the Kaiser had issued to all ranks above those of dead men. The blade was wickedly sharp because it always had to be, and when he had gingerly cut the tripline, he delicately passed it under the lacquered toe of a black shoe and tied it to the high heel. Said into a pretty ear, 'Please don't move your foot. Not a millimetre. Just think of it as a bomb.'

Giving her a fatherly pat on the shoulder, he straightened up to tower over them, a shabby giant without his fedora, and the music went on and on all around him, the music . . .

Ange-Marie Rachline was now standing just beyond and to one side of the prompter's box. Ignoring her as best he could, the conductor took the orchestra through its paces, the sound of the cellos diving spiritedly into *Zaddle-zaw, taw, daw, dah* . . . until it filled the air.

For an instant their eyes met and Kohler shook his head. 'He's below us,' he said, mouthing the words for her and pointing downward.

The music pounded in her ears as she headed straight for the east wing, and when Kohler caught up with her to take her firmly by the arm, he said, 'Don't try to stop him madame. Please don't. Let us get to him first.'

'He will not listen to you! He will destroy the things he loves the most. You *must* let me talk to him. *Please!* I beg it of you. In his own way, Henri might still consider me a friend. Maybe . . . maybe he will listen to me.'

Over and over again the melody came to them as they joined the others. Beneath the stage there were timbered posts, a forest of them with cross-pieces for bracing. There were steamer trunks, old suitcases, stage props, cobwebs. The beam of Leiter Weidling's torch pierced the darkness.

They were all on their hands and knees and scrambling madly through this place until . . . 'Henri . . .' she managed.

'Louis, don't let her go to him.'

'Don't any of you move,' shrilled Charlebois. *'I'll do it! I will!'*

Weidling swore as his light found the Salamander and he saw the uniform of a Wehrmacht corporal. A corporal . . .

'Don't shine it into his eyes,' hissed St-Cyr. Ah *merde!* Each hand tightly clutched a fist-sized brown glass jar of phosphorus in water. Charlebois was sitting right beneath the cellos, with his back against a post. The line of gut was still wrapped around his right hand and it ran from there up to a tiny hole in the floor.

'Monsieur . . .' began Louis.

'Henri . . .' pleaded Madame Rachline. 'Henri, let me come to you.'

He must have thought this over, for he gave her a brief, sad smile before shaking his head. 'It's too late. It's over, Ange-Marie. Tell them I'll give you time to escape but only yourself.'

There was gasoline on the floor and when she reached it, she hesitated, for it was all around him and he sat right in the middle of it. 'Henri . . . *Chéri*, listen to me, please. Martine . . . You know how much she loved to play in the orchestra.'

His face stiffened. The jars were raised threateningly. 'Only because I made her,' he said. 'Me, Ange-Marie. *Me*, the brother who loved her more than anyone.'

The music of Haydn went on and on, over and over again. 'No . . . no, that isn't true, Henri. After her Max was killed, she threw herself into her music and her teaching. They were the only things that took the pain away and you know it. Don't destroy the theatre she loved.'

'As grandfather did?' he snapped back at her acidly.

St-Cyr let her go ahead of him. He tugged at Weidling's sleeve and finally whispered, 'Put the gun down where he can see it.'

'*Dummkopf*, don't be a fool!'

'If you shoot, the jars will break and we'll never get out of here alive.'

Hermann was working his way around to one side. Momentarily the woman blocked the torchlight from the Salamander but then its beam fell on Charlebois again so that they could see the jars more clearly.

'Ah *nom de Jésus-Christ*, Louis, he's got the lids off!'

He had.

St-Cyr motioned to Weidling to stay put and began to ease himself away and around in a flanking motion. They'd have to try. They had no other choice. They were in too deep . . . too deep.

He brushed a cobweb from his face. With difficulty he eased himself under a crosspiece. Hermann was now some two metres to the other side of Charlebois; Leiter Weidling still perhaps four metres towards the entrance; Ange-Marie Rachline was resting back on her heels in front of her childhood friend.

'Henri, do you remember Concarneau?' she said.

The thought brought only despair. 'How could I ever forget it?'

She brushed her tears away and tried to smile at him. 'The smell of the sea, the sound of the waves, Henri.'

'You would let Claudine hold your hands and I would pass the flame over her until . . .'

'Until I told you where to touch her.'

'Ah Jesus, *Louis!*'

That name was strung out for ever as the melody began again its strident surge. The tripline would be yanked, the bottles would be thrown . . . They could not get to them in time . . . time . . . Flames . . . There'd be engulfing flames . . . Phosphorus . . . searingly hot . . . Blinding . . . The stench of garlic . . . garlic . . . White smoke . . . dense white smoke and erupting gasoline . . .

Gently the woman took the jars from Charlebois's hands and set them carefully to one side, 'Bless you, Henri,' she said, a tender whisper. 'Your memory will live for ever for not having destroyed this place.'

'Then shoot me!' he screamed, and it was done as the sound of the cellos rose above them.

Paris was just not itself. Gripped in the iron fist of winter and that of the Occupier, the city was more than ominously silent. St-Cyr paused as he turned the corner on to his beloved rue Laurence-Savart. He knew the house at Number Three would be a shambles—shattered windows and splintered boards, the front wall and yard a wreck, a mistake . . . a Resistance bomb. Yet he was too tired and depressed to care. Lyon had left its mark on him and Hermann . . . Hermann had *not* wanted to share a belated bottle of the Moulin-à-Vent or to spend a moment in holiday salutations no matter how late.

Instead, hungry for his little pigeon and his Dutch *hausfrau,*

he had made feeble excuses and had left the Sûreté's little Frog
to his own designs.

Gabi was still away at the château, the invitation for him to
join her but a painful memory. The house, as he was just saying,
was . . . 'Ah no, Hermann *No!*'

In their absence, the Organization Todt, which did all the
building for the Reich, had completely rebuilt the place! Three
days, four days . . . what had it been?

In spite of knowing the street would now hate and distrust
him as never before—A collaborator and why not, eh? Just look
at what has happened!—he had to marvel at the job and to
wonder how much Hermann had paid them.

There was a note tucked into a beautifully painted brand-new
door. 'Louis, go out and get laid. You need it.'

'Ah *merde*, Hermann . . .' Eyes smarting, he searched the
long, narrow canyon of the street in hopes of seeing his partner,
only to know the Bavarian would be sound asleep in his flat
with a woman on either side of him.

'Monsieur the Chief Inspector . . . ?'

It was Dédé Labelle, whose mother took in laundry. 'Monsieur, my friends and I, we wish to . . . to beg your forgiveness.
We are sorry we have not given you the benefit of doubt in the
matter of your . . . your collaboration. The people who have
fixed your house, fixed the windows of all the others and gave
them also the pleasure of burning the scrap boards.'

He went out to the boy and opened the brand-new gate for
him. 'That's all right. You are forgiven. Come . . . come in.
Let's have a look at the workmanship, eh? The Boches—hey,
those lousy Krauts, Dédé, there are some things they can do
very well.'

The boy was not smiling and had no desire to enter. 'What is
it, Dédé? Is something the matter? Come, come, my partner
and I have just finished a most difficult case in which a Salamander, realizing that a German fire marshal was hot on his
trail, set fire to a cinema killing 182 innocent people and a

priest who knew all about him. Unfortunately the fire marshal's wife, who had been lured to the cinema by a friend of the Salamander and who also knew too much, was not locked in the toilets as planned and failed to die in the blaze.'

'Monsieur . . .' The boy broke into tears. Ah *nom de Dieu*, what was this?

'My sister, Monsieur the Chief Inspector . . . Joanne, she is missing now these past two days and we . . we were afraid she has . . . *Grand-mère*, she says Joanne, she should *never* have answered the advertisement in the *Messages Personnels*, that these days mannequins are no longer in demand, and that even if a girl is ripe and beautiful, no one would have the money to buy the film with which to take the necessary photographs of her.'

St-Cyr gazed down at the crumpled scrap of newsprint. Little Joanne, missing . . . ? He saw her as a babe in arms, as a toddler playing with her friends, saw her as a schoolgirl in her blue smock and beret, and saw her in the shop where she had found a job. 'Eighteen . . . she'd be eighteen now,' he said aloud, but to himself and then sternly, 'It's a matter for the préfet, Dédé. It's Paris. It's his turf.'

Ah *nom de Dieu*, how could one explain the politics and territorial insanities of policework to a boy of ten who was desperate?

'Let's go inside, eh? Let's have a cup of that wretched coffee we all have to drink, and you can tell me everything while I have a wash and a shave.'

'She . . . she wanted so much to be a mannequin, Monsieur the Chief Inspector. It was to be her great escape. She was going to buy us all so many wonderful things. A new bicycle, a—'

'Yes, yes, the coffee first, eh, Dédé? You can make it for me while I telephone my partner.'

'There . . . there was also a bank robbery.'

'Pardon?'

'And a murder, a shooting.'

'Please don't pile it on. Let's just stick to the disappearance. Let's find her first before it's too late.'

'But . . . but she will have seen the robbery and the shooting? That's what we all think, all of us. The other boys and myself.'

A bank robbery and a shooting . . . 'How much was stolen?'

Blinking away his tears, the boy looked steadily up at him and for a moment there was only the silence of honesty between them. Then, 'Eighteen millions, Monsieur the Chief Inspector. Eighteen.'

One for every year of her life . . . 'Good. My partner's broke. That will be enough to tempt him out of bed at such an early hour.'